PRAISE F...

'*Life Before Us* is a wonde...
love and characters so fully...
E...

'A warm, insightful story about new beginnings and the power of kindness'
Rachael English

'A cracking yarn ... Meaney can excavate the core of our human
failings and present it to us, mirror-like on the page ... Which
makes her utterly credible, utterly authentic, utterly irresistible'
Irish Independent

'Roisin Meaney is a skilful storyteller'
Sheila O'Flanagan

'A real treat ... Meaney wraps her readers in the
company and comfort of ordinary strangers'
Sunday Independent

'Meaney weaves wonderful feel-good tales of a consistently
high standard. And that standard rises with each book she writes'
Irish Examiner

'It's easy to see why Roisin Meaney is one of Ireland's
best-loved authors'
Bleach House Library

'This book is like chatting with a friend over a cup of tea ...
full of all the things that make life interesting'
Irish Mail on Sunday

'Delightful ... a cosy read for any time of the year, be it
in your beach bag or sitting curled up in front of the fire'
Swirl and Thread

Roisin Meaney was born in Listowel, County Kerry. She has lived in the US, Canada, Africa and Europe but is now based in County Clare, Ireland.

She is the author of twenty novels and has also written books for children.

www.roisinmeaney.com   @roisinmeaney

ALSO BY ROISIN MEANEY
Life Before Us
The Book Club
It's That Time of Year
The Restaurant
The Birthday Party (a Roone novel)
The Anniversary
The Street Where You Live
The Reunion
I'll Be Home for Christmas (a Roone novel)
Two Fridays in April
After the Wedding (a Roone novel)
Something in Common
One Summer (a Roone novel)
The Things We Do for Love
Love in the Making
Half Seven on a Thursday
The People Next Door
The Last Week of May
Putting Out the Stars
The Daisy Picker

CHILDREN'S BOOKS
Puffin with Paulie (with illustrator Louisa Condon)
Don't Even Think About It
See If I Care

Roisin MEANEY

A Winter to Remember

HACHETTE
BOOKS
IRELAND

First published in Ireland in 2023 by
HACHETTE BOOKS IRELAND

First published in paperback in 2024

1

Cataloguing in Publication Data is available from the British Library.

ISBN 9781399711456

Typeset in Arno Pro by Bookends Publishing Services, Dublin
Printed and bound in Great Britain by Clays Ltd, Elcograf S.p.A.

Hachette Books Ireland policy is to use papers that are natural, renewable
and recyclable products and made from wood grown in sustainable forests.
The logging and manufacturing processes are expected to conform to the
environmental regulations of the country of origin.

Hachette Books Ireland
8 Castlecourt Centre
Castleknock
Dublin 15, Ireland

A division of Hachette UK Ltd
Carmelite House, 50 Victoria Embankment, London EC4Y 0DZ

www.hachettebooksireland.ie

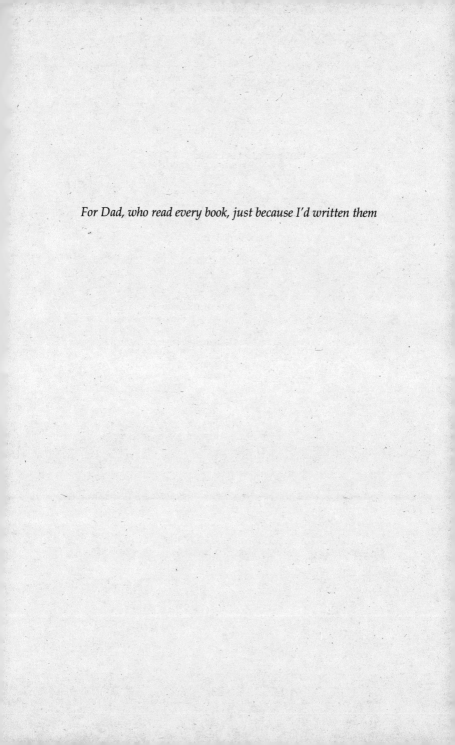

For Dad, who read every book, just because I'd written them

Christmas Day

THE COLD WOKE HER. THE DUVET HAD SLIPPED OFF her shoulders: she must have been tossing about. She pulled it up and lay still, eyes closed, deepening her breathing as she tried to coax her body back to sleep, but thoughts insisted on sidling in. Thirty-five mornings since she'd woken beside him, her brain keeping stubborn count. Thirty-five days since they'd last spoken, last touched. It felt like a decade.

She listened for rain, and didn't hear it. No sound at all: birds still tucked into nests, her housemates still slumbering. She fumbled for her watch on the bedside locker and peered at it, blinking until its fluorescent hands came into focus. Not yet seven, a while to go till daylight. She thought of little children all around the country who were already wide awake, rushing upstairs to show the presents that Santa had left under the tree.

She wondered if Pip had woken yet. She imagined him snuffling his way into consciousness, eyes cloudy, cheeks rosy from sleep, mouth open as if in astonishment, every single morning, at this remarkable turn of events. How often she'd stood by his cot observing just this, and marvelling at the miracle of him.

Her limbs were heavy with tiredness, and still sleep remained stubbornly elusive. Eventually she gave up and pushed aside the duvet, and padded wearily to the window to pull at one of the curtains, allowing light from a streetlamp to slide in. She dressed in the chilly gloom, having showered the night before so she wouldn't disturb the others with early morning water rushing through pipes. In the kitchen she made coffee and toasted wholegrain bread and spread it with passion fruit curd. A new recipe, too sweet: she wouldn't make it again.

She stood at the sink, toast in hand, regarding her image in the dark window above. It wasn't inspiring. Hair whose curls wouldn't be tamed, face hollowed with shadows from too much sadness and too little sleep. A mouth that had forgotten how to smile.

She ate without tasting, breakfast a chore needing to be got out of the way. She thought of the navy jacket lined with soft grey fleece she'd found back in October, a Christmas gift for Bill. She remembered patting herself on the back for being so organised – and now it sat, still in its shop bag, still with its tags attached, on a shelf in her room.

After washing up she tipped kibble into Barney's bowl and refilled his water dish. She opened the back door and stepped into the darkness, wrapping arms around herself as she breathed in the cold air, willing it to clear the sludge of sleep that persisted. Her exhalations were clouds that drifted and vanished, and she thought, *So this is Christmas*, and immediately the notes of the song she hadn't been conjuring up began to play in her head.

She heard a rustle in the bushes and out padded Barney, ready for his breakfast. She followed him into the house, closing the door behind them. She leant against the worktop and listened to his hungry crunching, envying the simple life he lived. All he asked for was food when it was needed, a space to ramble and hunt, and a safe place to sleep. 'You're lucky,' she told him, but he wasn't listening.

No stir from upstairs, which she hoped meant that her brother Daniel and his partner Nora were still asleep: Nora had been having trouble sleeping lately. Emily set the table for them, putting out the grapefruit marmalade with cardamom that Daniel liked, and the brown sugar that Nora added to her cereal.

Barney finished eating and leapt onto a chair and began to wash himself. Emily spooned filter coffee into the machine but didn't switch it on. She tiptoed back upstairs and collected the bag she'd filled last evening – clothes for later, shoes, make-up, scent – and brought it downstairs.

She tore a page from the phone pad and wrote *Happy Christmas! I woke early so I'm going to the restaurant to get a head start. Hope to see you later.* She signed it *E xx* and propped it against a cup on the kitchen table.

Would they come? She'd have to wait and see. Much as she

loved her brother, and much as Nora was becoming like the sister she'd never had, she was relieved not to meet them this morning, glad that she didn't have to paint on a smile and pretend she was happy it was Christmas.

The truth was, she regretted her impulse to host today's dinner at The Food of Love, the restaurant she'd opened more than four years ago. The truth was, she was not at all sure she could muster up the good humour that would be needed to play hostess to however many of her invitees showed up.

Three of them would be missing for sure, another two were uncertain, and as for Heather and her gang – well, that was anyone's guess. Was Heather even her friend any more? *See you tomorrow*, Emily had texted the night before, and no response had arrived.

Last year Heather had invited her and Bill and Pip to Christmas morning brunch at the house she shared with partner Shane and their blended family: his two sons, her daughter, and the child they'd made together. They'd eaten Nutella pancakes – a special request from the younger diners – and cocktail sausages, and little triangles of Shane's homemade pizza. The adults had made their way through the bottle of Moët that Heather had produced, and the cat under the table had feasted on the various spillages, and there had been lots of laughter and much joy.

She hated what had happened between her and Heather, but right now she didn't have the energy to try and fix it.

On her way out she paused at the open sitting-room door and looked in at the tree she and Daniel had decorated last week with some of the same baubles they'd hung as children. Christmas trees, she thought, always looked so disappointing in the daylight. Trying hard to enchant, but unremarkable without their twinkle. Like stars, only coming to life at night.

She took in the small heap of packages under the tree, some having arrived from her parents in Portugal in the past week or so, others added by Daniel and Nora, more by Emily herself. She'd open hers later, when her day was done.

She walked to the restaurant because she had time, and because it would be early enough when she was making her way home again, with dinner scheduled for three thirty. Besides, even muggers took Christmas Day off, didn't they? And no rowdy streets, with the pubs closed.

By this time the streetlights had winked off, and the sky was streaked with purple and yellow and grey. A couple passed her, walking a small white dog. The woman wore a beautiful red coat. 'Happy Christmas,' she said, and Emily repeated it. A car drove by, and another. Two little children, boy, girl, both swaddled in puffy jackets, pedalled shiny new tricycles along the path, accompanied by a man who trotted to keep up. Emily stepped aside to let them pass: he gave her a smile full of weary gratitude.

She halted outside a church, still three blocks from the restaurant. Without having planned it she climbed the wide stone steps and pushed open the heavy door. The air inside was still and frigid, thick with incense and wax polish. She made her way up a side aisle and slipped a coin into a brass slot and lit a candle. She knelt in front of the crib, where a plaster baby had been added the evening before.

No words came to her.

Holland Street, where the restaurant was located, was quiet. Emily knew all the occupants of the homes that were slotted between the businesses. No young children left in them, no need for anyone to be out of bed this morning. She glanced up and saw curtains closed in the windows of the apartment above the restaurant, her tenants still asleep too. She hoped she wouldn't wake them, working underneath.

She unlocked the front door and went through to the kitchen. She stowed her bag on a shelf and changed into her indoor shoes and pulled a clean apron from the pile. She lit the larger oven and took the turkey and stuffing from the fridge. She pulled open a long drawer in the dresser and lifted out the heavy white linen cloth she kept for special occasions, along with a rolled-up runner. With a pang, she realised that the last time she'd used the tablecloth was in April, when she'd hosted a meal for Astrid's family and friends after the funeral.

And this day last year, after the champagne brunch at Heather and Shane's, she and Bill had been preparing Christmas dinner together in Bill's house, and Astrid had attended as their guest. How different, how much sadder, this Christmas Day would be.

She shook out the cloth over the big oval table in the dining room, allowing it to billow and settle before moving it first one way then the other to centre it. Next, she unfurled the dark red runner, eighteen inches wide, and again she fussed and tweaked, coaxing it in both directions until it was perfectly situated.

In the centre of the table she set a heavy squat glass vase that held sprigs of berried holly and trailing ivy she'd gathered from the garden yesterday. She positioned a pair of long white candles in dark green holders on either side of the vase. She scattered little silver coloured stars along the runner, allowing a few to spill onto the white cloth.

One by one she set out the slate tablemats she'd picked up in an end of summer sale. She would lay the table for the twelve diners she'd anticipated – any fewer would look too spaced out. She'd seat her guests next to one another as they arrived, and leave the empty places together at one end.

As she moved about, polishing cutlery before placing it precisely, she heard bells begin to sound a recurring series of descending chimes from the church she'd visited on her way. They always seemed extra joyous to her on Christmas morning, pealing out their good news to anyone who cared to listen: He's born! He's born! Come and see! Come and see!

She collected side plates from the kitchen dresser and put them out. She worked slowly, taking her time. Three o'clock, she'd told everyone, to ensure that the last of them would have arrived by half past, when the turkey would be resting, and her selection of starters – salmon blinis, twisty cheese straws, melon and prosciutto, figs wrapped in bacon – plated up and ready to serve.

She returned to the kitchen and oiled and seasoned the turkey. She stuffed the breast cavity, slid the bird into the hot oven and set the timer for the first basting. She took red wine from the cool larder to bring it to room temperature.

She put glasses on a large tray and transported them carefully to the dining room. When every place setting had been furnished with the requisite glassware she went out to the corridor and studied the two high chairs under the stairs, kept for the rare occasions they were required. People didn't generally bring children to The Food of Love. Both should have been pressed into service for today's dinner, but now she wasn't sure that either would be needed. She left them where they were.

As she was placing crackers on plates, her phone rang. She saw her mother's name.

'Hi, Dol.' They'd never been Mum and Dad: she and Daniel had always called them by their first names, Dol for Dolores, and Patrick.

'Emily – just calling to wish you happy Christmas. Thank you for the patio rug, clever of you to order it online.'

'Easier than trying to post from Ireland. I haven't opened your presents yet, saving them for later.'

They'd lived in Portugal for the last ten years, decamping when Daniel was nineteen and Emily twenty-two. They saw their children roughly three times in the year: it suited everyone. Daniel still lived in the family home, and the furthest Emily had moved from it was to the apartment above the restaurant, just under a mile away. Brother and sister had always been close, more so when their parents had emigrated.

And for the past thirty-five days they'd been living under the same roof again, after Emily had left Bill's house.

'What's the weather like?' she asked her mother.

'Not bad at all – mild and wet, occasionally sunny. We went for a dip yesterday – the locals think we're crazy. Are you getting ready for your big dinner?'

'I am. I'm at the restaurant now.'

'Well, I hope you enjoy it. Here's your father.'

Patrick came on, and they exchanged Christmas greetings, and he told her that he and Dol had bought each other shares in a racehorse for Christmas. 'Between us,' he said, 'we own about two and a half legs and a tail. How are you getting on?'

'Fine,' she said, knowing that was what he wanted to hear. 'Doing OK.'

'That's good. You might come out to us once Christmas is over, take a few days off?'

'Oh … I might. I'll have a look at the January flights.'

A change of scene – why not? Dol and Patrick had bought a two-bed apartment that overlooked a pool, with the sea in the distance. It would do her good to hang up her apron and inhale some salty air, and feel what bit of sun there was on her skin. January was generally quiet in the restaurant, and Bernice, who stood in when Emily needed time off, might be glad of a week's work. She'd have a think about that.

After hanging up she put her phone on the windowsill and set out the last of the crackers. She positioned salt and pepper cellars, and glass dishes of mustard and cranberry sauce, with gravy and bread sauce to follow later. She placed trivets for the hot dishes.

Finally she stood back and surveyed the table. It looked good, festive and welcoming. She would make a supreme effort. She would smile and chatter and attend to her guests' needs, and hopefully she would pull it off.

Her phone rang again. She picked it up and saw a name that caused an almost painful lurch in her chest. The screen wobbled and blurred; she lifted the end of her apron and blotted her eyes.

The phone rang on and on until finally it stopped.

THE PREVIOUS
SEPTEMBER

Emily

'I DO BEG YOUR PARDON,' THE MAN SAID, HURRYING into the little waiting room, maroon file wedged under an arm as he fastened the buttons on his navy suit jacket. Dark grey hair stood bristle-stiff on his head. His cheeks were threaded with red, his eyes between brown and green. Double chin. He looked to be around Bill's age, Emily thought. Early fifties, or maybe a little beyond.

'My last meeting ran on,' he said. 'I hope you helped yourselves to coffee.'

'We did,' Heather told him, raising her paper cup in evidence. 'We couldn't find the doughnuts, though.'

'Ha!' A short bark of a laugh. His teeth were even and large, and more creamy than white. 'Sorry about that, must do better! Duly noted, Ms …?'

'Taylor. Heather Taylor.' She introduced Bill and Emily. Handshakes were exchanged: his was enthusiastic. He thanked them for coming and told them he was Derek O'Sullivan, and he was at their service. 'Do call me Derek. Come this way, if you please. Bring your coffees.'

He led them down a corridor into a larger room that housed a long, polished table of dark wood around which a dozen or so padded chairs were ranged, and a rolled-up projector screen on its stand in a corner. Shelves were set into the far wall, which held an array of files and books. A white mug sat on a windowsill beneath one of the four sash windows. Emily smelt coconut, or imagined she did.

'Sit, please sit.' The solicitor undid the buttons he'd just closed and walked around the table to take a chair across from them with his back to the windows. His tie, grey like his hair, had a small whitish mark on it in the shape of a tiny crescent moon. He set down his file.

'Might we have a window open?' Emily enquired. 'It's so warm.'

He leapt immediately to his feet. 'Of course, of course – extremely warm today indeed. Indian summer, for sure.' He pushed up two of the windows before resuming his seat and opening the file.

'Now,' turning pages, 'as I mentioned in my letters to you' – glancing up, his gaze swivelling among them – 'I've called you here in relation to the will of the late Mrs Astrid Carmody.'

The late Mrs Astrid Carmody. The words caused a pang. Five months after her death, Emily could still forget she was gone –

maybe because it had occurred so swiftly, so out of the blue. The last time they'd spoken she'd been her usual bright self, climbing carefully into the waiting taxi outside The Food of Love, having just eaten Sunday lunch there. See you on Tuesday, she'd said – the day they always brought Pip to see her – as Emily had tucked in the trailing end of her scarf and closed the door, but Tuesday hadn't happened.

I tried to wake her, the taxi driver had said, reappearing at the restaurant half an hour later, as Emily was clearing up. Scrubbing at his hair with a trembling hand, fighting tears. I – thought she'd just fallen asleep, so I – I called her, I tried for a bit, I shook her by the shoulder, just a little shake, but I couldn't get her to wake up, so I brought her to the hospital.

The words had stuttered out of him, his voice wavering, threatening to break. I thought I should come back and tell you – I thought you'd want to know. She's there now, I can bring you, I can wait till you're ready – but by the time they reached the hospital, Astrid had been officially declared dead.

Are you family? Emily was asked, and when she'd said no, but a close friend, she'd been shown into the anteroom where Astrid's trolley had been wheeled, and the hand that Emily touched was still warm. A peaceful death; what everyone hoped for.

She'd made it to her ninety-fifth year, a long life – and happy for the most part, Emily thought. Born Astrid Finklebaum, her family had got out of Austria just before the Second World War, coming to Ireland and making a home here. She'd married an Irishman, a farmer, who was long dead by the time she'd happened on The

Food of Love one lunchtime, aged ninety-one. They may not have known her for a long time, but the four of them had been close.

'Emily.'

Bill's quiet voice brought her back. 'Sorry,' she said. 'I was just … remembering.'

The solicitor regarded her sympathetically. 'I was only saying that Mrs Carmody had a great regard for the three of you. Her best friends, she told me. A great regard altogether.'

'We were fond of her,' Bill agreed. Forty-four years between him and Astrid but they'd bridged that gap easily, never stuck for conversation anytime they found themselves at the restaurant table together. Emily wondered suddenly what the solicitor made of herself and Bill, knowing them to be living at the same address, but with an obvious age gap there too. Let him think what he liked: they were happy, and Pip was the icing on their cake.

'Astrid was a sweetheart,' Heather put in. 'I cleaned her windows every two weeks. They didn't need doing that often, but I guess she thought I could use the cash.'

She certainly hadn't needed it. My folks both came from money, she'd confided to Emily, once their friendship had become grounded enough for confidences. It makes things easier for sure, but I don't believe it ever brings happiness. She never talked much about her childhood, but Emily gathered that happiness hadn't featured largely in it, despite the wealth.

The solicitor glanced down at his document. 'Well, in the first instance, Mrs Carmody wanted her house left to Master Philip Geraghty, whom I understand to be your grandson, Mr Geraghty.'

Utter silence followed. They looked at one another, and then back at the solicitor.

'Her house?' Heather.

'Pip?' Emily, at precisely the same moment. 'She left it to Pip? Are you sure?'

'Assuming by Pip you are referring to Master Philip Geraghty—'

'Yes, Philip.'

'In that case, I am very sure. Mrs Carmody was quite definite on that point. I realise that the child is young – this will was written at the end of last year, and as I recall he was still under a year old at the time, so now he must be …?' Looking questioningly at Bill.

'He's a year and four months,' Emily said, when Bill made no response. She could see him still trying to take it in, trying to assess what it would mean for Pip. 'He won't be two till next May.'

'Yes, thank you – so because he's so young, it was Mrs Carmody's wish that you three, her very good friends, would look after the house until Philip reaches the age of twenty-one. She instructed me, assuming you were all willing, to set up a trust, which would authorise you to act as caretakers of the house.'

More silence as they digested the news. Of course Emily was pleased for Pip – what a difference it would make to his life, to have been gifted Astrid's lovely little cottage – but whatever way you looked at it, it was hard to explain, given the history between Astrid and Pip's mother Christine. What could she have been thinking?

'OK,' Heather said, shifting a little on her chair, placing her palms on the polished table. 'OK. Let me get this straight. Astrid,

Mrs Carmody, has left her house to Pip, and she wants us to keep it safe for him until he grows up.'

'Exactly. They were precisely her wishes.'

'She wants us to look after her house for the next twenty years.'

'Well, not quite—'

'For the next nineteen years and eight months.'

'Er, yes. That's correct.'

'Wow,' Heather said. 'I mean, don't get me wrong, I'm OK with it, it's just … surprising, that's all.'

Surprising for sure, Emily thought – but maybe after all it wasn't so inexplicable. Astrid had left her house to Pip, not to Christine. She'd doted on the child from the first time Emily and Bill had brought him around to see her as a tiny infant, a week or so after Christine had run away. She'd knitted little blankets and cardigans for him in her tight, careful stitches. Maybe they should have expected exactly this from her, making generous provision for a boy whose mother had run out on him.

'As regards financial considerations,' the solicitor went on, 'the gift of the house to Philip will unfortunately incur capital acquisition tax – quite a lot, in fact, as there's no family connection between Mrs Carmody and her heir. However, as this tax will not become payable until Philip comes into possession of the property, it may be offset in the meantime through rental income, so I would strongly advise you to consider such a course of action.'

'You're saying we should let the cottage,' Emily said.

'Yes. You would advertise the property in the usual way

and secure a tenant, or tenants. Mrs Carmody set aside some monies to cover expenses along the way, running repairs, the aforementioned advertisement, et cetera. She was most anxious that you would not be out of pocket.'

It all sounded so organised. Again, typical of Astrid. Emily found herself wondering who'd been in line to inherit the property before Pip had come along, Astrid and her husband never having had children. Her nephew, most likely – or, rather, her husband's nephew. He and his wife had visited Astrid occasionally, bringing fresh duck eggs from their farm, and whatever vegetables were in season at the time.

Emily had met them both at the funeral. Astrid told us about your restaurant, the wife had said to Emily, and how much she enjoyed calling in. Had the husband expected the little house to pass to him though? Would he resent the fact that Astrid had decided to make a boy with no family connection her heir instead? She hoped not.

'You'll maybe want to have a think,' the solicitor said. 'You'll need time to decide if you're happy to take on the business of looking after the house.' He made it more of a question than a statement, and they told him no time needed, no thinking required.

'Right. Right, that's good. I'll set the wheels in motion for the trust then.' He turned more pages in the file. 'Now, in a separate clause, Mrs Carmody has bequeathed the sum of one thousand euros to each of you. Once probate has been sorted I can arrange payment by whatever method you each prefer.'

Her parting gift to them, as giving in death as she'd been in life. No money worries, she'd told Emily once, well provided for by her husband's careful investments, and by the sale of their home after his death, the little house she'd replaced it with costing far less. She hadn't needed much to live on, her only extravagances, if you could call them that, the lunches she'd eaten every few days in The Food of Love, and Markus, the Polish gardener, who'd taken over when outdoor work had got too much for her.

And of course her fortnightly window cleaner, whom she'd insisted on paying.

The solicitor turned pages, came to the one he wanted. 'Mr Geraghty,' he said to Bill, a quieter, more cautious note entering his voice, 'there's one more matter to discuss, and since it is … of a delicate nature, you may prefer we do it in private.'

'Delicate?'

A polite little cough. 'It concerns your daughter, Christine Geraghty. Mother of Master Philip.'

Emily saw the tightening in him, the new wariness at the mention of her name. It always caused this change in him, this tensing up while he waited for what followed, and it usually wasn't good. But this was different, wasn't it? A reference to Christine in a will couldn't be bad, could it?

Bill evidently thought the same. 'You can say whatever you have to say here.'

'Very well.' He dipped his head and read: 'I bequeath to Christine Geraghty my pearl necklace, to be held for her by her father Bill until she is in a position to claim it.'

For the second time that morning Emily was astounded. Astrid had left her precious necklace to the very person who'd stolen it from her two years ago. Never mind that Christine had subsequently returned it after Bill, suspecting that she'd been behind the theft, had tracked her down and confronted her angrily – this gesture of Astrid's made no sense at all.

The solicitor spoke again in the same soft tone. 'I was led to understand that Miss Geraghty's whereabouts were unknown at the time of Mrs Carmody making this will. Perhaps that has changed now.'

Bill shook his head wordlessly, and Emily wanted to weep. No change, his daughter's whereabouts still unknown. No contact at all with her father in almost a year and a half, and still he checked the landline's answering machine each time he got home. How could she continue to hurt him like this, when he had done nothing in the world to deserve it?

Christine was twenty-seven, a young woman with potentially so much life left – but having succumbed to drugs aged just sixteen she was sabotaging it as fast as she could. A period of sobriety following a stint in rehab hadn't lasted beyond the pregnancy that had been uncovered there – no man ever named as the father – and there was no way of knowing where she was now, or how she was living.

Still in Ireland, more than likely: following her departure from the house, Bill had found her passport in a dressing table drawer. When a week had gone by with no account of her he'd reported her as a missing person, which meant she was on a list somewhere, so if and when anything happened to her, the news would find its way back to him. Ireland was too small for the remains of any of its citizens, regardless of circumstance, to stay unidentified for long.

'I'll take it,' Bill said. 'The necklace. I'll look after it for her.'

'Thank you, Mr Geraghty. I'll let you know when it becomes available to claim.'

The meeting drew to a close. The solicitor walked them to the lift and shook hands with each of them, and bade them good day. 'I'll be in touch,' he promised.

As the lift doors slid closed they looked at one another.

'Unexpected,' Bill said, pulling out his car keys.

'Which bit?' Heather asked.

'All of it.'

Emily hitched her bag onto her shoulder as they reached the ground floor. 'Good for Pip.'

'It is,' Bill replied.

She waited for him to add some comment about Christine, but he didn't. She wondered if his daughter would ever get to claim her inheritance, or even be made aware of it. She thought it unlikely.

On the path outside, Heather checked her phone. 'I have forty-five minutes of freedom left. Who's got time for a coffee?'

Bill shook his head. 'I should get back to work.'

'I have time,' Emily said, fishing sunglasses from her bag. 'Mrs Twomey said no rush picking up Pip,' so they waved off Bill and walked in the sunshine to a café up the street that was owned by a pair of cheery Latvian brothers.

The door was propped open with a chair. 'Hello, darlings!' one of the brothers exclaimed as they entered. Dark haired, brown eyed, bearded, loading plates with a practised hand onto a tray. 'You find a table, I send the waiter, OK?' Their running joke, referring to each other as the waiter.

They sat by the wall, all the window tables being taken. Despite the open door, the air was laden with heat. After they'd ordered two iced coffees and one almond pastry, Heather planted her elbows on the table and regarded Emily.

'Will you say it or will I?'

'Christine?'

'Damn right Christine. She gets the family pearls? What the hell is that about? What was Astrid thinking?'

'Maybe she wanted to let her know she was forgiven.'

'But that's just it – she won't know. She'll never find out.'

'You think she'll never show up?'

'You think she will?' Heather countered.

Emily shook her head. 'Bill still lives in hope.'

'Of course he does. Will he try to find her again now?'

'I'd say so.' Astrid had just given him an excuse to renew his search, not that he needed one. More ads in the paper.

'I guess Pip will end up with the necklace as well as the house. That's a bit weird too, right? Leaving the house to Pip.'

'Well, it's certainly unexpected.'

'And not a mention of my girls.'

Emily looked at her. Heather stared back. 'What? It would have been nice if they'd been remembered, that's all. Even if she'd just left them a trinket or whatever. Nothing valuable, just something to show they hadn't been forgotten.'

She was hurt. Emily could understand it. Heather had brought the girls regularly to the cottage; Astrid would have known them almost as well as she'd known Pip. 'I suppose she thought Pip was the more deserving.'

'Well, sure.' But they both knew that wasn't the point.

Their order arrived, the iced coffees in tall glasses. Emily watched Heather dividing the pastry in two. 'I wonder if there are any of Astrid's relatives left in Austria – distant cousins, maybe. I know she never spoke of any, but it might have been hard to track people down after the war.'

Heather placed Emily's half on a napkin and slid it across the table. She licked her fingers and wrapped her hands around her glass. 'I guess I need to tell you about Astrid,' she said.

Emily bit into the pastry. 'What about her?'

'She didn't leave Austria before the war, like she told us. None of her family did.'

Emily shook her head. 'No, you're wrong. She said they had friends in Ireland, remember? That was why they came here.'

'They didn't,' Heather replied. 'They didn't leave. They were going to, they'd planned it, but they were rounded up before they had a chance.'

'No, that's definitely not right. I remember distinctly—'

'Emily.' Quietly, but with a note in it that made Emily stop. 'Astrid told me herself. It was about a month before she died. We were in her house, I'd cleaned the windows and we were having tea afterwards. I don't remember how it came up, but I asked her the same question you asked just now, about possible family left in Austria, and ... she told me everything.'

The little café was too hot. Emily's chest felt tight. She breathed in, breathed out. 'I don't believe it. I don't believe she lied to us. Astrid wouldn't lie.'

'Hey, don't look on it like that. The truth was too hard for her, that was all. Or maybe she didn't want to burden us with it. Maybe she saw it as a kindness, not telling us.'

'Everything OK, ladies?'

One of the brothers had returned. They looked wordlessly at him until Heather said, 'Yup, fine, thanks.'

When he'd gone, Emily pushed aside the rest of her pastry. 'So tell me.'

'You sure you want to know?'

She wasn't sure, not at all, but she said yes, so Heather told her. In the overheated café that smelt of coffee and cinnamon, Emily learnt of a young girl coming home from an after-school dance class to find her entire family – parents, brother, grandfather – gone from the apartment where they lived. She learnt of a terrified wait, alone in the apartment, until darkness fell, and then a panicked rush to the home of a near stranger, and the long, frightening years of hiding that had followed.

She sipped the cold coffee. She touched the glass to her hot cheeks in turn. 'And – did they survive, her family? Did she find them after the war?' But she knew the answer, didn't she? She didn't have to wait for Heather's silent shake of her head. 'All of them gone? Everyone?'

'Everyone. The apartment too, bombed by the Allies. There was nothing left for her, no photos, not a thing – apart from the string of pearls that she'd thought to take with her before she left. It had been passed down through the females in the family for generations.'

'Yes …' Emily remembered hearing the story of the necklace, after it had been stolen and returned. At least one thing was true. How precious the necklace must have been, quite apart from its monetary value – doubly precious after the loss of her family. How Astrid must have treasured it, her only keepsake.

And now it belonged to Christine. Emily felt a surge of anger that she tried to quash. She couldn't be angry, not when it was what Astrid had wanted to do. She must respect it, unpalatable as it was.

Horrible to think of the young Astrid living through that nightmare. Incredible for her to have emerged as the generous, positive person they'd known, despite those experiences. For one who had every reason to be bitter and cynical about the ways of the world, she'd been neither.

'Had she no other relatives at all?'

'None. Her father's brother, who would have been her only uncle, died young in a skiing accident. No aunts on either side.

Her three other grandparents were gone before the war – I think she said her father's parents died of the Spanish flu.'

Shocking that she'd kept all this trauma, all this sadness to herself. Why hadn't she confided in them, the people she'd claimed as her best friends? Wasn't that what friends were for?

But she *had* told someone. She'd told Heather. 'So what did she do then?'

'She got some kind of secretarial qualification and left Austria. She moved to England, worked in a typing pool in London. It was there she met her husband.'

'But … wasn't he an Irish farmer? How could she have met him in London?' Emily had a sense of it all sliding away, a crumbling of everything she'd believed to be true about Astrid.

'He wasn't farming then. He'd joined the British Army at the start of the war. He was in the process of being demobbed when they met. He brought her to Ireland and took over the family farm then.'

So much to process, so much mental reshuffling to do. Emily pushed back her chair, feeling unsettled by the account. 'I'd better collect Pip.' She needed to hold him, to nuzzle into his soft warmth, to take comfort from the innocence of him. He might be Christine's son, but he was also Bill's grandchild, and he was happy and sweet-natured, and Emily loved him every bit as much as she loved Bill.

'I'll ring you,' she told Heather, 'in the next few days. We must get together and sort out what we'll do with Astrid's house.' It might be best, she thought, not to say anything to Bill about this revelation, this true account of Astrid's history. What was the point in telling him? The truth would only bring him sadness. She wished Heather hadn't told her either.

To distract herself on the way home she tried to think what she and Bill should do with the money Astrid had left them. Nothing sensible: frivolity was called for here. Astrid would have wanted them to have fun with it.

That evening she asked Bill if he'd fancy spending it on a holiday. 'We could do with a break. I wouldn't mind Scotland – I'd love to see Loch Lomond. We could rent a place for a week, do a bit of walking.'

They were washing up after dinner. Bill wiped a plate and returned it to its shelf. 'Actually,' he said, 'I was thinking of using mine to have another go at tracking down Christine. I could try more ads first, and if nothing came of them I might hire someone.'

Hire someone. He'd pay a private detective to find a woman who didn't want to be found. Emily lifted cutlery from the water and dropped it into the holder on the draining board. 'OK,' she said, 'it was just an idea.'

'Emily—'

'Really, it doesn't matter. You must do what you feel is best.' She pulled out the plug and let the water swirl away. She peeled off her rubber gloves.

'I know you think it's a waste of time,' he said, picking up another plate.

She shook her head, unable to put a denial into words in case he heard the insincerity of it. 'I hate to see you disappointed, that's all.'

She couldn't bear the thought of him wasting his money on a wild goose chase. Could he not see that even if Christine was found she'd simply take the necklace and sell it, or trade it for more of the poison she was putting into her, and disappear again? Was he so blinded by fatherly love that he honestly thought a necklace would bring her back to him and make everything right?

Then again, wouldn't Emily feel the same if Pip was missing now instead of Christine? Since she'd moved in with Bill to help him raise his tiny grandchild, Pip had snuggled naturally into Emily's heart, and it had been a perfect fit for him. Wouldn't she move heaven and earth to find him if the unthinkable happened and he went missing? How could she object to Bill wanting to do the same for his child?

'Of course you must try to find her,' she said. 'We'll go to Scotland another time.' They'd go, she thought, when no trace of Christine was found, when Bill finally gave up the search again. A holiday would be needed then.

The following day, as she was cleaning up after the lunchtime session at the restaurant the doorbell rang, and she left the kitchen to answer it.

'Right on time,' she said to the couple waiting outside.

Lil

SHE STEPPED BACK TO LET THEM IN. SHE LOOKED older than Lil, thirty or so. Curly-haired too, but hers was shorter, and shot through with coppery lights that Lil immediately envied. A cream apron covered her clothes, a long affair that went right to her calves. She wore flat shoes the colour of primroses that looked soft and comfortable.

'I'm Emily,' she said, 'and you must be Tom and Lil,' and they shook her hand and agreed that they were. The corridor they stood in smelt savoury – onions, garlic, spices. Lil hoped their new accommodation wouldn't smell like that all the time. A staircase hugged the left wall directly in front of them. Wallpaper, trailing pink roses and leaves in shades of green, ran up along that wall: the rest of the hall was painted white.

'We're interrupting you,' Lil said. 'You're working,' even though the time had been agreed in advance – and Emily, reaching behind to untie her apron, said no, no, lunch was over. 'I'm free till we start dinner prep, about half four. Let me show you the garden before I bring you upstairs.'

She draped the apron over the banister – sleeveless yellow top, pale blue cropped trousers – and led them along the corridor. 'Restaurant kitchen through there,' she said, indicating a door on the right, 'leading to the dining room at the front.' She opened the back door and they stepped out onto a paved area with a small cast iron table and two chairs on it, and various pots with flowers. Herbs grew in a raised bed below the kitchen window – Lil recognised parsley and mint, coriander and sage.

Beyond the patio a clothesline strung between poles held two large squares of white that moved gently in the breeze, and several smaller squares, also white. Sheets and handkerchiefs? But then she remembered the restaurant, and decided they must be tablecloths and napkins. Further down the garden was a wooden shed painted dark green, with one window. Between line and shed there was a patch of lawn, and at the end of the lawn an assortment of shrubs.

Walls, four foot high or so, bordered the garden on each side. An end wall, slightly higher, had an iron gate set in it, reminding Lil of the gate at the bottom of the long garden behind her family home in Fairweather that led out to the cliff path. The restored cliff path, after a vicious summer storm last year had caused a chunk of it to tumble into the sea, along with the little community library Gran had set up at the bottom of the adjoining garden.

Already she missed Fairweather, having left it just two hours before. She missed the Atlantic, the power of it, the sound and smell of it, the heart-stopping shock of the cold water when she would plunge in. She missed the feel of sand under her bare feet, the sharp tang of seaweed, the sweet scent of candyfloss drifting from the summer stalls on the prom.

Staying there wasn't an option though, not after she'd decided to become a librarian, having cut her teeth in Gran's. The problem was, Fairweather didn't possess an official library, which was why Gran had stepped in. Moves were finally afoot to provide one, after the public outcry that had followed the loss of Gran's, and Lil was reasonably sure she'd secure a job there once recruitment began, but in the meantime she'd looked for and found work in another library, as close to Fairweather as she could get. Not close enough to commute, but they were only living here until such time as the new library opened, and not a minute longer.

'I'm giving you keys for the front and back doors,' Emily was saying, 'so you can come out here whenever you want. You'll find more chairs and things in the shed – and please help yourselves to the herbs. Right, I'll take you up and show you the apartment.'

It was small: that was Lil's first thought. One double bedroom, not large, a bathroom, and a kitchen-cum-living-room. She'd never lived in a place so small. She'd never lived anywhere but the house where she'd grown up – and Gran's house next door, where she'd fled after the accident. Her bedroom window in both houses had offered a view of the sea: here, their room overlooked a street that was filled with other buildings.

'It's lovely,' she said, because even though it was small it *was* lovely. It was bright and clean and uncluttered, and the furnishings suited it. And it was her and Tom's first place together, and they would turn it into a home. 'Thank you for letting us live here.' Tom had gone down to get the rest of their things from his Jeep, leaving the two women alone.

'I hadn't really planned on letting it,' Emily admitted. 'I should have. With places in such short supply these days, it did feel wrong to have it lying empty. I suppose I was a bit worried about putting strangers in – but when Judy told me her new library assistant needed a place to live, I couldn't say no.' She gazed about. 'I loved living here. It belonged to my grandmother – she had a hat shop downstairs, years ago – and she left it to me in her will, so I decided to open a restaurant, and I moved in here.'

She didn't say where she lived now, and Lil was too shy to ask. She thought it was a good omen that the apartment had been passed to Emily from her grandmother, given her own bond with hers.

'You must drop in below for a meal,' Emily continued. 'Your first will be on the house.'

Lil thanked her and promised they would. 'So are you from this town?' she asked.

'Yes, born and bred less than a mile away. And Judy tells me you're from Fairweather.'

'That's right.' Did she know about the accident? If she did, she gave no sign.

'Well, best of luck with the job. I know Judy's delighted to be getting an assistant. And Tom's a Dubliner, by the sound of him.'

'He is. He grew up in the city. We met when he came to live in Fairweather for a while.'

'And what does he do?'

Lil shrugged off her jacket. Still so warm; an Indian summer they were having. 'He's a freelance web designer – he's amazing on the computer – and he works as a handyman between commissions. He likes the balance.'

But Emily had stopped listening. 'Is that an engagement ring?'

'Oh … yes.' She was aware of the familiar little heart swoop, the small flip of anxiety whenever she thought of the wedding. She offered her left hand to Emily, who gazed at the ring.

'Congratulations, it's beautiful. When are you getting married?'

'Not till next June.'

'Lovely. A summer wedding.' She gave a laugh then that wasn't really a laugh. 'I nearly got married once, but it wasn't to be. My groom got cold feet.'

'Oh … I'm sorry.' Lil was thrown, the remark landing so suddenly between them.

Emily shook her head. 'No, it was a good thing, I had a lucky escape – and I'm with someone far better now. You were saying about Tom. He designs websites?'

'Yes – and he does odd jobs too, in his spare time. He's very handy.'

'Is he? I can spread the word in the restaurant – a good handyman is always in demand.'

'Oh, would you? Thanks so much. He's got leaflets – he can print some out for you.' And hopefully Judy would let her pin one on the library noticeboard too.

'Absolutely,' Judy said, the following morning. 'That's what it's for. And bring in a bundle to put on the desk too, so people can take one when they're checking out books. Now, you said in your interview that you'd done some storytelling in your grandmother's library.'

'Yes. My sister and I took it in turns every week.' The pang she always felt at the reference to Hollie. Softer than before, time rubbing away the sharpness, but the pain still there.

Judy, like Emily, gave no sign that she was aware of Lil's association with the Fairweather tragedy. Lil was relieved that people had moved on from it: she'd had enough pity and concern then to last several lifetimes.

'So what about a fortnightly storytime here, every other Saturday? Would you be happy with that?'

'I would, very happy.'

She loved telling stories to children, one of the few times she didn't mind being the focus of attention. She was charmed by their enthusiasm and innocence. She loved drawing out the quieter ones, seeing herself in their timid smiles.

She wanted one of her own, more than one. She wanted to fill her old Fairweather home with the sound of children, to create new family memories there.

'Good,' Judy said. 'That's settled. Let's begin on Saturday week, to give people plenty of notice. You might do up a little leaflet that we can display – time, date, age group, that sort of thing.'

'OK.' Tom would help.

'So how did you find Emily's apartment? Are you pleased?'

'We are, it's perfect, and she left us a sponge cake in the fridge.'

'Ah, very kind. Poor Emily has had her troubles. I don't know if she told you about being left at the altar on her wedding day.'

'She mentioned it.'

'She's with an older man now. He's the caretaker in the nursing home on Courthouse Street, a very courteous man. They have a baby – not theirs, his daughter's, but they're looking after it.' She spoke of Christine and her addiction, and her abandonment of her little son. 'She used to come to the library with her mother as a young girl, but the mother died when Christine was in her teens, and everything went wrong after that.'

Sounded like Emily had her hands full, with another woman's child to raise and a restaurant to run – and now tenants in her apartment too.

'Come on,' Judy said, 'let me show you around.' She walked Lil through the library, pointing out the various areas. It felt familiar and different at the same time. Gran's library had been on such a smaller scale, and not computerised at all, but Lil loved being back among books, in the hushed atmosphere that rooms full of them seemed to demand.

'Take your time this morning,' Judy said. 'Get to know the place,' so Lil wandered about, returning stray books to their rightful shelves, restoring order to the picture-book displays, stacking magazines and newspapers, and generally learning where everything lived. Occasionally Judy would call her to the desk to introduce her to a library member, and Lil tried to store the names in her head.

In the afternoon, as she took up her position behind the desk for the first time, she was approached by a bearded, fair-haired man in a navy uniform who told her he was Karl. 'Dogsbody,' he added gloomily. 'Officially I'm security, but they have me carrying boxes and running errands and whatnot from morning till night. They're lucky I'm so obliging.'

And Judy, overhearing from her little office behind the desk, called out that he was the lucky one to have a job. 'Dogsbodies are ten a penny, I'll have you know.'

'Right, boss,' he called back, and turned to give Lil a sudden grin. 'I knew she'd have something to say to that,' he whispered, and she realised he wasn't gloomy at all.

Everyone was friendly. Everyone she met welcomed her to the town and wished her well in her new job. Lil felt she was going to enjoy it, for however long it lasted.

During a mid-afternoon break she checked Dublin train times

and booked a return ticket for the following Thursday, her first day off, before she could change her mind.

She'd tell Tom she wanted to check out the shops for ideas for the wedding. He'd probably think she was crazy, with the day still so far away, but she knew he wouldn't question it. Not that it was a lie exactly: she planned to do a bit of browsing after she'd taken care of what was really bringing her to the capital.

She was going to track down Tom's father, George McLysaght, a man she'd never met. She hadn't met him because he and Tom were estranged, or pretty much. His father phoned every week, and Tom picked up the call but said little – Lil would overhear, 'Yes,' and 'Mm-hmm,' and 'OK,' and not much else. He never spoke of the calls afterwards, and Lil had learnt to let them go.

She knew the reason for the estrangement. Tom had told her late into the night about eight months ago, just before he'd proposed. She'd known there was a story, a reason why she'd met his brother Joel, and Joel's wife Sarah and their children, but not the widowed father he hardly ever mentioned. She'd held her tongue, content to trust that Tom would tell her when the time was right, and he had.

There are things about me, he'd said, that you should know – and then he'd spoken, haltingly, of Vivienne.

We met at Joel's wedding – she's a first cousin of Sarah's. We went out for three years, we lived in London, and then we got engaged, but not long before the wedding ... he'd paused here to let several seconds pass by, staring into the distance ... I found her in bed with my father, in my father's house.

More silence. Whatever Lil had been expecting, it wasn't that.

I got out of there and went to a bar. I drank so much ... I got into a fight, I don't remember it, but I hit a man, and I ended up in jail. I lost my job, lost everything. It was a nightmare.

Lil had heard his pain beneath the words, his reluctance to revisit that time. She couldn't imagine him hitting anyone. How shocking it must have felt, to be betrayed by both of them. Little wonder he'd been a broken man when he'd shown up in Fairweather, several months afterwards.

My father tried to visit me in jail, but I refused to see him. Now he phones and I answer, but that's all. I'm telling you this because I want you to know. I don't want secrets between us.

He'd asked then if she'd consider marrying him, and she'd said yes, and his father wasn't mentioned again – but Lil had wanted to know more, so the next time she and Tom met Joel and Sarah, she waited until she and Sarah were out of earshot, and she asked for more.

None of us could believe it, Sarah said. Tom and George had been very close, as close as a son and father could be. We couldn't get our heads around how George could have done it. Tom stayed with us for a few months after he came out of jail, but he was in a really bad way. Joel was worried about him. He didn't want him to go to Fairweather, it was so far away and he knew nobody, but that was precisely why Tom chose it.

What about Vivienne? What did she do?

Sarah shrugged. She went back to London, but after a few months she moved to the States. We don't have anything to do with her now, but her mum is Dad's sister, so we hear stuff.

And Tom and Joel's father? Do you still see him?

Here Sarah hesitated. Yes, we do. Maybe we shouldn't, but it's tricky. He's good to the children, and we feel it would be punishing them if we cut ties with him. But we never talk about what happened. We just don't go there.

What's he like?

He's charming. Loves going out on the town, knows everyone who's anyone. Likes a nice meal and a good bottle of wine. He's a consultant cardiologist, very well respected. He cut back on his hours when he turned sixty – he's sixty-three now – but he's very active, plays golf and does a bit of sailing. He still lives in Merrion Square, where the two boys grew up. Their mum died when Tom was in college, and Joel was starting his business – you probably know that.

Yes.

Sarah began scrolling through her phone. He's good-looking, she said, showing Lil a snap. This was taken on the night of the engagement party he threw for me and Joel at his house.

The photo showed Tom and Joel on steps that led up to a tall red-brick house, an older man positioned between them. Good-looking without a doubt, clear-skinned and dark-eyed, a bit of Tom around the mouth, Joel's high forehead and square chin. The three men looked happy, arms around each other's shoulders,

Tom and his father yet to make the acquaintance of Sarah's cousin Vivienne.

The estrangement saddened Lil, and worried her too. Could there be another layer to Tom's seeming inability to forgive his father? Was it possible that he still had feelings for Vivienne, the woman he'd first proposed to? Was that why Tom's wound remained open, two years after the event? If, as he claimed, he was truly happy now with Lil, wouldn't he find a way to let the other go?

The worry persisted, gnawing at her whenever she thought of their plan to marry. Maybe she was being paranoid, but she needed to know for sure that Tom was over Vivienne. She felt driven to act, to do something, anything, to resolve the situation. If she could somehow figure out a way to bring Tom and his father back together, it would be a good indication, she thought, that Vivienne no longer had a hold on Tom.

Not telling him of the real reason for her trip to Dublin was risky, she knew that. If he were to discover it, Tom might well regard her covert behaviour as another betrayal. It might even spell the end of them. But the fear she felt drove her on. She must do something. She must.

Tom didn't quite react in the way she'd expected when she told him that evening of her plans. 'Just a look around at what's out there,' she said. 'Dresses, shoes, bags, maybe hats. I know it's still ages away, but I thought it might be fun.'

She waited for a response that didn't immediately come. Could he possibly suspect her real reason for the trip?

Eventually he nodded. 'Sure,' he said. 'Whatever you want.' He hesitated. 'It just … brought something back, that's all.'

'What do you mean?'

He shut his laptop, sat back in the chair. 'Look, it's daft, but I'm just a bit … allergic to the whole wedding-prep stuff. Given what happened before.'

Given what happened with Vivienne, he meant. Lil's heart sank.

'Sweetheart, I'm sorry,' he said gently. 'I know you're nothing like her, I know that. She went completely overboard – it was crazy.' He smiled. 'Take no notice of me. Go to Dublin, look at stuff, have fun. You want me to come?'

It was the last thing she wanted. 'You can't,' she said. 'It's bad luck for you to see anything beforehand.' She was pretty sure browsing together wasn't bad luck, but he nodded.

'I'd be useless anyway. So let's go out to dinner when you get home on Thursday – what about dropping in downstairs?'

'We should,' she agreed, relieved at the change of topic.

The days passed pleasantly, the work in the library enjoyable, Judy and Karl amenable workmates. If she couldn't be in Fairweather, Lil thought, she was in a perfectly acceptable substitute. She loved the anticipation of seeing Tom as she walked home each day, loved the evenings they spent exploring their new neighbourhood or curled up in front of a film on telly – and most of the time she managed to push her worries away when they were together.

On Thursday morning Tom drove her to the station. 'I can walk,' she said, 'it's not far, and it's dry,' but he insisted. 'Have fun,' he told her as she climbed from the car, and she felt bad to be keeping him in the dark. She wasn't planning to have fun.

All the way to Dublin she wondered what she would say to Tom's father, if and when they came face to face. She really hadn't thought it through, hadn't thought beyond locating the house and ringing the bell – but she'd taken it this far, and she would press on, and hope inspiration hit at the right time.

On arrival in Heuston Station she decided to walk, in no rush to encounter George McLysaght. As she made her way along the quays, keeping an eye on the directions she'd requested on her phone, she conjured in her mind's eye the photo Sarah had shown her, hoping she'd identify the house from the details she remembered – three steps leading up to a black front door, black wrought-iron balconies at the ground-floor windows. If not, she'd have to ring doorbells until someone pointed her in the right direction.

At length she reached Merrion Square and walked slowly along its west side, but found museums and art galleries rather than houses. At the corner she turned onto the north side, and immediately felt that the layout, the buildings, were more in keeping with what she was looking for. It must be here. As she progressed slowly, checking each façade, her attention was suddenly caught by the loud slam of a door up ahead. She turned to see a dark-haired woman rushing down the front steps of a nearby house. Black jacket, black trousers, lime green scarf slung over one shoulder.

She strode rapidly towards Lil, heels clicking loudly on the path. Her right hand clutched the gathered strap of a black bag; with the other she held the edges of her jacket together. Close up, Lil saw with alarm that she was weeping openly, mouth contorted, tears running freely. As she brushed blindly past Lil the green scarf slid off, and would have dropped to the ground if Lil hadn't grabbed it in mid-flight.

'Your scarf,' she called, but the woman hurried on, either not hearing or not caring. Lil repeated it, more loudly, and still the owner didn't turn. She stood and watched her rapidly retreating figure, debating whether to run after her, and deciding against it.

She examined the abandoned scarf. It was feather light and delicately woven, intended more for decoration than warmth. She tied it to the closest streetlamp and moved on, wondering what had prompted the woman's flight in such a distraught state.

She could see the house from where she stood. She took in its black front door and black balconies. Could it be the one she was looking for? She moved closer, and decided it was. Everything tallied with the image in her head. She would ring the brass bell and see what happened.

She put her foot on the first step – and stopped. She glanced back up the street: the woman had disappeared from view. What if she'd just had a blazing row with George McLysaght? He might be in no mood to entertain Lil, or anyone.

And really, what was she doing there? What could she possibly achieve by this random visit? Already she felt uneasy about it. Even if her motives were good, she was butting into Tom's personal life without his permission or knowledge. And now that she thought about it, it was Tom she needed to persuade, not the man who phoned him every week, and who clearly wanted to reconcile.

She took her foot off the step. She turned and made her way back to the scarf she'd tied to the pole. She loved that shade of green – and what were the chances of the owner coming back to retrieve it? Minimal, surely – in her state, she probably wouldn't have a clue where to look for it. Much more likely that it would be claimed by someone else – and Lil *had* tried to return it.

She glanced around; nobody nearby. She quickly untied the scarf and pushed it down into her bag. She spent the following couple of hours trying on hats and shoes absently, her mind still on Merrion Square and the man she hadn't met after all, and the crying woman who'd emerged so dramatically from his house.

Eventually she made her way back to Heuston Station and caught her train, and sat opposite two women in identical navy jackets who didn't once look up from the books they were reading. She felt deflated, having achieved nothing. On the other hand, she hadn't done anything she'd have to hide from Tom – apart from stealing another woman's scarf, if you could call it theft. She mightn't mention that.

She pulled it from her bag and ran her hand along its length. No label on it, nothing to tell her what it was made of, but the soft wispy feel of it pleased her, and it was narrow enough to use as a hair wrap, if she wanted to tame her curls.

'Didn't see anything I liked,' she told Tom when she got home. The truth, with her mind miles away.

'Nothing to please you in the whole of Dublin?' he teased.

She laughed. 'Well, I didn't exactly do the whole of Dublin. I think I just wasn't in the mood. I decided it's too early to start looking.'

'Fair enough. Are you hungry for dinner?'

'Starving.'

It was past six, and she'd skipped lunch in her distraction, and the smell of food drifting in now through their open window was tantalising.

'Come on,' he said, and they descended the stairs.

To access the restaurant they had to exit the building through their front door and use the public entrance. They stepped inside and paused to take in their surroundings.

A big oval table dominated the small space. It was covered with a white cloth and set for about a dozen. Salt and pepper cellars were dotted about, and jugs of water, and little vases with flowers in them. The walls were painted pale lemon and decorated with framed watercolours.

There were five people already seated, two men at one end of the table, one male and two females at the other. A sign just inside the door instructed them to sit anywhere. Lil looked at the vacant seats in the centre of the table, wondering where best to position themselves. Not too close to either group – making small talk with strangers seemed like too big a challenge after her day.

'Hey there – come and join us.'

A dark-haired woman of what Gran would have described as generous proportions was already pushing out the chair next to her. She was part of the group of three, her seat facing the door. 'One here,' she said, patting the vacant chair, 'and one across, so we can chat.'

American accent. Lil didn't see that they had much choice, so she took the offered position, and Tom seated himself at the other side as instructed.

'Newbies,' the woman said. 'So easy to spot. We're all friends here – you'll feel at home in no time. I'm Heather. I was Emily's very first customer, and I just had to keep coming back, so I'm like part of the furniture now. And I've just made the acquaintance of Corey and Patricia here, on vacation from Canada. Corey's a housepainter and Patricia's a landscape gardener.'

She was like the hostess at a party, making sure all her guests were taken care of. Lil introduced herself and Tom, and added that they'd just moved in upstairs.

'Oh, hey – you're Emily's new tenants. Glad to meet you. Married?'

A bit direct. 'Next summer.'

'Well, congratulations. Look, Patricia – such a pretty ring. Planning kids?'

'… Not just yet.'

'No rush – you're young. So what do you do?'

'I work in the library.'

'Very worthy. I'm not much of a reader, I'm afraid – best I can manage is a flick through a magazine.'

'I'm starting a storytime,' Lil told her. Might as well begin spreading the news. 'The first one's on Saturday week at half past eleven. If you know anyone with young children you could mention it to them.'

'Well, that's me – I have a small girl. I should bring her along. And what do you do?' she asked, turning to Tom, and he told her he designed websites.

'Hey, lucky you – that's where the money is. I'm from California – my mom's family has a company in Silicon Valley.' She went back to Lil. 'So what do you think of our little town?'

'Very nice. We're just getting to know it.' To head her off from more questioning – one mention of Fairweather and she'd probably ask Lil if she knew the people who'd been killed in that terrible accident – Lil enquired if she'd lived long in Ireland.

'Oh yeah, long time. I got two girls who were born here. My eldest is eleven going on ninety – her dad did a runner when I told him she was on the way. I was just seventeen, he was a year older. Two kids having a kid. Haven't set eyes on him since. He was German – well, he probably still is, if he's still alive, ha-ha.'

She paused to take a forkful of her dinner. 'Emily will be right out,' she went on, mouth full. 'This is so good – it's the chicken pie. There's a choice of three dishes every evening. Just two when she opened, but now it's three.'

She gestured with her knife towards a blackboard on the wall, and Lil read *chicken pie* and *lasagne* and *butternut squash* and *chick pea curry*.

'Everything's good here,' the American told them. 'I've never once had a bad meal – and wait till you taste the desserts. Sometimes I skip dinner and just have two desserts – you know to look at me, right?'

'Er ...'

She took another mouthful, and again talked around it. 'Anyhow, my current partner is a paramedic, and we knew each other way back, long story. He was married before and has three kids from that, and we've had a daughter together, so we're a real Brady Bunch now. His older girl, just turned twenty-one, moved out last year, but his two boys are still at home with us. Luckily, everyone gets on OK – well, most of the time. Wouldn't be a real family if nobody had fights, right? Oh, and we have a cat too, just in case the house isn't quite crowded enough.'

Lil wondered if she ever stopped for breath.

Heather

SHE WAS TALKING TOO MUCH. SHE COULD HEAR herself running on and on like a Duracell bunny. She was wound up, tight as a banjo string. She'd been wound up since morning, when Jo had woken her too early, red-cheeked from sore gums – and when Heather had quietened her with a teething ring from the refrigerator and gone to crawl back into bed for the thirty precious minutes she had left, she discovered she'd got her period during the night, and Shane wasn't due home from work for another couple of hours, so guess who got to yank the sheet off.

To replace it she had to pull the stepladder out from under a pile of junk in the garage and haul it up the stairs so she could reach the top of the airing cupboard where the laundered sheets lived, and by the time she'd remade the bed and tossed her pyjamas into the laundry basket it wasn't worth getting into a clean pair and going back to bed, so she'd made coffee and burnt her tongue on it.

And the day had gone downhill from there.

A row with Lottie over breakfast when Heather had ordered her to bring Tinkerbell into the living room, as if she hadn't said a million times that the cat needed to be out of the kitchen when they were eating. Lottie did her usual 'you always blame me' grumble, even though Tinkerbell was her cat. Lord knew what she'd be like when she hit her teens.

And more moments of gladness after that: a bowl of Cheerios toppling from Jo's high chair to land with a splat on Eoin's rucksack; an electricity bill in the post that couldn't possibly be right; a last-minute search for Jack's football shorts, finally located at the bottom of the laundry basket, stiff with mud from his last game. Heather had brushed them clean as best she could and bundled them into his kit bag, ignoring his protests.

By the time she'd ferried Lottie and Jack to school in silence, and dropped Jo to Madge until lunchtime, all the while conscious of a familiar cramping pain in her abdomen, she was ready to go right back to bed, and she would have – she would happily have cancelled the few things she'd planned for today and crawled back under the duvet, with the radio and a couple of Wagon Wheels for company, if it hadn't been for the fact that Shane would be under it too.

Over the last while – a few weeks, maybe more – she'd gone

off him. There was no other way to put it. Everything he did was an irritation, from the way he brushed his teeth – *not* side to side, goddammit – to the sound of his laugh, too high-pitched for a man.

He was so pernickety about things too, always picking up after the kids, constantly wiping down worktops, hanging Heather's car keys on a hook if she left them out of her hand for one damn second – how had she ever thought any of that charming?

And he was such a doormat when it came to his ex. Yvonne wanted Jack to go to boarding school when he started secondary next year, when it was abundantly clear to Heather that Jack, sweet and sensitive and useless at knowing who to avoid, would be ideal fodder for bullies. Might as well paint a target on his jacket right now.

Where do *you* want him to go? Heather had asked Shane, and he'd said he'd much prefer the comp down the road, where Lottie was headed – and where she, fearless and feisty like her mother, would be on hand to keep him out of any bully's way. So put your foot down, Heather had said, and Shane had shrugged and told her he'd rather a quiet life, and maybe it would do Jack good to be away from home. Honestly, that man needed to grow a backbone.

And of course, of *course*, when she'd told him about Astrid leaving the house to Pip and nothing at all to her girls, he'd said he could understand it, with Pip having been deserted by his mother, and nobody knowing who his father was. And Heather had gritted her teeth, having wanted him to sympathise, and to agree it had been hurtful for Astrid not to leave the girls anything, when even Christine had got a necklace. Why did he have to be so *reasonable*?

She should talk to him, she *knew* that. She should tell him how she was feeling, point out the things that annoyed her. He had so many good qualities – she'd point those out too, for balance. He was a brilliant father to all the children, including Lottie, who was mad about him. He was helpful at home, even when he looked drained after his night shift. He bulk-cooked dinners on his days off, because Heather was rubbish at cooking.

He was a good man – no one could argue with that. Paramedics were heroes, dealing with stuff that would send anyone else running for the hills. He was generous and kind, and it wasn't fair to keep him in the dark about her passing discontent.

But … what if this wasn't a passing thing? What if they simply didn't work any more? What then?

She still had her old house across town, the little two-up, two-down terraced red-brick that she and Lottie had been living in when Shane had come back into her life. The one Shane's father had lived in until his death, and left to Heather in his will as a thank-you for working as his carer. She loved that little house, so different from the soulless mansion she'd grown up in.

She'd put it up for rent eighteen months ago, after the move to Shane's house, but the woman who'd taken it, a widow who'd returned to Ireland after the death of her Swedish husband, had herself died in June, and Heather hadn't yet got around to looking for a new tenant, so it was lying empty.

She could move back there with her girls, if it turned out that she and Shane had run their course. It was small and humble, but the three of them would manage – and she could always sell it down the line and buy something bigger, if they needed more space as the girls grew up.

And in the meantime, here she was eating dinner at The Food of Love, after a stupid row with Shane about tablemats, of all things. She'd put out dinner plates without them: when she'd spotted him going around slipping them underneath the plates she'd lost it, and ended up stalking out after telling him what he could do with his dinner.

It was roast chicken too, which she loved.

Here she was, frazzled and wound up and talking too much to folk she'd only just met. And maybe she was imagining it, but suddenly it seemed that they were all giving her the kind of guarded look you'd send in the direction of someone you saw muttering to themselves in a shopping mall. Probably wishing they'd chosen any other night to come in.

Emily appeared, and Heather took the opportunity to shut up and finish her pie, for once not having the heart to stay for dessert. 'It was real nice to meet you,' she said to everyone as she rose, having asked Emily to box up a portion of the cheesecake for Shane. Peace offering.

'Might see you in here again,' she added to Emily's new tenants, and the curly-haired woman, who looked like she wouldn't say boo to a goose, agreed that she might. Her fiancé had the kind of face you remembered, all cheekbones and striking eyes. If Heather were free, she'd be drawn to that face.

Halfway home her phone rang, and she saw Mom on the screen, and her mind automatically did the calculation. Middle of the day in California.

'Hi, Mom.'

'Hello, Heather.' Always Heather, never honey or sweetheart, never anything but Heather. She'd never been that kind of mom. 'How is everyone?'

'Everyone's fine. How are you and Dad?'

There was a little pause. 'I have news, Heather.'

Not good news, by the sound of it. 'Is Dad OK?'

'He's fine. We're both fine. We're getting a divorce.' Said so matter-of-factly that for a second it went by Heather, until it screeched to a halt and came back.

'What? You're divorcing? You and Dad?'

She shouldn't have been surprised. The only surprise should have been that they'd taken so long about it. For as far back as she could remember they'd been a mismatch, with Mom too needy and tempestuous, and Dad too busy with other stuff to pay her the attention she craved. Heather remembered blazing rows full of flying crockery and accusations and insults, invariably followed by angry silences that could go on for days. There must have been periods of calm, when nobody was name-calling and peace reigned, but it was the other times that stood out. A real barrel of laughs being their only kid.

So news of a divorce shouldn't have pulled the rug out from under her, but for some reason it did.

'I've had enough, Heather,' her mother said. 'It's time for us to split. My shrink agrees. We're toxic together.'

'Wow.' How long had they been husband and wife? Heather was twenty-eight, and dimly aware that she'd been a late addition to the marriage. Thirty-four, thirty-five years maybe. 'Well, I'm … sorry to hear it.' Was she sorry, or still too astonished to take it in? 'So what now? Have you moved out?'

'I certainly have not. He has. He's taken a suite at the Four Seasons.'

Of course he had. His favourite hotel in San Francisco, all polished wood and thick carpets and impeccably groomed staff. Every birthday meal, every family occasion that Heather could remember had happened in the restaurant at the Four Seasons. His suite probably had a Golden Gate view.

'I hope it goes well – I mean, as well as it can.'

'It'll go how it goes, Heather. These things are never pleasant. I've got a top attorney, Tina Mendez. You went to school with her son, Danny.'

'Right.' Heather didn't want to imagine the legal bills. Tina would be laughing all the way to the bank. She vaguely remembered Danny, one of the nerds, hiding his braces and acne behind a computer. Probably coining it in Silicon Valley now.

'I'm thinking of coming to Ireland for a while,' her mother said.

Uh-oh. 'What? You mean now, or when it's all over?'

'Now, to get away from it. Let Tina fight it out – I have no appetite for it. I've told her what I want, and I won't accept anything less.'

Poor Tina. Poor rich Tina. How long did divorces take? With a couple as moneyed as her parents, and with two strong personalities between them, Heather guessed it wouldn't be quick. 'You know we'll be happy to see you.' Lottie at least would be delighted: she loved the glamour of having American grandparents. 'I'll book you into the hotel.' The town still had nothing better to offer than Fleming's, three stars on a good day.

'I'd really prefer not, Heather. I don't enjoy staying in a hotel on my own. Too public.'

'An apartment then – I'll see if I can find an Airbnb.'

'Would it be serviced? I'd need staff.'

She would. 'I doubt it, Mom. They don't really do that here.'

Silence fell.

'I was thinking,' her mother said, 'that I could stay with you.'

'With us? Well, yeah, of course you— Well, it's pretty crowded. We only have one bathroom.'

More silence. Was Mom seriously willing to share a bathroom with six others? It would appear that she was.

'Well, if you're sure you want to slum it with us, we'll fit you in.'

Where, though? They barely had enough room for themselves. Jo was in a cot with Heather and Shane, Eoin and Jack were in bunks in the second bedroom, and Lottie was in the tiny box room that had been Jack's before she and Heather had moved in. There was the dining room which they never ate in but which the kids had taken over, with the table serving for homework and table tennis, and a telly in the corner, and Lottie's karaoke machine, and Eoin's guitar, and Jack's sports stuff.

And even if they had all the space in the world, could she and Mom live under one roof for any length of time without wanting to shoot each other? Very doubtful – but now it was said, now that the rather lukewarm invitation had been extended, she could only hope that it would be turned down.

It wasn't. 'We'll cope,' her mother said. 'You know I don't expect a fuss.'

Heather knew nothing of the sort. Mom was the most high-maintenance person she knew. She thrived on people fussing around her.

'When were you thinking of coming?'

'I could get a flight to Shannon Airport on Sunday, arriving Monday morning your time.'

Monday. Today was Thursday. Lord. 'OK, let me have flight details when you book, I can pick you up at the airport. Don't bring too much luggage – we don't have a lot of storage. See you soon.'

After hanging up she rang her father and got his voicemail. 'Call me,' she said, 'anytime before midnight my time.'

When she got home she found Shane alone in the kitchen emptying the dishwasher. 'Where's everyone?'

'Jo's asleep, the others are in the den.' The dining room den. 'Plenty of leftovers, if you want them.'

'I ate at Emily's.' She produced the cheesecake. 'Sorry, time of month.' Chickening out again, able to talk about anything except what mattered.

'Poor you.'

'I'll finish that, you go eat.'

So he ate the cheesecake while she stacked plates and returned pots to their shelf. 'Mom rang, by the way.' She told him about the divorce. 'She wants to hole up someplace far away while the lawyers fight it out, and with her only child being here, she picked Ireland.'

'You OK?'

She looked at him. 'I'm fine. A divorce is long overdue. I'm afraid I told her she could stay here – she didn't give me much choice. I offered to book her into Fleming's, but she didn't want a hotel, or an apartment unless it came with a maid.'

He didn't bat an eyelid. 'So when does she arrive?'

'Monday morning.'

'We can put her in Lottie's room. Lottie can have the fold-up in the den.'

'You don't mind?'

'Course not. She's family.'

More charitable towards her mother than Heather was. Then

again, he hadn't grown up in the battlefield Heather had called home.

After he'd left for work she broke the news to the others, and got the enthusiastic response she'd expected from Lottie. 'She'll be staying here, so you'll have to sleep in the dining room, on the fold-out bed' – and Lottie said great, probably thinking of the TV she could watch when everyone else was asleep.

Half an hour later Heather's phone rang as she was putting her feet up with a vodka and Coke. 'Dad – thanks for calling back.'

'Anything wrong?' he asked.

Anything wrong? Had he forgotten his wife was divorcing him? 'I spoke with Mom. She told me you're splitting up.'

He laughed. He actually laughed. 'Heather, your mother's being your mother. She's looking for attention, that's all.'

'She's got a lawyer on the case.'

'Tina Mendez? Please. They play tennis together.'

Talk about denial. 'She says you've moved out.'

'I gave her some space, that's all. I'll be back when she starts making sense again.'

'She's coming to Ireland. She's arriving on Monday.'

'Is she?' Still sounding amused. 'Couldn't handle her own company. How long is she staying?'

'As long as it takes, she says.'

He laughed again. For a man on the verge of losing his wife of

thirty-something years he seemed a bit too happy, so she gave up
and told him of Lottie's haircut and Jo's emerging teeth, and he
spoke of the new wing for the local hospital he was sponsoring,
and the yacht he was thinking of buying, which could probably
hold her little red-brick house on its deck.

'Better go,' he said then. 'I got a meeting with the board.'
She didn't bother asking which board – it would mean nothing
to her. As she was debating the merits of a second vodka, her
phone beeped with a text from Emily.

Hope you're OK. You seemed a bit off when you were here.

Even rushing around serving meals, Emily was able to assess
her mood. *All good, just fancied a bit of me time.* She hadn't said
anything to Emily about going off Shane – saying it aloud to
anyone might turn it into something she needed to act on.

Another beep: *See you Sunday.*

She'd almost forgotten. They'd arranged to get together for an
hour in the afternoon to decide what to do about Astrid's cottage.
They were meeting in Bill's house – or Bill and Emily's house, as
it was now.

She remembered when Emily had moved in with him a year
and some months ago, the timing dictated by his daughter's
disappearance. He needs me to help look after Pip, Emily had
said – and despite this somewhat unromantic start, it was all
working out nicely. Anyone could see they were nuts about each
other, and Pip was the sweetest little thing.

Heather's only concern was how close Emily and Pip had become. Wonderful, of course – but what if his mother was to reappear? Heather couldn't imagine Emily ever wanting to hand him back. It was a tiny concern, with no real likelihood of Christine showing up again, but it was there.

On Sunday afternoon she packed Jo into the car and drove to Bill and Emily's. Coffee was made, and just-baked sesame biscuits served – and it quickly became apparent to Heather that she was surplus to requirements.

'Are you agreed,' Bill asked her, 'that we should put it up for rent?'

'I guess so. Sounds like a no-brainer. Like the attorney said, we need to make the money to pay that tax demand.'

'We do,' Emily agreed, 'and Bill is going to take care of whatever has to be done.'

Heather dunked a biscuit in her coffee. 'Does stuff have to be done? The place always seemed fine to me. A bit old-fashioned maybe, but that's OK.'

'I'd like to check the wiring and the plumbing,' Bill replied, 'to be on the safe side. And we should investigate the boiler, and fit a few smoke alarms. Stuff like that.'

'Well, sure, but apart from—'

'And we were thinking of seeing what's underneath the carpets,' Emily said. 'If there are old boards, it would be a shame not to uncover them. And the whole house could do with painting, inside and out – and the kitchen units are so dark.'

Sounded like they were just going to pull it to pieces and put it back together again. Heather looked from one to the other. 'Have you been there since the will?' she asked, and Emily told her they'd dropped over the day after to have a look.

Nice of them to tell her.

She pushed aside the stab of irritation. No point in falling out, not when they were supposed to be managing the house together. She wondered suddenly why Astrid had included her in this arrangement – weren't Bill and Emily demonstrating right now that they could do fine without her? – but she *had* been included, so she would play her part.

'I can help with the painting,' she said. 'I've done heaps of it.'

'Not at all,' Emily said. 'You have enough on your plate, with Jo and the others. Bill can do it – and if an extra pair of hands is needed we thought we could ask Tom to pitch in.'

Huh. 'Who's Tom?'

'My new tenant. You met him and Lil the other night in the restaurant.'

Mr Cheekbones. She'd forgotten his name. 'I thought he was in computers.'

'According to Lil, he's handy as well – and Astrid did leave money to use on the house.'

Great. They'd rather pay a stranger than let Heather help. She made one last attempt. 'I'll clean the windows. I can do that much.'

Emily looked at Bill. Was she waiting for his permission? 'We'll give a shout so,' he said, 'when the rest is done.'

Pushed out, it felt like. You're not needed, so bugger off till we call you. Heather drained her mug and stood up. 'I should get going. House needs cleaning before Mom lands in the morning.'

Emily looked at her in surprise. 'Your mother's coming? You never said.'

'Right, I forgot you didn't know. There's been a development.' She told them about the divorce as she got Jo back into her jacket. 'Mom's getting out of the way while her attorney does the wheeling and dealing.'

'And she's staying with you?'

'Yup.'

'How long for?'

'Until it's done, however long that takes. Dad's in denial, waiting for her to change her mind and come back to him.'

Emily studied her. 'Are you OK?'

'I'm OK.'

But she was not OK. She couldn't be in the same room with Shane for more than five minutes without wanting to throw something, and her mother was coming tomorrow for what might be a long stay. She was most definitely not OK.

Emily walked out to the car with her, Pip in her arms. As they approached Heather's car an older woman walked slowly by. 'Two lovely children,' she said, 'and their mams.' Heather waited for Emily to correct her but Emily just smiled – delighted,

Heather knew, to be mistaken for Pip's mother. Wasn't the first time.

It was on the tip of her tongue to say something to her friend – a caution, a warning, a reminder that he didn't belong to her – but she said nothing, knowing it wouldn't be well received.

It was a concern. Tiny, but there.

Christine

'WHAT TIME'S YOUR TRAIN TOMORROW?' SHE ASKED, rinsing lettuce leaves. Trying to sound casual, like she was just making conversation, because Bernie was scrubbing potatoes at the big sink and pretending not to listen, but of course she was listening. Bernie would have it all over the house before dinner, if she thought there was anything going on.

'Eleven,' the chef replied, chopping a cucumber so fast it terrified her. 'Leaving here half ten.' He'd shown her how to chop like that, how to position and move the knife, how to tuck in her fingertips so she wouldn't cut them off, but she wasn't half as fast as him. Just takes practice, he'd tell her. Keep at it and you'll get the hang. You'll be a pro in no time.

He was a good teacher. She'd learnt a lot from him. He'd

qualified as a chef ten years ago, got a job at a fancy restaurant in Dublin. Its name had meant nothing to Christine. Worked hard, played hard, he told her. Started on cocaine – literally everyone on the payroll was using. Got out of hand, moved on to bigger and better. Lost my job, kicked out of my place when I couldn't pay the rent. Went on the street. You know yourself.

She knew herself. She knew how it went, how your old life, the life you'd always taken for granted, began a slow slide away from you, how every day you lost a bit more of it. She knew the craving that would come at you, the clawing hunger that would worm into the marrow of your bones, the fierce need that would shove everything else out of its way and drive you to do things you'd never thought you would. She knew all about it. Been there, done that.

But not any more, not ever again. Now she was clean, and she was staying clean. Rehab hadn't worked for her the first time – it hadn't had a chance, not after she'd found out she was pregnant within forty-eight hours of arriving at the clinic. Health check, they'd told her, routine for anyone coming in – and just like that, she was told she was six weeks gone. It had felt like a sick joke, with her as the punchline – especially when she realised who the father must be. The cocky dealer who'd taken advantage of her desperation to get what he wanted, who'd smirked while she'd pleaded with him, promising to pay the next day. You can pay me now, he'd said, and she had.

But she'd stuck it out in rehab, still wanting to get fixed. She'd attended the meetings, taken part in the activities, kept the diary

– but her focus was lost. A baby was the last thing she needed. A baby, a creature wholly dependent on her, when she couldn't look after herself. Even worse, a baby by a man she loathed. A constant reminder of how deep she'd sunk.

She'd decided to get rid of it as soon as she was out of rehab, but when she'd told Dad – having no choice, because he'd have to pay for it – he'd talked her out of it. Promised he'd help her to raise it, promised she'd cope – but he'd lied because she hadn't coped.

The remaining months of pregnancy had been worse than any rehab, the constant gnawing pain in her gut and in her limbs adding to the nausea and backache and heartburn that had plagued her.

And then there was Emily, making eyes at her father whenever she came to the house, thinking Christine was blind as well as pregnant. She would always ask how things were going, smiling and letting on to be concerned, bringing salads and hummus and stuff, but you could see she wished Christine wasn't there, so she could have Dad all to herself.

And the baby, after the horror of his birth, after the endless knifing agony that had reduced her to a screeching, howling animal, after all that, when Philip was placed damp and bawling on her chest, she'd looked at his screwed-up red face, his matted dark hair, and thought: Is that it? Was all that for this? She'd waited for the rush of love that she'd assumed would come, even though she hadn't wanted him, but nothing at all came.

Again she'd tried, letting a nurse show her how to change his disgusting nappies, how to bathe him – so slippery, so scary – and how to feed him with a bottle, Christine having been too rundown and underweight for breastfeeding to be an option. Back home, Dad had done as much as he could to help, but less than a week later she'd taken off, unable to handle this weird new situation, craving the oblivion again.

She'd told herself she was doing everyone a favour by getting out of their way, leaving her son with a grandfather who loved him, giving Dad and Emily space to go wherever they were going together. Dad would be upset, she knew that – but in the long run it was for the best.

Emily would have been over the moon. Were they still together? Christine had no idea. Were they settled and cosy with Philip, or had Emily found someone her own age and left Dad to raise his grandson alone?

He would slip into her thoughts now and again. Her baby, her child, who was growing up without her. She would try to conjure up his infant face, but her time with him had been too brief for her to recall it. Blue eyes, she thought, dark hair, but no clear features materialised. Did he have teeth now? Could he sit up? Was he crawling? Would he be speaking? She hadn't a clue, and it saddened her. She'd run out on him, his mother had let him down – and when she thought of how loved she'd been by Mum, she'd have to push all thought of him away, or go mad.

And Dad – how was he doing? Did he hate her for running away from him for the second time, and for leaving Philip to be looked after? So many times she'd wanted to get in touch, to tell him she was OK, even when she wasn't, to say sorry – but she'd never done it. Too scared of his reaction, or too reluctant to get his hopes up, when they'd probably be dashed again. She'd hurt him enough; she'd leave him alone.

But now everything was different. Now she was getting ready to start again. Now she had Ethel, twenty-two years out of addiction and working in the rehab clinic. Lovely motherly Ethel, set to become Christine's sponsor when she left the transition house.

. And now she had the chef. He was the miracle she'd never expected. Encountering her on the streets of Galway when she'd been begging for money, crouching down to talk to her, the first person in weeks apart from fellow addicts to make any kind of connection with her. There's a better way, he'd said quietly – and because he'd looked her straight in the eye, because for the first time in so long someone's gaze didn't slide away at the sight of her, she'd listened. Trust me, he'd said, and she'd seen something in his face that told her she could.

He'd saved her. He'd got her somehow into the rehab place where he'd already done his time, and from there she'd come here, the transition house for recovering users who had no place else to go, where he'd been working as a chef for the past eighteen months, in between trying to help others like Christine.

And within a week of her moving in, he'd asked if she'd like to be his assistant in the kitchen. Seeing something in her like she'd seen in him that very first time he'd spoken to her. Hardly able to believe that anyone would want her, wasted and pitiable as she'd been, but it seemed that he had.

We need to build you up, he'd said, making her French toast when she told him she used to love it as a kid, tempting her with bowls of chicken noodle soup, and buttery croissants warm from the oven, and pancakes filled with softly stewed berries and topped with cream. In his company she felt treasured, cherished. In his company she began to gain the weight she needed.

He was the only one here who knew about Philip, the only one she'd told. The people in charge must know of her pregnancy – she was in the system; it had to be on her file – but nobody had brought it up, and she hadn't mentioned it. They probably thought she'd lost the baby, or given it away for adoption.

But when the chef had asked, when he'd said, Tell me everything, she'd told him. About losing Mum when she was sixteen, and everything going wrong after that. About Dad and how he'd tried to hang on to her, and failed. About her years on the street, and the baby conceived in addiction, and left in the care of his grandfather when he was just a week old.

She'd wanted to lay herself bare before him, to show him all that she was, even if it meant risking him turning away from someone who'd abandoned her child – but to her astonishment and delight, he didn't turn away. To her great relief, the news of Philip's existence hadn't put him off.

You're a mother, he'd said. That's amazing – and when he'd said it, when he'd put it like that, she'd begun thinking that maybe it *was* amazing. She was a mother, a mum. Maybe if she tried again, now that she was clean, she'd get the hang of it. Maybe she'd come to have feelings for Philip, if it wasn't too late to reclaim him.

She wished Mum was still around to help her. She'd tried not to think about Mum when she'd been on the streets: it was too painful. But she wouldn't have been on the streets, would she, if Mum hadn't died? She wouldn't have tried that first pill if she hadn't been missing Mum so much it hurt everywhere.

She and the chef had to be a secret in the house. No relationships between residents had been drilled into them. Nothing for three months after you leave here – that was another golden rule. Get yourself strong first, they were told, before you commit to anyone else. But she'd already committed; they both had. They'd bloomed in private, stealing kisses when nobody else was around, whispering promises to each other. Making plans.

And tomorrow he was taking the train to Dublin, because he'd been offered a job in a cousin's bakery, and he was urging Christine to leave too. Make contact with your dad, he said. Ask him to help you get back on your feet. Get to know Philip. It's time, Chrissy.

But what if Dad didn't want her back? He'd almost cut her out of his life once before, when Christine had stolen the old woman's necklace. I can't deal with you any more, he'd said. I can't watch you destroy yourself. Don't come home, he'd said, meaning don't show up every couple of weeks for a shower and a change of clothes, like she'd been doing – and the shock of hearing that from him, the first time he'd pushed her away instead of trying to hang on to her, had been enough to turn her around, to make her agree to try rehab.

But now, after her second tumble from grace, her second

middle-of-the-night flit from home, there was a real danger that he'd follow through this time – and where could she go, if the only home she'd ever known was denied to her, and if she and the chef had to stay apart for three months?

She'd have been happy to ignore that advice. Three months felt like an eternity – but the chef was adamant. We need to do it right, he'd said. We need to make sure we're both strong enough, so we'll stay clean together. It'll be worth the wait, he'd said – and to make it a little easier, he'd come up with an idea. We'll send postcards, once a week. I'll give you my address in Dublin, and you can write the first one when you're out.

'Don't take too long,' he said, as he was leaving the next morning. 'Come out soon. I'll be watching for that postcard' – and she wanted more than anything to bury her face in his jacket and cling to him, to stop him from going, or to go with him, but because they were within sight if not earshot of Cathy, who was driving him to the station, she kept her hands in her pockets.

'I'll miss you,' she said, and he echoed it and climbed into the car, and she smiled and waved, and then went for a long walk so nobody would hear her crying her eyes out, and nobody would see her, when she'd finally managed to stem the tears, sitting on a low stone wall and staring bleakly at the photo of him she'd taken the day before, right after he'd taken one of her.

And three days after that, when she was trying to screw up her courage to go to the office and tell Ethel she thought she might be ready to leave, Bernie said, 'You're in the paper.'

'What?'

'Someone's looking for you,' and she'd felt a leap – the chef, not able after all to live without her – but it wasn't the chef.

Seeking the whereabouts of Christine Geraghty, daughter of Bill and the late Betty, in relation to a will bequest. Please get in touch with your family.

'I thought you said you had no family,' Bernie said, clattering dishes in the sink. Bernie always sounded angry when she worked, banging and thumping. A wonder the crockery survived.

'I didn't think they'd want to know me.'

'Well, someone's left you something. Might be worth your while getting in touch.'

Christine didn't believe in signs – or she hadn't, up to now. Hard to think this wasn't a sign though, coming right when she was trying to find the courage to face Dad, to take the first step in her departure from the house. The ad had no name attached to it, but he had to be the one who'd put it in – which meant, didn't it, that he hadn't disowned her, and he wouldn't tell her to get lost if she showed up?

When she showed up.

In relation to a will bequest. She wondered who'd died, and what she'd been left in the will. With a skip of her heart she thought *he* might have died, and someone else – his sister Grace? – might have been responsible for the ad. But she had no number for Grace, who lived in England, and who hadn't come to see Philip when he was born.

Or it might have been Emily who'd put the ad in, if they hadn't split up. She didn't want it to be Emily. She'd just have to hope it was Dad looking for her.

She was nervous and excited and hopeful. So many feelings colliding with each other. So many challenges ahead. So much possibility. She thought of the Dublin address, tucked inside her pillowcase where nobody would find it.

Later that day she went to the office.

OCTOBER

Emily

'LOOKING GOOD,' SHE CALLED, AND FROM HIS ladder Tom turned his head.

'Hi, Emily. Yeah, nearly there. Another hour or so should finish it.'

They'd been lucky with the weather. Not a drop of rain in the past two days, perfectly timed to allow Tom to paint the outside walls while Bill wrapped things up inside.

Between them, in just under two weeks, they'd given the entire house a facelift. They'd replaced the old oil boiler and two ancient radiators. In the kitchen they'd sanded the dark-wood cabinet doors and painted them white, and ripped out the lino and put down tiles. They'd got rid of bedroom carpets and restored the old floorboards beneath. They'd changed washers in taps and filled cracks in plaster. They'd oiled hinges and locks and given a fresh coat of paint to every wall and ceiling.

While all that was going on, Emily had organised new pillows and mattresses and bed linen and cushions and rugs. She'd chosen new window blinds for the bathroom and kitchen, and crockery and saucepans to replace ones that had served their time. She did it all with mixed feelings: while she enjoyed seeing the house becoming fresher and brighter, it was saddening to think they were erasing traces of Astrid.

That blue teapot with the daisies, and the chip on the lid; so many cups of tea Astrid would have made in it, for herself and her visitors. The mattress they'd replaced on her bed, the kitchen lino, the carpets, the wallpaper they'd painted over, had all been part of her life here. But they had their memories, and they'd never be erased.

They'd used gravel and a raised bed in front of the house to make the space low-maintenance, knowing that a tenant might not appreciate having to upkeep the grounds, but the back garden, which Astrid had nurtured and cherished, was staying the same. They were taking nothing away, the fuchsia and lavender and broom and the rest of it would flower again as it had in the days when she'd been there to enjoy it – and her old gardener Markus, whom Emily had tracked down through the local garden centre, had been recruited to call once a month to handle any upkeep over the autumn and winter. The garden feeds my soul, Astrid had said once to Emily. That, and my music.

Her music was gone now. The mahogany record player – too

big really for the little sitting room, but a lovely solid piece of furniture – had been picked up before the renovations started by her husband's nephew, when Emily had got in touch to ask if there was anything he'd like from the house. I remember my mother admiring it, one time I brought her to visit, he said. I'm going to surprise her with it. He'd also taken Astrid's music collection: not much point in leaving it behind, with nothing to play the records on.

If he resented not having inherited the house, he gave no sign of it. She told me about that little lad, he said, and about her plan to leave him this place. She asked if I'd be OK with it, and I told her the house was hers and she should leave it to whoever she wanted. She was happy here, he said. She certainly loved that garden of hers.

Emily wondered if he'd known anything of the trauma of Astrid's past. Her husband surely had known, but maybe it hadn't gone further. To take the place of the record player she found a smart little cream unit with two drawers and a wooden top. She put a houseplant on it, an aloe vera in a white pot, and a verbena-scented candle.

An older person, she thought, a widow or widower would be a reliable tenant. Or maybe a young couple, just starting out. If Tom and Lil weren't in the apartment, they'd have been perfect. She was nervous of letting strangers in here, as she had been with the apartment. They'd just have to hope that whoever moved in would look after it.

'All done,' Tom said, putting his head around the door later, as

Emily was stowing the last of the new cutlery in a clean drawer. 'Hope the rain holds off a while – I don't like the look of the clouds.'

'Fingers crossed.' Emily took her phone from her bag. 'Thanks so much, Tom. Bill will be in touch about payment.'

'No rush. See you soon.'

After he'd gone she rang Heather, and again her call went unanswered. Three calls this week, and none of them returned. No sign of her in the restaurant either. I'm not around, her voicemail said. You know what to do after the beep.

She'd be busy, of course, with her mother staying. Emily knew their relationship had always been rocky. She'd met the mother, met both parents when they'd flown over to spend Christmas with Heather and Lottie a couple of years ago, and she'd found them to be perfectly polite and charming. Don't be fooled, Heather had said. Dad's fairly normal, but Mom's hard work – and now with a divorce in the offing, who knew what state her mother was in?

Still, it wouldn't take much to pick up the phone. 'Hope things are OK,' Emily said. 'Hope your mother's visit is going well. Just letting you know that Astrid's house is ready for a tenant – all that's left is the window cleaning, if you still want to do it. And we'll need to word the ad too – give a shout when you're free.' She'd have to respond to that.

She's hurt, Bill had said, after their last meeting with her, when Emily and Bill had told her of their plans for the cottage, and she'd seemed a little off to Emily. It's understandable, Pip getting the house, such a huge gift, and her girls not mentioned at all. I can see her point.

Bill always saw everyone's point. It was one of the many things Emily loved about him, his ability to empathise, to put himself in another's shoes, despite whatever difference of opinion there might be between them. It was this very empathy, Emily knew, that must torture him so much when he thought of Christine. It must kill him to imagine her life now.

He'd put an ad in every one of the national papers looking for her. He'd paid for it to run three days a week for six weeks. Seeking the whereabouts of Christine Geraghty, it read, daughter of Bill and the late Betty, in relation to a will bequest. That was the carrot he was dangling, the thing he hoped would bring her back to him.

It made Emily cringe every time she read it. Two weeks it had been running so far, and not a sign of a response, not a whisper – and if she'd been a betting woman, Emily would have put a substantial sum on the possibility that all six weeks would go by without Christine showing up, and Bill's money would have been thoroughly wasted. And what then? The private investigator he'd hinted at, she supposed, just to use up the rest of Astrid's gift to him.

And the awful thing, the horrible secret she had to keep from him, was that she was hoping Christine wouldn't be found. How selfish was that, knowing how desperately Bill longed to see his daughter again? But if Christine did come back, if by some miracle she reappeared, there was a chance, a tiny chance, that Emily and Bill would lose Pip, and that didn't bear thinking about.

Pip was like a gift Emily had done nothing to deserve, but one she'd accepted gladly. Right from the first day she'd taken him in her arms she was lost, completely in thrall to him. She loved whenever anyone mistook him for hers – and in another year or two, she and Bill would begin to give him … well, in reality she supposed they'd be his uncles or aunts, but to all intents and purposes they'd be siblings. She couldn't wait.

She locked up the cottage and got into her car for the drive home. Today was Tuesday, one of her closed days, and she and Bill had decided to treat themselves to dinner at Borelli's, their favourite Italian restaurant. Emily would have cannelloni tonight, and Bill would probably go for lasagne, like he usually did.

But they didn't go to Borelli's that evening. They didn't go anywhere that evening.

Lil

SHE PUT HER KEY INTO THE LOCK AND TURNED IT, glad as always, after a day spent mostly on her feet, to be back at the apartment. She still thought of it as the apartment: it hadn't yet become home in her head. Perfectly understandable, Gran said, that Fairweather still had a hold on her.

It did have a hold on her. She missed Gran, and the friends and locals she'd grown up with. She missed the sea, which had been such a massive part of her life. She was as much at home in the water as she was on land – more so after the accident, when something stronger than herself had pulled her back there, day after day. The shock of the icy water – her family had been year-round swimmers – had been the only thing that could distract her from the grief, the only thing that could lift, even temporarily, the unbearable sadness that had threatened constantly to engulf her, to render her completely insensible. Living away from the sea now was so hard – she had to keep reminding herself that this was temporary.

Her family home was let. She'd advertised it as soon as she'd got the job here, and three young musicians had signed a six-month lease and moved in the day after Tom had moved out. We need a quiet space to write songs for an album, they'd told her. This house is perfect.

Happily, Gran approved of them. They're polite, she'd reported. They called round to ask if I'd mind if they played music in the garden. I must say I quite enjoy it. And when Lil and Tom returned to live there, they'd give the house a facelift. It needed a new kitchen, and much of the furniture could do with replacing, and they were going to check out solar panels.

And hopefully, they'd fill it with children.

'Lil?'

Halfway up the stairs, she turned to see their landlady at the restaurant kitchen door, aproned as usual. A little after five: she'd be in the middle of dinner preparations.

'Someone phoned here,' she said, 'about an hour ago. She said she was just checking that she had the right address for Tom. Said she was a friend.'

'Did you get her name?'

'No – she didn't give it.'

'Did she leave a number?'

'No – it came up as private on my phone, and she hung up before I had a chance to ask for it.' She gave an apologetic grin. 'Sorry – it's not much of a message.'

'No problem. I'll let him know. Thanks, Emily.'

She and Tom had been back to the restaurant a few times since their first visit, feeling under a slight obligation. It was no hardship though: the food was always tasty – and with Tom by her side Lil felt less self-conscious among strangers. There had been no further sightings there of Heather, the American woman they'd met on their first night, but she'd shown up at Lil's storytimes since then with her chubby baby. Lil had thought her quite overbearing, but in the library she came across as friendly and funny, and just as ready to laugh at herself as at anyone else.

Upstairs, Lil unpacked groceries before getting out of her work clothes. Judy had never said she had to wear skirts, but they put her in a more businesslike mood. She showered and changed into sweatshirt and loose trousers, and slipped her feet into soft leather pumps – not robust enough for the Irish climate but perfect as house shoes – that Hollie had brought her back from a trip to Greece about five summers ago.

She wondered about the woman who'd phoned looking for Tom. Checking that she had the right address, Emily had said. Was she planning to call on him? Send something to him? Odd that she hadn't given Emily her name. A friend, she'd said, which didn't really narrow it down much. Lil thought of Olga married to Fintan, neighbours from Merrion Square, who still sent him a card at Christmas, and Birgit and Ursula, a couple he'd worked with in Dublin before he'd moved to London.

She supposed it could have been Olga, organising this year's Christmas card list and looking for where to send Tom's. October was a little early to be doing that, but she might be one of those very methodical people who bought their Christmas presents in the January sales.

As she was slotting lemon wedges and shallots between chicken fillets she heard Tom's step on the stairs, and a smile came unbidden. She scattered oregano and drizzled oil, and slid the roasting dish into the oven just as he walked in.

'Hello,' she said, lifting her face for his kiss, and returning it. Taking the bunch of flowers he offered, finding the vase for them. He brought flowers home every week from a little florist on the corner of the street whose owner wasn't afraid to mix her colours. Today's mix was dahlias as ruby red as wine – Lil dipped her head and smelt chocolate – and beautiful orange and yellow irises that Gran grew in her garden, and a fluff of something blue and frothy. Somehow they worked together – the florist knew what she was doing.

'Can I help with anything?' Tom asked.

'No, all set.' When he'd kicked off his boots and washed his hands and opened a bottle of beer for her, and taken another from the fridge to the couch, she told him of the woman who'd phoned Emily without leaving a name.

'Odd.' He yawned, stretching his arms wide. 'Joel phoned a while ago.'

She was glad the brothers at least were close. 'Did he? Any news?'

'Nothing much. Harry had his first sleepover. Big excitement.'

'Sleepover? Harry's six.'

'It was harmless – the pal lives two doors away. Joel and Sarah were waiting for the parents to call and say he wanted to go home, but he lasted all night.'

'Little dote.'

She'd wanted to include them in the wedding day, so Harry was to be their pageboy and his sister Emily, almost four, flower girl, but Sarah had warned Lil that she could back out at the last minute. Lil wasn't bothered either way. The lack of a flower girl – or a pageboy, come to that – wouldn't make or break the day.

Their guest list was short, just fourteen in total, four of whom were children. The hotel was in Italy, located in a village on the Amalfi coast. Tom had found it on the internet. It was small and family run, and it sounded lovely. The wedding would be out of doors, since sunshine was pretty much a given in June. They'd exchange vows under a flowered archway, and the meal would be eaten on a vine-covered terrace, with views of the sea.

And whenever she thought about the day, Lil had mixed feelings.

Would they still be together next June, or would Tom say, between now and then, that he had something to tell her? Would he talk about Vivienne and break her heart? And even if that didn't happen, if they made it to the day without a hitch, she dreaded the sadness that she knew to be lying in wait, preparing to hijack and possibly overwhelm her. Sadness would be inevitable, with the absence of the people she most wanted to be there.

Her sister Hollie should have been the first of them to marry, with Lil as her bridesmaid. Pat Danaher and Hollie had been a couple since their schooldays, destined to end up together. They'd be married now if Hollie was alive, and Hollie would be preparing to be Lil's matron of honour. She might have had a son and daughter to act as pageboy and flower girl for their aunt Lil.

Mum would have loved the fuss of a wedding. A trained chef and well able to bake, she'd probably have made the cake, and she and Hollie would have helped Lil to get ready on the day. A bottle of champagne might have been opened. A hairdresser might have called to the house. And Dad, of course, would have walked her up the aisle to Tom.

But none of that could happen.

The hotel where the wedding was to take place would supply the cake. The two friends Lil had invited – not bridesmaids: she couldn't countenance a bridesmaid who wasn't Hollie – would help with her preparations. And instead of Dad, Gran's partner Mark would walk her to the flowery arch. Like Lil, he was Fairweather born and bred, and she'd known him for as long as she could remember, and he would be mindful and tactful, and the day would be a mix of happy and sad.

She'd thought going away might make the whole thing easier. She'd hoped that putting distance between her and Fairweather would soften the feeling of loss – but anytime she visualised the wedding, she was aware of another rush of loneliness, and she knew that no matter where she was, she would miss them on the day.

But she must focus on the positive. She was dying to marry Tom, and she would be thrilled if all her fears were imaginary, if everything went to plan and she became his wife in Italy.

The kettle boiled. She poured water onto a waiting stock cube and stirred, her back to him. 'I was thinking about the wedding,' she said. 'I was just wondering if you might change your mind about inviting your father.' No harm, she thought, to give it another try.

Silence. She turned, the fork still in her hand. He was regarding her with the blank expression she'd seen every time he looked at his ringing phone and saw his father's name. 'I just think,' she added, 'you might regret it in the future.'

He took a swallow of beer. 'Nope,' he said, 'I won't.' Such a hard note all of a sudden in his voice. Don't argue, the note said. His father not forgiven, nowhere near being forgiven yet. Leave it, the note said – but she couldn't.

'How can you be sure, Tom?'

He stared at her. 'Lil, I told you what he did' – and she thought of two people she'd never met, in a bed they shouldn't have been sharing.

Go on, a voice in her head commanded. Ask him about her. Ask him. Have it out, once and for all – but she couldn't. 'Do you think you can ever forgive him?' she asked instead.

'I *have* forgiven him. I just can't – I just don't want to see him.'

'It doesn't sound to me like he's forgiven.'

He sighed impatiently and turned away from her. He went to the window and looked out, but she knew he wasn't seeing what was out there. 'Sorry, Tom. I know you don't like when I bring it up.'

No response.

'I suppose it's just … losing my own parents, and him still being alive, and the only grandparent our children would have …' She let it drift away, and he turned then, but kept his distance.

'Look, I understand,' he said. 'It was horrible, what happened to you. My experience was trivial in comparison—'

'Not trivial,' she said, but he ignored it.

'I know I must seem very harsh to you, but he's not coming to the wedding. I don't want him there, end of story. And I can't tell what'll happen in the future, but right now I can't see a time that I'll want to meet him. OK?'

'OK.' She stooped and took the chicken dish from the oven. She was adding the hot stock when the doorbell rang – and while Tom was gone to answer it, her phone buzzed with a call.

'I wanted to let you know,' her grandmother said, 'that Mark and I are considering a cruise over Christmas. I'm wondering how you'd feel about that.'

'Oh … I think you should go for it – why not?'

Mark, seventy-two, and Gran, two years his senior, had been a couple for well over a year now – hard to say when it had begun, with no official announcement – but they didn't live in the same house. Too independent, both of them. 'When would you be sailing?'

'We're looking at the twenty-third of December, for five or six days.'

'And where are you thinking of going?'

'Maybe the Caribbean, out of Florida.'

'Sounds lovely.'

'I'm just afraid I'd be letting you and Tom down.'

'Not at all. Don't worry about us, we'll be fine.'

They hadn't made Christmas plans, assuming they'd spend the day with Mark and Gran at Gran's house, as they had done the previous Christmas, with Mark's son Fred and his family dropping in afterwards – but it might be good to do their own thing.

'It's a shame,' Gran said, 'that you can't spend it with Tom's family.'

Gran knew the story. Lil had filled her in, after Tom had told her she could. Gran was the best secret keeper she knew. For a second she was tempted to tell her about the trip to Dublin, and the woman who'd rushed in a state from Tom's father's house, but decided against it. Nobody need ever be told about that.

And she knew what Gran would say if she shared her worries about Vivienne. Ask him, Gran would insist. For goodness' sake, just ask him outright. Gran would, if she was in that situation, because Gran was fearless. Lil wished she was too.

After hanging up she set the table, wondering who had rung the doorbell. They'd had no visitors, not a single one, since moving in – and no post either, apart from the Happy New Home card Sarah had sent, and a few junk mail things. Might be someone looking for Tom to do a job, although his address wasn't on the leaflet, just his number.

When he hadn't reappeared after ten more minutes she turned down the oven and went in search of him. The street door was closed – would he have left without telling her? Surely not. She walked down the corridor to the back door and found him in the garden, standing at the edge of the patio, hands in pockets, turned away from her.

'There you are,' she said, and he swung around – and for an instant, before his face adjusted, it felt like he didn't recognise her. 'I wondered where you'd got to. Who was at the door?'

He didn't reply, just went on looking at her. Had he heard?

'Tom?'

He gave a small toss of his head then. 'No one,' he said.

'No one? Someone rang the bell.' Why was he behaving oddly?

'Selling calendars,' he said then.

She stared at him. 'Calendars, in October?'

He laughed. Did it sound a little forced? 'I know, right? I told them to come back in December. I was wondering about eating out here tonight.'

The abrupt change threw her. 'Out here? We'd have to bring

it downstairs … and is it warm enough?' She didn't think so, autumn definitely in the air, the light already seeping from the sky.

'Maybe not, just an idea. Come on then,' he said, slinging an arm around her shoulders. 'I think I have half a bottle of beer waiting for me.'

They climbed the stairs together. They ate dinner, and the evening passed like any other, and she decided she must have imagined the moment when he'd looked at her like he had no idea who she was.

Emily

GONE SEVEN O'CLOCK – SHE'D HAVE TO GET A MOVE on. The reservation at Borelli's was for eight, and she wanted a shower, and Pip would have to be bathed and put to bed before Mrs Twomey arrived to babysit. Bill would happily have attended to Pip, but she hated to miss the bedtime routine on the nights she wasn't working.

She pulled up outside the house. Darkness closing in, the days shorter now that October was here – and the nights would arrive earlier again when the clocks went back at the end of the month. She didn't mind: dark nights made restaurant dinnertimes cosier, with lamps and fairy lights about the place, and the wall heaters on to give incoming diners a welcome waft of warm air.

And winter didn't bother her, with Christmas right in the middle. She loved that time of year: buying gifts, putting up decorations, scouring the internet for twists on Christmas dishes to offer in the restaurant. Watching films she'd seen so often, and would never grow tired of.

Last Christmas Bill had laughed when she'd produced a little stocking to hang at the end of Pip's cot. The child isn't one yet, he'd protested, but Emily knew nobody was too young for the magic – and sure enough, Santa had slipped a soft blue rabbit into the sock, and it had become Pip's best friend.

As soon as she opened the front door she heard the murmur of voices from the kitchen. Mrs Twomey was early: poor thing must crave a bit of company, living on her own.

An unfamiliar jacket hung on the hallstand. She'd never seen Mrs Twomey in yellow: maybe it had been on sale. She hung hers next to it and entered the kitchen. 'There you are,' Bill said – and before she saw who was with him, something in his voice, the way he said the words, told her it wasn't Mrs Twomey.

'Look who's here,' he said, in that same too-hearty tone, and Emily saw Christine, seated at the table with a cup of something in front of her.

Christine.

Her long hair was gone. The short choppy style drew more attention to jutting cheekbones. She didn't appear to be wearing make-up, apart from a red shine on her lips that only served to emphasise the lack of colour in the rest of her face. Little silver rings in her ears, another in one nostril. Her eyes were enormous – Emily had forgotten that. Brown like Bill's, but a shade lighter.

And Pip was beside her, in his high chair.

No. No.

The child, the toddler Emily loved fiercely, was sitting next to the mother who'd deserted him. 'Emwy,' he said, raising his arms on seeing her. She crossed the floor and lifted him from the chair and pressed him to her like she always did, conscious of two pairs of eyes watching.

'Hello, Emily,' Christine said. Her smile was barely there. She didn't quite meet Emily's eye. She wore a sky blue sweater with a loose neckline, and long sleeves that covered half her hands. Still biting her nails, by the look of them.

'Christine … This is a surprise.' Putting what felt like a terribly false smile on her face. Holding Pip close, cradling the back of his head. Keeping him from her. Keeping him safe.

Was she high? Would Emily even know if she was? Bill would, she thought. He'd recognise the signs.

This wasn't happening. It couldn't be happening – but it was. It was happening. Against all her expectations, Christine had returned.

Emily saw Bill's dog Sherlock lying under the table with his head resting on Christine's feet. Sherlock, who'd hardly left her side all the time she was pregnant. Emily could imagine the welcome she'd got from him – and from her father.

'She saw the ad,' Bill said, taking another cup from the press, pouring tea that Emily hadn't asked for. 'Just the other day.' Every word a plea, Emily could hear now. Every word beseeching her to be nice, to speak kindly to his daughter. She hated how ill at ease he was, how nervous of her reaction.

'That's good … Has Pip been fed?'

'He has indeed. Here,' he said, pulling out a chair. He was overjoyed to see Christine again: she could see that. For his sake, she'd make an effort.

She sat, positioning Pip on her lap so he was facing away from Christine, but he craned to see her, curious about the visitor, so Emily turned him the other way. 'How are you?'

Christine gave a little nod. 'I'm OK … I'm clean.'

Also wary of Emily. It wasn't fair that Emily was made to feel like the one they both had to tiptoe around. 'That's good,' she repeated. 'I'm glad to hear it.'

'She's done more rehab,' Bill put in.

Look at him, bursting with pride. 'That's good,' Emily said, for the third time, but it wasn't really that good. She'd tried rehab before, and gone back to drugs. Emily poured milk, wondering where to take the conversation. 'So … you saw the ad in the paper.'

'Someone else did. They told me about it.'

'And you've heard about Astrid's will?'

'Yeah.' Shifting a little on her chair, a faint colour seeping into the pale cheeks. Knowing that Emily must have been told that she'd stolen the pearls. Probably as bemused as they were at the notion that they belonged to her now.

Emily turned back to Bill. 'You'll need to get the necklace from the solicitor.'

'I picked it up a few days ago,' he told her.

'Oh ... OK.'

He'd said nothing to her. She understood why, but still it hurt.

'Would you mind,' he asked, 'if we didn't go out to eat tonight?'

'Of course not.' They could hardly go and leave her with Mrs Twomey. 'There's plenty in the fridge.' They had a constant supply of leftovers that Emily brought home, packaged into single portions for Bill to have on the nights she was working.

She turned to Christine. 'You'll have dinner with us' – and Christine threw a look at her father before nodding. At least she hadn't just taken the necklace and bolted. 'You need to cancel Mrs Twomey,' Emily told Bill.

'I'll pop over,' he replied, making for the back door, and was gone before Emily could say anything to that. She regarded Christine over Pip's head. 'We have shepherd's pie,' she said. 'Lasagne. Chicken curry. What do you fancy?'

'I don't mind. Anything.'

Emily rose, transferring Pip to her hip, not wanting to relinquish him. She took containers from the fridge and set them on the worktop. She turned on the oven before resuming her seat.

'Thank you for looking after Philip,' Christine said. Philip, not Pip, the pet name Bill had put on him when he was just a few weeks old. So much she didn't know about him.

'I didn't have a whole lot of choice,' Emily replied. 'Bill would never have managed on his own.' Keeping her voice light, but again the colour rose in Christine's face.

'I know. I'm sorry.'

'He was heartbroken, Christine. Bill, I mean, when you left.'

'I know.' A small sharpness in that – or did Emily imagine it? 'I never … wanted to hurt him.'

Was she talking about Bill or Pip? 'He looked for you, did he tell you? He put ads in the paper then too. Every time he came home he'd check the answering machine for a message.'

No response. Pip lunged suddenly, reaching a chubby hand in the direction of an earring: Christine jerked her head away.

'Could you not have let him know you were still alive, at least? Could you not have done that much? Just a quick phone call would have been enough.'

'It's not – I can't explain.'

She sounded sulky now. Emily tamped down a surge of anger. Didn't she understand that she'd changed their lives, that she'd forced change on them? Granted, Emily and Bill had eventually been going to live together, but Christine's disappearance had taken the timing out of their hands – and with Bill eaten up with anxiety in the weeks following her departure, and with a tiny baby to take care of, his and Emily's relationship had definitely shifted to second place. Would they even have stayed together if it hadn't been for Pip needing both of them?

To her relief the back door opened again, and Bill reappeared. 'Mrs Twomey says to call in and say hello tomorrow,' he told Christine.

Tomorrow? Emily looked at her. 'Are you staying nearby?' she asked – and immediately wished it unsaid. Of course Christine wasn't staying nearby.

'I've told her she can spend the night here,' Bill said. 'Sorry, I forgot to say. I hope that's OK.'

'Of course it is,' Emily replied swiftly, setting Pip down on the floor. 'I didn't think. I'll make up a bed. The oven is on. Put the food in in five minutes – and you'll need to cancel Borelli's, if you haven't already.' She left the room before he could see the mix of feelings – confusion, anger, hurt, fear – that were jostling for space within her.

Upstairs she took sheets and pillowcases from the hotpress, her thoughts spinning. Was Christine moving back permanently, just like that? Had Bill already told her she was welcome to live with them? Or worse, far worse – was she planning to stay one night and then leave with Pip?

The thought was horrifying. They couldn't let it happen. They wouldn't let it happen – but would they have a choice? Was his birth mother legally entitled to him, even with a history of addiction? Surely the fact that she'd absconded so soon after his birth would go against her, if it went to court.

If it went to court. Emily closed her eyes, hugging her bundle of linen, inhaling its clean scent, forcing herself to breathe slowly in an effort to calm her galloping mind. Stop. Stop jumping ahead. Christine might not even want him. It didn't look like she wanted him. She couldn't possibly feel any bond.

She wasn't getting him. It wasn't going to happen.

She made up the bed in the room that had been unoccupied for nearly a year and a half. She took towels from the hotpress and set them on the chest of drawers. She flicked a duster over the dressing table that still held the things Christine had left behind – a hairbrush, a few tubes, a half-full container of cotton buds, a little dish of hair clips. She cracked open the window and pulled the curtains closed. She tweaked the bedside rug straight with a foot and left the door ajar to let out the stale air.

On her return to the kitchen she found Bill and Christine on their feet, and Pip in Bill's arms. 'We'll put him to bed,' he told Emily.

We'll. She felt another dart of panic. He was getting Christine to interact with Pip: he wanted them to get to know one another. 'Can't you do it? Let Christine take it easy.'

'I don't mind helping,' Christine said, and they walked out, and Emily felt something hard and cold settle inside her. She set the table, visualising the bedtime routine. His bath, his clean nappy afterwards, his pyjamas. Brushing the teeth, tucking him in, reading his story. Blue Rabbit in the cot.

Christine had no idea how important Blue Rabbit was. She had no idea how to look after him. Had she even changed his nappy during the time she'd had with him, or had a nurse, and then Bill, taken care of all that?

A scratch at the back door announced the arrival of her cat Barney, looking to be fed. It had taken a while for Barney and Sherlock to come to an understanding that eventually saw cat and dog sharing Sherlock's big basket in the utility room. Everyone adapts, Emily thought. Given time, we all accept what we can't change.

No. She would never accept Pip being reclaimed. Never, never, never.

As she shook nuts into Barney's bowl, her phone rang. Heather, finally returning her calls. 'Christine is back,' Emily said without preamble. Keeping her voice low, alert for steps on the stairs.

'Hey – wow. She is? When?'

'She was here when I got home from Astrid's. She's staying the night, Bill told her she could.'

'So she saw the ad?'

'Someone did. Heather, what if she wants to take Pip?' Just voicing it aloud made her feel sick.

'Has she said?'

'No, but she's gone up with Bill now to put him to bed.'

Pause. 'How is she?'

'She looks OK. She was in rehab – she said she was anyway. I don't think she's on anything. But she can't take him, Heather. I know she's his mother, but she's an addict – she can't be trusted to look after a small child.'

'Hang on, slow down. Where is she living now?'

'I don't know. I'm afraid Bill is going to ask her to move back in here, and of course she won't stay, she'll disappear like she did before, and I can't have him going through all that again – and it could totally mess up Pip too.'

'Hey, let's not count any chickens, right? Talk to Bill when you're alone, express your concerns and see what's what.'

She was right. Emily sagged into a chair. 'I never thought she'd come back. I really didn't think we'd ever see her again.'

'I guess she was curious about the will.'

'That's another thing. Bill collected the necklace from the solicitor a few days ago, and he didn't say anything to me.'

'Well, that's hardly surprising, is it? He knows how you feel about her. He probably thought you wouldn't want him talking about it.'

'I know, I *know* that, it's just ...' Just what? 'I'm afraid, Heather.'

'I get it, but—' Heather broke off.

'But what?'

'Emily, she's his mom, whether you like it—'

'Only in name. She left him – have you forgotten? She walked out on him, she didn't give a damn!' In her distress it came out too loudly – but did she care if she was overheard?

'Emily, I know it's difficult, but you've got to tread carefully here. You always knew this could happen.'

'No, I didn't – and neither did you. In the coffee shop you said she'd never find out about the pearls.'

'Well, I guess I was wrong. But now she's here you've got to deal with it – and falling out with her, or with Bill, isn't going to help.'

Emily made no response.

'Can you just hang on till you see what's happening? Can you do that, Emily?'

'... Yes.' She wasn't at all sure she could.

There was another pause. 'Astrid's house,' Heather said then, in a new voice.

Astrid's house, the reason she'd rung. Emily tried to pull her thoughts back. 'Yes, it's ready. You want to clean the windows?'

'Sure, I'll clean them – but that's not what I meant. I'm thinking it would be perfect for Christine.'

'What?' Emily asked sharply. 'What do you mean, perfect for Christine?'

'I mean, she might not be the tenant we would have chosen, but if she needs a place to stay …'

She was joking. She was making a bad joke. 'Heather, are you seriously suggesting we let her move into the house? Astrid's house?'

'Look, I'm just putting it—'

'No way. No *way*. She's not even living in this town.'

'You said you didn't know where she's living.'

Emily shook her head impatiently. 'She's not – she *can't* be anywhere close by, or she wouldn't be staying the night here, in this house.' Would she? Breathing was becoming difficult. She dipped her head, trying to pull in air, trying to marshal her scattered thoughts. She couldn't believe Heather would consider allowing Christine into Astrid's house. She searched for a compelling objection, and found it.

'We need someone who can pay rent. We need to make money for the tax Pip will have to pay.'

'Well, I'm guessing Bill would pay the rent until she finds a job. Just think about it, is all I'm saying.'

Emily didn't want to think about it. She couldn't bear the thought of Christine living in Astrid's house. It would be a mess in a week.

'Look at it this way,' Heather continued. 'It's going to belong to Pip eventually – it would make sense in Bill's head for his mom to live in it now. It would give her security, a roof over her head.'

'She *had* a roof over her head – she was here, in this house, and she still left.'

'Sure, but maybe she's more ready to put all that behind her now. And she'd be close by, which would suit Bill.'

He wouldn't, he couldn't suggest making Astrid's house available to his daughter – but even as she thought it, as she silently and adamantly resisted the notion, Emily knew he could. If Christine was looking for a place to stay, the cottage would seem like the logical, the obvious place for her to go. An empty house, newly done up and waiting for someone to live in it.

And yes, he'd pay her rent. Of course he would.

And if she intended moving back to the town, wouldn't it be better for her to have her own place? Emily propped an elbow on the table and sank her forehead into her palm. She didn't want to deal with this. She wanted it to go away and never come back.

'Talk to Bill,' Heather said again. 'It's just an idea, something to consider. I might not be right, it mightn't have occurred to him, but if that's what he wants, you can tell him I won't object. Listen, I've got to go – I hear Jo kicking up, and Mom's not great with babies. I'll call you soon,' and the conversation was brought to a close with a click, and no goodbye, and Emily felt mad at Heather for being so willing to hand Astrid's house over to Christine, and guilty for forgetting to ask after her mother.

Dinner was a challenge. Emily felt stiff with tension, and the short bursts of conversation sounded stilted and too polite. To her relief, Christine announced she was going to bed directly afterwards, having left more than half of her shepherd's pie uneaten. They wished her goodnight and were silent as they listened to her climbing the stairs.

Emily wondered suddenly if she'd go into their room, where Pip's cot was. She had to fight an impulse to rush upstairs, to protect him again. She felt knotted with tension.

'Sorry about Borelli's, love,' Bill said. 'We'll do it soon.'

A missed meal at Borelli's was the least of her worries. Bill reached into a cupboard and brought out a bottle of red wine. 'We could use a glass,' he said, rummaging in the cutlery drawer. 'Why don't you go into the sitting room, and I'll bring it in?'

She didn't move. 'Bill, what's going on? What's happening with Christine?'

He opened the bottle and filled two glasses. 'She's been in rehab,' he said, handing one to Emily. 'She's clean.'

'I know that. Where is she living now?'

'In a kind of halfway house near Galway, attached to the rehab clinic she was in. She's been there three months.'

One month in rehab, three in a house. 'And she's been clean all that time?'

'Yes.'

So trusting, so eager to believe everything Christine told him. Galway was two and a half hours up the road, and she couldn't let her father know she was there. In four months, with her head clear, she couldn't pick up a phone so he'd know she was still alive. Emily took a gulp of wine, and it hit the back of her throat with a woody kick. 'So she's living with other addicts.'

'Recovering addicts,' he corrected gently. 'Yes, I could gather that's the case. They're helping one another. She found rehab good, better than the last time, and she likes the house she's in now. She's got a sponsor too, an older woman. A bit like a mother, she said.'

Again she could sense the quiet joy he was feeling, the joy she'd wished for him for so long. Now it seemed to mock her, this happiness. She couldn't believe in it, couldn't see it lasting, and already she was bracing herself for his heart being broken again.

She loved him, deeply and fervently. It had taken her by surprise, this love. It had grown slowly, out of friendship, and she had welcomed it, knowing it to be real and lasting, and healing. She loved his generous ways and his pure, trusting soul, and she couldn't bear how Christine had abused his generosity, and thrown his trust back at him.

'How long is she planning to stay at the halfway house?' she asked, searching his face.

'Well, she says she's ready to leave now. She was thinking about it before she saw the ad.'

The words brought renewed panic that she fought to hide from him. She took another sip of wine, and it went down a little more smoothly. She felt it putting warmth in her stomach. She rubbed at the furrows in her forehead.

'Emily, I know this is hard for you. I'm sorry.'

She went to him then. She took his glass and set both on the worktop. She laid her head on his chest, and she felt his arms coming around to enfold her. 'I can see how happy you are to have her back again,' she said, feeling the warmth of him.

'I am. I couldn't believe it when I saw her. I wish—' He broke off and dropped a kiss on her head, and she didn't ask what he wished. They stood like that for several moments, and then she eased away and tipped her head to look up at him.

'I'm afraid, Bill,' she said. 'I'm so afraid of her hurting you again – and I'm afraid she'll want to take Pip from us. I know she's his mother, but I don't know that she can be trusted to look after him. Not like we can.'

'I know. I understand that.'

'I can't bear the thought of losing him. He's like my own child. Like our child, Bill.'

She watched the struggle in his face. In so many ways he was being pulled. He loved Pip as much as she did – more, maybe. He'd feel every bit as fearful as Emily was now, but he'd also want to do right by Christine. He was torn, she could see that.

'I was thinking,' he said – and she knew Heather had been right. And as she listened to him wondering aloud if maybe they could let Christine stay in Astrid's house for a while, just until she found her feet, and he'd be happy to pay her rent until she got a job, as she listened to his tentative plan, her heart broke a little.

'Heather had the same idea,' she said when he'd finished speaking. 'She phoned while you were putting Pip to bed. She thought Astrid's house might suit Christine.'

'And you?' he asked tentatively. 'What do you think?'

She took a breath. 'I think … it's worth a try,' she said, because what else was there to say?

Lil

THE MORNING WAS QUIET, AS WEEKDAY MORNINGS tended to be in the library. Lil was cataloguing a box of new arrivals when she heard someone approach the desk. She glanced up from her computer screen.

'Excuse me. I'm looking for Lil Noonan.'

A husky quality to the voice, not unattractive. Polished English accent. Glossy black hair falling past the shoulders of a grey leather jacket, unbuttoned to reveal a shirt in palest pink beneath. Full lips painted plum, flawless skin, deep blue eyes underlined darkly. Taller than Lil by a few inches. Quite stunning.

'I'm Lil. How can I help you?'

The woman blinked, and didn't return Lil's smile. She made a slight movement with her shoulders, no more than a twitch, and reached up to bring the edges of her jacket together. Nails a darker shade than the mouth, almost black. 'I wonder,' she said, in the same quiet beautiful tones, 'if we might ... have a talk. When you're free.'

'A talk?' Lil held her smile in place, although something was beginning to feel not altogether right. Clearly they hadn't met, but the woman had asked for her by name. Some Fairweather connection? 'May I ask who you are?'

A beat passed. 'I'm Vivienne. Tom's ex.'

Vivienne.

Tom's ex.

Lil felt the blood draining from her face. Tom's ex, the woman she feared might have the power to decide her future, was standing in front of her, wanting to have a talk. Worse, she was beautiful. If she'd come to reclaim Tom, Lil wouldn't have a hope against her. She felt horribly exposed, as if somehow Vivienne had learnt of her insecurities, and had come to prey on them.

And then anger took over. The nerve. The brass neck. How dared she, the woman who had almost destroyed Tom, who had ruined his relationship with his father, turn up unannounced at Lil's workplace? How could she be so brazen as to think Lil would want to talk to her?

'I know you'd rather I hadn't come,' Vivienne went on, studying Lil's face. 'I expected that. The trouble is' – and here she faltered – 'I'm a bit desperate, and I thought I might – I thought you might help me.' She pressed her lips together.

Lil's disbelief and anger swelled. Her skin prickled with it.

'Help you?' Struggling to keep her voice down, aware that Judy was possibly within earshot. 'Why on earth should I help you? If Tom knew you were here—'

'I know. I know he'd be angry. He wouldn't talk to me yesterday. Please, I just need you—'

Lil stared at her. 'Yesterday? You phoned him?' He'd said nothing.

Vivienne shook her head. 'I went to your apartment. I'm sorry, I know it must seem like an intrusion, but I really needed to talk to him. I tried to explain, but he wouldn't listen. He told me to go away, so I had no option but to stay the night in the hotel and come to you now.'

She was the person selling calendars – except that she hadn't been selling calendars. Tom had lied to Lil. He'd gone downstairs when the doorbell had rung. He'd opened the door and Vivienne had been standing there, and when Lil had found him later in the garden he'd been odd.

He'd lied to her. The library was heated but she felt cold.

'How did you know where we live? How did you know where I work?' The words came out in angry, breathless little bursts.

'I'm a cousin of Sarah's, Tom's sister-in-law. Perhaps you didn't know that.'

'Of course I know that,' Lil snapped. 'I also know that Sarah and Joel want nothing to do with you, after what happened.'

Vivienne's face seemed to collapse. 'Yes,' she said, in a voice so low Lil hardly heard. 'I'm aware of that. My mother is in touch with her brother. Sarah's father.'

Of course she was. Regardless of rifts, families talked and news travelled. They're living above a restaurant in such and such a town, Sarah might tell her father. Lil's enjoying her new job at the library. Her father might repeat it innocently to his sister, who might then share it with her daughter, if asked. A few degrees of separation, that was all.

Lil didn't think she'd ever been so angry. If someone annoyed or offended her, her instinct was to ignore or placate, or to walk away as a last resort. Anything rather than confrontation, words spoken in anger that might well serve to inflame a tricky situation – but not this time, not when placating was the last thing she wanted to do, and when walking away was not an option. How dare this woman invade their lives?

She longed for someone to interrupt them, anyone at all, but nobody did. The small scattering of library users browsed shelves and ignored them, and Judy must be out of earshot after all. And where was Karl, the security man, when she needed him?

She took a breath in an effort to steady herself. 'If Tom didn't want to talk to you, I certainly don't,' she said in the same tight undertone. Beneath the counter her hands squeezed of their own accord into fists. Her toes curled in their shoes. Everything felt like it was contracting, drawing in on itself. 'You're the last person I'd want to help. I'd like you to leave now, or I'll be forced to call security and have you escorted out.' Would Karl do that, if Lil told him she was being harassed? She had no idea.

Vivienne's eyes filled with tears. 'Please,' she said, 'if you would just listen to me, I can explain. I'm asking for a few minutes, that's all.'

'Why should I listen to you?' Lil hissed. 'Why should I give you any time at all, after what you did?'

'Because you're happy,' Vivienne said in a rapid whisper, making no attempt to wipe the tears that brimmed over and ran down her perfect face, 'and I'm not. I've paid for what I did – believe me, I've paid every single day since it happened – and I'm tired, I'm so tired of being sad, and since Tom refused to listen to me, you're the only one who can help me. You're my last hope.'

Lil was her last hope? What was Vivienne going to ask her to do – finish with Tom? She saw a tear drop from Vivienne's chin onto the leather jacket, making a splattery dark stain – and out of nowhere, a memory returned of a woman rushing in distress from Tom's father's house, her green scarf drifting off as she hurried past Lil, who'd caught it.

This was the same woman: she was suddenly certain of it. *I saw you in Dublin*. She left it unsaid, still unravelling its implications. Vivienne had been at Tom's father's house, the same house where they'd betrayed Tom two years ago, and been caught. Vivienne was still in touch with George McLysaght – and now she was here. What on earth was going on?

'Will you let me explain?' Vivienne asked again urgently, blotting her face now with a tissue she'd taken from some pocket. 'Will you, Lil? Truthfully, I wouldn't be here unless I could see no other way. I'm begging you.'

Her anger, Lil realised, was ebbing. Was it because of the other's tears? Was she being swayed by what might well be some very clever acting? Was she being manipulated? But Vivienne in Dublin had looked just as distressed, when she'd had no idea who Lil was.

And didn't Lil need to find out why she was here now? Mightn't a conversation with her, however Lil might dread it, provide the answers she wanted?

'Please. Please, Lil. I promise it won't take long, fifteen minutes out of your lunch break. There's a little coffee shop just down the street – I could wait for you there.'

'What do you want? I have to know what it's about.'

'I can't go into it now, not here. But I'm not trying to come between you and Tom, I promise. Please, just trust me.'

'But I don't trust you,' Lil said. 'Why on earth should I help you?'

Vivienne gave a small sad smile at that. 'I don't know,' she said. 'I don't deserve it' – and that at least rang true, and Lil found herself agreeing to fifteen minutes in the coffee shop at noon.

After Vivienne had left she retraced their conversation, picking it apart for clues, and finding none. Had she done the right thing, agreeing to listen to whatever Vivienne wanted to tell her? What would Gran say if she knew Lil was going to meet the woman who'd broken Tom's heart? What would Tom say?

And what was she to do with the knowledge that he'd lied to her yesterday?

I'm not trying to come between you and Tom, Vivienne had

said. Lil clung to that as the clock crawled towards midday, and finally reached it.

She took the blue wrap she'd stowed under the desk – not the lime green scarf: that was washed and folded and sitting in a drawer, as yet unworn – and draped it like a barrier around her. She told Judy she was meeting someone for lunch, and left the library with a heart that hammered its objection all the way to the café. Just because she wanted the truth didn't mean she was looking forward to hearing it.

Vivienne was seated at a corner table for two, a cup before her. She looked gravely at Lil as she approached. 'Thank you for coming,' she said. 'What do you want?'

For an awful moment Lil thought she was offering to pay for the return of Tom. *How much will it take to give him back to me?*

'Coffee? Tea? Can I get you a sandwich?'

Lil unwound her wrap and draped it over the back of her chair. 'Tea,' she said, still on her feet, still in two minds whether to stay or go.

'Anything to eat?'

'No … thank you.' She was hungry, but she couldn't imagine being relaxed enough to face food.

'Please sit.'

As Lil lowered herself slowly into the chair Vivienne lifted a hand – and instantly a young waiter, eighteen at the most, was there. Clearly taken with the beautiful customer, smiling bashfully at her as she handed him her empty cup and placed an order for two teas, one to be peppermint.

'Thank you,' Vivienne repeated, when they were alone again. 'I truly appreciate it. I know how little you must think of me for what I did to Tom. For what we did,' she amended, 'George and I. It was despicable.'

'Why are you here?' Lil asked, in no mood to rehash the past. Every impulse still screamed at her to get up, to leave. 'What can you possibly want from me?' The chair was too hard, her posture on it too stiff.

Vivienne folded her hands on the table, and Lil's eyes were briefly drawn to the perfect dark ovals of her nails. 'The fact is,' she said, finding and holding Lil's gaze, her words slow and deliberate, 'the *truth* is, Lil, I'm in love with George.'

It was the last thing Lil had expected to hear. In love with George? Had she heard it properly? Or had Vivienne made a mistake, and named the father instead of the son? She would have met both of them on the same day, at Sarah and Joel's wedding.

'I love George,' Vivienne said again, 'and he loves me. We've loved one another for a long time.'

Lil found her voice. 'Tom's father?'

Vivienne nodded. 'It wasn't something I planned – I'm not like that, despite what you may think. It just happened. You don't choose who you fall in love with, right?'

Right. Neither Lil nor Tom had been looking for love when they'd met, or not consciously. They'd both been more concerned with not falling apart – but love had happened.

'I was going to break off my engagement,' Vivienne went on in the same measured tones. 'When I finally admitted to myself how

I felt about George, I knew I had to break up with Tom but ... I dragged my heels, because, well, I thought – I assumed I wouldn't see George again if Tom and I split up. I didn't realise then that George also had feelings for me.'

The waiter reappeared. They sat in silence as he set little pots and cups on the table, waited until he was out of earshot.

'You stayed with Tom, even though you didn't love him,' Lil said. 'You stayed just so you wouldn't lose contact with his father. You used him.'

'Yes.' Her direct gaze began to unnerve Lil. 'I'm not proud of that. My behaviour was deplorable. I'm heartily ashamed, but I'm being honest with you, Lil – and I need you to listen, please. There's more.'

Lil added milk to her tea, glad of something that would give her an excuse to break from that solid blue gaze.

'That weekend, I'd come to Dublin ahead of Tom. You probably know that. I stayed in George's house, like we always did when we came over.'

'I don't really want to—'

'But I must,' Vivienne broke in urgently. 'Please, I must explain, I need you to understand.' Her words running along more quickly now. 'I didn't plan what happened – I swear to you it wasn't planned. I just wanted to be close to George, to be in his company, but he – well, he confessed that he'd fallen in love with me. He said he accepted that I was going to marry Tom, and he would have to find a way to live with that.' She stopped. She curled her hands around her cup. 'So,' she went on, the urgency gone now, 'I told him how I felt.'

'And then you went to bed with him.'

Vivienne shook her head. 'It wasn't – it sounds bad, I know it does. We hadn't – we didn't want to hurt Tom. Neither of us did. I told George I'd break things off as soon as we got back to London, and then we decided we'd wait a while, maybe a few months, maybe longer, before ... starting anything. We honestly didn't intend what happened that night, but ...'

She lifted her head to regard the ceiling, and when she lowered it, her eyes shone with more tears. She blotted them with a napkin as she continued to speak. 'It was a nightmare, Tom coming in. I couldn't believe when the door opened and he was there. George rushed downstairs after him, but he was gone. I got dressed and left the house. I couldn't talk to George, I didn't know what to do. I went to a friend's house and spent the night there.'

Listening, Lil was torn between distaste and relief. While their betrayal of Tom was still outrageous, it would appear, if she was telling the truth, that she had no feelings left for him – if she'd ever had them. She wasn't here to reclaim him. Whatever she wanted from Lil was something else entirely – but what?

'I returned to London the next day. I didn't contact George, and I didn't hear from him. I hadn't expected to hear from him – I knew how close he and Tom had been.' More tears welled, again blotted before they could fall. 'I did try to ring Tom. I was beside myself with guilt, and frightened for him, but I couldn't get through. I eventually heard what had happened to him, and I hated myself.

'I left our apartment in London, just packed my bags and walked out, and moved back home with my mother. I found out later that Joel had come over and sorted things out, cancelled the apartment lease, returned Tom's company car, brought Tom's things back to Ireland.'

Her tea remained untouched, her herbal teabag still sitting on the saucer that held her teapot. She rocked a little as she spoke, a tiny movement. She'd stopped making eye contact with Lil; her gaze was directed downwards now, into the teacup or onto the table. Her voice was dull and monotone, all animation gone from it.

'For a long time I wanted to die. I had ruined Tom's life, maybe ruined both their lives. Ruined mine too, come to that. I still went to work, but I'd completely lost interest in it. I went through the motions, got away with it. I stopped going out after work, lost touch with friends. Eventually I asked my boss to send me to the office in LA. I felt I had to get away, try to start again.

'I met a man soon after I arrived in America, and within weeks we were engaged. I thought it might help me to move on, but inside I was as sad as ever, and eventually I realised I would be marrying him for all the wrong reasons, so I broke up with him and went back to London. I heard that Tom had left prison and was living in the west of Ireland. I hoped he was OK. I knew nothing of George – I'd heard no news of him, but I thought of him constantly. I grieved for him, and for what we might have had.'

'I saw you in Dublin,' Lil said, the words out before she could stop them. 'A few weeks ago.'

Vivienne looked at her, frowning. 'You saw me? Where?'

'You were leaving ... Tom's father's house.' She wouldn't mention the state Vivienne had been in.

'But you didn't know who I was.'

'No, not until this morning.'

The puzzled expression remained. 'Why were you there? Were you going to see George?'

Lil hesitated, beginning to regret her blurted admission. 'I – yes, I had planned to call on him. I thought I might be able to help.'

'Help?'

'To ... mend things between him and Tom. I'd tried talking to Tom, but ...' She drifted off, hearing how nonsensical it sounded.

Vivienne stared at her. 'You went to *George*?'

'I can see now,' Lil admitted, 'that I was wrong. I didn't think, I just—'

'What did he say?'

'Oh – I didn't see him. I decided—' She halted, remembering that it had been Vivienne's appearance, her emerging in such a distressed state from the house that had caused her to lose her nerve. 'I decided against it,' she finished. 'I realised it would achieve nothing.'

'But it's Tom,' Vivienne insisted, the intensity returning to her voice. 'It's Tom you must convince. You must, Lil! This is why I came,' she went on eagerly, the tears gone as she leant once more across the table towards Lil. 'I came to ask you – well, I-tried asking Tom directly, but when he wouldn't talk to me I came to you. I need this to happen, Lil. I need them to reconcile – and clearly it's what you want too.'

She was so earnest, searching Lil's face intently. Again Lil found it unnerving. 'You want me to persuade Tom to forgive his father?' I have forgiven him, Tom had said yesterday, but he hadn't, not really.

'Yes! Yes!' Uttered so forcefully that a woman at a nearby table turned to stare at them. 'Look,' Vivienne went on, lowering her voice again, 'I went to see George that day, because I couldn't get him out of my head. I told him I still loved him, and he told me he felt the same but he said nothing more could happen between us. We could never be together because of Tom, and everything we'd caused.

'I tried to reason with him. I said I'd go anywhere with him,' spreading her hands over the table. 'We could live anywhere in the world – I didn't care as long as we were together. I reminded him that Tom had moved on and met someone else, but he kept saying no, kept insisting it would hurt Tom, and he couldn't do anything that would cause more hurt. He said he was still trying to reconnect with Tom.'

That much was true. 'So you want me to persuade Tom to forgive his father, and also to give his blessing to your relationship?'

'Yes,' Vivienne replied. 'I know it won't be easy, and I have no right to ask you, but you're my only hope. I can't ask Joel – and anyway, I'm not sure Tom would do it for Joel, but he might for you.'

She wanted Lil to be the go-between, to act as her emissary in this skewed triangle. Lil had already tried and failed to persuade Tom to allow his father to come to the wedding: how on earth was she supposed to convince him to accept a relationship between the very people who'd caused all the trouble? There wasn't a hope of that happening.

But it didn't need to happen, did it? All that needed to happen was for Lil to report this conversation to Tom. His reaction to the news that Vivienne was in love with someone else – the fact that it was his father was almost by the way – would tell Lil everything she needed to know, and had been too afraid to find out for herself. Ironically, it was Vivienne who had unwittingly given Lil the perfect opportunity to learn the truth.

She got to her feet, gathering up her wrap. 'I have to go,' she said. 'I'll do what I can. Please don't contact me again.'

'Thank you,' Vivienne replied, remaining seated. 'I appreciate it, Lil' – and Lil left without another word, or a backward glance, and all afternoon she tried to figure out how she should approach this with Tom. She'd need to ease her way in. She'd need to tread softly, with such a delicate subject.

He was preparing dinner when she got home, stirring onions in a pan. On the worktop she saw an open can of tomatoes, and a waiting heap of chopped aubergine and courgette, and balsamic vinegar and sprigs of thyme. Once a week he made ratatouille, a dish she'd taught him.

'Smells good,' she said.

'Hi there,' he said brightly, leaning in for a kiss. 'How's my favourite girl?'

'Fine.' She set down her bag, aware that her heart had begun to beat faster. 'Any news?'

'Nothing much. Phone call looking for a house to be painted, told them I could do it next week.'

'That's good.' She shrugged off her wrap and filled a glass with water at the sink as he scooped the contents of the pan into a bowl and added more oil.

'Forgot the basil,' he said. 'You'll have to imagine it.' He whistled a snatch of something, or tried to. He couldn't whistle. He tossed in the waiting vegetables and gave the pan a shake. 'Want a beer?' he asked, crossing to the fridge. 'Split a bottle?'

'Tom, Vivienne came to the library this morning. She told me she'd been here yesterday.' Calm voice, inner turmoil.

He stopped dead, the smile slipping off his face. His arm, raised towards the fridge door handle, lowered. 'She called to the library?'

'Yes.'

He swore, which he hardly ever did. She saw his face harden. Still so much emotion there. 'I hope you sent her packing,' he said.

His response caused a flare of anger. 'Why didn't you tell me she came here? Why did you say it was someone selling calendars?'

He drew a hand across his mouth. He inhaled, exhaled. He

returned to the pan and turned off the hotplate. He leant against the worktop, arms crossed. 'Sorry,' he said, not sounding sorry. 'I didn't want you involved. I can't believe she went to the library.'

She threw calm out the window. 'Not involved? Tom, we're supposed to be getting married – or had you forgotten that? Like it or not, I *am* involved. Your ex came to see me because she needs help. I don't like it any more than you do, but that's the situation.'

His face remained grim. 'She doesn't deserve our help.'

'I agree – but at least I listened to her.'

'Easy for you,' he shot back.

'No, it wasn't easy! I asked her to leave, more than once, but I didn't have a door to slam in her face like you had. I was at work – so short of getting her thrown out, I hadn't much choice but to listen.'

Her anger, which he saw so rarely, seemed to soften him a little. 'Go on,' he said more evenly.

Lil took a breath, trying to pull herself back, to regain control. 'She told me she's in love with your father. She says he loves her too, but he doesn't want to cause you more hurt, so he can't be with her. She wants you to tell him you're OK with it. That's basically the message.'

He stared at her in silence. She searched his face for evidence of how he was taking the news that Vivienne was in love with someone else, and that the someone else was his father – but his expression was unreadable.

Finally, he pushed off from the worktop and crossed again to the fridge. He took out a beer and cracked it open. He flicked the top into the sink and took a long swallow. 'Let me get this straight,' he said. 'Vivienne says she and my father –' he stopped, closed his eyes briefly '– are in a relationship.' His mouth twisted, as if he'd tasted something sour.

'No, that's not what she said. Your father won't agree to it, because it would hurt you. He doesn't want to hurt you, Tom.'

'Bit late for that.'

It was laced with bitterness. Lil's anger left as quickly as it had arrived. She hated having been the cause of banishing his good mood, presenting all this mess to him.

'Vivienne thinks if you say you're OK with it—'

'Vivienne thinks,' he repeated loudly, cutting across her. 'Since when have you become Vivienne's messenger?'

'What?' The unfairness stung her, causing anger to rear up again. 'I can't believe you—'

'Lil, she's lying! She's using you, using us.'

'Why? Why would she do that?'

'I don't know – how would I know? Maybe she wants to split us up. Maybe she knew it wouldn't go down well when you told me.'

This brought her up short. Could Vivienne be trying to do just that? Was Tom the one she loved? Had she concocted this story simply to drive Tom and Lil apart?

No, it was preposterous. It couldn't be true. What about the day Lil had seen her in Merrion Square?

'I believe her,' she said. 'There's something I haven't told you.'

She hadn't been going to reveal it. She'd planned never to let him in on it, but suddenly it seemed imperative that he know the whole truth.

He narrowed his eyes. 'What?'

The suspicion in his face unnerved her, but she continued. 'When I went to Dublin a few weeks ago I said I wanted to look at wedding things, but that wasn't the real reason.'

He didn't react, just kept on looking at her with that awful expression. 'Tom, I feel so bad about you and your father – I wanted to see if there was anything I could do to help. I didn't tell you because I knew you'd say no. I realise how foolish it was now – and in the end I didn't meet him. But I did see Vivienne.'

She briefly described the scene in Merrion Square. 'Her story adds up. It ties in with what I saw that day.'

He shook his head. 'You went to see my father.'

'Oh, for God's sake – that's what you focus on? Get over it, Tom!'

'You lied to me.'

'And you lied to me, remember? You said Vivienne was a person selling calendars!'

He turned abruptly and yanked his jacket from the back of the door.

'Tom, don't just walk away—' but he opened the door and banged it after him, and she sank onto the couch and dropped her head into her hands as his feet thumped downstairs.

They'd kept the truth from each other – what kind of a relationship was that? In his eyes now she was no better than Vivienne, just another woman who'd deceived him – and she didn't know if he was more angry about her hiding her reason for going to Dublin, or the idea of Vivienne being in love with his father. After this horrible scene, she was no closer to knowing how he felt about his ex.

He'd sent Vivienne away yesterday when she'd turned up here, but the encounter had shaken him so much that he'd had to go to the garden to pull himself together before facing Lil again. Would it have affected him like that if he felt nothing for her?

Was he in a bar now, getting drunk like he'd done on that other night? Was he reliving it all?

He'd come back and tell Lil he couldn't do this. He'd say he'd made a mistake, and he'd call off the wedding. He'd move out of the apartment and she'd never see him again. She moaned in her distress, wanting the comfort of her family, hungry for her mother's arms around her.

The light faded slowly from the sky. The room darkened and she didn't move, ignoring the pangs of hunger – nothing eaten since breakfast – and straining to hear sounds of his return.

What if he didn't return? What if he'd already left her?

As she was on the point of calling Gran, needing someone to reassure her, to tell her that she and Tom would survive this – not that she was at all sure Gran would say that – she heard his step on the stairs. Her hands were icy. She sat up and waited for whatever was going to happen.

He opened the door and came in. He flicked on the light and saw her. For what felt like a long time they stared at one another. He seemed sober. His gaze was clear and unsmiling.

Finally he spoke, and his voice was low and weary, his anger spent. 'Sorry. I'm sorry, Lil. We shouldn't have fought. We're on the same side.'

On the same side. Relief filled her. She blinked hard, once, twice. Tears were perilously close, and now was not the time for them. He pulled out a kitchen chair and turned it to face her. He sat on it, arms folded.

'I'm sorry I lied to you yesterday,' he said. 'I messed up, I should have been honest.'

'I'm sorry I didn't tell you why I went to Dublin,' she replied.

A beat passed. Neither of them moved. What now? she wondered. Would they just do nothing, pretend this day, and the one before it, never happened?

Finally he got to his feet. 'She's not going to contact you again, is she?'

'I asked her not to.'

'That's good.' He took off his jacket and dropped it onto the chair. He regarded his dinner preparations, precisely where he'd left them. He took out his phone. 'Pizza?' he asked.

'OK.'

Despite her hunger, she wasn't sure she could stomach anything. She listened while he ordered the pepperoni, olives and pineapple toppings they both liked. She watched him spoon the half-cooked vegetables into a container and stow it in the fridge.

It wasn't fixed. Nothing was fixed.

Heather

'MOM!' A SHOUT, TRAVELLING DOWN THE STAIRS.

'What is it?' Heather yelled back.

'I can't find my yellow sweatshirt!'

'Look under the bed!' Lottie's clothes could end up anywhere.

'Must you bellow like that?' her mother asked, putting her hands to her ears. 'It's so *grating*.'

Heather crossed to the door that led into the hall, Jo clamped to her hip. *Yes, I must bellow, because she's upstairs and I'm downstairs.* She was doing a lot of silent responses these days.

'Not there!'

'Check the laundry basket!'

Muffled stomps. Her daughter, who couldn't weigh more than sixty pounds, walked like someone in concrete boots. 'Nope!'

Heather sighed. She deposited Jo in her high chair and gave her a spoon and an empty plastic bowl. 'Knock yourself out,' she told her. Knock your grandmother out while you're at it. Three weeks under the same roof was two weeks and six days too many.

'She'll yell as soon as you leave the room,' Heather's mother said, taking muesli from the press, and halfway up the stairs Heather smiled when Jo obliged.

Breakfast was the usual mayhem of spilt milk and squabbles and burnt toast, and Heather demanding to know who kept turning up the toaster, and threatening to install a camera on the ceiling. Her mother removed herself from the melee and perched with her cereal on the windowsill, a faraway expression on her face. Probably doing one of her visualisations: walking along a deserted beach, or lying on a hammock by a babbling brook. *Good luck with that, Mom.*

Thank the Lord for Eoin, mopping spills and organising lunch boxes before disappearing to catch the bus to Limerick for his paramedic studies course in UL. Following in his father's footsteps, which of course had delighted Shane.

'Hello, all' – and here came the fully qualified paramedic, home from his night shift, shucking off his boots at the door. 'How's everyone this fine morning?'

Heather couldn't understand how he always returned in such good humour. Paramedics didn't have it easy – early on in their relationship he'd shared stories that had stopped her in her tracks – but he rarely showed up after a shift without a smile on his face.

He deposited a white cake box with a flourish on the table. *Shane the paramedic* was written in biro on the lid. 'Now,' he said.

'What's that?' Lottie demanded.

'Open it,' he told her – and she did, to reveal a cake iced in white, with *thank you* spelt out in blue.

'From the daughter of a woman I brought to hospital a few days ago. It was left at the desk for me yesterday, when her son came to bring her home.'

'Isn't that nice,' Heather's mother said, having left her windowsill to inspect it. 'And so well deserved.' Shane was the golden-haired boy. If Heather left him, she knew who Mom would side with.

'Can we have some?' Lottie asked.

'You can not,' Heather told her. 'You and Jack have exactly twenty seconds to get your asses into the car.'

'You want me to take them?' Shane asked, and Heather was tempted but said no. He was pale with tiredness, blue shadows beneath his eyes.

'Sit and keep Mom company,' she told him, ushering Jack and Lottie towards the door. 'Get Jo down for a nap if you can – I'll be taking her out later.'

She was taking her to Astrid's house. She was on a spying mission. Christine had been living there for just over a week now. Heather knew this because of a terse text message that had arrived from Emily, two days after Christine's unexpected return. *She's moving in next Friday*, the message had said, just that, and Heather hadn't needed to ask who or where. *Fingers crossed*, she'd replied, and Emily hadn't come back, and since then there'd been no communication.

She could see how it made a peculiar kind of sense to have Christine living in the house earmarked for her son. She wondered what arrangement Bill and Emily had worked out with her, if any conditions had been laid down for her tenancy. So much for the three of them managing the house: Heather was definitely a sleeping partner in this enterprise.

She'd gone around to clean the windows the day before Christine was due to move in, using the patio door key Astrid had given her. Nobody had been about. She'd walked through the house, noting the changes, and she'd been hurt all over again that everything had gone ahead without her. She couldn't deny that the place looked good, all fresh and bright, although she still thought the cottage in its old state had been perfectly fine.

Astrid's windows cleaned, she'd texted Bill afterwards – Bill, not Emily, she wasn't sure why – and he'd responded with a simple *Thank you, Heather.*

But whatever about the wisdom of letting Christine live there, surely the next logical step, if she stayed clean, would be for her to reclaim Pip. She could hardly live in the same town and *not* lay claim to him, and that wasn't going to sit right with Emily, not at all.

For the past week, Christine living at Astrid's had been on Heather's mind, so because nobody had bothered to tell her how things were going, today she was going to call there and see for herself. She was bringing Jo deliberately, to observe how Bill's daughter was around young kids, and get an idea of how prepared or otherwise she might be for looking after Pip.

She wondered how big a risk it would be to let her care for Pip, even occasionally. She could well imagine Emily's fear, and Bill's too, if they had to surrender him. And in addition to worrying about Pip's welfare, Bill must be terrified of her relapsing like before. It wouldn't be easy.

'Mom – are you listening?'

She shook her thoughts away and looked at Lottie in the rear-view mirror. 'Yep.'

'What did I say?'

'I wasn't listening then, but I am now.'

Lottie gave the raised eyes look she'd begun using lately. 'I *said* I'm going to Charlene's after school. Her mom will drive me home.'

'OK. Don't be late for dinner.' She found Jack in the mirror. 'Sorry about the shorts.' Another laundry basket lapse.

'Tom Burke will laugh at them.'

'Tell Tom Burke to go stick his head in a bucket – and give them back to me the minute you get home.' The school came into view and she pulled in fifty yards away from it, Lottie having instructed her some time ago not to drop them right outside. Having a growing-up daughter was such fun.

She returned to the house to find her mother and Shane drinking coffee and eating cake. 'We couldn't resist,' her mother said.

'It was all her doing,' Shane added, causing her mother to pout and call him a tattletale. She positively flirted with him.

'Want some?' Shane asked Heather.

She shook her head as she scooped the cat off the worktop. Why was she always the one to do it? 'Is Jo down?'

Her mother nodded. 'This hero got her to sleep in two minutes. The cake was his reward.'

Heather regarded Shane. 'Go to bed – you're wiped,' she said.

He gave her a thoughtful look before finishing off his cake and taking a final swig from his mug. 'Going now,' he said. 'Have a good day, you two.' He left the kitchen without looking back.

'You could be nicer to him,' her mother said. 'It wouldn't kill you.'

Heather counted to five while she poured what was probably lukewarm coffee from the machine. 'I wanted to ask you,' she said, 'about Christmas.'

'What about it? That coffee's cold – you should make fresh.'

'It's fine. You and Dad were coming here, remember? For Christmas?'

That had been the plan. Shane's boys were spending the holiday with their mother, and his daughter Nora was planning to do her own thing with her partner, which left just Shane, Heather and the two girls at home, so in a weak moment Heather had invited her parents to come visit – but what now?

'Of course I remember, Heather – I'm not senile. And I may well still be here at Christmas, at the rate those attorneys are going.' She threw Heather a sharp look. 'Have you had enough of me? Would you rather I left now?'

'Mom, don't be crazy.' Heather crossed her fingers. 'You know we all love having you. I'm asking because I spoke with Dad last evening—'

'You called him? What on earth for?'

'Mom, he's my dad. He'll still be my dad after the divorce.'

'Don't be flippant, Heather.'

'I asked him if he was still planning to come for Christmas, given the change in your circumstances—'

'And he said no, since I'm going to be here, right?'

'Well, not exactly.'

'What does that mean? Is he coming or not?'

'He is. He wants to see Lottie and Jo – and me, I suppose.'

Her mother looked scandalised. 'I don't believe it. He's just doing it to annoy me. So typical of him.'

'I'm sure he's not, Mom. But you're welcome to make other plans if you think you'd feel uncomfortable having him around. You could always come back to us in the spring.'

'I'm not going to change my plans to suit him. I have no intention of it. He's not going to stop me doing whatever I want.'

They were like stubborn children, both of whom needed spanking, or at the very least a spell in the time-out corner. 'So you think you'll be able to be civil on Christmas Day? I really don't want trouble between you, Mom – and I'm not going to choose one of you to spend the day with, so you'll have to be together.'

'If there's trouble, you'll know who to blame,' her mother said, and Heather dropped it, and began filling the dishwasher while her mother tapped on her iPad. She spent a lot of time on the iPad. Heather guessed she'd gone online with her shrink – she didn't make a move without his go-ahead – and she probably had plenty of FaceTime conversations with friends back home.

There must be contact with Tina the attorney too, not that Mom ever spoke of it. Just as well: Heather had no wish to hear how her parents' marriage was being carved up. However ill-judged that union had been, she felt curiously reluctant to contemplate the end of it.

After lunch she packed Jo into the car and drove her mother to the salon where she'd booked an afternoon of treatments. Facial, manicure, top-to-toe massage – and had a mud wrap been mentioned? Salons were her mother's happy places, right after cocktail bars, and boutiques that only let you in with an appointment. The fancy bars and swanky boutiques might be in short supply in town, but Mom was happily doing the rounds of the salons.

As she drove on to the cottage, Heather thought back to her last visit there. It was April, and Astrid had pointed out the blossoms on the cherry tree at the bottom of the garden. This is my favourite time of year, she'd said. Everything coming into bloom, new life wherever you look.

The weather had begun to soften around the edges after a harsh winter, a weak sun doing its best that day. Bundled into two of Astrid's wraps, they'd sat on the little patio, cradling cups of hot chocolate. They'd spoken of Pip, turning one in a few weeks, and Jo, just beginning to sit up on her own. Astrid had laughed at a photo of Shane dressed as the Easter bunny when he and other paramedics had called with a delivery of chocolate eggs to a crèche beside the hospital.

And three days later, Emily had rung Heather in tears to tell her that Astrid was gone.

She pulled up outside the cottage and sat in the car looking out. The small patch of lawn in front had been replaced by gravel in pretty shades of pink and sand and white. Heather, who sneezed if she stood on grass for more than twenty seconds, had approved of this development when she'd seen it the week before. A new raised bed, a foot in height, ran along by the wall that divided the property from its neighbour. Various growing things had been installed in it, none of which Heather could identify.

She scanned the front windows – sitting room, spare bedroom – and saw no movement within. 'Come on,' she said to Jo, releasing her from her car seat, 'let's see who's at home.' She rang the bell and waited, and rang it again when nobody appeared. Was she out? She shifted Jo onto her other hip and flapped the letterbox. 'Hello,' she called. 'Anyone home?'

Still nothing. She wouldn't leave without exploring all options. She walked down the side passage and around to the patio door. Inside she saw a woman who had to be Christine sitting at the kitchen table with an open book before her.

She rapped on the door. The woman's head snapped up. Yes, Christine.

'Hi there!' Heather called brightly. Christine looked blankly at her for a second before getting to her feet. 'The bell must be broken,' Heather said, when the door was opened. The bell wasn't broken. She'd heard it – and Christine must have heard it too. 'I hope I didn't startle you.'

Christine – pixie haircut, arresting eyes, nose ring – stood mutely, unsmiling. Heather sailed on.

'I'm Heather, a friend of Emily and your dad, and this is my daughter Jo. We actually met a few days after Pip was born – I called around to your dad's house for a visit. You were just out from the hospital. Maybe you don't remember.'

Christine shook her head. Did she speak? She sure looked different now. Better fed, for one thing, although still on the skinny side. Better-groomed, brighter-eyed, nicer clothes – and short hair suited her.

'Sorry for turning up unannounced, but Emily told me you were living here now, and I knew where the house was, because I used to come every two weeks to clean Astrid's windows.' Was she going to have to tell her life story before being invited in? 'I just happened to be in the neighbourhood, and I thought maybe I'd take a chance that you'd be home, and see how you're settling in.'

Christine scratched at an elbow, looking hunted. Could she be on something? Having come this far, Heather wasn't about to leave without at least seeing that the kitchen hadn't been trashed.

Finally, Christine spoke. 'Who did you say you were?' Not a hint of a smile.

With an effort, Heather kept hers in place. 'Heather, good friend of Bill and Emily's, and Astrid's when she was alive – but hey, if this time doesn't suit, we could come back another day. I wouldn't mind using your bathroom though.' She grimaced, gave a half-laugh. 'Drank too much coffee at lunchtime, as usual.'

At this, Christine stepped aside – grudgingly, it felt like – and Heather entered. The kitchen was spotless, with no dishes in the sink or on the draining board, and not a crumb to be seen anywhere. Heather glanced at the book, still open on the table. Did she spend her days reading?

'You know where the bathroom is?'

'I do indeed. Would you mind—?' She offered Jo, and after a tiny hesitation, Christine took her and held her awkwardly. 'She might act up, but I'll be quick,' Heather promised. Don't drop her, she added silently.

She scooted out to the hall, also spotless. One jacket hanging on a row of hooks, an umbrella beside it, a scarf beside that. Nothing on the floor, no clutter anywhere. The house's new tenant certainly seemed to be looking after it.

The bathroom was no less orderly. On a shelf Heather saw shampoo and conditioner and bath foam, a tumbler with a single toothbrush and paste, and lavender-scented air freshener. Toilet rolls stacked neatly under the sink, beside a bottle of bleach and a bathroom cleaner. A candle on the windowsill, a matchbox hiding behind. Tampons in the little unit above the sink, with a tube of face cleanser and cotton buds.

No meds of any kind, not even a headache pill.

The hand towel was clean, the bath towel draped over a rail. The room smelt faintly of the lavender spray. Heather counted to twenty, flushed, and went out.

No sign of Christine, no sound from Jo. She halted at the closed door of what had been Astrid's room. Would she be caught if she snuck a peek inside?

'You want tea or coffee?'

She'd materialised at the kitchen door, silent as a ghost, Jo looking unbothered in her arms. Heather quickly fixed her smile back in place and came forward to reclaim her daughter. 'I was just remembering Astrid. Lovely lady. Tea would be great, thank you. I think I've had my fill of coffee for the day.'

The kettle had been plugged in and was already starting to sing. The book had been closed and moved from the table to the worktop. Heather read *Bringing up Baby* on the cover. It reminded her of a book she'd taken out of the library when she was pregnant with Lottie. Boy, she'd pretty much memorised it, not having anyone to ask. Looked like Christine was planning to take her son back. Emily wouldn't be happy, but at least the book was a good sign. She was doing her homework.

She watched as Christine scalded the pot – a new white teapot, no sign of Astrid's daisy one – and dropped two teabags in before setting out cups, plates, sugar bowl, milk jug, all new, all white. 'Want some help?' Heather asked, more to cut into the silence, but Christine shook her head and turned to take a tin down from a shelf. Weird to think she was now familiar with Astrid's kitchen. Strange and sad not to have Astrid pottering around here.

Christine was slim, maybe a little too slim. Never think she'd had a baby, hips narrow as a boy's. The jeans she wore would probably fit a boy. She looked younger than her age, which Heather knew was twenty-seven, just a year off her own. Not stop-you-in-your-tracks pretty, not exactly glowing with health – must take a while for that bloom to come back after years of not being healthy – but the haircut suited her, and the eyes were definitely her best feature.

The tin turned out to contain buns, topped with yellow icing and sprinkled with hundreds and thousands. Made by Emily, Heather guessed, and delivered by Bill – she couldn't see Emily visiting.

'So,' she said, when it became apparent that unless she spoke, nobody would, 'how are you getting on here?'

'Good. It's a nice house.' Her nails were bitten all away, every one of them. 'How old is your baby?'

'Eight months – and there's also eight months between her and Pip. Emily and I have decided they should marry when they're older.'

For a second Christine didn't react, then a tiny smile appeared. 'Do they see each other much?'

'Not lately, I've been busy' – how long had it been since she'd brought Jo to Bill and Emily's for a play date? Too long – 'but normally they meet once or twice a week.'

'You're American.'

'I am, born in California.'

Christine lifted the pot and filled their cups. 'Would you like a bun?'

'Sure.' Heather took one and bit into it. She tasted lemon sponge, light and zesty. 'This is wonderful.'

'I made them,' Christine said, her face going a little pink.

'Did you? Good job. I can't bake to save my life, or cook either.'

'I like to cook,' Christine said. 'At least, I like to try. I'm learning.' The colour deepened in her cheeks. 'Does Jo ... eat buns?'

'She eats whatever she can get her hands on,' Heather said, breaking off a piece of hers and offering it to Jo, who grabbed it and stuffed it in. 'Just don't tell my mom. Maybe I could have a little milk for her?'

Christine jumped up and found a mug. 'Is this OK? I don't have ... baby ones.'

'That's fine. Just a little will do.' She needed some kiddy apparatus, but Bill would help with that. Heather decided to bite the bullet. 'Would you like to have Pip back with you?'

She nodded. 'Dad got me a book,' she said, pointing. 'And I go over when ... he's there, and help him with Pip.'

When Emily wasn't there, Heather would bet. 'That's good. The more preparation you have, the better.'

'We're thinking,' Christine said, 'I might take him for a night next week.'

'That sounds like a plan. One step at a time and you'll be fine.'

Time now for Emily and Bill to consider having one of their

own – and with Bill in his fifties, it might be best not to let it go
too long.

Christine was shy, Heather decided. Not unwelcoming, just
not used to life outside rehab. Happier to leave the doorbell
unanswered, not able yet to deal with people. Heather would
prattle on, and hopefully put the girl at ease. 'Poor Lottie – that's
my older daughter – didn't taste a decent home-cooked meal till
my partner Shane and I got together. He's a good cook.'

'So he's teaching you?'

Heather laughed. 'No way – he wouldn't dare suggest it. I can
manage shepherd's pie, just about.'

'Do you … have other children?' Hesitant. Afraid of asking the
wrong question.

'No, just Lottie and Jo, but Shane had three kids before we got
together, two boys and a girl. Nora, the eldest, moved out last year
to live with her boyfriend. Shane wasn't too impressed, because
she was just twenty, and her boyfriend's eight years older. He's a
good guy, though. He's Emily's younger brother, Daniel. Maybe
you've met him.'

Christine shook her head. No, Emily wouldn't have been
rushing to introduce them.

'He was into the ladies big time before Nora, but he's a one-
woman man now. And for the record, Shane is almost twelve
years older than me, but still he's upset that Daniel is eight years
older than Nora. I guess that's fathers and daughters for you.'

She kept going, asking Christine if she'd met any of her
neighbours: 'You should bring them buns – they'd love you.'

Telling her of the community that had rallied around Heather when she'd moved into her first house as a single mother with an infant daughter: 'Couldn't have been kinder, every one of them. I felt totally at home there.' Making Christine smile with her account of living with her soon-to-be-divorced mother: 'You wouldn't like a little company, would you? I'm sure she'd love your spare room – so much cleaner than my house.'

Little by little, she drew her out. Bit by bit, it got easier. Christine spoke of the online NA meetings she attended every morning on her phone – 'There aren't any actual ones here in town' – and the sponsor who checked in with a call every couple of days, and the park she walked around when the weather allowed.

'What about work?'

She picked at the end of her sleeve. 'I'm not sure ... what to look for. I'm not qualified for anything. I don't even have a Leaving Cert.'

She was twenty-seven, and had yet to hold down any job at all. Heather, also without qualifications, had worked a dozen different jobs since the age of sixteen. Carer, window cleaner, dog walker, painter, car washer, pizza-delivery girl, envelope stuffer, leaflet distributor, and a few others along the way.

'What kind of work would you like?' she asked.

Christine shrugged. 'I like cleaning,' she said. 'Cleaning houses.' A little defensively, as if she was afraid Heather might laugh.

Heather didn't laugh. She looked around the spotless kitchen. 'Know what? You're very good at it. I sure could use you in my house – but you'd probably run a mile.'

'No, I wouldn't.' Quickly. 'I mean, if you're serious.'

Heather had never considered getting a cleaner – but why not? It would give Christine a start. 'Really? You want it? I warn you, the place is beyond messy. Three bedrooms, three adults, four kids. It's a disaster zone.'

'I wouldn't mind.'

'Great – you're hired. Will we say two hours, twice a week, maybe Tuesday and Friday, see how you go?'

'Honestly?'

She looked delighted. She looked like Heather had just told her she'd won the lottery. Wait till she saw the house. 'I'm about a mile from here – I can come pick you up on my way home from the school run, around about nine thirty.'

'I can walk.' She didn't even think about it. 'Give me your address, I'll find it.'

'Well, if you're sure … and payment. Let's see …' Minimum wage was eleven-something, wasn't it? Heather could do better than that. 'Would you be happy with sixteen euro an hour? We needn't tell the taxman.'

'Yes, that's perfect. Thanks.' Christine went right on looking thrilled, and Heather felt pretty pleased too. The more she thought about it, the more sense it made. Why on earth had it never occurred to her to get someone in to clean?

Mom would be impressed. Since her arrival Heather had caught her taking in her surroundings with a look that would have curdled milk. She'd had the sense to say nothing to Heather, but the look said it all. Never lifted a finger to help, but clearly disapproved of her surroundings. News of a cleaner would go down very well indeed.

Bill would be happy too when he heard that Christine had a job. Heather hoped Emily wouldn't see it as some kind of betrayal. She'd have to consider the bigger picture, and realise that employing Christine was a good thing.

She dipped into the tin again. 'I'm going to have a second bun. It seems the polite thing to do – and Jo agrees.' She told Christine of the storytelling that had started up in the library. 'The woman who does it is renting Emily's apartment above the restaurant with her fiancé. I've brought Jo to the storytime: it's good fun.'

Christine looked doubtfully at Jo. 'Is she not too young?'

'Never too young to expose kids to books. I'm not a reader, but I'd love her to be. She doesn't have a clue what's going on, but she gets a kick out of watching the other kids, and being in a new place. You should bring Pip along – and you could become a member while you're there, and borrow books to read to him.'

Christine picked at the paper case of her bun. She'd eaten about a third of it in the time it had taken Heather to polish off two. 'I used to go to the library,' she said. 'When Mum was alive, we'd go at the weekends.' Bleakness in the smile that followed.

For all her troubled years, her life on the streets, there was an innocence, an air of vulnerability about her. It was crazy for Heather to feel motherly towards someone just a year younger than herself, but she did. 'You were how old when she died?'

'Sixteen.'

'Must have been rough.'

'Yeah ... that was when I – when it all started. The drugs, I mean.'

'Right.'

Heather remembered asking Bill about children when they first became acquainted, and he said he had a daughter, and then changed the topic in a way that told Heather not to return to it. An estrangement, she'd thought at the time. His wife dead and his only child distanced: how sad.

'Emily says you were in a kind of halfway house before coming here.'

'Yes.' Another pause while she examined her nails, or lack of them. Did the mention of Emily make her uncomfortable? Heather thought it did. 'I spent three months there. I was lucky to get a place.' She nibbled briefly at a nail that had nothing left to give.

'What was it like? If I can ask.'

'Brilliant.' The word, quietly uttered, was unexpected. 'I ... met someone there,' she added, a tentative smile blooming now on her face.

'You met someone? Someone nice?' Like drawing out a scared child.

She nodded. 'He got me off the streets – he was the one who got me into rehab.'

'Fantastic. What's his name?'

'Chris.' She gave a little giggle. 'Chris and Christine. He was the chef there. He taught me. I was ... sort of his assistant in the kitchen.'

'So was he in recovery too, or just a chef who happened to work there?'

'In recovery. He trained as a chef, before he got into drugs.'

'And is he still in the house?'

'No, he's in Dublin now. He left the house just before me, a couple of weeks ago. His cousin and her husband have a bakery, and they gave him a job. He's living with them until—' She broke off. 'Well, until he finds a place of his own.'

'Great.'

So Christine had followed him out of the house. He'd given her the push she'd needed, maybe, to take her chances in the world again. But what now for them, with him in Dublin and her on the other side of the country?

'We're meeting in January,' Christine said, answering Heather's unspoken question. 'We're not supposed to – be with anyone for three months after coming out.'

Giving one another time to acclimatise before taking the chance on a life together – or at least a relationship. Making sure they were both ready for it. The odds stacked against them, Heather thought. Two needing to be strong, not just one.

She wondered if he was Christine's first love. It was a question for another day, when Heather knew her better.

'Are you in touch with him?'

'Well, we said we wouldn't, except … we send postcards, once a week. Just to check in.'

'That's so romantic. I really think that's great, Christine. It gives you both something to aim towards. Does he know about Pip?'

Her face softened. 'He does. I was scared of telling him, in case ... but he says he can't wait to meet him.' She dropped her gaze, smile dimming. 'I miss him,' she said quietly.

'Sure you do.'

'Don't tell anyone,' she said. 'I haven't said it to anyone, not even Dad.'

'I won't breathe a word,' Heather promised. 'And now I must get going. I've got to collect two kids from school' – and Christine put buns in a freezer bag for the kids while Heather wrote down her address for her new cleaner.

'Thank you,' Christine said, her earlier shyness returning, causing her to trip over her words. 'For the, I mean, for the work. The cleaning job. I'm, honestly, I'm so, well, thank you. Really.'

'Hey – I'm the one should be thanking you. See you Tuesday.'

Impossible not to want all good things for her and the chef, who couldn't wait to meet Pip. Fingers crossed for Chris and Christine.

On impulse, Heather called Emily from the car. It was beginning to feel like they were avoiding each other, and that wasn't good. 'Hello, stranger.'

'Heather – long time no see. How are you getting on with your mother?'

'Bearing up. Listen, I've just come from a visit with Christine. I was curious to see how she was getting on.'

'You called to the house?'

'I did, and all is well. The place is so clean – there wasn't even a spoon in the sink waiting to be washed. And get this: I offered her a job as my cleaner. Not planned – I never thought of getting a cleaner. I said it as a kind of joke, just because she was keeping hers so nice, and she jumped at it. How funny is that? She starts next week.'

A moment passed. 'Well,' Emily said stiffly, 'that's kind of you.'

'Listen, kindness doesn't come into it. Mom will be delighted – I think she feels she's landed in a pigsty.'

Another little pause. 'Listen, before I forget, I've decided to do Christmas dinner at the restaurant this year – will you come? You and Shane and the girls – and your mother, of course, if she's still here.'

'What? You're going to open the restaurant on Christmas Day?'

'No, just a private dinner, family and friends.'

'So who have you invited?'

'Daniel and Nora, and I'm going to ask Lil and Tom, my tenants. And obviously Christine will be there.'

Daniel, Nora, Lil, Tom, Bill, Emily and Christine. Seven around the table already, before the addition of Heather and her crew. 'Look, I appreciate the invite, but I think you have enough without us – and my dad's coming over too. You know he and Mom were planning to spend Christmas with us, before this divorce kicked off. I didn't think he'd still want to be here, but he says he does.'

'Bring him too – there's plenty of room.'

'Are you really sure you want us all there? You want all that work?'

'I'm sure. Pip and Jo will be in high chairs, so everyone will fit.'

Where would Pip be living by Christmas? Heather was definitely not about to voice the question. 'In that case, I guess you have a deal. Hope you won't regret it on Christmas morning.'

'I won't.'

Christmas at the restaurant. As long as her folks were seated well apart from one another, it should work.

Assuming, of course, that Heather and Shane were still a couple by then. Otherwise, they'd need a whole new plan.

Christine

HE'D STOPPED DEAD AT THE SIGHT OF HER.

They'd stood there, just looking at one another, for – well, probably not long at all, but it had felt long, and she honestly hadn't known if he was happy to see her or not.

It had taken so much courage to walk up the path and ring the bell. Her legs had felt shaky all the way. And she'd thought when he'd come to the door that things would take care of themselves, but they hadn't, not straight away.

And then she'd said, I saw the ad, and at the same time he'd said, You came, and she'd wanted to hug him so much then, but she was afraid he might not want it, and he'd made no move to hug her either, so maybe he was afraid too.

You cut your hair, he'd said, and that had made her sad, because she'd first had it cut over a year ago, in a place where hairdressers gave free cuts to homeless people. For all that time she'd had different hair, and he hadn't known.

I saw your ad in the paper, she'd said again. I was planning to come and see you anyway. I've done another month of rehab – the words galloping out now, making up for the silence at the start – and I'm living in a place for recovering addicts, but I want to leave it. I think I'm ready, I mean. I've been there for three months. I wanted to come and see you, and Philip. She'd stopped to breathe. I'm clean, she'd said, her eyes filling, dashing tears away before they could fall. I'm clean, Dad. Honestly I am. I've been clean for four months, I swear to God.

He'd made no response to that, and she couldn't blame him for not believing her. Finally he'd stood back. Come in, he'd said, so she had, and Sherlock had appeared while Dad was hanging up her coat, and he'd whined, tail wagging, and butted his head up against her. At least he'd been glad to see her.

And then they'd gone into the kitchen, where a little boy sat on the floor surrounded by a scatter of toys. A little boy, in little boy's clothes. Not a baby any more.

This is Pip, Dad had said.

Pip, not Philip. They'd changed his name. His hair was lighter than she remembered, straight on top with the ends finishing in soft little curls. His T-shirt had a Superman S on it. He'd stuck his thumb into his mouth and looked at her.

Pip, your mum is here, Dad had said, and Christine had felt a small shock at being called that. She'd crouched and said hello, conscious of Dad watching her. It had been unreal, coming face to face with her child, like a dream she'd soon wake up from. She'd pictured him as a baby whenever she'd thought about him. She didn't think he looked much like her, but she couldn't see anything either that reminded her of his father, which was good.

It was sad they were strangers though. She'd put a tentative hand on his head, just as Sherlock had bumped against him, toppling him over. Christine had gasped in fright, but he'd just laughed and bobbed up again like a skittle, and his laugh sounded like there were bubbles in it, and his teeth were tiny, like a doll's teeth.

Dad had put him into a high chair and given him a little tub of yogurt and a plastic spoon, and by the time the kettle boiled it was all over his hands and face, and in his hair. As Dad had cleaned him up, doing it in a way that showed Christine he was used to it, he'd told her that Astrid had died in April.

Who?

The woman you – did a bit of work for, in her garden, he'd said, without looking at her, and she'd recalled then the tiny old woman with the foreign accent whose hedge Christine had attempted to cut but had instead destroyed, high as a kite, and whose spare front door key Christine had pocketed before she'd been sent packing.

She left you the necklace in her will, Dad had added, and Christine didn't need to ask which necklace. The one she'd taken when she'd returned and let herself quietly into the empty house, having seen the owner leave in a taxi. The necklace she'd surrendered to Dad when he'd found her out before she'd had a chance to sell it.

And now it belonged to her. She hadn't known whether to laugh or cry. She didn't even like pearls. Had she been left it as a final joke, or as a way to make her feel ashamed for having stolen it? Or was it a sign of forgiveness from the woman who'd been kind to Christine, kinder than she'd deserved?

Dad had gone upstairs to get it while Christine had stared at her son. Pip, she'd said, trying it out, and he'd looked at her, and she'd smiled but he hadn't smiled back, and the smile had frozen on her face as he'd gone on regarding her solemnly. Judging her, it had felt like, for leaving him. Sherlock had settled with a grunt on her feet, and she'd scratched his head the way she knew he liked.

You'll stay the night, Dad had said, after Christine had slipped the necklace quickly into her pocket – she'd felt embarrassed to examine it with him there – and she'd said she would if that was OK, and then Emily had arrived.

Emily, who, it turned out, lived there now.

And Emily hadn't been happy to see her.

The way she'd looked at Christine when she walked into the kitchen, like Christine was the bad news she'd been dreading. The way she'd scooped Pip from his chair, as if she was afraid he was going to catch something from Christine – and then lecturing her when Dad had gone next door to Mrs Twomey's, as if Christine didn't know exactly how much trouble she'd caused.

She'd gone to bed that night wondering if she and Emily

could possibly last three months in the same house, assuming she'd be invited to stay there until she and Chris found a place together in January – but in the morning, after Emily had left for the restaurant, Dad had told Christine about Astrid's house, and how it would belong to Pip when he was twenty-one, and in the meantime he and Emily, and another friend of Astrid's, had been put in charge of it.

And while she was still trying to get her head around the idea of her son, who wasn't even two, being left a house, a whole house all for himself, Dad had said, as casually as if he was offering her another slice of toast, You could live in it now, if you wanted. I don't know if you remember it, a little bungalow, and we've done it up, and it's in a nice quiet area about a mile from here.

Christine had stared at him, not understanding. How could I live in it? You said Philip – Pip – won't get it till he's twenty-one.

Her dad had explained about the tax bill. We're going to let the house till Pip takes possession, to raise money for the tax.

So I'd have to pay rent.

She might have known there'd be a catch. She had to sort out money – the rehab office had forms she'd have to bring to Social Welfare – but she was pretty sure she wouldn't get enough to rent a full house on her own.

I can pay your rent, Dad had said, for the moment. Until you get fixed up with work. You'd need to look after it, keep it clean and tidy. And stay off the drugs. You'd have to promise me, Christine.

I promise, she'd said, thinking of Chris. It was like a present, a wonderful unexpected present. She'd been half afraid to believe it was really happening. Thank you, she'd said, again wanting to hug him, but again she hadn't.

And maybe, he'd said, when you're settled, you might take Pip for a night now and again, see how you get on.

Christine had looked at her son, feeding a crust of bread to a little blue rabbit. Yes, she'd said, but the idea of having him on her own, with nobody to tell her what to do and what not to do, was terrifying.

Not until you're ready, Dad had said, so she must have looked as scared as she'd felt. We could have a look at the house this morning, he'd said, before you go back.

Are you not working?

I'm part-time now, three days a week. I switched after— And then he'd broken off, and she heard *after you left*, as clearly as if he'd said it aloud. The changes she'd caused. Emily moving in, Dad going part-time, Mrs Twomey looking after Pip when both of them were working. And still Dad was doing everything he could for her. He'd forgive her, she thought, if she murdered someone. He'd stick up for her no matter what she did.

They'd washed up the breakfast things together, and then he'd put Pip into a little puffy jacket and driven them both to the house that Christine barely remembered, and there had been nothing about it that she didn't love.

And three days later she'd said goodbye to Ethel and the others, and she'd come back and moved in.

She couldn't believe it. A house of her own, to do exactly as she wanted in it. Her own front door, and the key that opened it, and another key for the patio door at the back. A hall with two more doors, kitchen and sitting room. A corridor leading off the hall with three more doors, two bedrooms and one bathroom. Five rooms, seven doors and a key-ring with two shiny keys on it.

The bathroom had a bath. She hadn't had a bath in years. Now she had one every other night, with bubbles. She would light the candle she'd taken from the sitting room and set it carefully between the bath taps. She would turn off the light and undress, and wrap her hair in a towel – new towels! She would lower herself into the bath, as hot as she could bear, and lie back. She would close her eyes and breathe in the steamy scented air, still finding it hard to believe that she was here. It was like a dream.

She'd sent her first postcard to Dublin the day after she'd moved in. She'd made her writing as small as she could, to fit as many words as possible.

I'm out. I'm living by myself in a small house, and I'm going to take Philip for a day here and there to start. Everyone calls him Pip now, and I kind of like it. How is your work? I hope you like it. I'll look for work soon. I'm practising the recipes you gave me. Last night I made fish cakes, my first dinner in the house. I miss you. Here's my address.

At the end she put *C xx*. Reading it over, she thought it sounded awkward and childish; she'd never been good at writing. She'd wanted to say more about missing him, and how she thought about him all the time, but you couldn't be too personal on a postcard.

His answer had arrived just three days later. The postcard had a picture of James Joyce on it. Chris's writing was even smaller than hers, so she'd had to squint to make it out. He liked the name Pip. His bedroom was small, but his cousin and her husband were easy to live with. He enjoyed the work in the bakery, although getting up at four in the morning was messing up his sleep. Dublin was noisier and dirtier than he remembered, and way more expensive.

He was happy she was fixed up in a house. He said good luck with the job-hunting. He missed her too, and he wished January was closer, and he sent hugs to her and Pip. Chrissy, he called her, like he'd done in the house when nobody was nearby.

In his next postcard – a dog in a tutu on the front – he told her he'd found a ukulele in a skip and was learning how to play it from YouTube videos. He could manage 'How Much Is That Doggie In The Window?' very slowly. His singing wasn't great, but he was going to learn 'Rock a Bye Baby' so he could put Pip to sleep – or give him nightmares with the singing, one or the other.

She called to Dad's house often, usually when she knew Emily would be out, and he let her feed Pip and change him, and put him down for a nap, and he called her 'Mum' all the time in front of Pip. He'd also given her a book called *Bringing up Baby: the Toddler Years*, and she read and reread bits every day, wanting to learn everything she could.

And now she'd been in the house a full week, and an hour ago the doorbell had given her a fright. Nobody rang it except Dad, and he was working today. She'd ignored it, hoping whoever it was would go away, but the caller had just come around to the back, giving Christine another fright when she'd rapped on the patio door.

She was big and smiling, with a tumble of dark hair and a fat baby clamped to her side. A friend of Bill and Emily's, she'd said, and friendly with the old woman too, before she died, and Christine had decided she must be a spy, coming to see if the house was being looked after. She hadn't wanted to let her in, but she could hardly say no when she'd asked to use the bathroom, and practically shoved her baby at Christine.

While she was gone Christine had made faces at the baby, trying to get her to smile, but the baby had just looked bored. She thought she'd better be nice to the mother, or she might go back to the others and say things weren't good, and they might take the house away.

And it turned out she was fine. She was friendly, with plenty to say, and she seemed happy with how she found the house. And before Christine could stop herself she'd told her about Chris, and the postcards, and their plan to meet up again in January, and Heather was like, Oh, that's great, I'm so happy for you.

And best of all, craziest of all, she'd offered Christine a job, just like that. And cleaning was something she was good at; cleaning, she'd discovered – real energetic scrubbing and mopping and polishing like your life depended on it – kept the cravings at bay, so she'd become expert at it, and every inch of the house was always spotless.

And if Heather was happy with Christine's work she might spread the word, and there might be more job offers. Wait till she told Chris and Dad and Ethel.

And even though they'd only just met, it felt like Heather might turn into a friend. A proper friend, like her old girlfriends from school. They'd all melted away one by one when Christine had begun using; she'd destroyed all those friendships, and now she hoped not to meet any of them again, because of the shame and embarrassment she'd feel.

She'd made no friends while she was on the street. She'd hung around with other addicts at night because it was safer to be in a group, but they hadn't been friends. She hadn't connected with anyone in rehab, apart from Chris – people there weren't really looking for friends. But Heather felt like she might become a friend.

Her sponsor Ethel wasn't so much a friend as a kind of protector, but it was good to have her phoning to check in every couple of days. Stay well, she'd say at the end of every call. Keep attending the meetings. Stay strong, Christine. I have faith in you, so don't let me down. Ring me anytime you need to.

That evening, she called Dad to tell him about the job, forgetting he was at work. 'That's wonderful,' he said. 'I'm so pleased for you.'

'I'll be able to pay you something towards the rent. Not a lot, but—'

'Don't worry about that, wait till you get a bit more work. When do you start?'

'Tuesday. Tuesdays and Fridays, Heather said.' She took a breath. 'Maybe … I could take Pip on Wednesday night.'

Her father didn't miss a beat. 'You could. I'll bring him around to you about three, if that suits.'

'Fine.' And just like that, it was sorted. No going back now.

On Tuesday she made her way to Heather's house, feeling nervous. It was number twenty-four in a housing estate, with Heather's red Fiesta parked outside, and a blue Volkswagen in the driveway that must belong to her partner, whose name Christine had forgotten.

The door was opened by an older woman in a pale blue jacket and skirt, with hair that looked stiff. 'You must be the cleaner,' she said, in an accent like Heather's. 'Wait here' – and she disappeared, leaving Christine standing uncertainly in the hall. The mother wasn't friendly like the daughter.

'You found me!'

And here came Heather down the stairs, baby on her hip, just as she'd appeared at Christine's patio door. 'You've met Mom,' she went on, giving a silent grimace that made Christine smile. 'Let me show you around the mansion.'

Every room was full of too many things. Clothing, shoes, schoolbags, books, sports gear, dirty mugs. In the main bedroom a cot was wedged between double bed and wall, and the floor was littered with toys, and newspapers were piled on a chair, and the wardrobe doors swung open, unable to contain the load within. The bathroom had damp towels heaped on the bath edge, and an overflowing laundry basket, and toothpaste trails in the sink, and splashes on the toilet seat. Only the smallest of the three bedrooms was tidy. 'This is Mom's,' Heather said. 'I guess you won't have much to do here.'

The kitchen was the worst, table still cluttered with breakfast things, cupboard doors open to reveal jumbled contents, a cat licking something from the floor. In the living room, not quite as messy, Heather's mother sat on the couch with an iPad. She glanced up when they walked in, and ignored them after that.

'Hello!'

A sudden cheery call from the kitchen. 'That'll be Shane,' Heather said. 'He did the school run so I'd be here to meet you.'

Shane looked drained, as if he hadn't slept at all, but he gave Christine a friendly smile. 'You're a brave woman,' he told her, 'trying to put order on this house.' He looked older than Heather – had she said twelve years between them?

'You can start in the main bedroom,' Heather said. 'He'll be going to bed in about half an hour – he's just off night duty. Do what you can – you'll find what you need under the stairs.'

But under the stairs yielded very little. A bucket held a few bottles of cleaning products, two of them empty, another almost empty, and a crumpled bundle of cloths that didn't smell so good. An ancient Hoover sat next to a tired-looking mop. No sign of a duster or rubber gloves.

Christine did what she could, making beds, folding clothes

into drawers, finding space on shelves for books, stowing toys in the cot to clear the floor. She left the cloths alone and used a damp hand towel to clean skirting boards and surfaces. From the second bedroom she heard movement in the main one, and presumed it was Shane going to bed. She tried to remember what job he had, and couldn't. Maybe Heather hadn't said.

When she had done all she could upstairs she came down and entered the living room with her bucket, pulling the Hoover behind her. Heather's mother rose to her feet and walked out without a word. By the time Christine reached the kitchen, her last room, she found Heather wiping dishes, and no sign of her mother.

'Well – was it awful?'

'Not at all – but I could do with a few more products.'

'Write down what you need,' Heather instructed, passing her a pad, and Christine wrote bleach and toilet cleaner and furniture polish and window cleaner and bathroom cleaner and kitchen cleaner and duster and mop head and J Cloths. She thought a bit and added oven cleaner and sponge scourers and rubber gloves, size small, and Hoover bags. Was it too much?

Heather scanned the list. 'What are sponge scourers?'

'Um – they're for scrubbing. One side is spongy and the other is … wiry.'

'Wow. OK.'

'I put towels in the washing-machine – if they're done before I leave I'll hang them out and put another wash on from the laundry basket.' She looked up at the kitchen presses. 'I'd like to rearrange things in there, if that's OK.' She was itching to put order on their higgledy-piggledy state.

'Knock yourself out. Let me know if there's anything else I should do to make your job easier here.'

When the two hours were up, Christine was only halfway through the kitchen reorganisation. She'd happily have stayed longer, but Heather paid her and shooed her out. 'You've done your time – the rest will keep.'

'I can do better,' Christine said, afraid that what she'd managed to do might not impress, afraid she'd lose her job right after starting it. 'Once I get the other stuff, and find my way around a bit more, I'll make it really clean.'

Heather laughed. 'Slow down, Superwoman – I can guarantee you've done miles better than me. See you Friday.'

That night she lay in the bath, planning. On Friday she'd load the washing machine when she arrived, so she could get two loads done in the time she had. She could change the linen on two beds each time she was there, so they'd all get a turn in two weeks. And she'd ask Heather to get storage boxes so she could stow more things under beds and on top of wardrobes, and maybe there was attic space for stuff that wasn't being used. And air freshener for the bathroom – she'd forgotten to put that on the list.

The following day she answered the doorbell at five past three, her stomach leaping about like she was going on a first date. 'He's in the car,' her father said, his arms full of a flattened playpen. 'I'll set this up in the kitchen while you bring him in.'

There was a mountain of other luggage in the car, piled in

around Pip. A giant sack of nappies, a bag of clothes and toys, another bag of food in little jars, and plastic bowls and beakers and utensils, and a box holding baby wipes and Calpol and Sudocrem and nappy bags and more. In the boot she saw a folded-up cot and a white plastic bath and a changing table. It looked like a whole lot of stuff for one small boy. How would everything even fit in the house?

She leant in and unbuckled Pip's harness. 'Hi,' she said, and he looked at her unblinkingly. 'No smile?' she asked, and he held up his blue rabbit. 'Hi,' Christine said to the rabbit. 'Can you smile?' and this made Pip giggle.

He didn't resist when she lifted him out, and as she carried him in – the heft of him coming as the surprise it always did – she thought of all the ways he might die while she was in charge of him, and she wanted to hand him back to Dad and tell him he and Emily could hang on to him, she'd just come and visit.

'He doesn't really need this any more,' her dad said, snapping the playpen sides in place. He'd had to move the table and chairs a bit so it would fit in. 'We've stopped using it, but I thought it might be handy for you until you get used to having him around the place. He's quite happy in it.'

When Pip had been installed there and surrounded by his toys, Dad took a page from his pocket and handed it to her. 'Instructions,' he said, sounding apologetic, and Christine unfolded it and saw handwriting that wasn't his: *Feeding Routine* and *Bedtime Routine* and *Giving a Bath* and *Emergency Doctor Number* and *Things to Remember*.

Under the last heading she read, *Don't leave knives or scissors or anything sharp within his reach. Keep saucepan handles turned in to the wall when cooking. Don't leave the kettle flex, or any flex, where he can grab it. Cut grapes in half, and make sure they're seedless. No nuts, nothing hard that might choke him.* And more, and more, the two sides of the page covered.

'You know this stuff already, of course,' her dad said. 'Emily just thought it might help if it was all there in black and white.'

Christine sat down abruptly. 'I'm scared,' she said. 'Maybe it's too soon. Maybe I'm not ready.'

Her father folded his arms. 'You're ready,' he said. 'Pick up the phone if you have any problems, but you won't have,' and she looked at her son, the little person she'd made, and again the responsibility of keeping him safe almost overwhelmed her.

'You're ready, Christine,' Dad said again. 'Just keep focused, keep an eye on him.'

'Emily,' she said. 'What does she think?'

He scrubbed the back of his head. 'She'll take a while,' he said. 'She's very attached to him. She's a bit nervous, but she'll be OK.' He paused. 'One thing I have to ask you. Well, two things.'

'What?'

'Don't leave him alone in the house. Don't ever go out and leave him, even if he's asleep, even for a short while – remember he can walk, and he can move fast when he wants. And don't ever … take anything while you have him.'

'I won't.'

'You promise? You'll ring me if you ever … ?'

He didn't finish it. He didn't have to. *If you ever get the urge and can't fight it. If you ever decide to go back to that life.* 'I swear,' she said, an image of Chris's face flashing behind her eyes. She thought of the three of them, him, her and Pip, becoming a family. Everything to live for now, everything to stay clean for. 'Cross my heart, Dad. I won't let you down this time.'

And she could see he wanted to believe her, and she felt frightened still, but determined too. Pip cried after he left, and didn't stop until she opened a jar of apple purée, an hour before Emily's feeding routine said he should eat. She forgot to put a bib on him and his top got messy, but when she tried to take it off he cried again, so she filled his plastic bath even though it was nowhere near bedtime, and put him in with all his clothes still on, which distracted him enough to stop his tears, and while she was peeling off his trousers he toppled backwards under the water.

She grabbed him and hauled him up, heart hammering, and he spluttered and laughed and slapped the water with his little palms, and she flooded the bathroom floor when she lifted him out, afraid to leave him in any longer, and somehow she got him out of the rest of his clothes and into pyjamas without further incident.

And when she put him into his cot, hair still damp because she was afraid she'd burn him if she used the hairdryer, he cried again. 'Emwy,' he wept, 'Emwy,' clutching his little blue rabbit, until she remembered his soother, and plugged his mouth with it. 'Emily's coming soon,' she told him, and he looked at her with wet eyes, lashes spiked, and she hated that she had to lie to him.

She hunted for a bedtime story but couldn't locate the bag with books in it she'd seen Dad bring in earlier, so she sat on the floor by the cot and tried to think of a fairy tale that wasn't scary, and when she failed to come up with one that didn't have a witch or a wolf or a bear or a troll in it, she told him about Mary who had a little lamb, and Bo Peep who lost her sheep and Jack Spratt who ate no fat as he sucked his soother and watched her mouth moving.

And when he was still awake after that she sang about Old MacDonald who had the farm until she ran out of animals, and finally his eyes began to close, and she leant her head against the bars of the cot, feeling on the point of sleep herself.

She tiptoed from the room, leaving the door open. She mopped the bathroom floor, and was squeezing out his sodden clothes when she found his nappy, wadded up inside his trousers, and she realised that she'd forgotten to put a new one on him. She grabbed her bath towel and folded it, and snuck back into the bedroom where she inched it underneath him, holding her breath every time he stirred.

She hardly slept that night, too tense to switch off. Around four in the morning he woke and cried, and she grabbed the chance to put a nappy on him, leaving off his soaked pyjama bottoms and pulling out the damp bath towel. When he persisted in crying even after she'd fed him a pot of custard and held his beaker while he slurped milk – *no food after bedtime, just milk,* Emily's instructions read – it took her ages to figure out that he was looking for the blue rabbit that had fallen down the side of the cot. 'Waba,' he kept sobbing, 'waba,' but she didn't yet speak his language.

In the morning she sat bleary-eyed at the kitchen table while he chewed a finger of toast in his playpen, banging the spoon he'd refused to surrender against the wooden bars, his hair full of yogurt that she hadn't the energy to clean up.

But she'd done it. She'd got him through a night without poisoning or scalding or choking him, and only nearly drowning him – and if she could do it once, she could do it again.

Of course she could do it again. She was his mum, and every time she saw him she liked him better. He was growing on her, that was what it felt like – and in January Chris would be around to help her look after him.

Oh, the spark of pure joy that prompted. She imagined them bathing him together, bringing him to the park and to the beach, getting his first proper football. Teaching him stuff like how to be kind, how to say please and thank you. How to stand up for himself.

How to say no if someone offered him a pill at the school gates. How to keep saying no, every time it happened.

This was accompanied by an unexpected surge of fury that caused her grip to tighten on her coffee cup. If that ever happened, if she ever heard of that happening, she would find whoever did it and hurt them. Chris might not want to hurt them; he'd probably try to talk to them, but Christine would have no problem inflicting pain.

She pushed away the thought. Maybe Pip would be musical, like Christine's aunt Grace: she'd seen him jiggling along in Dad's house to a song on the radio. They could send him for piano lessons when he was old enough – or he might prefer the guitar.

She finished her toast and cleared the table. She yawned as she put Pip into a jacket and settled him in his buggy, and wiped with a damp facecloth at his sticky hair. Dad wasn't due to pick him up for another hour, so there was time to walk to the cemetery, fifteen minutes or so from the house. Pip might have been brought there already, but not by Christine.

When they arrived she pushed the buggy along the path till they came to the grave she wanted. 'Look, Mum,' she said, 'here's your grandson. Imagine, I'm a mum now too' – and the words brought tears spilling suddenly down her face. She couldn't bear to think of how sad Mum would have been if she could see how low Christine had fallen – but now it was time to reconnect.

'He wasn't planned,' she said through her tears, 'and I didn't do right by him at the start, but I'm going to make up for it now. I have a lot to learn, but I will. I will learn. I'll never be as good a mum as you were, but I'll do the best I can.'

She wondered what it would be like when she finally had Pip all the time. Would he cry for Emily every night, or for his granddad? She knew Emily would be sad to lose him. She wondered if they'd argued about Christine having him for the night – Dad was glad about it, but clearly Emily wasn't.

When they got back to the house she sat on a patio chair and watched Pip toddling around the garden, squatting every now and again to pull up tufts of grass and fling them into the air. She thought of the old woman who would have sat in just this spot, looking at the same garden. She thought of the string of pearls she kept under her pillow, not knowing what to do with them.

Mad, how she'd ended up in this house. Maybe Chris could move here in January, find a job in a local bakery. Maybe Dad would agree to let him move in with Christine and Pip. She didn't see why not, if they could pay the rent themselves.

Pip could grow up here, in this house. She could see it, clear as anything – and in a year or two, she might have another child. She thought of sharing a bed with Chris, and lit up inside. She didn't have to wonder if she'd love his child: she knew she would.

She looked at the postcard in her lap that had been waiting on the hall floor when they'd returned from the cemetery. The front of it had Charlie Chaplin leaning on his stick. She turned it over.

Hello from the capital! Dog tired here, will sleep for a week when I get holidays. Can now play 'You Are My Sunshine' and 'Rock A Bye Baby' on the ukulele, but my singing is still as bad as ever. Great news about your job, all the best. Hope your first night with Pip goes well too. We won't feel it till we're together again. Stay strong. Be happy. There are good times ahead for us, Chrissy. Cxx

So many good times, just waiting for them. All they needed was to stay strong.

NOVEMBER

Emily

THEY GOT ON FINE, BILL TOLD HER, EACH TIME he brought Pip back from an overnight visit with Christine. No problems at all – and it wasn't that Emily didn't believe him exactly, but she knew the bias would be there. The wanting his daughter to do well would be there, and he might close his eyes to any hint that she wasn't.

She signs in to online meetings every morning, he'd reported to Emily. Narcotics Anonymous, never misses one. I think she's on the right road at last. And Emily would nod and say, Fingers crossed, and she would try to sound enthusiastic.

Pip seemed happy enough with the sleepovers, never kicked up when Bill told him he was going to stay with his mum. Emily was the one who felt like having a tantrum, throwing herself on the floor and screaming until Bill promised never to take him to Christine again, but she had to hold her tongue. She had to tell herself it was good for Pip – and if his mother could stay healthy, it was good for him to be with her.

It just wasn't good for Emily.

You should come and see, Bill would say, when he was packing up Pip's things. She keeps the place spotless. It would do you good to see it – but Emily kept finding reasons not to accompany him, until he stopped asking.

Heather had visited the cottage though. Without saying anything to Emily she'd called there with Jo. Not only that, but she'd given Christine a job. And last time Bill had come back from the cottage, he'd said Christine wanted to collect Pip on Saturday morning to take him to storytelling at the library that Heather had told her about. It's your new tenant, he'd said, who tells the stories. Small world, isn't it?

It was selfish of Emily to feel jealous and betrayed, but hard not to. Heather had never once said she wanted a cleaner, so she'd clearly created the job to help Christine. And she'd never mentioned Lil's storytelling to Emily – not that Emily would be free to bring Pip on Saturday morning, but that wasn't the point.

She and Heather seemed to have grown apart. There'd been no sign of her at the restaurant since her mother had arrived. She'd rung Emily once, after calling to the cottage to meet Christine, and apart from that there'd been just the odd breezy hope-all-is-well text. Emily wondered if she'd upset her friend in some way, but then dismissed it – if Heather was upset, Heather would say so. She was busy, that was all.

And yes, yes, of course it was good that Christine was settling into the town and earning money – Bill had called Heather to thank her when he'd heard about the job – but the better her prospects became, the more likely she'd ask to take Pip back permanently. And try as she might, Emily couldn't face losing him.

She missed him so much on the nights he wasn't there. She would wake in the small hours and listen for his breathing, like she used to do when he was tiny, and a new and terrifying responsibility for them. He wouldn't die on her watch, she'd vowed, and the sound of his rapid little breaths would allow her to tumble back into sleep.

Now she lay sleepless because he wasn't there, and the absence of him was immense – and she knew, if Christine stayed clean, that he'd eventually be gone from them altogether, and she could only hope it wouldn't come too soon.

But it did. It did come too soon.

'I'm very grateful,' Christine said, a few days after she'd taken Pip to the storytelling. 'I am really. I appreciate everything you did for him – but you should get on with your own lives now.'

She'd called unexpectedly, finding both Bill and Emily at home on a Tuesday afternoon. Eight days into November, winter nudging in from all sides. Air cold enough to redden the tips of noses, rain with a sting in it, woolly hats and gloves resurrected, the last of the leaves from the acer tree in Mrs Twomey's garden blown across into Bill and Emily's by the wind of the night before.

Pip was upstairs napping, the baby monitor that was plugged in above the breadbin picking up his little snuffles. Emily was ironing tablecloths and napkins and aprons, glad of something to do while Christine and Bill sat at the table.

'What are you saying?' Bill asked, but he knew what she was saying. Both of them knew what she was saying.

'I can take him all the time now. I'm ready. I feel ready.'

Emily's grip tightened on the iron. I'm not ready, she said silently, pressing the same fold over and over into a napkin. I'll never be ready. From the monitor, a little sneeze erupted.

Bill shifted on his chair, not looking at Emily. He knew exactly how she felt, how unwilling she was to let Pip go, how afraid she was that he'd come to harm. He knew, because she'd told him often enough. But she had to be so careful, dancing around the topic, trying not to upset him by being too critical of Christine – so maybe after all he hadn't realised the strength of her feelings.

'We love having him, Christine,' he said. 'It's not a bother for us at all – and if we keep him for some of the time it leaves you free to look for other work. Why not let things stay as they are till after Christmas, and we can have another think about it then?'

Christine gave a toss of a shoulder as if she was shrugging something off it. She hadn't touched the water she'd asked for, hadn't gone near the plate of almond fingers Bill had put out. 'You've done enough. I don't want him to be a burden.'

'You know he's never that. What about when you go to Heather's house to clean, who'll look after Pip then?'

She chewed a nail. 'I can bring him,' Heather said. 'He can play with Jo.'

Emily swept the napkin off the ironing board and added it to the stack on the worktop. *Heather said.* Heather was facilitating everything, making it so easy for Christine. Didn't she know how Emily felt about Pip? Of course she did. She took another napkin and sprayed it with a loud puff of steam that made Bill glance over.

'Look, I want to do this, Dad. I've missed out on a lot – and I know it was my own fault, but it's time for me to take over now. Will you bring the rest of his things when you're dropping him to me tomorrow? You can come and see him anytime you want. Both of you,' she added, her eyes flicking briefly in Emily's direction. Emily could imagine being watched silently as she interacted with Pip, Christine seeing, and probably resenting, the bond Emily still had with him.

She wouldn't be calling there. Despite what Christine was saying, she knew she wouldn't be welcome.

'And you can bring him over to us,' Bill said, already giving in. Already accepting what Emily couldn't. Maybe, she thought suddenly, he'd known about this in advance. Maybe Christine had told him she was ready, and he'd said, Better come on Tuesday, and say it when Emily's there. 'Come as often as you like,' he said now, 'any time at all.'

But she wouldn't come, Emily thought. Bill would go to the cottage to see his grandson. He'd bring him back here for a visit if Emily asked him, she knew he would, but she wasn't sure she could bear just little snatches of Pip. The idea of him growing away from her, having a life that was separate from her, was unendurable.

'Did you know?' she asked Bill, after Christine had left, after Pip had woken and been brought down, after the ironing board had been folded and put away.

About to tie a bib on Pip, Bill looked up at her. 'Did I know what?'

'That Christine was planning to come here, and say – what she said.'

He shook his head. 'Not as such, but I could tell she was working up to it. We knew this day would come, Emily.'

She wound up the iron cord, her skin prickling. 'Hey,' Bill said, in a new voice, 'take it easy, buster,' and Pip laughed and slapped the tray of his high chair, and she realised then that she came second to Christine, and she always would.

That night she turned away from Bill in bed, and he said, 'Emily, we're not losing him. He's just going to live in another house. We can still see him – he'll only be a mile away,' and she squeezed her eyes closed and waited for him to stop talking. For much of the night she lay awake, listening to Pip's sleeping sounds and fighting tears. Their last night with him, their last time to share a bedroom with him.

In the morning she got him into his little blue jacket before leaving for the restaurant. He was going next door to Mrs Twomey till lunchtime, when Bill would come home from work and deliver him to Christine's.

She hugged Pip, unable to say goodbye. She kissed his cheek and tickled under his chin, and he giggled and ducked his head. She gave him another hug and turned away, and walked out of the house without looking at Bill. 'See you later,' he called after her, but she didn't answer.

Over the days that followed she kept busy. She was glad of the bustle at work, and her chef Mike's chatter as he prepped and cooked. She was glad of Sherlock to walk on her days off, when Bill was at the nursing home and all her chores were done. She was glad of her brother Daniel and his partner Nora, who never minded her dropping in to say hello.

Another distraction was the planning of the Christmas Day dinner – although she wondered now if she'd done the right thing. Hosting at the restaurant had seemed like a good way to dilute Christine with other people, and everyone she'd invited had accepted, including her tenants – but would she manage to be civil to Christine now, and would she and Heather be OK, given the distance that seemed to have opened between them?

Despite all her distractions, the sadness from the loss of Pip lingered. It ambushed her unexpectedly, caught her off guard and pulled her down into loneliness. Bill did bring him back to visit. Every few days he'd appear, straining from Bill's arms on seeing her, and it was wonderful for as long as it lasted, but saying goodbye each time caused her heart to crack again, and she wondered if the fresh pain was worth it.

'You'd miss him,' Mrs Twomey from next door said, when Emily had spotted her at her clothes line and called her in for tea and gingerbread, craving another diversion. 'He was a bit of fun around the place, wasn't he?'

'He was.'

Emwy he called Emily, not able yet to get his little tongue around the full thing. He loved her creamy rice pudding, and wouldn't touch tomatoes in any form. Liked pasta with no sauce, didn't fancy eggs unless she scrambled them. Would sometimes nod off while she was feeding him, head drooping in his high chair.

His chortle when she tickled his bare soles was a symphony. When she read him a story he would sometimes reach up and touch her mouth with his fingers, and she would pretend to gobble them, just to hear him erupt in delighted laughter. The perfect whorls of his ears, the curve of his cheek, the little dimples of his knuckles, all brought a rush of love and a lump in her throat.

'I hope Christine is staying well,' Mrs Twomey said, and Emily told her she was, neither of them mentioning drugs. But always, always it was a worry. One slip and she'd be lost again – and Pip could be put in jeopardy, his safety compromised. Emily didn't think she could bear it if any harm came to him through Christine's neglect. She'd kill her, or want to.

But it wasn't just the loss of Pip, it was more. It was her wish for a child of her own that had bubbled quietly within her for years, and had come rushing back in the wake of Pip's return to Christine. It was as if losing him had left a yawning emptiness far greater than she'd felt before he'd come into their lives.

She was changing sheets one afternoon when the doorbell rang. She went downstairs to find her brother there.

'Daniel – everything OK?' He rarely turned up without an advance phone call.

'Everything's perfect,' he said, stepping into the hall. 'Everything's hunky-dory. Have you a minute?'

'I have.'

She brought him into the kitchen and sat him down, and made coffee while he commented on the weather – frost on the ground that morning, sleety showers forecast – and asked about the restaurant, and enquired after Bill, and all the time she could see there was something waiting to be said, something he was hugging to himself until he had her full attention. He'd proposed to Nora, she guessed. They'd been in a relationship for two years, living together for the last one. A question had been popped, and the answer, clearly, had been yes.

She was wrong.

'Nora's pregnant.' He barely waited until she'd taken a seat. 'I wanted you to be the first to know.'

'Oh my God – Daniel, that's wonderful!' She rose and he did too, and she caught him in a tight squeeze. 'You're going to be a dad! When is she due?'

'May.' He looked so pleased with himself. 'We planned it,' he told her. 'It wasn't an accident.' He was the cat that got the cream. Her little brother, on his way to being a parent. 'You'll be an aunt. Aunt Emily. Auntie Em.' His delighted smile opened into a laugh. 'Hey, wasn't that Dorothy's aunt in *The Wizard of Oz*?'

'I think so. When are you telling Dol and Patrick?'

'We'll ring them tonight.'

They'd be thrilled. Dol had twice in the last few months told Emily about friends becoming grandmothers, and Emily had heard the envy in her mother's voice, and had pretended not to hear the unspoken question.

'Not sure how Shane will react,' Daniel went on. 'He's young to be a granddad – and he might think Nora's a bit young to be a mum.'

Shane had turned forty in June. His other daughter hadn't yet turned one. A young grandfather for sure. 'He'll get over it.'

And what would the baby make Heather, as Shane's partner? Officially, nothing – but in practice she'd be a sort of step-grandmother, at the ripe old age of twenty-eight. Emily wondered how she'd take the news. She must ring her, after she was sure they'd been told.

She and Daniel talked about morning sickness (bad at the outset, pretty much gone now) and finding out the gender (he didn't want to know; Nora might, closer to the time) and possible names (both in agreement, Chloë for a girl, Simon for a boy). Eventually she told him she needed to get back to the restaurant, and he hugged her goodbye and promised to pass on her congratulations to Nora.

Driving to The Food of Love, she digested the news. She'd thought she'd be the first of them to be a parent. Three years older than Daniel, engaged to be married at twenty-five, little dreaming how spectacularly wrong that would go. Now, when she'd found the man who would never hurt her like Ferg had, she wasn't even sure he wanted more children.

On her next birthday she would be thirty-three, and Bill would be on his way to fifty-two. It was time. It was past time.

When she reached the restaurant she took out her phone and found Nora's name. *Thrilled to bits at your news – congratulations! Talk soon – E xxx*

The text was hardly sent when the response came: *Thanks, Emily, I'm over the moon! N xx*

Heather rang later, much later, when Emily and Mike were clearing up. They've heard the news, she thought, when she saw Heather's name.

They had. 'Congratulations,' Heather said. 'You're an auntie in waiting.'

Emily propped the phone between chin and shoulder. 'I was going to ring you,' she said, trying not to make too much of a clatter as she returned clean cutlery to its tray. 'Isn't it marvellous? How did Shane take it?'

'Half delighted, half panicked. "Grandpa" isn't exactly a title he was expecting to inherit just yet.'

'No, but he'll make a great one – and you'll be Ireland's youngest step-granny.'

'I know. Relationships will be crazy. Jo will be its step-aunt.'

'Imagine … So how's everything?'

'Well.' Pause. 'We're a little … up and down at the moment.'

'With your mother there, you mean?'

'No, I mean me and Shane. Well, me really. I'm just – what? Just a bit discontented, I guess. But you're right, Mom being around isn't exactly helping.'

'Oh … sorry to hear that.'

'I'll push through. How are you?'

Emily switched the phone to her other shoulder as Mike mouthed goodbye. She gave him a wave and waited until the door had closed behind him. 'I'm lonely after Pip.'

'Of course – but you always knew you might have to give him back some day, right?'

Not what she wanted to hear. 'Doesn't make it any easier,' she said shortly, untying her apron. 'I hate the house without him. It feels so empty. I need—' She stopped, the apron still in her hands.

'You need a child of your own.'

'I do.' The apron had a small dark red splotch on it: blackberry juice from the crumble. 'I really do.'

'I get it. Obviously I didn't plan Lottie, but I was broody for Jo. What does Bill say?'

Emily dropped the apron into her laundry bag and pulled the drawstring. Her neck felt stiff when she reclaimed the phone. 'We haven't really … we never had a proper discussion about it.'

'You haven't talked about children?'

The incredulity in Heather's voice made her defensive. 'It wasn't … With the whole Pip thing, there just didn't … We never got around to it,' she finished, hearing how lame it sounded.

'You've got to talk to him, Emily.'

'I know.'

'Soon. You've got to do it soon.'

'I *know*.' Suddenly she'd had enough of the conversation. 'It's late,' she said. 'I'm tired, and I'm still at the restaurant. I need to get home.'

'Sure. Catch you later' – and she was gone, leaving Emily feeling cross. She drove home, trying to shrug off the irritation, knowing Heather hadn't really caused it.

Since Pip's departure from the house she'd been prickly with Bill. She knew it wasn't fair. He'd done nothing wrong, and yet she felt resentful. She blamed him, even though he was blameless – and in true Bill style he remained patient with her, aware that she was hurting, and that he was a convenient punch-bag.

They needed to talk, but she needed more time. She needed not to be annoyed with him any more.

He was asleep when she got home, so she told him Daniel's news the following morning over breakfast.

'That's great,' he said. 'They must be thrilled.'

'They are.'

'Do your parents know?'

'They will by now. He was ringing them last night.'

Her parents had taken some convincing, when Emily had told them she was embarking on a relationship with a man just a few years younger than her father. It had become easier, a little easier, when they'd met him, but they were still not entirely happy, she knew that. They'd have preferred someone her own age for her. She'd accepted it and set it aside, knowing she'd made the right choice.

Her mother rang that afternoon. 'Isn't it marvellous news,

Emily? We can't believe it. I'm finally going to be a granny!' and
Emily said yes, it was really great, and no, she hadn't seen Nora
since Daniel had told her the news, but she'd call on her in the
next few days, and yes, she was looking forward to having a niece
or nephew, and no, Daniel hadn't said anything about godparents,
and yes, of course she'd be godmother if they asked her, and the
call seemed endless.

The days passed. She worked on a December menu for
the restaurant with Mike. She gave the shed in the restaurant
garden a fresh coat of preservative. She walked Sherlock more
than he needed. She dropped by Nora and Daniel's, bringing a
congratulations card and a chocolate cake and a jar of bath salts.
She planted dozens of tulips in Bill's garden, and changed the
curtains in the sitting room, and moved pictures from one wall
to another.

Heather didn't show up in the restaurant, or phone. Emily
wondered if she and Shane were still going through a rough patch,
and if her mother was still staying with them, but she didn't ring
to enquire, not wanting to risk Heather asking if she'd talked to
Bill yet. She decided that she and her friend were going through a
patch of their own, and it would sort itself out when both of them
were ready.

And one Sunday afternoon, as she was walking with
Sherlock, she saw a woman coming towards her. Reddish hair
emerging from a grey furry hat. Tanned face – just back from a
sun holiday? A soft plumpness in the cheeks. Hard to make out
her figure, with a dark blue poncho draped like a blanket over

her, but broad in the shoulders, and a suggestion of heaviness in her measured tread.

As they drew level the woman halted, a quizzical look on her face. 'Is it Emily? Emily who owns the restaurant?'

'It is.' She must have eaten there. 'I'm afraid I can't—'

'I'm Therese. Therese Ruane.'

Therese Ruane. The reason Emily's fiancé had fled on their wedding day. The ex who'd broken up with Ferg and emigrated to Canada a month before he'd met Emily. Therese Ruane, who'd taken him back when he'd followed her to Canada after the wedding that never was.

Sherlock sniffed at the poncho. Emily pulled him away. 'So how's Ferg?'

Therese grimaced. 'I wouldn't know,' she said. 'We're not together any more. He wasn't really the settling-down kind, was he?'

That was a surprise. Emily had assumed they'd been destined for one another. Therese lifted a hand then and brought it to rest on her abdomen – and seeing the familiar gesture, Emily understood what bulk lay beneath the poncho.

'You're pregnant.'

She smiled. 'I am, due in January. I got married over the summer.'

'Congratulations.'

'Thank you.' Therese paused. 'I know Ferg messed you up – he messed up both of us. I hope you're happy now.'

Emily thought of Pip being taken from her, and the

conversation with Bill she kept putting off, and her younger brother who was awaiting the birth of his child. 'Very happy,' she said, hoping she sounded as if she meant it.

Later, in the restaurant, as she prepared that evening's desserts, she kept seeing Therese Ruane's hand drifting unthinkingly to her abdomen, compelled by some basic instinct. Therese Ruane was pregnant, and Nora was pregnant, and so many more women were pregnant at this time – and Emily knew she couldn't put it off any longer.

There was nothing to worry about, she told herself. She and Bill were in sync about everything: this would be no different. The fact that he'd never mentioned children meant nothing at all. There was no reason to feel nervous.

'Could you handle the clean-up on your own this evening?' she asked Mike. 'Would you mind? There's something I need to do.'

'No problem.'

'Thanks.'

At opening time she patted her cheeks to put colour into them. She redid her lipstick and took off her apron, and prepared for three hours of smiling and talking and pretending she wasn't filled with ridiculous foreboding.

After the last dessert had been served, while a few people were still sitting at the table, she told them she had to go. 'The chef is still in the kitchen – just tap on the door if you need more of anything.' She took payment for their meals and left.

She drove home, her mind elsewhere. A cyclist appeared, crossing in front of her – she braked sharply and he glared at her, and she realised she'd been about to drive through a red light. Focus, she told herself, and she did, and got home in one piece.

'You're early.' Bill looked up in surprise from his newspaper. 'Everything OK?'

'I left Mike clearing up,' she said, dropping onto the couch. 'Bill, there's something we need to talk about.'

He folded the paper and set it on the coffee table. 'What is it, love?'

She took a deep breath. 'We need to talk about children. Our children. We should have done it before this, but Pip came along – and now that he's gone, it's time we made our own plans.'

He laced his fingers together on his knees. She loved his hands, so capable, so gentle. She clipped his nails every month, filed away the sharp edges.

'I know I've been impossible since Pip left the house, and I'm sorry about that. I was feeling so empty, and so – well, let down.'

'By me?'

'Yes. I felt you should have put up more of a protest.'

'Emily,' he said gently, 'how could I object to her wanting him back? I understand your worries, but we have to let go. We have to trust her.'

She shook her head. They were going off on a different track. This wasn't about Pip. 'I want children, Bill. I know it's late in the day to be saying it, but I'm saying it now.'

'Emily,' he replied quietly, 'I'm sorry, but it's not something I want.'

Everything in her plummeted. She actually felt a fall inside, like a lift breaking free of its moorings and plunging down and down. 'What do you mean? You think you're too old? You're not too old. Lots of men have children at your age.'

He shook his head. 'It's not my age. I don't—'

'Look how you managed with Pip. You were as good a father to him as any child could want. You were better than a lot of younger fathers.'

'It's not my age,' he repeated. 'I know I can raise a child, but—' Something, some pain, crossed his face. 'I can't, Emily. I can't risk it happening again. I'm too frightened.'

'Risk what happening again?'

'Christine.' Just that. Just that one word.

She stared at him. 'Bill, that's – that doesn't make sense. Just because—'

He bowed his head. 'I know. I know it doesn't make sense.'

'She's better now. She's looking after Pip, she's working. You can see it yourself, she's fine.'

'I *know* all that, but I – I just can't go through what I went through again. I can't take that chance. I can't, Emily.'

'So that's it? You're saying no to children, ever?'

'I am. I should have made it clear to you, but I hoped I'd never have to. I'm sorry, Emily. I'm so sorry.'

He fell silent. She looked at his hands, the defeated hunch of his shoulders, the slope of his back, and she saw her future, their future, crumbling away. She saw the landslide of it.

She'd known, hadn't she? She'd known all along, right from when he'd told her about his daughter's descent into addiction and his frantic efforts to halt it, and his failure to stop it taking Christine away from him. She'd known, even as she'd been falling in love with him, that he might never have the courage to go down that path again. She'd known, when she'd seen what Christine's departure after Pip had done to him, how desperately he'd missed her, how stubbornly he'd clung to the belief that she'd come back. She'd known all that, and it had stopped her talking about children with him. It had made her push away her own yearnings for fear that he might not share them, until they became too strong to push away.

She'd known, and still she'd chosen to make a life with him.

She'd made the wrong choice.

She got to her feet. 'I can't,' she said, hearing the tremble in her voice. 'I can't stay with you, Bill – not if you deny me this. I'll leave in the morning. I'll sleep in the spare room tonight.'

He raised his head, 'Emily—' but she couldn't bear the anguish she heard in his voice, the pain that mirrored her own, so she walked out and climbed the stairs. She took her pyjamas from their bedroom and crossed the landing to the room that had always been Christine's.

She listened to him come up, twenty minutes after her. She heard the slow plod of his step on the stairs. When he emerged from the bathroom she heard him pause on the landing. She tensed, picturing him standing there, willing him not to come in – and when he didn't, she was devastated.

He was her soul-mate, her other half. Every line in every corny love song could have been written for them, and she was giving him up, she was choosing to live without him – and in leaving Bill, she was also leaving the only contact she had with Pip. She was losing two precious people, not one. She buried her face in the pillow and cried out her heartbreak, and fell asleep eventually, exhausted from sorrow.

She woke before the night had fully faded. She dressed silently in the clothes she'd taken off, her eyes sore with tiredness. She rolled her pyjamas into a ball: the rest would have to wait. She'd come back this afternoon, when Bill was at work. In the bathroom she put toothbrush and cleanser and makeup into a toilet bag. She tiptoed downstairs and slipped on her padded jacket.

It struck her, as she opened the front door as quietly as she could, that this was how Christine had left, on two occasions – and weren't their reasons similar, when you thought about it? Both in search of something they didn't have, something they hungered for that wouldn't leave them alone.

She put her things in the car and returned to the house. In the utility room she took Barney's carrier from a shelf and went out to the garden and called softly until he came. He gave a protesting mew as she lifted him into it – he wasn't a fan of the carrier, which generally signalled a visit to the vet. She retrieved his things from the utility room – bucket of food, bowls – and brought everything to the car.

She drove through empty streets, the town not yet woken up. She pulled into the driveway of her childhood home and parked next to the Jaguar that Daniel and Nora shared. Not a lot of money between them – the car was second-hand, and very old – but from what she could see, there was a whole lot of love, and now a baby on the way too. Lucky, lucky Nora.

It was too early to ring the bell. She'd wait until curtains were pulled apart and lights went on. She'd tell them she needed a place to stay, just until she found somewhere else, and they'd know not to ask questions. She'd look for shared accommodation to tide her over until Tom and Lil's lease ran out in February. She'd tell them she was sorry not to be able to renew it.

She wished she could ring Heather. She needed to hear her friend's voice, whatever words might come out, but it was too early, and Heather had troubles of her own.

She wondered what would unfold for her. She pushed away the prospect of the long, lonely months and years that might lie ahead. She knew there was a chance she'd meet someone else, have another opportunity to start a family, but the thought of being with anyone other than Bill was not something she could think about now. She must live in the present. She must keep on keeping on.

In his carrier Barney mewed, and she shushed him. 'We have to wait,' she told him. 'We just have to wait a while.'

Lil

IT WAS UNEXPECTED. IT DROPPED INTO THE EMAIL address that Judy had created for her, which was accessible to anyone who looked up the library website.

> *Dear Ms Noonan,*
> *I'm Alice Murphy. I know you've recently moved to the town so I'm not sure if you've seen my page in the* Bulletin. *It's called Happy Talk, and it's dedicated to neighbourhood good news stories that don't make the regular headlines.*

The *Bulletin* was the local paper. Half a dozen copies were dropped into the library each Friday, and Lil would flick through one during her break. She'd noticed Happy Talk, and thought it a nice idea. 'Accounts of everyday joy', the line under the title read, and how could anyone not approve of celebrating the little occasions of happiness that weren't considered important enough for the main headlines?

I've been contacted by a woman called Heather Taylor, who brings her daughter to your Saturday storytimes. She says it's very popular, and she thinks it might lend itself nicely to being featured on the Happy Talk page. Would you agree to that?

Heather had said nothing to Lil about contacting someone from the paper. Maybe she'd wanted it to be a surprise.

If you're happy for me to include you, I could come to the next storytime with a photographer. We'd have to get the go-ahead from the parents to take snaps, but it would be great if we could include them. Anyway, give me a shout and let me know if you'd be up for it.

It was signed Alice, with a happy-face emoji next to the name. Lil wasn't sure how she felt about appearing in the local paper. She'd had enough attention from journalists after the accident to last a lifetime, enough requests from people who wanted to interview her and Gran, to pick through their sorrow and put it on public view, just to sell a few more papers.

She read the email to Tom that evening. 'Great publicity for the library,' he said. 'Your boss will be happy.'

She would – but still Lil was undecided. The only good thing about moving out of Fairweather had been that she'd put distance between her and what had happened. Nobody she'd met here had made reference to the accident – but if mention was made in the article of where Lil had come from, would people make the connection?

She must be that Noonan, they'd say. Such a terrible accident – remember that awful photo of the car in the paper? Parents and daughter, wasn't it, and another daughter left behind? People might come into the library just to see the person who'd suffered such a loss.

'People have short attention spans,' Tom said, when she admitted her reservations. 'I'm guessing most people living outside Fairweather wouldn't remember the accident. This article will introduce them to Lil Noonan who works in the library and tells stories. You'll be in the news for a positive reason, not like before. That would be good, wouldn't it?'

It would. She decided to go ahead.

Hi Alice,
That would be lovely, thank you. My next storytime is this
Saturday at half past eleven. Feel free to come along.
Lil

The response was swift.

Lil,

Thanks so much for agreeing. The photographer and I will see you on Saturday. Would you have time for a few quick questions, either before or after?

Alice

A few quick questions. She pushed down a qualm.

Yes, 11.15 will be fine. I'll be setting up in the children's section.

Lil

On Saturday morning she chose her clothes with care, and pushed her hair back with a red band, and spent a bit longer on her makeup. 'Wish me luck,' she said, and Tom told her she didn't need it, and arranged to meet her for lunch in town afterwards.

Alice Murphy was petite and thirtyish, with pale streaks running through her light brown hair, and glasses with green frames. She was also extremely pregnant, wearing a jersey top that left the world in no doubt. She turned up promptly at the arranged time, and Lil brought her into the little break room.

'Thanks again for doing this,' Alice said, taking her phone from her bag. 'I had a quick chat with Judy on the way in – she has lovely things to say about you and the storytimes. I'll catch a few of the parents afterwards for quotes too.'

She paused then. 'Lil, I looked you up,' she said. 'I always do a

Google search on my subjects, to see if there's anything I can use. I'm so sorry about what happened – and obviously I won't go into it. We'll just focus on the here and now, OK?'

'Thank you.' It was a relief. Alice set her phone to record, and they spoke of libraries and books and children – and when Lil's engagement ring caught Alice's attention, the talk turned to marriage. Alice's own wedding, it emerged, had taken place in Italy, in the vineyard owned by her Italian mother and Irish father, and the minutes passed so pleasantly that Lil almost missed her starting time.

'You'll be in next Friday's paper,' Alice told her, as they left the little room.

'Great. And can I ask when you're due?' It seemed rude not to mention such an obvious state of affairs.

'Three weeks, give or take. You're my last column till after the event.'

'Congratulations. Hope everything goes well. Your first?'

'My first. My husband has a teenage daughter – she's almost as excited as I am.'

The storytime audience had assembled. Lil spotted Heather and gave her a wave, and Heather responded with a cheery thumbs-up. Alice asked if anyone would object to a photo of the children for her Happy Talk column: nobody did, so the bearded photographer hovering at the rear of the group took a few snaps of Lil in action before departing.

At the end of the session, as Alice was moving among the parents, Heather caught Lil's eye and beckoned her over. Hey, hope you were OK that I put you up for Happy Talk,' she said, manoeuvring her baby's arm into a sleeve. 'Maybe I should have given you notice.'

'No, that was fine. It was nice of you.'

'Boy, is that lady pregnant or is she pregnant? I was afraid she might have it right here.' She gestured towards her companion. 'You know Christine?'

Short hair, pretty brown eyes. Slender, boyish figure. A little child in her arms. Not their first time here. 'Hi,' she said shyly. 'Sorry, I need to change Pip – I won't be long, Heather.'

Lil had noticed her last time. Present but not present, eyes fixed on something beyond Lil, mind clearly elsewhere. Not, Lil had thought, a likely friend for Heather. So detached. So quiet seeming.

'Bill's daughter,' Heather said, snapping buggy closures.

'Bill?'

'Emily's ex.'

'Oh … I didn't know they'd broken up.'

So that was the daughter who'd gone astray – and the little boy presumably was the child Emily and Bill had been raising. Their relationship was over, and the boy reunited with his mother by the look of things. Big changes for Emily.

Lil tried to recall when she'd last seen her landlady. A few days ago, Thursday maybe. They'd exchanged hellos, Lil going upstairs, Emily coming in from the garden with an armful of greenery. Not a long enough encounter for Lil to notice a change in her demeanour.

'I believe you and Tom will be joining us for dinner at the restaurant on Christmas Day,' Heather said.

'Oh – yes, we will.'

The invitation had come out of the blue, shortly after Gran's news of the Christmas cruise. Friends and family, Emily had said, and Lil had been touched to be included, even as she'd baulked a little at the notion of being surrounded by strangers, or near strangers, on Christmas Day. She was glad Heather was going too.

At lunchtime she walked to the café where she was to meet Tom, and found him already there.

'I have something to tell you,' he said, as soon as she'd sat down.

He looked ill at ease. Lil felt a clutch of fear. There had been no mention of Vivienne in the time since her separate encounters with them, but that wasn't to say he'd put the episode behind him, as he'd said he would – and Lil certainly hadn't. Something told her it was about to resurface. 'What is it?'

He slid the salt mill an inch to the right and back again. He planted his palms on the table, replaced them with his elbows. 'It's my father. I'm meeting him tomorrow.'

Meeting his father. Not what she'd expected to hear. Before either of them could speak again they were approached by a waitress, and Lil fumbled through her order.

'I rang him this morning,' Tom said when they were alone again. 'I've been thinking about what you said, what Vivienne told you.'

Her name, uttered so matter-of-factly. She'd haunted Lil since they'd met, the beautiful tragic face drifting in and out of her thoughts by day and hijacking her dreams at night. She'd donated the green scarf to a charity shop, wanting to be rid of it, and still the woman Tom had loved first refused to leave her alone.

You're not yourself, Gran had said, last time they'd talked on the phone. Gran never missed a trick. I'm fine, Lil had told her, just a bit low in energy, and Gran had suggested a tonic, and Lil had wished a tonic was all she needed.

'Say something,' Tom said, watching her.

'I don't know …' She couldn't collect her thoughts, so many jostling for her attention. 'What made you decide to meet him?'

He lifted his hands. 'It needs sorting,' he said. 'I need to sort it.'

She didn't know what he meant by that. 'You want to find out if it's true, what … she said.' She couldn't say the name aloud, not to him.

'Yes.'

'Does he know? Have you told him?'

'No.' He shrugged. 'I felt it should be done face to face.'

'OK.'

He was telling her nothing really. He was telling but not telling. She'd wanted them to meet, to put the past behind them, so why was she feeling so apprehensive now? She answered her own question: because Tom's only reason for meeting his father was to find out how he felt about Vivienne, to discover if there really was something between them. He wanted it so badly he was willing to meet the man he could barely talk to on the phone.

He was still invested. He hadn't let it go. Hadn't let her go.

'Lil, will you come with me? I want you to come.'

'Yes,' she said. She needed to be there, to hear what he had to say. She needed to put an end to this. 'Where are you meeting him?'

He mentioned a well-known hotel in the midlands. 'Two in the afternoon, leave here about half twelve.'

'OK.'

Their food arrived. Lil ate her chicken sandwich without tasting it. He asked about the storytelling, and if Lil had met the journalist, but it felt like an afterthought. When they'd finished eating he set his plate aside and gazed at her.

'I'm sorry,' he said.

'What for?'

'For not being uncomplicated. For having horrible baggage.'

She tried to smile. 'I'm not exactly uncomplicated myself.' But they both knew her baggage was different. Her baggage didn't threaten to destroy everything they had, everything she hoped for. Tom had come into her life when she'd thought she'd lost everything worth living for. He'd given her new hope, new courage to face the future – and increasingly she felt like it might all be snatched away again.

Back in the library she kept busy, filling shelves, filing returns, updating databases. Anything to make the time go faster, to keep her thoughts at bay until tomorrow, to push back the dark clouds that kept threatening to descend.

'Penny for them,' Karl said at one stage, and Lil thought he wouldn't thank her if she took his penny and told him all that was in her head.

At half past four she walked home. The rain that had been forecast started to fall on her arrival at the restaurant. As she climbed the stairs the kitchen door opened and Emily emerged, accompanied by the smell of frying chicken. 'Lil,' she said, 'could I have a quick word please?'

She looked miserable, her spark gone, her lightness missing. Her smile was a faint echo of what it had been. 'Of course.' Lil leant against the banister and waited.

'It's just that – well, I don't know if you've heard, but I've separated from my partner,' she said.

Lil, unable to pretend, nodded. 'Heather told me. I'm so sorry.'

'Thank you … The reason I'm mentioning it is that I've moved out of his house, and I'm currently living with my brother and his partner, but … well, I'm afraid I won't be able to renew your lease when it runs out in February.' She brushed something off the front of her apron. 'I'm really sorry, Lil. I'll need the apartment back for myself.'

'I understand,' Lil said, but it was a fresh blow. Just when they'd begun to make their lives together, their first home was being taken away. 'We'll find somewhere else,' she said, not at all sure that they would. She'd say nothing to Tom until tomorrow was over. One challenge at a time.

He was quiet all evening. They watched a film on TV – or rather, they sat in front of it. Lil's thoughts were far from the action on the screen, and she imagined Tom's were too. His father wouldn't be expecting her to turn up: she thought it might not be what he wanted. She tried to conjure up the face she'd seen in the photo Sarah had shown her, but all she could recall was dark eyes and hair.

The rain of the day before was still falling when they got up. It continued as they read the Sunday papers over scrambled eggs and coffee, but it stopped while they were getting into the old Jeep, and before they reached the end of the street a weak November sun had slid out from behind a cloud. An omen, Lil thought, as they left the town behind and headed for the motorway.

They didn't talk much. They turned on the radio, and turned it off again an hour later because the reception, never great in the Jeep, got worse the further they travelled.

When they stopped for petrol Tom went inside to pay, and came back with a scratchcard for Lil. She won five euro and thought, Another omen. She smiled across at Tom – 'A fiver,' she said – but he barely glanced at her, his mind clearly elsewhere.

Was she losing him? Was this how it would happen? They sat close together, but it felt like he was moving further from her with each mile they covered. She looked through the window and watched fields and trees fly by, and she wished herself back in Fairweather, making her way along the cliff path to the beach. She wished she'd never met him – but that thought was unbearable too.

They reached the hotel with a few minutes to spare. They parked around the back, where several other vehicles stood. 'He's not here,' Tom said, looking around. The first reference to his father today.

They entered the hotel through a rear door and took seats at a low table in the lobby, and when nobody appeared to take an order, Tom went off in search of coffee. It was quiet, just a couple of other tables occupied. Conversations were muted by thick carpeting. Logs burned in a large fireplace.

Lil felt self-conscious, although nobody was looking in her direction. She drew her phone from her bag and set it on the table – and after a few seconds put it away again. As she was lowering the bag to the floor a man came through the revolving front door, and Lil knew him instantly.

A sprinkling of grey in the hair, plenty of dark left. Olive-green sports jacket, black jeans. Trim and tall, like Tom. Attractive, undeniably: more striking than either of his sons. An air of confidence in how he held himself. He was aware of his good looks.

A woman's man she'd thought, on first seeing him in Sarah's photo, and she thought it again now. The man Vivienne claimed to love – yes, they would make a handsome couple. She watched him casting about for the son he hadn't seen in over two years. What should she do?

She lifted a tentative hand in his direction. He caught the movement and glanced behind him before raising his eyebrows and gesturing towards his chest in a silent question. She gave a single quick nod and he advanced, while she prayed for Tom to return.

'Hi,' he said, a quizzical half-smile on his face. 'I'm not sure if you were summoning me.'

His voice was deeper than Tom's. She could imagine him

reassuring his patients with it. 'I'm Lil,' she told him, rising, 'Tom's fiancée,' realising as she said it the significance that phrase must hold for him. 'I think you're his father.'

If he was surprised to see her, he hid it. He regarded her calmly, unhurriedly, making her feel assessed. Was he comparing her to Vivienne, wondering how Tom could possibly have chosen her?

'Lil,' he said finally, extending his hand. His grip was warm and strong. 'George McLysaght, happy to make your acquaintance. I didn't think our paths were going to cross today.'

Perfectly composed. She thought of Tom's edginess as they'd travelled here, and her own misgivings and apprehension. She saw no sign of such anxiety in his father, no evidence of this man being in any way ill at ease. Maybe he was practised at hiding his feelings. Maybe his job had taught him that. Nobody wanted a cardiologist who showed any sign of uncertainty or foreboding.

'Tom asked me to come,' she said.

'Well, I'm glad he did.'

He smelt good. His teeth were even. His hair was longer on top and swept to one side, and held there, she thought, with wax or gel. He wore a gold ring on the little finger of his right hand. His nails were immaculate. He looked directly, unwaveringly, at her, and she was glad she'd worn the lilac wool dress Tom had taken her shopping for on her last birthday, not long after they'd got engaged.

'Tom is getting coffee,' she told him, resuming her seat. Would he get two or three? 'He won't be long.'

'Right.'

He took a seat across the low table from her, the one Tom had occupied a minute or so before, and crossed his legs. 'You probably know the story,' he said. 'Tom would have told you, yes?' Not smiling now. His voice low, but the words clear.

She nodded, hoping he wouldn't go into it, not wanting to have that kind of conversation with him directly after meeting him.

'You must think—' He broke off, gaze shifting to look beyond her, and she knew Tom had reappeared. She didn't turn.

His father got to his feet again. 'Tom,' he said, in a different voice, not offering a hand, and Tom must have nodded his reply, because Lil heard nothing. Face to face after two years, give or take.

A cup was placed before her. Tom took the seat next to her, across from his father. Two cups, not three. 'You've met Lil,' he said.

'I have indeed,' his father agreed, resuming his seat, his gaze flicking towards her for an instant before returning to Tom.

'If you want coffee you have to get it from the bar.'

'I'm fine.'

Not looking quite so relaxed now, Lil thought. No crossing of the legs this time, forearms resting on his thighs, a small inclination of his upper body towards them. No, towards Tom. She felt as if she'd been dismissed.

'It's good to see you, son,' his father said. 'You're looking well.'

Tom tapped the table once with his fingertips. Come to order, the gesture said. Cut out the small talk. 'We had a visit from Vivienne,' he said.

Jumping right in. Lil lifted her cup and sipped, compelled to do something. Now she would hear. Now she would learn. She held on to the cup, head slightly bent, watching them covertly.

Tom's father sat back, laced his fingers together. Impossible to tell if the news surprised him. Face like stone now, giving no sign that the mention of her name affected him. 'Did you,' he said. Not a question.

'We did.'

His father slid an index finger along the bridge of his nose, pushing up invisible glasses. Maybe he wore them normally, Lil thought. Maybe the gesture was instinctive. 'And what has this got to do with me?' he enquired mildly.

Tom touched his cup but didn't lift it. 'You don't know? You have no idea?'

'I have no idea.' Calmly. Impassively. If he was lying, he was good.

'Have you met her since that night?' Tom asked. He rapped it out sharply. Lil found herself holding her breath.

'I have not.' Same even, measured tone. 'This is beginning,' he said, 'to feel like an interrogation.' His tone remained mild. He even gave a slight smile that went nowhere near his eyes.

Silence followed. Tom lifted his cup and drank. He lowered it and sat back and folded his arms. 'She was seen,' he said, deliberately and clearly, 'coming out of your house in September.'

His father did something with his mouth then, a quick twist. 'Tom,' he said, a softer note entering his voice, 'I don't see what—'

'Did she come to see you?'

A long, slow sigh. 'She did come to see me, yes. Uninvited.' A hand lifted to flick away the information. Not important, the hand said.

'So you lied.' Tom sounded almost thoughtful. His gaze remained steadily on his father. Lil set her cup back on its saucer, feeling distinctly uncomfortable. Wishing again for the safety of Fairweather.

His father gave a kind of shrug to his head then, a flash of something – anger or impatience, she thought – passing across his face. 'Look,' he began, and stopped. His gaze flicked up to Lil, causing her to look away quickly. 'You want your fiancée to stay for this?'

Your fiancée. Lil felt invisible, irrelevant.

'She's staying,' Tom said, not looking at her. Part of her wanted to get up and walk away from this awful scene and leave the two of them at it. The other part knew she had to stay.

'Go on,' Tom said, his voice harsh and flinty.

'I hadn't seen her since that night.' His father made another rapid little grimace. Ill at ease now for sure. Rattled now. 'No contact after that.'

'So she turned up at your house out of the blue, nearly two years later.'

'She did.'

'What did she want?'

His father sighed. 'Tom, what's the point of digging all this up? Why don't you just—?'

'What did she want?'

His father slid his palms slowly up and down the black jeans. 'If you must know,' he said, 'she wanted me to … she wanted to enter into a relationship with me.'

'And what did you tell her?'

'I told her no. I told her what had happened was wrong, and it should never have taken place. I said it was a moment of insanity, and I would regret it for the rest of my days.' He spoke rapidly. He rattled it out.

It sounded to Lil as if the subject was distasteful to him. She thought back to what Vivienne had told her of their conversation in Dublin. *I told him I still loved him, and he told me he felt the same.* Two different accounts. One of them had to be lying – but which one?

'*She* told Lil,' Tom said, 'that you want to be together. She told her that you're refusing to be with her only because it would hurt me. She wanted Lil to talk to me, to persuade me to give you my blessing. She had to go through Lil, because I sent her away when she called to our apartment. She went to Lil's workplace.'

His voice was calm and measured, his confidence seeming to increase as his father's discomfiture became more evident. 'She told Lil that she loved you, that you loved each other.'

His father listened, eyes narrowed, forehead creasing in a frown. 'She said that?' Turning to Lil. 'She told you that?'

'Yes.'

His eyes, she thought. They were Tom's eyes, but without Tom's warmth. It occurred to her that maybe what she'd taken earlier for composure was actually lack of feeling. Even with the son he professed to love, the son he hadn't seen in so long, there was little evidence of affection, let alone love. She guessed he had no trouble attracting women – wealthy man-about-town, good-looking, intelligent, eligible widower – but she wondered if there was any depth to him, any sincerity beneath the charm.

She didn't like him. That might change if she got to know him better but right now, it was the truth of it.

He leant towards Tom again. 'Tom, listen to me,' he said, more urgently. 'You must listen, and you must believe. The woman means nothing to me. She means less than nothing. I have no idea why she would seek you out and say what she said, why she would imply that I have any feelings for her. I left her in no doubt that I never wanted to see her again. She couldn't possibly have misunderstood me. You must believe me, Tom.'

Tom shook his head. 'I don't know what to believe. Why would she lie about it? What would she have to gain?'

His father gave a shrug, a small careless lift of one shoulder. 'Only she can tell you that. I repeat that it's not true. I have no feelings for her. I never had.'

Tom said nothing to that. They sat without speaking, the three of them, as a woman at a nearby table laughed loudly and said at the end of the laugh, 'Not this again!' and a pair of children dashed into the lobby ahead of a couple who called them back.

Finally Tom spoke, regarding his father steadily. 'You took her because you could,' he said tightly. 'You took the person I loved, the person who meant everything to me, even though she meant nothing to you. I'll never understand how you could have done that to me.'

His father shook his head. 'Tom,' he said, 'it was a mistake, a stupid mistake, but it's in the past now. Don't let her come between us again. Don't let that happen.'

A beat passed. 'But she *is* between us,' Tom said slowly. 'She never left. I'm not sure she ever will.'

She never left. Lil heard, and mourned. They were over, she and Tom. It was finished, whatever they'd had – and however his father felt about Vivienne didn't matter in the least.

'You said you forgave me,' his father said.

'I did,' Tom replied, getting to his feet. 'I did forgive you, because I couldn't move on without doing that, but we can never go back. I see that now. We can never be the same, you and me. I'd rather you didn't phone me again.'

'Tom—'

But he had turned to Lil. 'Coming?'

She lifted her bag and glanced at his father, prepared to nod a goodbye, but he was focused on Tom. 'Please don't leave like this,' he said, but Tom took Lil's hand and walked off.

They got silently into the Jeep. As Tom reversed and drove out, Lil spotted a Dublin-registered black BMW, and thought it was probably the kind of car George McLysaght would drive.

They made their way back towards the motorway, Tom looking straight ahead. Lil tilted her face towards the sky, too disheartened to talk. The rain had stayed away, but overhead there were banks of grey that looked dense and impenetrable.

She was glad to see it: the way she was feeling, a blue sky would have been cruel.

So what would happen now? Would she stay on alone in the apartment? Would Tom move back with Joel and Sarah until he found another place to live? Would he look for Vivienne, try to rekindle what they'd had?

She thought of the wedding that would have to be cancelled, the ring she would slip off and return to him. The pity she would see in Gran's face next time they met.

'He was my hero.'

It was said half to himself as they took the slip road for the motorway. Lil closed her eyes. What did it matter now? What did any of it matter?

'From the start, I thought he was perfect. The eight-year gap between Joel and me was a lot when I was small, but Dad … I wanted to be just like him. He loved going out and about, he and Mum both. Their photos were always in the paper, at some event or other – and after she died I thought he'd stop, or cut back a bit, but he didn't. Within a few weeks of her funeral he was going out as much as he always had. I was in college, and still living at home. It threw me, seeing him with other women so soon after … It was the first time I was conscious of something about him making me uncomfortable. But then I told myself to grow up. He was a free agent and he wasn't doing anything wrong.'

She listened because it was impossible not to. She kept her eyes closed, felt the movement of the Jeep as he changed lanes, speeded up, slowed down. Heard the whoosh of other cars as they passed.

'When I got involved with Vivienne, I was delighted they got on so well.' A sound that wasn't a laugh, more a puff of incredulity. 'And I'm not sure, but I think *him* doing what they did was almost worse than her doing it. It was like … the person I'd looked up to, the man I had *worshipped* pretty much all my life had tried to find the way he could hurt me the most.'

She wanted him to stop talking about Vivienne. She wanted him to stop.

'And sitting there today, listening to him talking about how little she meant to him, pretty much *admitting* that he'd done what he'd done just because he could, that he'd almost destroyed my life for no good reason …' Another puff, and then he fell silent.

After a minute or so Lil opened her eyes. The car ahead of them was a blue Ford, Galway registration, one year old. A black dog in the back looked glumly out at her.

'Lil?'

She turned.

'You OK?'

She shook her head, not trusting herself to speak. She looked through the windscreen again. The Galway car had moved into the fast lane; she watched it overtake a bus and disappear.

'Lil, what is it? What's wrong? Look at me.' She couldn't look at him. She turned her head away, biting her lip to refuse the tears that burnt behind her eyes.

'Lil, please talk to me. Tell me what's wrong.'

At that she swung back, fury bubbling up, nothing to lose now. 'What's *wrong*? Are you seriously asking me that?'

'What?' He looked genuinely bewildered. 'Is it something I said?'

'Something you *said*?' Why was he tormenting her like this? 'You still love her – don't try to deny it!'

There – it was out, it was said, but the words, bottled up for so long, brought no relief. Still she churned inside, still she felt like bursting into tears, or throwing up, or both.

Tom was shooting incredulous glances at her. 'What? *Jesus*, Lil – is that what you think?'

'It's true – I know it's true! I heard what you said in there!' Rage seared through her, pushing her on. 'You arranged to meet him because of her – *she* was the reason we came here today!' And when he didn't answer, she persisted: 'Wasn't she? You'd never have met him otherwise – you could barely talk to him anytime he rang!'

He flicked down the indicator, and she saw an exit approaching. 'We need to stop,' he said. 'We need to talk.'

She clamped her mouth shut, blood racing inside her. He took the exit ramp and turned left at the roundabout and pulled into the forecourt of a service station. He bypassed the pumps and parked by a wall. He switched off the engine and turned to face her.

'Lil,' he said gently, 'you've got it all wrong.'

She stared at him mutinously. She would not cry. He would

not be the cause of tears – not until she was alone. 'You're still in love with her,' she insisted. 'You *said* it yourself – you said she's still between you and your father. You said it, I heard you!'

'You've got it wrong, Lil,' he repeated. 'I—'

'You said she never left, and you're not sure she ever will.'

'God,' he breathed. 'I'm so sorry if you took that to mean … Lil, listen to me. Please, just listen to me. Will you? Will you let me explain?'

She remained mute, not wanting to hear him try to weasel out of it, but too spent from her anger to protest.

'Lil,' he began, looking steadily at her, 'I *was* in love with Vivienne, I can't deny that. She blew me away when we met – I thought I'd hit the jackpot with her.'

She didn't want to hear, but she couldn't walk away from him in the middle of nowhere. He didn't attempt to take her hand – on the contrary, he was as far as he could get from her, leaning against the driver's door, folding his arms, like he'd folded them in the hotel. Keeping her at bay, it felt like.

'Our relationship wasn't perfect. We had rows just like everyone else. There were things I would have changed about her – she was careless with money, and very messy, and high maintenance – and I'm sure there was plenty she'd have changed about me, but on the whole we were very happy. I can't deny that, Lil.'

He stopped again. He looked beyond her. 'That night,' he said, his voice faltering now, 'what I saw that night – I felt like my life was ending, and in a way it did end, *that* life did. Things were never the same after. My job went, our flat went – London was over for me. All the people I'd known there, colleagues, friends, neighbours, everything was gone. I never went back.'

She knew all this, but she remained silent. Get to the point, she demanded silently – and as if he had heard, he did.

'Lil, I don't love her any more, I swear it. I haven't loved her for a long time. It didn't just switch off that night, although it should have. It took a while for those feelings to die, but they did die, completely. I'm not sure when exactly I got to that point, but I remember Joel telling me she was engaged again, I think it was about eight months after … we broke up, and when he told me, I felt nothing. Well, maybe a bit offended that she'd done it so quickly –' here he broke off, a small bitter smile flashing briefly across his face '– but nothing else, and I knew then that she didn't mean anything to me any more. She'd lost the power to hurt me. That's the truth, Lil, I swear it. It was my *father* I couldn't accept losing. Even though I told myself I hated him, I didn't really. It wasn't possible for me to hate him. It still isn't. I don't.'

He looked intently at Lil then. 'It was all about him, Lil. Today was all about him, never about her. After you told me what she'd said about him, about them wanting to be together, I couldn't get it out of my head. I thought if it was true, if they had real feelings for one another, it might excuse what they'd done – what *he'd* done. Well, not excuse it, but at least – I don't know, give it some context, or something. Make it … less cruel.'

Another bitter, faraway smile. 'I was hoping to let him off the hook a bit, I suppose. He was still my dad, my one-time hero. That was why I decided to meet him. I had to *know* – I had to sort it out in my head. I needed him to look me in the eye and tell me he loved her – but he didn't do that.'

He drew in a breath, looking unutterably sad. 'How did he put it? A moment of insanity – that was all it was for him. When I heard him saying that, I knew what little regard he had for me. He slept with my fiancée just because he could.' He shook his head slowly. 'So when I said she was still between us, I meant that he had done nothing today to change my attitude. That night was still what had broken us, him and me, and it always will be. He's lost to me now, like her.'

He paused, his eyes on her face. 'Lil, I'm sorry you thought I still had feelings for her. I mustn't have been attentive enough to you. I mustn't have shown you properly how I feel about you. How much you mean to me. How much I love you deeply. Truly I do, Lil.'

She found her voice then. 'You did,' she said. 'You did show me, you did tell me, and still I was afraid. After my family died, I felt … abandoned, and when you came along, and when I realised how much you'd come to mean to me, I was so afraid you'd leave me too. I couldn't let myself believe that you'd stay. And then, when I met Vivienne, when I saw how beautiful she was, I felt even more afraid.'

'Oh, Lil,' he said softly, 'you're far more beautiful to me. I will never, ever leave you – even if you get so sick of me you beg me to go. I'm going nowhere, Lil. You're stuck with me till we're old and grey, like it or not.'

He reached for her hands, and she gave them to him, half laughing, half crying, and slid over so she could nestle into him. 'You saved me,' he whispered, kissing the top of her head, arms wrapped around her, making her feel so protected, so loved. 'My beautiful, kind, generous Lil. I'll never know what I did to deserve you.'

More words were murmured, more promises given, tears shed on both sides for what they'd lost, and what they'd found. Eventually they resumed the journey, silent for the most part, each content to be quiet, now all that needed to be said had been said. The rain came, and she didn't care. Let it rain all it wanted. Let it rain from now to eternity.

And out of the peaceful silence, out of the blue, a thought came to Lil. It arrived fully formed, and she looked at it from every angle, and tweaked it a little as they covered miles of motorway, and the more she considered it the more sense it made, and the more it seemed to her exactly what they needed, both of them.

She waited until they were half an hour from home. 'Tom,' she said.

He shot her a glance.

'I've had an idea.'

It might take a bit of persuading. He might think it too impulsive – it *was* impulsive – but he was a captive audience for the next thirty miles or so. She had time.

She began to speak.

Heather

'ALL DONE,' SHE SAID, RUBBING HER HANDS together as she entered the kitchen. 'Chilly out there today.' She looked down at Jo, bashing two wooden spoons off the floor. 'Hope you've behaved yourself for Auntie Madge.'

'That little lady couldn't misbehave if she tried.' Madge was taking mugs from a press. 'Sit down, the Bovril will heat you up – and I made a tea brack.'

'Wonderful.'

Heather had been unsure about Bovril at the start. A bit heady, a bit too enthusiastically meaty – but now she loved it, especially on a day like this, when a wind from somewhere very cold had whistled around her as she'd cleaned the outside of Madge's windows.

'So how's everything?' Madge asked, when they were settled

with steaming mugs and buttered tea brack, with a slice cut up for Jo.

'Everything's fine. Jack turns eleven tomorrow – his party's on Saturday. Shane's taking them bowling, because the house just wouldn't fit any more people right now.'

'How's Shane? Any news?'

'No news, all well with him. Working hard, on nights a lot of the time.'

'Ah, the poor thing. Tell him I said hello.'

'I will.'

Madge had known him right through his childhood and adolescence, and had been the most thrilled of all the neighbours when word had got around that he and Heather were an item. Even if Heather wanted to share her current ambivalent feelings about him – she didn't – Madge was not the person to confide in. Madge, like Heather's mother, was a paid up member of the Shane fan club.

'And how's my Lottie?'

'Lottie's great. Getting a bit cheeky.'

'Oh, it's all ahead of you.'

Madge, whose own four children were long grown up and gone, whose husband had left her while they were all still in primary school, had been Lottie's babysitter when Heather and Lottie had lived up the street. Now Madge took Jo anytime she was called on, and flatly refused payment, so Heather showed up with her bucket every two weeks, whether the windows needed a wash or not.

'How's your cleaner working out? What did you say her name was?'

'Christine. She's a marvel. She's transformed the place. She doesn't just scrub and polish – she's totally reorganised the kitchen cabinets, and she washes clothes and irons them, and she asked me to get storage boxes, and half our clutter's in the attic now. I never thought I'd say this, but I can kinda see why Mom always had a housekeeper.'

'And how are things with your mother? Is it getting any easier?'

Heather made a face. 'Mom is Mom – there is no easier. I tune her out when I can.'

'She's been with you a long while now.'

'Nearly seven weeks, feels like a lifetime. I literally can't remember the house without her in it. She's like another kid – doesn't lift a finger to help, expects to be waited on hand and foot. But Shane gets on well with her, and she thinks he's just wonderful—'

'He *is* wonderful.'

Oops. 'Yes, so he's cool with her staying, which is just as well, because there's no sign of her going home, not a word – and obviously I can't ask.'

'How's the divorce coming on?'

'Nothing sorted yet, which doesn't surprise me. Attorneys making big bucks by the hour, probably. At this stage, I'd be surprised if it's sorted before the end of the year.'

'And is your father still talking about coming over for Christmas?'

'He's not just talking – he's bought his air ticket. He's arriving a few days before Christmas.'

'Christmas Day is six weeks today.'

'I know. Comes around faster every year.'

'Where will he stay? Fleming's, I suppose.'

'Not much choice. I booked him a room.'

'And what about Christmas Day? Didn't you say you were going to your friend's restaurant for dinner – what's her name?'

'Emily. Both my folks are invited too, so that should be fun.'

She felt guilty about Emily. These days they hardly spoke, and Heather knew it was every bit as much her fault as Emily's. They both had stuff going on, but they should still make time for each other, especially now.

The break-up with Bill, coming so hot on the heels of Pip going back to Christine, had hit Emily hard. She'd phoned Heather the day after it had happened, sounding so defeated. Heather had been surprised when she'd heard that Bill wasn't keen on fathering another child. Sure, he'd gone through hell with Christine, but to rule out any more kids on the grounds that they might become addicts too was a little extreme.

Still, if that was how he felt, that was how he felt. Very tough on Emily though – anyone could see she was made to be a mom. Pip had been a lucky little boy to have her waiting in the wings when Christine had run out on him.

Come out for a walk, Heather had suggested. Come this afternoon, just for half an hour – but Emily had said no, she wanted to lie down, she hadn't slept well. And no, the next day wouldn't suit either, she had to go to the cash and carry, so Heather had said call me when you have time, and the call hadn't come, and the walk had never happened.

And in the ten days or so since then, Heather had texted – brief *how-are-you* and *thinking-of-you* texts, and Emily's responses had been equally brief – *I'm coping* and *Busy today* – but they hadn't spoken again, or met up. Emily would be missing Bill and Pip so much: Heather really must make time for her.

She thought it was a good thing Christmas dinner in the restaurant was going ahead. Emily would need to be surrounded by people on that day, even if two of her guests would probably be spending their time willing the other to choke on a turkey bone.

And Bill's heart was broken too. Heather had bumped into him at Christine's house the other day, when she'd brought Jo around for a play date, and his loneliness was palpable. Shame, such a crying shame that a couple who fitted together so well, far better than Heather's parents ever had, couldn't find a way around this.

'I'm thinking,' Madge said then, 'about your house.'

'I know what you're going to say. I must get another tenant.'

'Well, not exactly – but you should have someone in it, so I'm wondering if it would suit your mother while she's here.'

Heather's mouth dropped open – and then she laughed. 'That's a joke, right?' Her parents had visited her house. They'd come to dinner there two Christmases ago, their first and only time in Ireland until now – and even though they'd said nothing, Heather was pretty sure they'd pitied her for living in what they probably regarded as the equivalent of servants' quarters. The idea of installing her mother there and leaving her to fend for herself was completely absurd. 'Totally out of the question. A non-starter, Madge.'

'Hang on – let's think about this. She'd have her own place, and you'd have her out of your hair.'

'Madge, she'd never cope on her own. She'd need a maid, or a cook, or both. And my house—' She broke off, realising that any criticism she levelled at her little terraced house would also apply to Madge's identical one. 'She's used to more luxury,' she said. 'More space. My house is fine for normal folk, Lottie and I loved it when we lived there, but we're not talking normal with Mom.'

'Well, I hope you won't mind me saying this, but she doesn't have a lot of luxury or space where she is now, does she?'

'Good point, but she'd still need someone to look after her. She can hardly open a tin, let alone operate a washing machine.'

'Well, what about your cleaner? If there was someone coming in every day, even for an hour or two, it might give her the feeling that someone was looking after her. And I could mind the cleaner's little lad, like you do when she goes to you. She could drop him in to me on the way. And yes, the house is small, but she'd be there on her own, so I bet it would feel bigger than where she is now.'

She made it sound like it was perfectly feasible, but Madge hadn't met Mom. Even with Christine doing a daily visit, Heather still couldn't see it.

Then again, she couldn't say for sure, could she, until she looked at it from all angles?

One of the few things Mom could do was make coffee, so

breakfast was sorted with a box of muesli. Christine could arrive after that, do a couple of hours' cleaning and prepare a simple lunch – soup or salad was all Heather offered – before she left. And Mom could order in dinner, or come to Heather and Shane to eat. And she'd still have her salons and shops on the doorstep, and taxis to ferry her wherever she wanted to go.

And it would mean more money for Christine. Mom was impressed with her, said she beat her own housekeeper Gloria on the cleaning front. A break for Heather, which would be much appreciated, and a bathroom of her own for Mom, which might well seal the deal.

Would it work?

It just might.

'Leave it with me,' she said. 'Mom will probably say no right away.'

'You won't know till you ask her.'

'True.'

Heather could give the house a fresh coat of paint and a good scrub. Christine could help with the preparations: another bit of cash for her. They could have it ready in a few days.

The more she thought about it, the more possible it became.

She left Madge's and wheeled the buggy down the street, and fished her old house key from her bag. She was due a visit, over two weeks since she'd looked in, and now she wanted to visualise Mom in there, to see if it could possibly happen.

She pushed the buggy ahead of her into the tiny hall. After having been vacant for the best part of five months, the place smelt musty, neglected. It was time to set the heating to come on at night, and crack open the upstairs windows to get some air in.

She closed the front door and bent to pick up the small bundle of stuff that had been posted through the letterbox. Junk mail or utility bills: that was all that came here these days. She flicked through the leaflets – a candidate in the local election, someone looking to clean her gutters, someone else offering to check her hearing – and came to a white envelope that wasn't the right shape for a bill.

She turned it over and read her name and address in unfamiliar handwriting, and saw a foreign stamp. The house number was missing from the address, but that hadn't been a problem for Conor, who'd been delivering mail on this street as long as Heather had lived in the house.

And in the top left corner, in smaller script, she read *M. Töller*, and an address in Munich, Germany.

M. Töller.

Manfred Töller.

Lottie's father.

She stood unmoving in the little hall, her gaze fixed on the envelope. Manfred, getting in touch after more than ten years. Remembering the street name after all that time. What the hell?

She'd met him within weeks of her arrival in Ireland, shortly after she'd landed the job of live-in carer for Shane's father in this very house. She remembered sneaking out to meet Manfred after she'd put her charge to bed, praying that his son or daughter-in-law wouldn't drop by unexpectedly and find that she'd absconded.

She recalled being walked home at the end of every date, she and Manfred wrapped around each other, dawdling past Madge's house and the others, not wanting the night to end.

She'd never brought him past the front door. They'd kissed goodnight there, whispering the nonsense all lovers whisper before she'd gone inside, still spinning from the wonder of him. Floating up the stairs to dream about him in her single bed.

And then the discovery, only months after they'd met, that she was late. The worry, the nail-biting panic while she'd waited for blood that refused to flow. I'm pregnant, she'd finally said, watching his face, terrified he'd deny it was his and finish with her. She remembered the relief when he'd hugged her and told her he'd support her and their child. He'd marry her, he promised, as soon as they could arrange it – but he hadn't done any of that.

He doesn't work here any more, the manager of the pub had told her when she'd gone there three days later, after no further word from Manfred, after so many failed attempts to reach him on his phone. Where did he go? she'd asked, and he'd shrugged and said, No idea, he just left, and she'd heard a soft laugh, or thought she had, as she'd turned and rushed out, blinded by sudden tears of shock and fright.

And in all the years since then she'd heard nothing from him, not a word. Manfred, who had caused such a swoop in her belly every time she'd seen him, every time he'd said her name in his foreign accent, every time he'd touched her, whispered to her, promised her he'd be careful. She'd been so trusting, in love for the first time, letting him do everything he wanted, never questioning, never asking just how careful he was being.

Not yet eighteen when Lottie was born, Heather had been a single parent alone in a foreign country, terrified of this tiny creature who was totally dependent on her. Reading up on how to change a diaper, how to feed and bathe a baby, how to recognise signs of illness. How she got through those first years without losing her sanity remained a mystery, but she had. She'd managed without him.

She put the envelope into her bag, not sure whether to rip it up or send it back to Munich unopened. She put him from her mind and walked through the silent house, trying to see it with Mom's eyes. It was difficult to picture her living there – but like Madge said, she wouldn't know if Mom would go for it till she asked.

She'd do it today. She figured it was worth the risk of Mom being mortally offended at the suggestion. Come to think of it, Mom might get so offended that she'd high-tail it straight to Fleming's, or back to California.

She'd definitely put it out there.

She set the timer on the boiler and pulled the old sash windows down an inch in the upstairs rooms. Burglars didn't worry her, with nothing of real value here, sentimental or otherwise. She'd never been into things, just people.

She wheeled the buggy from the house and locked the door. She walked home with her sleeping daughter, her thoughts back in the past, all the memories she'd buried pushing up at her.

The sound of his chuckle, rich and deep, that had always put her in mind of Santa Claus, even though he'd only been a year older than her. The black leather coat he wore that he told her had belonged to his grandfather, who'd fought in the Second World War and survived it. The red socks he favoured. The pattern his boxer shorts waistband imprinted on his skin. The Bayern Munich scarf she would unwind from his neck and wrap around hers, just to inhale his smell as she walked.

The feel of his face in her hands, the thrill of the prickle of his stubble. The undulations of his ribcage, the curls of hair on his chest. The German words he would murmur when they got physical, knowing she loved to hear him speak in his native tongue.

He didn't know if Heather was alive or dead. He didn't know if he was father to a German-American child or not.

No. Lottie wasn't German-American, she was American-Irish. He had no claim on her, no right to call himself her father – but Heather was getting ahead of herself. He might not be writing to claim ownership of his child: he might have a whole other reason. Maybe he'd won the German lottery and wanted to say sorry, with a fat cheque, for running out on her.

She decided not to tear up his letter, or return it unopened. She'd open it tonight, after Shane had gone to work, when the kids were in bed and Mom was watching Netflix. She'd die of curiosity otherwise.

Should she say anything to Lottie? Definitely not at this stage, not until Heather learnt what he wanted, or didn't want. Lottie had asked about her father when she heard other girls talk about theirs, and realised that hers was missing. Heather had told her truthfully that she hadn't seen him in a long time and she didn't know where he was.

Why not? Lottie had wanted to know – six or seven years old – and Heather had thought fast. We had a fight, she'd said, and he went away because he was cross, and he didn't tell me where he was going.

What was the fight about?

Oh, something silly. I can't even remember now – and Lottie had been young enough not to ask more questions.

'I was going to call you,' her mother said, when they got home. 'You were gone so long.'

Heather counted to five as she eased Jo out of her purple cocoon. She'd been counting to five a lot over the last seven weeks. 'We dropped into my old house after I'd cleaned Madge's windows, to make sure everything was OK. I was pleased with how it's looking. You didn't need me for anything?'

'That's not the point, Heather. Never mind, you're here now.'

She's bored, Heather told herself. She's away from home and all her buddies are back in California. She deposited Jo in her high chair, then gave her a teething ring and a rice cake.

'You're feeding her? Aren't we having lunch soon?'

'She'll eat lunch. Nothing wrong with her appetite.' Good job she didn't know about the slice of tea brack at Madge's.

'Her appetite is what's concerning me, Heather. If you don't mind my saying, she could lose a few pounds.'

Heather laughed. 'Mom, she's a baby – they're supposed to be fat. She'll lose it all when she starts walking. I'm the one who could drop a few pounds.'

No response. A loaded silence, you could call it. One, two, three, four, five. 'We could go for a drive this afternoon, if you like, after I pick up the kids.'

'A drive? Where to?'

'Anywhere. Out into the countryside. We could have a walk and then find a bar, and you could have a martini.' Honestly, it was like humouring a child. She wondered if a country bar would appreciate an order for a dirty martini.

'I don't think so – it looks like it might rain again, so I should think a walk is out of the question. And you know I don't like to drink during the day.'

Heather knew nothing of the sort. What about the charity lunches with her friends, everyone as moneyed as herself, that went on all afternoon? You could bet they weren't sinking cups of tea for four hours. 'What about the cinema? We could check what's on.'

'Oh no – that cinema's a little grubby, don't you think? I wasn't at all comfortable when we went before.'

'You never said.'

'I don't like to complain.'

Another silent count to five. If prizes were given out for complaining, Mom would have a cabinet full of them. 'You might find something on Netflix then.'

Her mother sighed and patted her hair. Heather took a jug of chicken soup from the fridge and tipped it into a saucepan. Do it now. Go on.

'Mom.'

'Yes?'

'I've been thinking. I mean, it's so crowded here, I feel bad that you have to share the bathroom with all of us. And your room is so tiny.'

No response. No 'Thank you for taking me into your already crowded house.' She was waiting for the punchline. Heather lit the hotplate. 'And we don't know how long the divorce is going to take, so you could be here for quite some time.'

'What's your point, Heather? Have I outstayed my welcome?'

'Of course not – I'm just sorry you don't have someplace nicer to stay, with your own bathroom and all. So I had an idea.' She took an inner deep breath. 'I was wondering if you'd like to move into my house. My old house.'

'*Your* house? That tiny house?'

Little bubbles started to pop on the surface of the soup. Heather lowered the heat and turned around. 'It's been lying empty since my tenant passed, and I'd much rather someone was in it. It just occurred to me that it might suit you.'

'That tiny house,' her mother repeated, but she wasn't saying no. Her own bathroom was giving her something to think about. Heather moved on to her second trump card. 'And I had another idea. You think Christine does a good job here, right?'

'I do, but I fail to see—'

'I'm sure she'd love to clean for you too. If she popped in to you in the mornings she could do whatever needed doing, and maybe prepare lunch before she left – and you could come to us for dinner, or order in. You want bread with your soup?'

'No, thank you.' She rose and took a green bottle of water from the fridge. No tap water for her – she'd been scandalised when Heather had offered it. 'Your house is still in good condition?'

She was thinking about it. Heather fished for spoons in the cutlery drawer. 'It really is. There's no sign of damp or anything, and today I set the heating to come on every night. It's so easy to heat, with houses on either side. It's really cosy in the winter. And the neighbours are lovely.'

'You have Wi-Fi? And a television?'

Mom wasn't interested in the neighbours – but boy, would they be interested in her if she moved in. Heather could imagine the conversations over the back walls. Madge would be the one with the information, delighted to be doling it out.

'Yes to the TV. I cancelled the Wi-Fi when we moved out, but I can easily get it reconnected. I could also paint the rooms to freshen them up: that would take just a couple of days. And I'm sure Christine would help to give it a good clean before you arrived – if you did think of moving in.'

And unexpectedly, as she placed the bowls of soup on the table, Heather felt a pang of guilt. The woman was going through a divorce, even if it made total sense, and currently living in an overcrowded, noisy house that contained none of the luxuries she was accustomed to – and now Heather was trying to sell her the benefits of an even more basic place.

She might not have been the best mother, or even a fairly good one, but she was still Mom. That counted for something.

'You know you can stay here as long as you like, Mom. You *know* that, right? I might not always sound as if I'm happy to have you here, but I am. I'm just – busy with the kids and stuff. We're both happy that you're staying here, Shane and I – and Lottie really likes having you around. Please don't feel like you're being pushed out.'

Her mother picked up her spoon. 'Thank you, Heather. I do appreciate your hospitality – but you're right, it *is* a little cramped here, so I think on balance I might take up your offer of the house.'

'Really? Are you sure? You want to come see it?'

'No need, I remember it. If Christine's happy to come in and see to things, I think I should manage.'

'I'll talk to her this afternoon.'

All through lunch she had to tamp down a flick of excitement. Mom in her own place, Lottie back in her room. Order of a sort restored, and Christine twice a week keeping things in an orderly state. If she agreed to clean for Mom – and Heather was fairly sure she would – they'd have to juggle her hours here, which wouldn't be a problem.

It occurred to her, as she drove to Christine's later, that with Mom installed in her old house she would have nowhere to go with the girls if she decided that she and Shane had passed their best-before date. No matter: she could find a rental till Mom went home. There was always a way out, if you really wanted one.

'The house is a lot smaller than Shane's,' she told Christine, 'so you'd have no problem with the cleaning. Mom thinks you're wonderful, but she's not the easiest to work for. And I've sort of said you might do lunch, but that would be something simple, like soup or a salad. Shane could make a batch of soup, and all you'd have to do would be reheat it.'

'What about Pip? Would I be able to bring him?'

'Well, not to the house, but I was talking about it to one of my old neighbours, and she said she'd be happy to look after him. She's just four houses away, and she's like the best kind of gran. She looked after Lottie when she was a baby, and now she takes Jo any time I need her.'

'How much would she charge?'

'I wouldn't worry, it won't be much – and I'll make sure Mom pays you enough that you can afford it.'

'Wow.' Christine looked a little dazed. 'Honestly, this is huge, Heather. You're being such a help.'

'So you'll take it? Two hours every morning, even at weekends?'

'Of course I'll take it. Can I still clean yours?'

'You bet – I'm not about to give you up. You can switch to afternoons with me. And will you help me paint and clean the old house before Mom moves in? You'll be paid, of course' – and they came to an agreement before Heather left to collect Lottie and Jack from school.

The rest of the day flew by. Shane woke up and cooked a pasta dinner, and Lottie and Jack treated them to a performance of the song they were planning to sing at the school's Christmas concert in a few weeks.

The cat threw up in the laundry basket – better than on a pile of clean clothes, Heather figured – and after she'd sorted that out, and Jo was down for the night, and Shane was supervising Lottie and Jack's homework, Heather told her mother that Christine had agreed to work for her in the little house.

'The going rate for that kind of service here is twenty euro an hour. I've told her you'll pay her in cash once a week. I can get it out of the bank for you.'

Her mother nodded absently. Heather was sorry she hadn't said thirty an hour. 'You want to pick out paint colours? I'm free to make a start tomorrow.'

So they went online, and for an hour or so there was harmony as they considered and rejected paint shades, and her mother settled finally on a chalky cream throughout, not unlike what the walls already wore.

And finally, after Shane had dropped a goodbye kiss on her cheek and left the house for his night shift, and her mother was choosing which spy thriller to watch, and Eoin had come in from rugby training and was taking a shower, Heather went to her room and sat on the side of the bed with just the lamp on, so Jo wouldn't wake.

The stamped date on the envelope was too blurred to read. The letter could have been sitting on the hall floor for two weeks. She opened it and pulled out the folded pages.

Was she sure she wanted to do this?

No. Not sure. Not the smallest bit sure.

She unfolded the pages.

Dear Heather

I do not know if you will receive this letter. I do not know if you are still living in the same house. I remember you were a sort of nurse for an old man, so maybe he is dead and you are in another house, or maybe you are back in America, but I hope that this letter will locate you.

It will be a surprise to hear from me, after such a long time. You were very angry maybe when I left without telling you. It was a very bad thing I did, and I am very sorry. I was a young and stupid boy, and I was afraid. Believe me, I am very, very sorry. I did love you, but I was afraid.

I don't know if you had the baby, or if you had an abortion. I don't know if you are married now, but I think maybe. I know I have no right to ask for any information, but I would really like to know. I think about it a lot. I think about you a lot, my beautiful American girlfriend. I think about if you are happy. I hope so.

I am living in Munich, you can see from my address. I am a businessman, helping people to put money in different places. My dictionary tells me it is investment broker. I like the work, but I am alone. I am not married, and I have no girlfriend right now. I have girlfriends sometimes, but they don't remain for a long time. I think they are not so good as you!

My father died five years ago, aged fifty-eight. He was on a train and it crashed. Maybe you heard about it. Twenty-six people died, it was bad. My mother lives now with her sister in a town called Heidelberg. She went there after my father died. I see her every month when I visit her, or she comes to Munich. She is well.

Heather, I would really like if you want to talk to me. Maybe you can forgive me for the terrible thing I did. I am older now, and I think I am a better man. I hope! If you like to contact me, I will put my email address at the last of this letter, or you could write a letter to my address – I mean my address in Munich.

I hope you will contact me in some way. I remember the nice time we had in Ireland.

Yours truly,

Manfred

Please excuse my English, I don't have the chance for speaking it, so it's not very good.

And below, his email address.

Heather let out the breath she'd been holding. She went back to the beginning and read it again, and then she read it a third time.

I did love you, but I was afraid.

My beautiful American girlfriend.

I remember the nice time we had in Ireland.

She sat with the pages in her hand. She heard the bathroom door opening and Eoin crossing the landing to the room he shared with Jack. After a while she returned the letter to its envelope and slipped it back into her bag. What should she do? Ignore it? Rip it up and post the pieces back to him?

I was a young and stupid boy, and I was afraid.

I am very, very sorry.

She had no reason to disbelieve anything he'd written. He had nothing to gain by lying to her now.

I am older now, and I think I am a better man.

She resisted the idea of telling him about Lottie. Maybe technically he had a right to know, but hadn't he forfeited it by bolting? Tough call. She didn't want to be spiteful, however much he might deserve it.

And what about Lottie? She had a German grandmother and great-aunt – *My mother lives now with her sister in a town called Heidelberg* – and maybe there were more family members. Maybe cousins, uncles and aunts – who knew? And even though he hadn't mentioned children there was a chance, wasn't there, that Manfred had fathered others? Maybe Lottie had half-siblings.

She picked up her phone and opened her email app. She had to get his letter out again to find his address. On the point of typing it in, she stopped. What was she doing?

Nothing much. Nothing incriminating. She wouldn't tell him anything that could come back to haunt her. Jo whimpered in her sleep, and Heather said, 'Ssh.'

She and Shane hadn't had sex in a few months. She'd had no loving touches, no tenderness, pretty much no displays of affection from him. She knew it was her fault – she'd made it clear that she wasn't up for it – but all the same she missed being held, being kissed. She missed feeling the way Shane, and Manfred, used to make her feel.

She wasn't planning an affair. That wasn't who she was. She was just … having a look around. Seeing how the land lay.

She clicked 'compose' and put in his address. *Manfred*, she began – and then deleted it. Too friendly to use his name. Too personal. After more consideration, she tapped at the keys again.

I had the baby. That is all I want to say about that.

I'm sorry about your father.

Heather

There. Short and polite, nothing fancy. About to press *send*, she adjusted it.

I had the baby. That is all I want to say about that.

I'm sorry about your father.

Thank you for your apology. It was very difficult for me after you left, but I coped.

H

H was better than Heather. H sent its own message.

She sent it off, and immediately placed her phone face down on the dressing table, half appalled at what she'd done. Would he insist on his rights, whatever they were? Could he demand joint custody? She grabbed her phone again and tried to undo the sending but it was too late. Maybe it had already arrived in Germany; maybe it was landing in his inbox right now.

She should have slept on it. No, she should have torn up the letter the second she'd realised who the sender was. Damn, damn, damn.

He had the address of her old house – and now he knew she still had some connection with it. She pictured him turning up on the doorstep and being met by Mom. That might not be a bad turn of events: she could imagine the hauling out he'd get once he revealed his identity to Lottie's grandmother.

She got into pyjamas and visited the bathroom. She moisturised her washed face and climbed into bed with the letter, and read it through again. An investment broker was a surprise: he'd told her he wanted to own a bar some day, and he'd also wanted to write a book, a novel with a football team at its centre. Did he work in an office? Did he wear a suit? Was he a commuter, sitting silently among strangers on a train every morning and evening?

Did she care? Not really.

She didn't think so.

Investment broker was about as far from a paramedic as you could get. She tried to compare him and Shane, but her experiences of both men were too separated in time, and she'd been a different person in the Manfred days. Younger, more foolish, more gullible.

Freer. More willing to dare. More excited about the future.

She put the letter back into her bag and switched out the light and slept. Her night was full of muddled snatches of dreams, and murmured guttural words.

And over the days that followed, this happened:

Dear Heather

I am so happy to see your email and to hear that I am a father! I can't believe it. This makes me very happy – and also sad, because I was not there to see my child growing up. Can you please tell me if I have a son or a daughter?

Yours truly,

Manfred

Daughter. Her name is Charlotte, but everyone calls her Lottie.

H

Lottie – I like that. We also have this name Charlotte in Germany, and sometimes it is Lotte. Thank you for the informations, Heather. I am happy we are in communication again.

Yours truly,

Manfred

Christine

'JUST TO LET YOU KNOW,' HER DAD SAID, PIP ON HIS knee, 'Emily and I have separated.'

Separated. It came as a surprise. Christine had wondered why he'd stopped taking Pip back to his house to see Emily. She hadn't asked, any talk of his ex making her uncomfortable, but she'd thought it strange, with Emily so attached to Pip. A separation hadn't occurred to her – although now that she thought about it, he *had* seemed quieter.

'When?'

'A little while ago. Couple of weeks.'

'You never said.' And Heather, who must have known, hadn't said anything either. Maybe she'd thought it wasn't her place to tell Christine.

Dad jiggled a leg, making Pip bounce. 'Bit hard to talk about it,' he said, not looking at her, and she felt bad for him. She assumed Emily had been the one to put an end to things. Looking for someone younger – or maybe she'd already found him.

She hadn't exactly rejoiced when Dad had told her about Emily, shortly after she'd come out of her first rehab. The fact that Emily was just a few years older than Christine felt like he was being disrespectful to Mum, like he was insulting her memory.

But as the months had gone on and Emily had stayed around, they *had* seemed like a good fit, despite the age difference. Emily made Dad happy, anyone could see that – even Christine, who hadn't wanted to see it, so this news wasn't good.

He set Pip down then and went to look out the window. 'We just couldn't agree on things,' he said, his back to her, even though she hadn't asked. It was vague and told her nothing, but she didn't push it. Pip asked for a bun – he liked her buns – and she cut one up into little mouthfuls and put them on a plastic plate for him, and filled his beaker with milk.

Dad would be OK. Given the age difference, it was probably for the best. But he seemed so dejected, standing there hunched like an old man. It reminded her of how he'd looked anytime she'd turned up on his doorstep in search of a shower and a change of clothes, back when she was living on the streets. Back when she was breaking his heart, day after day.

To distract him, she told him about Heather's old house. 'You should see it. It's on Elm Street, behind the bus station. A little red-brick house, like the ones on *Coronation Street*.'

'I know it,' he said. 'I was there while Heather lived in it.'

'We painted it,' she told him. 'Me and Heather. And guess what – her mother's going to live there for the rest of the time she's in Ireland.'

'Michelle is moving into Heather's house?' He stared at her. 'Are you serious?'

Michelle seemed almost too normal a name for Heather's glamorous mother. 'Yes, I'm serious. It's too crowded at Heather and Shane's, and since the house is empty, it makes sense.'

'But how long more is she staying in Ireland?'

'No idea. I don't think Heather knows either.'

He shook his head. 'I just can't imagine her living there. I mean, the way Heather described it, her parents' home in America is very fancy.'

Yes, Christine had guessed there was money. The way Heather's mother dressed, and the perfume that smelt expensive. And Christine had overheard her on her phone at Heather's, making appointments for massages and stuff. And once she'd come home from town in a taxi with bags from fancy shops, and the taxi driver had carried them into the house for her, so she must have tipped him well.

'And here's the best bit,' she said. 'She wants me to be her cleaner too.'

'Does she? That's good news.'

He didn't sound enthusiastic. Maybe he'd wanted more for her than cleaning people's houses, or maybe he was just distracted, upset about Emily.

'Who'll look after Pip while you're working there?'

She told him of the arrangement with Madge, who'd sounded very nice when Christine had rung her. I'm looking forward to meeting him, she'd said. I do love little children in the house. When Christine had enquired about the cost, she'd named a sum that had sounded very reasonable. Christine thought she might give her a bit more. She could afford it, with Heather's mother paying her twenty euro an hour, for fourteen hours a week – imagine. Christine had been gobsmacked when Heather had told her.

She was a bit scared of Heather's mother. She still pretty much ignored Christine when she was at Heather and Shane's house. Hopefully she'd keep out of Christine's way in the other house too, and hopefully Christine wouldn't mess up the lunch. It sounded simple enough. She must tell Chris she was now a cleaner *and* a chef, next time she wrote. He'd get a laugh from it.

'I'll be able to pay some rent,' she said to Dad, 'when I start the new job,' but he said no, no, wait until things were more settled.

'Let's leave it as it is till Christmas,' he said, 'and we'll see how you're fixed after that,' and Christine said OK and thanked him, and resolved to slip money into his coat pocket as soon as she started getting paid by Heather's mother.

She washed Pip's hands and face, sticky after the bun, and put on his jacket while Dad folded the buggy and put it into the boot of his car. He was driving them to the library so Christine could return the picture books she'd borrowed after the last storytime, and take home some more.

I love to see young children being exposed to books, Lil had said when Christine was checking them out. Lil was friendly without being pushy. She'd seen Christine flicking through a recipe book and she'd said, Let me know if you want me to make copies of any of those for you, so Lil had picked out macaroons – Dad had said Pip liked coconut – and spinach and blue cheese pie because she loved blue cheese, and apple crumble cake because Chris's favourite desserts were ones with apple in them.

Judy, the head librarian, was fine too. Christine remembered her from years ago, when Mum would bring her to the library – but there was something about people who'd known her from before. Those people, when they met her now, treated her a bit too politely, as if they were afraid the wrong word would send her running back to drugs, and Judy was one of them. To Lil, who didn't know anything about her past, Christine was just another library user.

On impulse she gave Dad a hug outside the library. They hadn't hugged since she'd come back, not properly, but today he looked like he needed one, so she put her arms around him and squeezed, and after a second he hugged her back, and when they stepped apart his face looked as if it might collapse in on itself.

'Thank you,' she said.

'For what?'

'For everything. For not giving up on me.'

He smiled tiredly. 'I'm your dad,' he said. 'That's part of my job. And I'm proud of you, love. Look how you've come on, and how you're doing so well with Pip. Mum would be proud too' – and all she could do was hug him again.

She waved him off from the top of the steps, after he'd carried up the buggy for her. He had helped so much, was still helping. She must have him around to dinner, now that he was on his own. She'd arrange it soon. He'd be her first dinner guest. Maybe she'd invite Heather too, since she and Dad were friends.

She might try the spinach and blue cheese pie.

That evening, when Pip was asleep, she wrote a postcard.

I cooked your lemon chicken last night. It wasn't as good as when you made it, but Pip didn't complain. He called me Mum today for the first time, and it made me feel like crying because it reminded me of my mum. I got him new orange wellies and he wears them all the time. He wanted to wear them in the bath, so I let him. The bathroom was flooded – he kept kicking – but he was so happy it was worth it. I start my new cleaning job in two days. I'll be cooking lunch too, so you're not the only chef any more. Hope you're doing OK. Miss you.

C xx

She wished she could put things better. She wished he was there with her. She looked at his photo on her phone and tried to feel his arms around her, tried to hear his voice. They deliberately hadn't exchanged phone numbers – he'd said that would feel like cheating. She'd said, What about the postcards? and he'd said they were different, they weren't direct contact.

She yearned for direct contact with him. She'd give anything to hear his voice, to cradle the phone and close her eyes and listen to his words, to be able to ask a question and get the answer right away. To hear him call her Chrissy, instead of seeing it written down. Even if they could text, if she could send him a message and wait for the ping of his response. That wouldn't be direct contact, would it? Maybe he'd thought they wouldn't be able to resist calling if they had each other's numbers, and he was probably right.

Over the last few weeks she had discovered something. It wasn't that drugs gave her what she craved: it was that they took away what she found too hard to bear. They banished all the rubbish stuff, the anxiety and grief and loneliness and shame and guilt. They allowed her to forget it all for a while, to be free of everything that dragged her down.

Now, without drugs, she had nothing to keep the bad feelings away. They usually came late at night if she was tired and missing Chris, and they were fierce and frightened her, and sometimes she felt she would do anything, anything, to have them gone again, even for a while, but she stayed determined. She'd been lost and she was found, like in the hymn, and she had Pip and she had Chris and she had her dad and Ethel.

When she told Ethel on the phone about feeling bad, Ethel said maybe she should consider counselling. It wasn't the first time she'd mentioned it. You're doing so well, she said, but we can all

do with a bit of help. I can give you names. You could do it online
or in person – and Christine had promised to think about it.

When she went out she was careful to avoid places she might
meet anyone she used to know on the streets. If she came across
someone sitting on the path with a paper cup in front of them,
like she used to do, she'd scatter coins into the cup without
looking at the face behind it, and hurry on. If Chris were there
he'd probably stop and try to talk to them, but she didn't think
she'd be any good at persuading someone to change. She didn't
feel she'd reached that place yet, and maybe she never would.

Her first day in the new job arrived. She woke earlier than
she needed and made tea while Pip was still asleep. She drank
it standing at the patio doors, thinking of her mum. 'Come with
me,' she said aloud. 'Make sure I don't mess this up.' Mum would
have loved Pip – she'd have taken him out for walks and brought
him to the cinema: she and Christine had often gone – and she'd
have made a fuss of his birthdays and spoilt him rotten, like grans
were supposed to do.

'Right on time,' Heather's mother said, when Christine arrived.
Unsmiling, but that was normal for her. Christine wasn't on time,
she was five minutes early, but she thought it best not to point it
out.

'Heather has shown you around, so I'll just leave you to it.
There's a container of soup in the fridge for my lunch, it just needs
reheating. I eat at noon sharp.'

Christine would have to keep an eye on the time. 'Where will
I find the cleaning things?'

'I believe Heather has left them in the spare bedroom.'

She scuttled upstairs and located a box of the same products she used at Heather's, along with a Hoover and a mop, both of which looked brand new.

Half an hour after she started, having resolved to tackle the upstairs first, Heather's mother called up that she was going to an appointment and would return for lunch, and Christine relaxed as she scrubbed and mopped and hoovered.

By ten to twelve, the little house shone. She wondered what she would find to clean when she came back tomorrow, and worried that Heather's mother would decide she didn't need a cleaner every day. She washed her hands and tipped the soup, which was coloured orange, into a saucepan. There was no sign of bread, or even a breadbin, so she supposed it wasn't part of the menu.

She set a place at the table – the good thing about the tiny kitchen was that you could find everything easily – and filled a glass with water from the green bottle in the fridge before worrying that it might get too warm, so she was attempting to pour it back into the bottle, half of it slopping into the sink, when the front door opened. Christine glanced at the clock on the wall and saw that it was a minute to twelve. She hurriedly refilled the glass and set it back on the table.

'Thank you, Christine. You may go,' Heather's mother called, and Christine heard her ascending the stairs.

'Goodbye,' she called, but no response came. The soup was simmering: should she put it out or leave it in the pot? She remembered Heather saying her mother expected to be waited on hand and foot, so she filled the soup bowl and cleaned the pot rapidly and returned it to the press under the sink. She gave the spoon a polish with the tea-towel and replaced it carefully beside the bowl. She gathered up her things as quietly as she could and left, pulling the door softly closed behind her.

Easier than she'd been expecting.

As the days went by she felt a kind of contentment settle over her. She thought it must come with routine, with having your day, or part of your day, already sorted before you woke up. Heather's mother remained aloof, speaking to Christine only when necessary, which suited Christine fine as she cleaned rooms that were already spotless.

Preparing lunch was routine too, soup alternating with an undressed salad, made from whatever ingredients she found in the fridge. Her most challenging task in the kitchen was to hard-boil an egg.

She switched to afternoons for Heather's house, which worked out fine. Lottie and Jack would arrive home from school while she was still there, and would help to peg clothes on the line or bring them in when they were dry. Lottie had moved back into the small bedroom, which made cleaning the dining room a lot more straightforward.

Things were going well with Pip too. He seemed happy to be living with her, and she couldn't imagine not having him there. He didn't look for Emily as often now, which Christine thought was good in one way and sad in another. Any time she thought about Emily she felt guilty – but what could she do?

She wondered if she'd have the courage to call to the restaurant and invite Emily to Pip's second birthday party. It wasn't until May so there was plenty of time. She'd wait and see.

At the end of her first week working for Heather's mother there was an envelope on the kitchen table with her name on it, which she pocketed without opening. On her way home with Pip she brought him into a café she hadn't been to in years and ordered two ice-cream sundaes. As soon as they arrived she realised she should have got one between them – they were enormous – but she couldn't very well give one back, so she handed him a spoon and let him at it.

She'd left his bib at Madge's, so he got as much of it on him as in him; she could see other customers looking, and probably judging, but she didn't care because he was enjoying it. On the way home he threw it all up, and she felt bad for overfeeding him. Emily, she knew, would be horrified.

'Not to worry,' she said, pushing the buggy faster. At home she filled his bath and poured in lots of bubbles. She stripped him off in the kitchen and threw his clothes into the washing machine. She put back on his orange wellies – he still wore them all the time: she'd had to buy a second pair so she could dry out one while he wore the other – and lowered him into the warm bubbles. She washed ice-cream out of his hair as he kicked and laughed and soaked the floor again, and out of the blue she thought, I'm happy. It just came floating into her head.

I'm happy – and she was.

Chrissy,

I'm sure your lemon chicken was great. Pip sounds like a boy after my own heart. Wellies in the bath – what a good idea. I must try it. Busy here, sleep still crap, but I'm coping, although I really miss you. Not too long more, and we'll be glad we waited, I promise. Can I come and see you first? I want to meet Pip, and see your house, and I'd like to meet your dad too, and tell him what a winner of a daughter he has, but he probably knows already. Hope the new job is going well. Take care, thinking of you.

C xx

DECEMBER

Emily

WHAT HER MOTHER SAID: 'IT'S FOR THE BEST, EMILY. I know you don't want to hear this now, but mark my words, you'll look back some day and realise that I'm right. And I'm not for a second denying he was a nice man – a real gentleman, so mannerly and thoughtful – but we did think he was far too old for you. I'm being honest here, Emily. And look at all that trouble with his daughter – and who's to say it won't happen again? You'd be expected to put up with it, and to row in if you were needed, just like before. I'm not denying you did a wonderful job looking after that little baby when she deserted him, but see where it got you, with her swanning back in when she felt like it, and making you hand him back. And I'm glad she's doing well now, obviously – but I wonder if she appreciates all you did for her little boy. No,

I think this is the best thing that could have happened, I really do. And you'll meet someone else, you're still a young woman. You've certainly been unlucky, first that Fergal who was such a disaster, and now things going wrong with Bill, but you'll find the right one, just wait and see. I know you will.'

What her father said: 'Sorry to hear it, love. I liked Bill, we had a lot in common, but I don't mind telling you that I worried about you. We both did. I know you said the age difference didn't bother you, but I felt it might go against you in the future. I can say it now. Your mother and I are sorry we're not there for you, but we're glad you're with Daniel. It's good to have family around when you're feeling low.'

What Daniel said: 'Em, I wish there was something I could do … but please stay here with us till your apartment is free again – you'd be crazy to rent another place when you don't have to. You know we're both happy to have you and Barney, and there's plenty of room. It's a shame, I really thought you and Bill … Well, anyway, it's too bad. Just say, won't you, if there's anything we can do?'

What Nora said: 'Please make yourself at home here, Emily – I'd hate you to feel like a visitor in this house. We'd love you to have dinner with us on your days off – although my cooking isn't a patch on yours or Mike's! But do whatever makes you comfortable. I'm so sorry, Emily.'

What Heather, the only one who knew the real reason for the split, said: 'Better it's happening now than later, sweetie. You've still got years to be a mom, and if it wasn't to be with Bill, then you need to find the right guy. It may not seem like it now, but your time will come, believe me. Tell you what – come out for a walk, just for half an hour. I can drop Jo in to Madge, she won't mind,' but Emily had made an excuse, not feeling up to talking to anyone.

Everyone was being kind. Nora brought cat treats home for Barney, and put flowers in Emily's room. Daniel brought her up coffee in the morning, and accompanied her to the cash and carry when he was free. Her parents emailed her a gift voucher for her favourite boutique, and her chef Mike presented her with a pack of the homemade Christmas cards his girlfriend sold online. Emily put her head down and ploughed on, and kept pretending she was doing OK, anytime anyone asked.

And then, on a day that the restaurant was closed and the morning yawned in front of Emily, Heather turned up on the doorstep with Jo in the buggy.

'We're walking,' she said. It didn't sound like it was up for discussion, so Emily got into her outdoor things and they made for the smaller of the town's two parks, and they talked – or rather, Heather talked.

Having enquired how Emily was doing, and Emily having given her the same response everyone got – even with her closest friend she felt compelled to put a brave face on it – Heather said, 'I have a secret to tell you. I'll implode if I don't tell someone, and I know you won't blab to anyone else.' A lime green elephant fell from the buggy: without breaking her stride Heather scooped it up and returned it.

A secret. Mild curiosity stirred within Emily. With Heather you never knew what was coming. She wondered if she'd be able to pretend to be happy if Heather announced she was pregnant again.

She needn't have worried. 'It's Manfred,' Heather said.

Manfred. Lottie's father, the runaway German. 'What about him?'

'He wrote me, to my old house. Can you believe it, after all this time?'

'He did not. A letter?'

'Yeah. An actual letter, in an actual envelope.'

'How did he remember the address?'

'No idea.'

'How did he know you'd get it?'

'He didn't – I guess he just took a chance. He said he was sorry. Very, very sorry, he said – and he asked if I'd had the baby.'

'The nerve.'

'Yeah, well …'

'Is he still in Ireland?'

'No, back in Germany.' Heather looked up at the sky. 'He called me his beautiful American girlfriend.'

'Did he.'

Heather looked at her. 'I hear how you feel about him, and I completely understand it, but I need you not to get mad. Promise you won't get mad.'

'Why would I get mad? What have you done?'

'Nothing much, honest – but I thought maybe he had a right to know that he was a dad. He's not married, and he didn't mention any other kids, so I thought … Well, anyway, I sent him a real short email, just telling him he had a child. I didn't give him any more information.'

Emily frowned. 'Not sure that was such a good idea. What did Shane say?'

'I haven't said anything to him. I told you, there's nothing to it.'

Emily stared at her. 'Hang on. Your daughter's father contacts you out of the blue, and you respond, and you don't think that's a big deal? You don't think Shane should be told? What the hell, Heather?'

Heather's face took on a mutinous look that Emily had seen before. 'Shane and I are going through a patch,' she said, a little sharply. 'I told you that.'

She *had* told Emily, and Emily should have followed it up, but then she and Bill had ended, and everything else had stopped mattering. 'Well, I'm sorry things aren't good between you and Shane, but do you really think that makes it OK to keep him in the dark about this?'

'There's no *this*,' Heather insisted. 'I get a letter out of the blue from a man I knew years ago—'

'A man who just happens to be the father of your daughter.'

'Oh, for goodness' sake – and I answered a question he asked because I thought it was the right thing, the decent thing to do. And yeah, maybe I would have said it to Shane if things were different, but at the moment he kind of annoys me. I mean, he's so … *pliable*,' she said crossly. 'Like a ball of clay, or something.'

The green elephant toppled out again. She picked it up and held on to it, swinging it by its trunk. 'But don't worry – I'm not planning to run away to Germany, ha-ha.'

She said ha-ha, but she didn't laugh. Neither did Emily. She was aware of a rising irritation with her friend. 'Shane is *pliable*? As in, he always does what you want?'

'Oh now, you're just making it sound—'

'In case you haven't noticed, Shane is crazy about you. He tries to please you by falling in with what you suggest. Is that what you mean? Is that what *annoys* you?'

Heather stopped walking. 'What is *up* with you? You're like a bear today.'

Emily stopped too. They faced one another, unsmiling. 'Did that man get in touch again?'

Heather gave a shrug, looking past Emily. 'Just a couple times.'

'A couple? You mean twice? He sent you two more letters?'

'Not letters, emails.'

'And did you respond?'

Heather glared at her. 'Look, it's just a few emails, right? I'm sorry I mentioned it now.'

'You *should* be sorry. You've got a wonderful man who loves you, and then this other rat gets in touch, who ran out on you as soon as he heard you were pregnant, while you were practically a child yourself, and you can't wait to become his penfriend.'

'I was almost seventeen when I met him,' Heather said loudly.

'Wow, all grown-up then – and by the way, in case you didn't know, the age of consent here is seventeen, not almost seventeen – he could have been up for rape.' She wasn't sure if this was strictly true, but Heather wouldn't know either.

'Oh please – there was no rape; I *did* consent, and he's sorry about the way it went.'

'Oh, he's sorry – well, that's OK, then. Go right ahead and forgive him, and tell him whatever he wants to know. I'm going to assume you haven't told him about Shane.'

Heather didn't reply, which gave Emily her answer. What was her friend thinking, fooling about with a man who'd treated her abominably? They walked on in strained silence for a bit. Emily kicked at a stone on the path, and missed.

'Did I tell you I moved Mom into my house?' Heather said then, the subject left behind. A coolness in her voice but she was trying, so Emily did too.

'No, you didn't.' Emily couldn't picture Heather's glamorous mother in the little terraced house. 'How long has she been there?'

Heather shrugged. 'A week, week and a half. Yeah, on her own apart from Christine.'

Emily frowned. 'Christine? What does she have to do with it?'

'She's her cleaner.'

'Is she?' Emily knew she should be happy that Heather was helping Christine, but all she felt was jealous. She wondered if Christine had been told about the reappearing German. 'Does she still clean Shane's house?'

'Yeah, we switched her to afternoons because she goes to Mom every morning for a couple of hours. No way is she needed there – that house takes about twenty minutes a week to clean – but Mom likes having someone she can boss around.'

'What about Pip?' Emily asked, the name conjuring an image of his face that caused a wrench. 'Who looks after him while Christine is working?'

'Madge, my old neighbour. She's mad about him.'

Everyone was mad about him. Emily missed him desperately. Every day she suffered the lack of him. It was the kind of pain, she thought, that the removal of a body part – a tooth, a limb, a kidney – might leave behind. She'd lost a bit of herself, it felt like, when he'd gone from her.

'By the way,' Heather said, 'I met Bill at the farmer's market on Saturday. He told me his sister Grace is having a hysterectomy.'

Something crumpled inside Emily at the mention of her other great loss. She'd met Grace over the summer, when she and her husband had paid a visit from Cornwall. They'd brought Pip a toothbrush with a monkey's head at the end of the handle. I'm so happy Bill has you, Grace had said. He deserved someone like you, after the way Christine turned out.

She walked through a clump of leaves, sending them scattering. 'I saw Bill,' she said. 'Two days ago.'

'Where?'

'Oh, just in town.'

She'd emerged from the library with a bag of books and there he was, walking right past the steps. He hadn't seen her, his gaze directed doggedly ahead. Hands pushed into pockets like always, feet turned slightly inward as he'd taken his usual long strides, shoulders hunched a little. He always walked as if he was late for some event he wasn't really looking forward to.

The familiar sight of him, so unexpected, had caused Emily to come to a halt on the steps, the thump of her heart suddenly too loud. Following some unknown impulse she'd begun to follow him, although he was going in the opposite direction to the one she'd been about to take. For a few minutes she'd shadowed him, watching his progress along the street, seeing him do a little hop to avoid a toddler in his path, watching him skirt a sandwich board, weave around a chattering group.

He'd entered a department store. She'd followed him across a carpeted floor, holding back when he'd stopped at a rail of men's shirts and begun flicking through the hangers.

Turn around, she'd begged silently. Look at me, look what you've done to me. Look how broken I am without you. She'd longed to see his face, wanting to witness an answering emptiness in it, a hollowness in the eyes that suggested nights as sleepless as her own, but he hadn't turned, not even slightly.

How could he not be aware of her? How could he be so close and not sense her there? She couldn't bear the thought of him shopping by himself, knowing how much he disliked it, how relieved he'd be whenever she arrived home with whatever he'd been reluctant to go hunting for.

She'd seen him select a shirt – not brown, she'd wanted to call out to him. Don't buy brown, it's too draining on you. After watching him make his way to the checkout, with a shirt that wouldn't suit him, she'd turned and left, and walked sorrowfully back to Daniel and Nora's.

After her first serious relationship had crashed and burnt, Emily had sworn never to leave herself open to that kind of heartbreak again. It had required a real leap of faith to take a chance on Bill, but she'd felt sure of him, blindingly trusting that he'd never break her heart like Ferg had. This is it, she'd thought. This is the real thing. I've finally cracked it – but she'd been wrong for the second time.

She knew now that love, the genesis of it, the blossoming of it, the nurturing of it, the success or failure of it, was either a matter of pure luck or a complete mystery, never to be solved. It was as simple, or as complex, as that.

'Emily, it's going to happen,' Heather said, as they passed a small playground where children swung and tumbled and slid. 'The town isn't big: you're going to bump into him now and again. You have to get used to that, and not let it upset you.'

She was aware of a jump of fresh irritation. She tamped it down. 'I know I do.' She just didn't know how.

'Why don't you come with me to Christine's some afternoon? We can call just for a short while, and you can get to visit with Pip. I bet he's dying to see you. What do you say?'

She considered it. If they chose a day when Bill would be at work, an accidental encounter couldn't happen. Emily would give anything to be with Pip again – and she couldn't deny she was curious to see for herself how Christine was getting on in the house.

No.

She didn't think she could act in a friendly way towards Christine, the reason for Bill's unwillingness to father more children, the reason Emily was alone now. She didn't think she could sit and smile, even if it meant she could see Pip.

'I think I'll pass,' she said. She'd had enough of this walk. It was churning things up too much.

'Emily,' Heather said, 'now you're just being silly.'

The words stung. 'What do you mean?'

'I mean you can't let your life come to a standstill just because you and Bill didn't work out – and, Jeez, it should never have gone as far as it did without having the babies talk.'

'What?' Her irritation turned to full-blown anger. 'You seem to have forgotten that your precious Christine was the cause of that! She didn't exactly give us a warning before she went running off, leaving Bill literally holding the baby.'

'So what are you saying?' Heather shot back. 'Because Pip was there, you couldn't talk to Bill about something as important as whether to have children? I'm sorry, honey, that's not enough of an excuse.'

Emily felt her face get hot. 'Well, you have some nerve lecturing me about relationships, when you jump at the first chance you get to go behind Shane's back!'

'Oh, come *on*—'

But Emily had had enough. Without another word she turned around and stomped off, and spent the rest of the morning feeling unsettled and grouchy, and unable to fix on anything. Her phone rang and she saw her mother's name, and ignored it. The last thing she needed was Dol telling her again what a good thing it was that Bill was off the scene. Emily would ring her back when she felt more up to it.

That afternoon she and Daniel drove to the cash and carry with the usual list. Now that December had arrived, The Food of Love was full each lunchtime with Christmas shoppers who dropped their bags and packages with weary, grateful sighs as they sank into chairs. Emily knew she could open for lunch seven days a week instead of five all through the month if she felt inclined, and every seat around the big table would be occupied, but although she'd welcome the distraction, and the added income would be nice too, she didn't have the energy for it.

But she did love Christmas. She'd put up decorations on the first day of the month as she always did in December, with Nora and Daniel helping her this year instead of Bill. A string of chubby smiling Santa lights framed the window, tinsel twined through it to create sparkle. Sprigs of holly poked from behind pictures, and more coloured lights criss-crossed the walls. Baubles were suspended from fishing lines that spanned the ceiling, the room being too small for a tree.

A blue ceramic Santa figure the size of a toddler was positioned just inside the entrance, a gift from Daniel the year she'd moved into the apartment upstairs, full of plans for a restaurant with a single big table that would feed diners who wanted company at mealtimes.

She'd hung a sprig of mistletoe just inside the door. She didn't think it would be pressed into much service – the restaurant occasionally had couples eating there, but mostly it was lone diners, the shy, the widowed, the lonely, or groups of friends, or parent-and-adult-child combinations.

The mistletoe reminded her of Bill. A lot of things reminded her of Bill. Thank goodness for Daniel and Nora, taking her in without question. Nora was becoming the younger sister Emily didn't have. There you are, she would say, whenever Emily returned to the house. She always managed to make it sound as if Emily was the person she'd most wanted to meet.

I'm just heating up some of your roasted red pepper soup, she might say – she'd become addicted to it since she'd got pregnant – or, I was about to make tea, or sometimes it would be Come and help me with this crossword, I'm absolutely stuck. She was very sweet, easily known she was Shane's daughter. Emily hoped Daniel appreciated how lucky he was, even if Heather seemed to have forgotten how lucky *she* was to be with Nora's father.

'Nora,' she said that evening, the conversation with Heather refusing to leave her head, 'how's your dad? I haven't seen him in a while.'

'Neither have I,' Nora said, rummaging in a drawer for something. 'He's been working a lot lately – they're short-staffed, and he usually volunteers when they look for people to do extra shifts.'

Emily wondered if the extra shifts had anything to do with his relationship going through a sticky patch: awful to feel he might be trying to stay out of Heather's way. 'Have you been talking to him?'

Nora pulled out a tape measure. '*There* it is. Sorry, what?'

'Just wondered if you'd been in contact with Shane.'

Nora frowned. 'Let's see – I spoke with him … maybe at the weekend, or was it Thursday? I just gave him a quick call.'

'And all is well?'

'Seemed to be. Jack was at the dentist – there's talk of him needing braces. Oh, and Heather's mother had them over to dinner some night last week.'

'Did she?' Heather had made no mention of it. Emily tried to picture them all in the tiny kitchen.

'She ordered pizzas, he said.' She laughed. 'I got the impression she's not a cook.'

'Definitely not.'

'Heather didn't go – she had a headache, so Shane brought the kids.'

A headache, real or imagined. Emily was concerned. With Heather and Shane going through a bad patch, the reappearance of Lottie's father might seem to Heather like it was meant to be. Dangerous timing.

Before she could change her mind, Emily rang Shane.

'Hi there. Anything up?'

He sounded like his usual cheerful self. 'I haven't seen you in a while,' she said. 'I was wondering if you and Heather would like to come to dinner at the restaurant on your next night off, my treat.'

'Aren't you good. What's brought this on?'

'Well, Nora tells me you're working extra shifts, so I thought you should have a night off dinner duty whenever you're free. The kids could get a pizza delivery – I'm sure they'd love it.'

'Thanks a million, Emily – that would be great. I'll say it to Heather.'

Heather would know perfectly well what Emily was up to, but it didn't matter. What mattered was that she and Shane stayed together. It felt important that they stayed together – and besides, Emily and Heather could do with a chance to make up.

'And speaking of Nora,' she said, 'congratulations on the granddad news.'

'Stop, I'm still getting over the shock – but no, we're thrilled really.' He paused. 'Heather told me,' he said, 'about you and Bill splitting up. I'm so sorry, Emily.'

'Thanks.' For some reason she didn't feel she had to tell him she was doing OK, maybe because he spent a lot of his time being with people who weren't OK. He could handle it. 'It's horrible,' she said, 'but I'm keeping busy.'

'That's good – and I'm glad you're staying with Nora and Daniel. Better that you're not alone. And how are your tenants getting on?'

'Fine,' she said. 'They come in to eat the odd time. They're nice.'

'As long as they pay the rent, and keep the place clean.'

'They do. So I'll be looking out for you and Heather soon.'

'Do. I'll say it to her when I see her. Thanks, Emily.'

A few nights later her phone rang as she got ready for bed, and she saw her mother's name, and realised she'd forgotten to return the other call.

'Hi, Dol. Sorry, I saw a missed call earlier in the week. I meant to ring back but it went out of my head.'

'Not to worry, I know you have a lot going on. Emily, your father and I have had a great idea.'

Emily felt wary. She and her mother didn't always agree on what made an idea great. 'What is it?'

'Come to us for Christmas. There's a gorgeous little restaurant just a short walk away, fancy but not too. We go there for any special occasion. What do you think? You could stay for a week.'

'Dol, I can't. I'm open until lunchtime Christmas Eve, and I told you I have a group of friends invited for Christmas dinner. I can't just cancel it.'

'Of course you can. Everyone will understand, with you and Bill … Anyway, I'm sure they all have other places they can go. And you know we'd love to have you.'

She wondered if anyone would care if she cancelled. Dol was right – they'd all find other tables to eat at. But then she thought about having dinner in a restaurant she didn't know with parents who thought Bill was too old for her, and who were relieved that Emily had left him.

'Honestly, it's a nice idea, and thank you for thinking of it, but I'd feel bad cancelling at this stage. I really don't want to do that, Dol.'

'Well, I'm sorry to hear it, and Patrick will be too. I hope you're not moping, Emily.'

Moping was just about all she was doing. 'I'm a little sad right now.'

'Of course you are, but it'll pass. And the invitation stands, so if you change your mind just hop on a plane.'

Did anyone actually hop on a plane? Even if she could get a flight this late, the airport would be a nightmare on Christmas Eve. Long queues, everyone frazzled, no room for hopping anywhere. Definitely not for her.

A few nights later, her tenants showed up again for dinner at the restaurant, their first visit since Emily had decorated it. 'This is lovely,' Lil said, looking around. 'Really festive.' Her hair looked newly washed, or maybe newly cut. In the coloured lights her curls gleamed softly.

'Evening, all.'

It was Heather, appearing with her mother. 'Michelle,' Emily said. 'Nice to have you back in Ireland again.' Better not mention the divorce. 'I was wondering when I'd see you.' It looked like she was coming in place of Shane.

'And you, dear. I'm happy to be back in your little restaurant – don't you have it looking nice? And Heather tells me we'll be eating here on Christmas Day too, which will be lovely.'

'And so will these two,' Heather put in, and introductions were made, and the four of them took seats together as the place began to fill. And all through the evening, with every opening of the restaurant door, Emily's heart insisted on quickening. Somehow it seemed that Bill must show up, with Heather here – and each time it wasn't him, she was crushed. Foolish to imagine he would suddenly appear, like a Hollywood hero's return in the final scene, coming to make everything right just before the credits rolled. Pathetic to keep on hoping, and still she did.

Towards the end of their meal Heather caught Emily at the kitchen door, out of earshot of her mother. 'Shane told me you offered a meal on the house. Thanks for trying to help, but I'm just not in the mood for a cosy dinner for two right now, so I told him Mom needed a night out.'

'This isn't exactly a cosy-dinner-for-two kind of place,' Emily pointed out.

Heather didn't smile. 'You know what I mean. And obviously I'll pay, since your offer was for me and Shane.'

'You don't have to pay – and sorry about the other day,' Emily said. 'I'm not the best company right now.'

'No worries, you just said what you thought – and I'd rather pay. Can I also get three spiced berry crumbles to go?'

She was still smarting. Emily wanted to ask about the German, but Heather clearly wasn't in the mood for confidences, so she returned to the kitchen and boxed up the desserts, and Heather paid in full, telling Emily she'd see her whenever. Definitely still smarting.

'Thank you so much,' Lil said, as she and Tom were leaving a few minutes later. 'Your food's really good.'

'Glad you like it.'

There was something about her, Emily thought. Something … suppressed, was it? Some secret she was hugging to herself. Another person with a secret. She watched Tom pointing out the mistletoe as they approached the door. She saw him pull his fiancée into his arms in front of the last few diners and kiss her. She saw Lil draw away, laughing. Shy about kissing in public, Emily guessed.

Maybe Lil was pregnant, like Nora, and waiting until the first crucial, dangerous weeks were past before announcing it to the world. If it turned out to be true it would be difficult not to feel as if Fate were taunting Emily, presenting her so cruelly with a parade of other women's pregnancies.

A little later, as she was about to lock up, the door opened and Daniel appeared.

Something had happened: she knew the instant she saw him. 'What?'

'Nora had a bleed earlier. I brought her to hospital. She might lose the baby.'

He stopped. How pale he was – how frightened he looked. Almost on the verge of tears, although she couldn't remember him crying, not ever.

'They've kept her in. I wanted to stay with her, but the nurse told me I'd be of more use if I went home and got some sleep. They'll phone if … anything changes.'

'Oh, Daniel,' Emily said, taking him into a hug. 'Poor Nora, and poor you. Sit and I'll make decaf' – but he said he'd just had a terrible coffee in the hospital and didn't want any more, so they sent Mike home and cleaned up between them, and got back to the house by midnight.

They opened the bottle of wine that Daniel's boss had given him when he'd told her that Nora was pregnant, and they talked a little and were silent in between. 'I was going to take her out to dinner at your place tomorrow night,' he told Emily, halfway through his second glass. 'I was going to propose right there at the table, in front of everyone.' He showed her the ring he'd bought, white gold because she preferred it to yellow, with an oval diamond set into it.

'Beautiful,' Emily said, 'and it'll keep until the time is right again – and I'd love if you still wanted to do it in the restaurant. I think it's a pretty safe bet she'll say yes.' He tried to smile as he slipped it back into its box and topped up their glasses, and they climbed the stairs just before two o'clock.

And as Emily was drifting to sleep, she realised that several hours had gone by without thinking of Bill or Pip. It was progress, she supposed, although it didn't feel like it.

And at eight in the morning, while Emily was making coffee and trying to persuade Daniel to wait for a cup before he went back to Nora, the call came from the hospital.

Lil

I CAN COLLECT YOU, GRAN HAD SAID. IT'S SILLY
coming on the bus when you don't have to, with everything you'll
be bringing down, but Lil had stuck to her guns and said the bus
was fine, and her bag was light, she'd have no trouble, and Gran
had said, You were always stubborn, and Lil hadn't risen to that,
although she was pretty sure it wasn't true. If anyone had been
stubborn, it was Hollie.

I should be with you by seven, she'd said, and Gran had
grumbled a bit more before saying she'd be at the end of the lane
to meet the bus, if Lil absolutely insisted on taking it, and Lil had
told her that would be lovely.

She could easily have walked down the lane. It would have
taken her six minutes at the most, even in the dark. She could

have walked it blindfold, knew every bend and turn. She'd always loved it, a strip of grass making a fat green stripe down the middle, the brambles that bordered the lane full of blackberries in late summer – Gran and Mum would make pies and tarts and crumbles; Gran still did – and beautifully peaceful in the winter, no traffic because it held just the two side-by-side houses, and petered out right after Gran's.

She could have walked it easily, but she'd won the bus battle. Let Gran have this one.

She hadn't learnt to drive, and didn't plan to. Partly because of how Hollie and her parents had died, but also because she didn't think she'd be any good at it. Despite being a confident swimmer – Tom said she must have been a mermaid in a previous life – she was clumsy in lots of other ways, and she couldn't imagine being coordinated enough to manage gears and pedals, horn and wipers and indicators with the ease other people did. Tom had offered to teach her, but she was happy to remain a passenger.

And she enjoyed bus journeys. She liked the idea of a collection of strangers brought together for a while, their lives travelling briefly on parallel lines as they moved in a common direction. Even if she never spoke to anyone – shyness often stopped her striking up conversations when she travelled alone, although she'd enter into one happily enough if someone else made the first move – a journey on a bus was still something she found pleasant.

And of course, this journey held a particular significance. Next time she travelled by bus, she would be fundamentally changed.

Not on the outside: nobody on this afternoon's bus would see a difference if they encountered her again on a future journey, but she wouldn't be the Lil Noonan who'd brought her weekend bag on board twenty minutes earlier, not wanting to trust it in the outside compartment.

And she was finding it very hard to keep the smile off her face.

'Are you going far?'

Her seat companion had just got on. Lil judged him to be in his fifties. He was wearing a black woolly hat and chewing something. He was accompanied by a tobacco smell, the nutty, dark scent reminding Lil of the thin cigars her father would smoke occasionally in the evenings.

'Fairweather,' she told him, 'just for the weekend.'

'From there, are you?'

'Yes, I am.' And steering away instinctively: 'How about you? Where are you off to?'

'I'm heading to Tralee to see my mother,' he told her. 'She was eighty last week, but I wasn't well enough to travel for the party. I've had radiation treatment for mouth cancer – it took it out of me a bit.'

'Oh, I'm sorry to hear it.'

'I'm on the mend now, but the mouth is very dry. The saliva glands don't work properly any more after the radiation. That's why I'm chewing the gum – well, that's mostly the reason.' He gave a sudden wink. 'I had a sneaky puff of the pipe before I got on the bus, and I'm not supposed to. Mam would give out to me.'

You never knew, Lil thought, even as she laughed along with

him, what others might be going through. Never knew what battles they might be fighting silently, what heartbreak might lie behind a smile. She thought of Christine, looking miles away throughout Lil's storytelling, her troubled past maybe haunting her still. She thought of her landlady Emily, alone and sad after breaking up with Christine's father, but having to paint on a smile every day for her diners.

Thinking of Emily reminded her of their situation, needing to hunt down alternative accommodation before the end of February. They'd been scouring websites and supermarket noticeboards, and discovering that there were alarmingly few possibilities, all more expensive than Emily's apartment. They'd make a renewed effort after the weekend.

The bus trundled on until it reached the outskirts of Fairweather. When it pulled in at her stop Lil retrieved her bag and said goodbye to her fellow passenger. 'Best of luck,' she added.

'Enjoy your weekend,' he replied, and she wanted suddenly to confide in him, to tell him what was bringing her back to Fairweather, but the driver was waiting for her to get off so she kept moving.

In the darkness she made out the shape of Gran's car, parked on the other side of the road, just up from the lane. She waited till the bus pulled away again before crossing, muscles stiff after two hours of sitting still. She opened the back door and slung her bag onto the seat. 'Hi Gran – here I am.'

No reply. Her grandmother's head was tilted slightly forward, hands in her lap. 'Gran,' she said, a little more loudly, reaching over the back of the driver's seat to touch a shoulder, feeling a small squeeze of alarm. 'Gran?'

At that, her grandmother stirred and looked around groggily. 'There you are. I must have nodded off.'

'You must have.' Lil closed the back door and slid into the front seat. 'There was no need at all to pick me up – it's not even raining.'

'There was every need, in the pitch dark. Let me look at you.' She scrutinised Lil. 'Too thin,' she pronounced, and Lil laughed.

'You always say that. I haven't lost an ounce since I saw you last – if anything, I've put on a bit. Judy brings treats to work nearly every second day.'

'Treats won't do you a bit of harm, provided you don't overdo them.' Her grandmother started the engine and drove slowly up the lane, Lil peering out at the familiar bends and landmarks until they reached the two houses.

There was a vehicle parked in the other driveway, and a second one pulled in close to the garden wall. The sight of the house where she'd grown up caused a familiar pang, memories good and bad jostling for attention. Lights were on inside.

'How are you feeling?' Gran asked as they walked up her path, their passage made easier by the sensor light above the door that Mark had installed the previous winter.

'I'm feeling good. Excited. I have butterflies.'

'I'm sure you do.' Gran pushed the key into the lock and steered Lil into the kitchen, where the table had been set with the good china, and something smelt tasty. As they ate tarragon chicken Gran told her about the cruise she and Mark had booked, with Christmas dinner to be eaten somewhere in the Bahamas. 'I hope they know how to cook a decent meal,' she said, and Lil had visions of her invading the kitchen if the food didn't live up to her standards. Someone should warn the chef that a retired domestic-science teacher was on the way.

They spoke of Alice Murphy – Lil wondered if she'd had her baby yet – and the Happy Talk piece on Lil that was attached with a magnet to the front of Gran's fridge. 'I saw it in the window of Olive's gift shop,' Gran said – Olive had been Mum's best friend – 'and apparently lots of people went in to say how delighted they were to see you doing so well.'

In the days and weeks following the accident, the locals had rallied around Lil and Gran in their various ways. Some had left items on Gran's doorstep, like flowers or sweets, candles or hand cream; others cut her grass, or delivered the daily paper, or took a grocery list from Gran and returned with a full shopping bag.

To this day Lil knew they were still keeping an eye out for her, still rejoicing in any good accounts of her. Maybe now her guardians could safely look away, as the road she'd been on since losing the others was levelling out, becoming smoother and wider. Still not without the occasional pothole, but nowhere near as bumpy as before.

'Any sign of that new library?' she asked Gran.

'Not a bit of it: they haven't even begun yet.' An old office block had been earmarked for the site, but much work would be needed. Gran had a friend on the council who kept her informed. 'It'll be next summer at the very earliest,' she said, and Lil had to accept that Fairweather wouldn't be seeing her and Tom back anytime soon.

After dinner they sat on, neither of them ready for sleep. Lil told Gran of the encounter with Vivienne, and the meeting with Tom's father that had come in its wake. 'We'll probably never know,' she said, 'which of them was telling the truth.'

Gran gave a slow nod. 'The truth,' she said, 'might be somewhere in between. When it comes to matters of the heart, or physical impulses, people can be capable of anything. Tough on Tom, though. You said he and his father were close when he was growing up.'

Lil hesitated. 'I'm not sure how close they were, really. Tom had him on a pedestal – but when they met in the hotel, the first time they were meeting since that night, I couldn't really see evidence of affection in his father. Maybe I was wrong, but that was how it seemed to me. I felt … he was cold. Detached.'

'Poor Tom.'

Now and again they lapsed into silence, their talk replaced then by the intermittent hooting of an owl outside. Lil didn't imagine it could be the same one she'd grown up listening to. Maybe it was its child, or its grandchild. Whatever generation it belonged to, she liked the idea of it living high in the nearby trees, bearing witness to all the goings-on below.

'Remember when Tom moved in next door,' she said.

'I do indeed, I remember it well. Terrible wet day. I knew he was troubled the minute I laid eyes on him. I remember thinking we had troubles enough of our own here, didn't need any more.'

Gran had been the one to show him around, Lil still locked in her speechlessness, a year on from the accident. She hadn't wanted anyone staying in her family home – she'd moved in with Gran after the funerals, unable to bear the place without the others – but Gran had talked her into it, saying it needed to be lived in.

She'd spied the new tenant from her bedroom window, the morning after his arrival. She'd watched him making his way down the garden to the little gate that led onto the cliff path. After that she'd encountered him on the path every now and again, nodding a reply to his greeting, taking some small satisfaction from the knowledge that he wasn't aware of her identity. She'd known him before he knew her.

'Well,' Gran said after another silence, 'this time tomorrow' – and Lil felt again the bubble of happiness that floated up in her now whenever she thought about her future. This time tomorrow she'd have taken a momentous step.

'They'd be proud of you, Lil.'

She looked at the woman who had insisted that life go on, when Lil couldn't think of a single reason why it should. When her loss of speech had persisted beyond a few weeks Gran had dragged her to one doctor after another. Do something! she'd demanded of them. Help her to speak! There must be something you can do – but there hadn't been.

Undaunted, Gran had ordered Lil to eat the nourishing dishes she'd cooked for her, and when she'd reopened the little library at the bottom of the garden she'd started up a few years previously, she'd told Lil – not asked, told – that she could help out.

She'd forced Lil to keep going when all Lil had wanted was to die too, and she'd done all this while she'd been going through her own mourning.

'I don't know what I'd have done without you,' Lil said. 'I don't know how I'd have coped.'

'Well, it's a good job you didn't have to then,' Gran said, getting to her feet. 'It's time we went to our beds,' so they did, and Lil slept a dreamless sleep, with air that smelt of shells and seaweed drifting in through the inch of window she'd opened, telling her she was home.

In the morning the sky was a uniform white, but the day was dry. Goosebumps rose on Lil's arms as she padded in her nightdress to the wardrobe and took from it the dress she'd hung there the night before. Not what she'd planned to wear on this day – she'd thought white linen in the heat of Italy, and short, but this was made of fine wool, and was pale blue instead of white, and it fell almost to her ankles, and it had cost her twenty-five euro in a charity shop near the library. It could have been made for you, the volunteer behind the counter had said, when Lil had tried it on.

She draped the dress across her bed and pinned Hollie's silver butterfly brooch to the front. The brooch had been a long-ago Valentine's gift from Hollie's boyfriend Pat: Hollie had worn it on the upturned brim of a straw hat in summer, and on a coat lapel in winter. After Hollie's death Lil had taken the brooch, but had never worn it. Today was the day.

Next to the dress Lil placed a deep red fur stole, Dad's last Christmas present to Mum, and another memento she'd held on to. She slipped his wedding ring into the little sequined bag she would carry, also from a charity shop.

They would be with her, the three of them. All day, they would be close to her. Italy, she'd realised on the way home from meeting Tom's father, would never have worked. She'd thought it would be easier to be married far away from them, in a country they'd never travelled to as a family, with no familiar things around her – but she knew now she would have been miserable in alien surroundings. Here was where she needed to be today.

She belted her dressing gown and found Gran already in the kitchen scrambling eggs, an apron over the turquoise wool dress she'd bought in the January sales last winter. Gran was a great one for the sales. 'Smoked salmon,' she said, chopping it and tipping it in. 'You won't eat again for a while. There's coffee in the pot.'

As they ate, Lil asked about her parents' wedding day, and Gran recalled good weather – 'Wall-to-wall sunshine at the end of August' – and Granddad's speech that she'd written for him, and the band that had played a song called 'Always' for the couple's first dance. 'Your mother was mad about the ones who sang it, I don't remember the name.'

'Bon Jovi.' Mum had danced around the kitchen with whoever was nearby anytime it had come on the radio. 'What about your own wedding?'

'Oh, I don't recall much, too far back, and weddings weren't a big thing then.'

'You must remember something.'

Gran thought. 'My father washed his car, a thing he never did – he was driving me to the church in it, and I think my mother probably nagged him until he gave in. The neighbours all clapped when I came out of the house, and when I got into the back seat I saw his wellingtons on the floor.' Lil thought it funny, and typical of practical Gran, that that was what would stay with her from the day she'd married Granddad.

The doorbell rang as they were washing up, and Lil went out to answer it.

'Chilly out there,' Olive said, hugging her, 'but still dry. I've come to get you into your finery.' In the bedroom she exclaimed at the dress, and pinned Lil's curls into a topknot, and wept a little when she saw Mum's fur stole. 'She would have loved to be here today,' she said, blotting her eyes so her mascara didn't run, and Lil didn't say, But she *is* here, in case Olive thought it strange.

On their return downstairs they found Gran's partner Mark alone in the kitchen. 'You look supremely beautiful,' he told Lil, lifting her hand and kissing it, and the gesture, which should have felt corny, was sweet in its sincerity – and Lil, who'd never in her life felt beautiful, felt it then.

'You look good too,' she told him, and he did. Grey suit, white shirt, polished black shoes. Blue and white checked handkerchief poking from his breast pocket.

'Your grandmother took me shopping,' he told her. 'Said she wasn't having me walking you up the aisle looking like a tramp.'

Lil could hear Gran saying it. 'Where is she?'

'Gone out the back to find something for the buttonholes.'

'Tom's here,' Olive put in, standing at the side window. 'He's just pulled up next door. Don't look out, Lil, bad luck. He's with a couple, and two little kiddies – oh, such a pretty little girl.'

Lil's butterflies were back. Her groom had arrived, and it was nearly time. Twenty minutes later she took up the bouquet of silk flowers that one of the craftspeople who supplied Olive's gift shop had made for her. She walked to the house next door on Mark's arm, Gran and Olive having gone ahead of them to furnish the groom and his best man with buttonholes.

They rapped on the front door: it was opened immediately by Joel's wife Sarah. 'The bride is here!' she told her children, and flower girl Emily, clutching a little basket of petals, looked shyly at Lil before hiding behind her mother. Harry stood his ground, clutching a small velvet cushion.

Lil introduced Mark. He dropped to one knee and shook hands solemnly with Harry, and took two gold rings from his breast pocket. 'Young man,' he said, 'let me have your cushion,' and he placed the rings on it. 'Here is your treasure,' he told the boy, handing it back carefully. 'Guard it well.' He turned to Emily, still half hidden, and told her she was the prettiest flower girl he'd ever seen, and Lil decided he would make a fine great-grandfather to her children, whether he married her grandmother or not.

'Ready?' Sarah asked, and Lil took a deep breath, and tightened her fingers on Mark's arm. 'Ready,' she said. Sarah crossed to the open sitting-room door and gave a thumbs-up – and a violin began to play 'Somewhere Over The Rainbow', one of Hollie's favourite songs, and the one they'd chosen to kick off the proceedings.

'You know what to do,' Sarah whispered to her children. 'Nice and slow, Harry, like we practised' – and she took Emily by the hand and they led the way into the sitting room, followed by the pageboy walking solemnly with his treasure. 'Best foot forward, my dear,' Mark whispered to Lil, and they advanced to the sitting-room door.

Lil halted on the threshold to take it in. The room had been cleared of its usual furniture and crammed with assorted kitchen chairs. Someone, Olive probably, had tied wide white ribbons around the chair backs. The music came from the top corner of the room, where Lil's three musician tenants were grouped in a huddle, conspirators in the preparations for today.

The priest who'd known her all her life stood at the top, his face breaking into a wide smile at the sight of her – and beside him was Tom, her love, her soon-to-be husband, flanked by his brother Joel, both of whom wore identical suits to Mark. There must have been furtive coordination.

The guests rose to their feet at her entrance. The music swelled as she and Mark took the half-dozen steps up the short makeshift aisle. The ceremony was brief and simple, as they'd requested. The priest spoke of the bittersweet day it was, but didn't dwell on it.

'Today we enter a new dawn,' he said, 'a new time of contentment, a new period of happiness for Lil and Tom, and for Beth too. The past will always be with us, along with the memories we treasure, but today we turn our faces to the future with great hope,' amid murmurs of assent, and much nodding, and some eye dabbing.

'Are there any objections,' he went on, 'to this marriage?' and Mark made a great show of getting to his feet, accompanied by a ripple of laughter. He cleared his throat and said loudly, 'None,' and sat again, to more mirth. Lil hoped Gran wouldn't be too hard on him afterwards – and looking at her grandmother's face, at the smile she was trying not very successfully to hide, she thought he'd get away with it.

Vows were exchanged, Lil's voice trembling as she promised to love and cherish Tom. Rings were presented by the blushing pageboy, and slipped on. And when it was all over, the musicians sang 'Love Is The Sweetest Thing' in beautiful unaccompanied harmony, and Mr McLysaght kissed Mrs McLysaght to loud applause, and Lil was married after all in the place where her happiest memories lived.

And she felt, or fancied she felt, the love of her lost ones in the room.

After that Gran ushered everyone into the kitchen, where plates were filled from the cold buffet – turkey, ham, salads – that had been laid out, and there was a general milling around the downstairs rooms as people found places to perch. Later, coffee was made and the wedding cake was cut – two tiers, baked by Gran: Tom's chocolate choice below, Lil's lemon drizzle above – and the children were given bowls of ice-cream. The music struck up again, and people sang, and others attempted to dance in whatever space they could find, and the newlyweds snuck out to the adjoining back garden to grab a moment to themselves.

The night was crisply cold, stars jostling for space overhead. She'd forgotten the marvel of the Fairweather sky. They sat entwined on the swing seat they'd given Gran last Christmas, underneath the coats they'd brought out with them. 'Wife,' Tom said. Slowly, as if he was trying it out for size. 'I have a wife,' he said. 'My wife is beautiful.'

Lil smiled in the darkness. 'Husband,' she said. 'I love my husband.' She leant into him, and they swayed for a while as the music and laughter from next door floated faintly out, and she thought of the father of the groom who should have been here today, and wasn't: the absences weren't only on her side. And it might be sadder for Tom, knowing his father could have been there, and wasn't.

She thought of the small envelope she'd slipped to Sarah, somewhere between the ceremony and the cake. Could you see that it gets to Vivienne? she'd asked, and Sarah had said she could, without questioning it.

Dear Vivienne

I'm writing to let you know that we met Tom's father, and Tom made it clear that he wouldn't stand in the way of any relationship, but his father wouldn't be drawn.

By the time you read this, Tom and I will be married. We wish you well in the future.

Lil

She'd shown it to Tom after writing it, not wanting any more secrets between them, and he'd said go ahead and send it if she wanted. It was formal and stilted, but it was the best she could do. It had seemed too cruel to report that Tom's father had denied any feelings for Vivienne, so she'd had to keep it vague.

Would they ever know how things panned out? Probably not.

'Tomorrow,' Tom said, 'we'll go to the sea. We'll do a beach walk.'

'We will.' She might swim, just a quick dip. She'd bring her togs to the beach in case she felt the pull of the ocean.

On their return to the town on Sunday evening, having spent their first weekend as husband and wife in Fairweather's smartest hotel – a wedding gift from Olive and her husband Fred – Lil sent an email.

Hi Alice
Lil here, of the library storytimes. I was Lil Noonan when I met
you, I'm Lil McLysaght now. I wanted to let you know that Tom
and I got married last Friday – we decided not to wait till June
after all, and we never got to Italy either. We had a lovely day in
Fairweather, and we're very happy – and Italy will wait.
Have you had your baby yet? I hope all is well.
Lil x

Alice didn't need to be told about the wedding. She hardly knew Lil, and she'd never met Tom – but for once Lil felt like standing up in the middle of a crowd and saying loudly: Listen to me!

Let me tell you what I've done! She wanted every head to turn towards her, and for them all to pay attention while she told them that she was now a wife, and she wanted them to applaud and cheer loudly when they heard the news.

And failing that, she was simply going to tell everyone she possibly could.

She began a text to Emily – *Just thought you'd like to know that Tom and I –* then decided against it. It might not be the right time for Emily to hear about a happily married couple.

She phoned Judy, and her boss called her a dark horse and promised cake and a special lunch in the near future.

She wished she had Heather's number: now *there* was someone who'd have made a fuss of a surprise wedding.

The following day, there was a response from Alice.

Lil,

I'm thrilled to hear your wonderful news, thank you so much for letting me know. Every happiness to you and Tom – wishing you years and years of love and good times. We have the best news here too: as they'd say in the Bible, I was delivered of a son at an ungodly hour (that bit isn't very Biblical!) last Thursday. He's tiny and completely adorable, and I'm terrified and exhausted and deliriously happy – we all are. I actually think I feel a little drunk, although I haven't touched a drop in about eight months, so it's either sleeplessness or happiness, or a bit of both!

We haven't named him yet. My Italian mamma is trying to steer us in the direction of Vittorio after my grandfather, and my husband George fancies Dan, his father's name. George's daughter Suzi wants Oscar, after her cat – but I think I'd like our little guy to have a name all of his own. We'll see.

Now I'll stop blabbing – he's asleep, and I need some food, and maybe even a bit of sleep too before he wakes up!

Keep in touch. I'd love to meet up for coffee and a chat one of these days, if I ever get to live in the normal world again!

Alice xx

Heather

Dear Heather

If you would like to tell me a little about Lottie, and about you too, I would be very happy.

Yours truly,

Manfred

Lottie is in her last year of primary school, so next year she will begin secondary, which is like American high school. She loves sports.

I didn't tell my parents about her until she was almost eight. I wasn't sure how they'd take the news but they were OK with it. We've visited them in the States and they've been here, and they get on well with her.

H

Dear Heather

Thank you for the informations. I am happy that your parents know about Lottie, and they are OK with it. I remember you told me of your parents in the big house in California. It is important to have enough money, for security.

It is a good thing that Lottie likes sports. I also like it, especially football, but I do not play, just watch! I hope it's OK if I ask some more questions. What is your job? Do you still look after that old man, or another person? Do you ever think about me, and does Lottie ever ask you about her father?

Yours truly,

Manfred

The man I was caring for died, not long after Lottie was born. I don't live in that house any more. My life is very different now. I work at various tasks in my own time. I prefer not having a schedule.

Lottie asked me a few years ago about her father. I told her the truth, that you left before she was born and I never saw you or heard from you again.

I have thought about you occasionally over the years. I have wondered if you were still alive, and now I know.

H

Dear Heather

I think that you still feel anger for me, and I understand. If there is anything I can do to show you how sorry I am I will try to do it. I am not a bad man really. Do you think you will tell Lottie that I have contacted you, and that we are writing now?

Yours truly,

Manfred

I'm not really angry any more. I was, for a long time. You were the first man I loved, and you broke my heart, and left me alone to deal with a major event at a very young age. I was sad and angry, and I was afraid I wouldn't be able to look after Lottie, and she would be taken away from me, but it didn't happen.

I am not sure if I will tell Lottie about this. I must think about it.

H

Dear Heather

I can say my heart was broken too. I said before that I loved you, and it is true. I think maybe I still do.

Do you think there is a chance we could meet? Do you think this is possible? I would really like it. And of course I would like to meet Lottie, but I understand if this is not something you want at this time.

I will be in London next week for my work. I could fly to Ireland, if you like. Best day for me would be Tuesday, but I can do another day if this one isn't good for you.

I am sending my picture so you can see how I look now. Maybe you will send me yours?

Yours truly,

Manfred

She stared at the message. She supposed she should have seen it coming, but the idea of meeting him again jolted her. She hadn't thought beyond this to-ing and fro-ing of information, this cautious rediscovery they'd embarked on.

He could fly to Ireland next week. It felt soon. They'd been communicating for such a short time – but a meeting needn't commit her to anything, right? Just a coffee somewhere, just a chat to see how they got on. And she certainly wouldn't be bringing Lottie along.

Was she tempted to revisit that whole scene? Did she want to risk putting in jeopardy the life she had now? Whatever about her ambivalence towards Shane, his sons had come to feel like hers, even though she was years too young to have been Eoin's mother. Lottie and Jack were best buddies too – and Jo was a kind of lynchpin, holding everyone together. They were all very … enmeshed.

Even the house was so much better now, with Christine

having brought order to the mess, and Mom moved out. Heather should be grateful for what she had and stop looking for something more, or something different.

Emily sure hadn't been impressed when Heather had told her about Manfred getting in touch – and of course she was right when she said Shane should be told about it, and Manfred should be aware that Heather was living with another man. Whatever about Manfred, Shane deserved to know about this. She *would* tell him when the time was right, just not yet. Not when everything was still so … up in the air.

Maybe Heather and Manfred had just met too soon. If they'd been older, the outcome might have been very different. They might have married, and had more children. She could have been living in Germany right now, mother of a bilingual family.

She clicked on the attachment – and he was suddenly, astonishingly there. Would she have recognised him if they'd met on the street? She wasn't sure.

His face was more heavyset than she recalled. A little network of lines, not deep, ran across his forehead. His hair was shorter – she used to gather it into a ponytail and tie it up to make him laugh – and at eighteen he hadn't had a beard.

Some things were as she remembered though. The pale blue eyes, the fair hair. The rather large ears that thankfully his daughter hadn't inherited.

She remembered how he'd gently eased her lips apart with his tongue, the first time they'd kissed. *Halb-offen deinen Mund*, he'd instructed her – half-open your mouth – a phrase that had lodged somewhere in her head. The feel of his hands on her skin, their furtive movements in the darkness of the cinema. His hot breath on her neck, everything racing around feverishly inside her, murmured words she didn't understand, but his desire had needed no translation. Oh boy.

She shifted on the edge of the bed.

She was tempted, no use in denying it. She was curious.

'Heather?' Shane, downstairs. 'Dinner's ready.'

'Coming.' She pocketed her phone and went down, and turned possibilities around in her head as she ate the chicken kebabs that were Lottie's favourite.

The following day it rained, so Heather dropped Christine and Pip back to the cottage after Christine had cleaned. 'Come in,' Christine said, 'I want to show you something' – and the something turned out to be the latest postcard from her chef. 'Four weeks till we meet,' she told Heather, the excitement plain on her face.

On the front of the postcard Heather saw a picture of a grinning donkey in a straw hat. 'You can read it, if you want,' Christine said – and because Heather knew she really wanted her to read it, bursting to share her happiness, to show him off to someone, she did. The writing was so small Heather had to squint to make it out.

Chrissy, missing you lots. Hope all is well, so happy you're enjoying the jobs. Busy here with Christmas coming, made ten full-sized cakes and a dozen puddings yesterday! Grabbed an hour for some shopping, got you a present that I'll save till we meet. Won't feel it, can't wait. Sleep's still rubbish, I'm like a walking zombie, but I'll survive. Hugs to you and Pip,

C xxx

He called her Chrissy. She was loved. He missed her lots, sent her hugs and kisses through the post. He'd got her a Christmas present. Everything was going right for her, with a secure place to live and her two jobs, and a man who loved her, and a father who'd never given up on her, and a son she was undeniably growing fond of.

Heather nearly told her about Manfred, but didn't. Christine wasn't the type to gossip – and didn't have anyone much to gossip with – but still she felt it might be wiser to hold her tongue. Enough that Emily knew.

'Shane's daughter had a miscarriage,' she told Christine. 'Everyone's sad about that. Nora's a darling girl.'

'I'm sorry. Is she OK?'

'Yes, she is. Devastated, obviously – they both are – but she's young. They'll have more chances.'

'You said her partner was Emily's brother?'

Heather nodded, surprised she'd remembered. 'Daniel. Emily's been living with them since she and Bill broke up.'

Christine hesitated. 'Do you know – did Emily tell you why they ended it? I asked Dad, but he wasn't really clear.'

Tricky. 'Well, they couldn't agree about – something.'

'That's what he said. About what, though? Is it private?'

She couldn't be the one to tell Christine that she'd scared her father off having more kids. 'It might be better if you had another conversation with Bill. Honestly, I'd feel I was breaking a confidence from Emily.' Would Bill tell her? Tough call for him.

That evening her mother came to dinner, as she did a couple of times a week. Heather made her usual shepherd's pie, and bought a cheesecake for afters. Her mother arrived with books for the girls and woolly hats for the boys and a bottle of good wine. She asked if Heather would be offended if she got a new rug for the sitting room in the little house, and maybe a throw to put over the couch, and Heather told her no offence would be taken.

After Shane had left for work and the younger ones had wandered off, Heather and her mother lingered at the table with the last of the wine.

'Shane is upset about Nora,' her mother remarked.

'He is. We all are.'

'These things happen. I lost two before I had you.'

Heather looked at her in astonishment. 'You had two miscarriages? You never said.'

'It's not something you discuss with your children, Heather.'

'But you could have told me when I was older.'

Her mother threw her a look. 'When you were older you were living here. We didn't know your precise location for years.'

Good point, and best ignored. 'Gee, Mom, I'm sorry to hear that happened to you and Dad.' She wondered suddenly if the losses had been the start of things going wrong between her parents. Maybe they'd been happy before that. Good job they'd tried again, and were successful with Heather.

'Would you have liked more kids?' she asked, half afraid of how the question would be received. She and Mom had never talked like this.

Her mother didn't reply immediately. She studied her nails – dark red, perfect – and then said slowly, gaze still directed downwards, 'I'm not sure it would have been a good thing. I wasn't exactly maternal.' She looked up. 'Well, you know that,' she said, unsmiling.

Here was another first: Mom admitting she'd messed up. Without thinking – because for the first time she saw vulnerability, for the first time she heard her mother speaking from someplace humble – Heather reached across and took one of the hands that lay on the table. 'You did the best you could, Mom.' It wasn't much of a validation, but she wasn't about to meet the truth with a denial that would be a lie.

It appeared to be enough for her mother. 'Thank you,' she said, giving a tiny squeeze to Heather's hand before withdrawing hers, and Heather wondered if that had been the first time they'd ever held hands, and thought it terribly sad that it might have been.

A car horn sounded outside, the taxi they'd called earlier. As she got into her coat, her mother spoke again. 'You and Shane,' she said crisply. 'You need to sort that out, Heather. If you're not careful,' pulling on a leather glove, 'you're going to lose him.'

This was her way of mothering, Heather thought. This was how she looked after her daughter. There was no tenderness in it, no softness, but it was the best she could do, and it was fine. It felt like they'd turned some kind of corner tonight. They'd never be close the way some mothers and daughters were, but Heather fancied they'd inched a little closer, and that was something.

Imagine if Mom knew about Manfred though. Boy, she'd sure have something to say then.

On Saturday she went with Christine and the two babies to Lil's storytime, the last one before Christmas – and directly afterwards, while everyone was still seated, Judy appeared with a bouquet of flowers and said, 'I want you all to put your hands together for Lil, who got married last weekend,' and Lil, wearing a Santa hat, took the flowers and blushed and smiled as they all applauded. Sweet, how completely happy she looked. More love in the air.

She wondered if Emily knew. They hadn't met since Heather had brought Mom to the restaurant for dinner, well over a week ago. The truth was, she was wary of meeting her friend alone, knowing that Emily would ask about Manfred, and Heather wouldn't be able to hide the fact that she'd decided to meet him.

Because the more she thought about it, the more reasonable and harmless a request it seemed. A trip down Memory Lane, that was all. They'd have lunch somewhere quiet, coffee not enough to justify a trek from London, with him having to hire a car after his flight and drive an hour to the town. Shane would be in bed when she was leaving the house, and hopefully still there by the time she got back, and she could drop Jo at Madge's on the way.

On Saturday evening, after Shane had left for work, she sent an email.

Tuesday is good for me. I can meet you for lunch. I'll attach directions from Shannon Airport to a restaurant in the town. See you at twelve thirty.
H

She scrolled through local restaurants and found Borelli's, an Italian one across town that she'd often visited when Lottie was small and Madge was babysitting. That would do. She booked a table for two and added directions to the email. She debated sending a photo of herself, as he'd suggested. She'd gained a little weight since Lottie, maybe more than a little. Never really lost all the pregnancy weight, truth be told, and Jo hadn't improved matters.

She checked her face in the dressing-table mirror. Her skin wasn't as fresh as it used to be. Lines were beginning to form in places that used to be smooth. Hell, she'd aged a bit, just like he had. Nothing wrong with that – but all the same she decided against a snap. Let him wait to see her in reality.

But she'd give reality a little help. Emily envied her eyelashes: might as well flaunt them with a bit of mascara, and pluck the stray eyebrow hairs she normally ignored. And she'd hunt out the maroon dress she'd bought for Shane's fortieth in June. Had she worn it since? She couldn't remember. Might be a bit of a squeeze, with summer full of ice-cream and takeaway pizzas, not to mention Emily's desserts, and that elderflower lemonade Heather's favourite coffee shop had sold – but so what if it was tight? She could sit up straight and pull everything in.

Madge would wonder why she was all dressed up. Heather would tell her she was meeting a friend she hadn't seen in a while, and wanted to look her best. No lie.

In three days she would be sitting in a restaurant with him. She tried to imagine their conversation, and couldn't. Would he bring her a gift? He'd better.

Tuesday was also the day her father was arriving. His plane touched down later in the afternoon, and he'd organised a car and driver to ferry him from the airport. He'd stayed at Fleming's before; he knew it wasn't the Four Seasons, but the staff were friendly and they had a decent enough restaurant.

How's your mother doing? he'd asked during their last phone call, and Heather had told him she was doing fine. He'd been tickled to hear she'd been installed in Heather's old house. Won't last two days, he'd predicted – and had seemed even more amused when she'd proved him wrong. Three weeks now she'd been there, and so far so good. God bless Christine.

Do you still think she'll change her mind about the divorce?

Heather had asked her father, and he'd said he'd bet his bottom dollar on it. He was playing a waiting game – and it looked like he was quite happy to wait.

Your father's being impossible, her mother had told Heather. Tina says he's putting every obstacle he can think of in the way of the divorce. And I've lost count of the times he's tried to call me. Tina's told me not to pick up – not that I would.

Heather would never understand them. Christmas Day at the restaurant would sure be interesting. She'd have a hard time forgiving them if they ruined it for Emily.

Tuesday turned out wet and wild and cold, the worst day of winter yet. Rain slapped angrily against the window, and Jo grizzled as Heather bundled her into the purple snowsuit. New teeth pushing through gums – or maybe she was just annoyed with the weather. 'You can go live in California with your grandma when you grow up,' Heather told her. 'She'd just love to have you.'

She changed into the maroon dress in the dining room, having brought it downstairs before Shane got home from work. It caught her under the bust and was stretched tightly across her mid-section, but it was still the best her wardrobe had to offer in the way of style. It would have to do.

She stood at the bottom of the stairs with Jo on her hip and thought of Shane, asleep in their bed. She told herself again that she was doing nothing wrong, just checking out how green the grass was on the other side.

'You're looking very swish,' Madge said, ushering them in from the rain. 'Where are you off to?'

'Meeting a friend for lunch,' Heather replied. 'I think I need to go on a diet – this dress is playing havoc with my circulation.'

'You on a diet? I'll believe it when I see it. Where are you eating?'

'Borelli's.'

'I know the place. I used to get my hair cut up the road from it. I always loved walking past, smelt wonderful.' She unzipped Jo's snowsuit. 'I had no Pip today,' she said. 'Christine rang to say he has a cold, so she's keeping him at home. She sounded anxious, poor thing.'

Not surprising. His first cold under her watch would be a big deal. Heather would give her a quick call after lunch, make sure all was OK. Mom wouldn't be pleased: imagine having to heat up her own soup. Heather hoped she wouldn't deduct from Christine's wages for the missed day.

She drove through sheets of rain to the restaurant. Her search for a parking space took her beyond their meeting time. She pictured him inside, watching the door every time it opened.

Before leaving the car she put on fresh lipstick and blotted it, and sprayed Tom Ford behind her ears. His new perfume, a glory of spices and flowers. One of her few indulgences.

She looked at herself in the rear-view mirror. Here goes, she thought. Nothing ventured. She climbed out and yanked up her umbrella. She was nervous, which was beyond ridiculous. If anyone should feel nervous, he should.

She hurried along the street, pulling at the dress that insisted on sticking to the back of her thighs, skirting puddles and swerving to avoid a deliveryman manoeuvring a trolley of boxes into a shop.

And suddenly she was there, outside Borelli's. She pushed open the door and walked in. A warm savoury smell hit her as she folded her dripping umbrella and placed it with the rest in the waiting metal basket. She turned and scanned the room.

He wasn't there.

It was nearly fifteen minutes after they'd arranged to meet, and there was no male sitting alone at any of the tables. Had he stood her up?

A waitress approached. 'Table for Taylor,' Heather said, because she was damned if he was going to stop her from eating lunch, tight dress or no tight dress. She was led across to the last vacant table, a little one by the wall. 'Something to drink?' the waitress asked, and Heather asked for a jug of iced water with lemon. She peeled off her coat and surrendered it, and breathed as deeply as the dress would allow as she took her seat and opened the menu.

'You are Heather?'

The voice was the same, rich and deep. She'd forgotten how he said her name. Hezzer, it sounded like.

She looked up. 'Hello Manfred,' she said.

His hair was wet, his face shiny with rain. Drops beaded in his neat little beard. The shoulders of his beige raincoat were dark with moisture. A black leather tote hung from a shoulder. 'I am very sorry to be late,' he said, taking a folded handkerchief from an inner pocket and dabbing his face with it. 'My aeroplane was late to arrive at Shannon, and after that it was a long time for me to get a car, and when I came here I could not find a place to put the car.'

Ze car. It was all coming back to her. She gave him a smile to relax him. 'No problem,' she said. 'I was late myself. Terrible day.' It felt surreal to be face-to-face again after so long. Was he shorter than she remembered? Hardly – but definitely broader. Maybe the beard was hiding a double chin.

He was shrugging out of the raincoat when the waitress returned with a jug and a bowl of breadsticks. 'Water is OK for me,' he told her in response to her query, and she spirited away his coat. He pulled out the chair across from Heather and dropped into it, and gave a grateful sigh as he raked his hair with both hands. 'Here we are,' he said.

'Here we are,' she agreed. He wore a tan sweater with a collar and a zip, and a white shirt under it with no tie. When she'd known him he was a leather-and-ripped-jeans sort of guy. Now he looked … settled. He appeared older than going on thirty. His hairline had receded at his temples.

'You look very beautiful,' he said, pouring water into glasses. 'The same like I remember.'

This was a load of horse manure, but she didn't argue. 'You look very different. I'm not sure I would have recognised you.'

He blinked at that. 'We are older. It is good to see you again, Hezzer.'

He was more serious than she remembered. He'd lighten up when they talked a bit more. 'Why did you get in touch?' she asked – but just then the waitress showed up again looking for their orders. When that was out of the way he took off the glasses he'd produced to read the menu and sat back, folding his arms, seeming to have forgotten her question, so she asked again.

'I was thinking about you,' he replied. Sinking about you. 'I wanted to know what was happening with you.' He gave a small tight smile. 'I never forgot you, you know. You were funny, and sexy, and always laughing.'

'You ran away. I was terrified. You knew I had nobody in Ireland. No family, no one I could turn to for help. I was seventeen, with a baby on the way.' She kept her voice light, but she didn't smile. It needed to be said, not just written in an email.

He cleared his throat, ran a hand again across his head. 'Yes, I ran away. I did a very bad thing, Heather. I am sorry.'

Let it go, she thought. It's said now. 'Have you told your mother about Lottie?' she asked, and he shook his head and said no, not yet, and she couldn't object to this, since it had taken her eight years to break the news to her parents.

'So tell me,' he said, 'how your life has been,' and she told him of Madge and Emily and Bill and Astrid, the friends she'd made in the town, and of Astrid's death in the spring, and of Lottie's best friend who happened to be a boy, and she left out the bit about the boy being the son of her current partner, and she made no mention at all of Jo.

Being in his company continued to feel strange, their conversation halting and polite. Here they were, in the same town where they'd fallen in love all those years ago. Here they were, making small-talk over water and breadsticks, while people at adjacent tables ate lunch and paid them no heed at all.

Heather had a sudden vision of getting to her feet and announcing to the room that this man, this ordinary man sitting with her, had for a while been the most important person in her life, until he'd made her pregnant and run out on her.

What would they do, these people occupying the same space as them? That trio of laughing women in running gear; that silver-haired man and solemn child, matching ice-creams before them; those couples, some speaking, others silent; that solo teenage girl making her steady way through a bowl of pasta, book propped against her glass?

She knew what they'd do. Their conversations would peter out as they turned astonished faces towards her – and then, one by one, their eyes would slide away, embarrassed, or dismissive, or maybe amused. There might be sniggers. She thought the runners would probably find it funny. The old man might send her a sympathetic look, or he might simply pity her and turn away too, and tell the child not to stare.

Their food arrived. Manfred shook open his napkin and tucked it into the neck of his shirt, which Heather always felt looked a little silly on an adult. On the other hand he'd opted for spaghetti, so maybe it was a wise move. She'd never order spaghetti on a date – but then, this wasn't a date. She wasn't quite sure what it was.

As they ate he spoke of his job, and again she pictured him sitting at an office desk, eating a lunchtime sandwich or tapping figures into a computer, or meeting couples who sat across the desk from him, listening as he told them where to put their savings. She thought it sounded like a dull way to make a living but he seemed happy with it.

'Did you ever write the book?' she asked.

He looked puzzled. 'What book?'

'You wanted to write a novel about a football team.'

He laughed. 'Did I? I forgot.' He gazed at her. 'It is so good to see you, Heather. I wish I did not live so far away.' And when she made no response, he added, 'But it is not so far, with planes. I could come to see you again, or maybe you could come to Germany.'

Did she want to see him again? Her jury was out. She was finding it hard to reconcile this man with the passionate lover she remembered. She couldn't imagine him letting go in bed – but maybe she was making a judgement call too soon.

He used a spoon to steer his spaghetti tidily around the tines of his fork. Every so often he would lift the end of the napkin and dab his mouth with it. He missed a small dot of sauce on one side of his beard. She said nothing.

Her phone rang abruptly, startling her. 'Sorry,' she said, taking it from her bag. She saw Madge's name. Madge, looking after Jo.

'I need to get this,' she said, and pressed the answer key without waiting for him to reply. 'Madge,' she said, turning sideways in her chair. 'What's up?'

'Heather, I'm sorry to bother you, but I'm worried about Christine. I've tried calling her a few times to see how Pip is, and she's not answering. I wonder what I should do.'

Christine.

Madge knew the story. Heather had filled her in when she was asking if she'd look after Pip while Christine was with Mom. Madge had sense enough to worry if Christine suddenly wasn't answering her phone when she should be at the end of it, at home with her sick child.

'I'll check it out,' Heather said, and hung up. Without looking at Manfred she called Christine, and let it ring and ring until it stopped. She set down her fork and took her napkin from her lap and dropped it onto her half-finished lunch. She got to her feet, casting around for the waitress. 'I'm sorry,' she told Manfred. 'There's an emergency. I need to go.'

He rose too, looking surprised. 'OK,' he said as Heather caught the waitress's eye, 'but please ...' He bent to his satchel, napkin still attached to him, and came up with a manila envelope. 'This is for you,' he said, 'I wanted to give you this.'

She thought it looked a little official for a gift, but she thanked him and slipped it into her bag, and took her damp coat from the waitress as he hovered around. 'Goodbye,' she said, 'sorry to leave so quickly. Thanks for lunch' – because he was paying, whether he liked it or not. She hurried away, not waiting for a hug or a handshake or whatever he might have offered, or been expecting. She left the restaurant, only remembering her umbrella when she was halfway down the street, and thoroughly soaked.

She phoned Shane from the car. 'Can you collect Lottie and Jack from school, and then swing by Madge's and pick up Jo?'

'I can – what's up?'

'I'm not sure – I don't know yet. Hopefully nothing.'

'Want me to come?'

'No – I'll be in touch later. Tell Madge I'll call her when I get a chance.'

She drove too quickly to Astrid's house, full of a sense of dread. It's nothing, she told herself. Phone out of battery, or in the wrong room when it rang, or the radio on too loud. Plenty of reasons for it to be nothing at all.

Let it not be Pip. Let it not be either of them. Let everything be OK.

She sat impatiently in a line of cars that waited for lights to change – why were they always red when you were in a hurry? Her wipers slapped as rain continued to pelt down. After far longer than it should have taken she pulled into the driveway and hurried out, shoes squelching as she approached the front door, which stood ajar.

She heard Pip crying inside.

Door ajar, Pip crying. Not good.

She followed the sound into the kitchen, where Pip sat in his playpen, fingers clamped on the bars, crying the way children do when they've been doing it for a long time, and are tired of it. Christine was slumped in a chair, head on the table. Oh, Lord. Oh, Lord.

She shook Christine's shoulder, and Christine lifted a blotched, swollen-eyed face. 'Have you taken something?' Heather demanded sharply, and Christine shook her head wordlessly and lowered it again. 'What's happened?' Heather asked, but this got no response, so she turned her attention to Pip.

She reached in and plucked him from his playpen and brought him into the bathroom. 'Poor guy,' she crooned, pulling off the orange wellingtons he'd become attached to, easing down his small damp pants and sodden, filthy diaper. She cleaned him and towelled him dry, trying not to get angry. Not yet, not until you know all the facts.

She put a fresh diaper on him. She brought him into Christine's room and set him, still sobbing wearily, on the bed while she hunted for dry pants.

Back in the kitchen, Christine hadn't moved. 'Pip needs feeding,' Heather said loudly. 'Christine, come on – you've got to look after him.'

Christine lifted her head an inch. 'Food in the fridge,' she mumbled, and Heather found milk, cheese, two eggs, a bunch of celery and a stack of little plastic tubs with no labels. She popped the lid on one of the tubs and sniffed the orange mush – carrot or sweet potato purée? Whatever it was, it would do. She quickly boiled the kettle, pacing the floor with a sobbing Pip while Christine remained unmoving. What could have happened to affect her like this?

She heated the contents of the tub, all the time soothing and shushing Pip – who, she realised, felt no heavier in her arms than Jo, eight months younger. Maybe Mom was right, and she needed to review her daughter's food intake.

After Pip had eaten she filled a beaker with milk and offered it to him, and he grabbed it and gulped, and slowly calmed while his mother, sitting up now, knees drawn to her chin, rocking and silent, watched them dully.

'OK,' Heather said. 'Talk to me, Christine. What's up? What's happened?'

Christine moved then, slow as a tortoise. She crossed to the cutlery drawer, and took something from it. She offered it mutely to Heather before resuming her seat and beginning to gnaw at a thumbnail that had nothing left to offer her.

Heather's heart sank at the sight of the postcard. The chef who missed her, who couldn't wait to see her again, and meet her child. The chef who called her Chrissy, who'd put three kisses at the end of his last postcard. Had it all been lies, just a bit of twisted fun to him? Had he broken up with her, just a few days before Christmas?

The front showed the Statue of Liberty with a Santa hat on it. She flipped it over. The address was in the same cramped handwriting as before, but someone else had written the message.

Dear Christine,
Please phone me when you get this.
Phoebe (Chris's cousin)

And below, a mobile phone number.

Oh no. Oh no. Oh no. Oh please.

Let him have fallen off the wagon and got high. Let him have lost his job, been kicked out of his cousin's house. Let the worst of it be that he would have to do more rehab, start again on his journey.

Or maybe it wasn't a glitch in his recovery. Maybe he'd been mugged, or in some kind of accident, and was too injured to write the message himself. Address already written – he might have addressed a bunch of postcards at the start.

She dropped into the chair beside Christine. 'What's happened? What did Phoebe tell you?'

Christine squeezed her eyes closed and shook her head. 'I can't ring,' she whimpered. 'I can't do it. I can't, I can't.'

She didn't know. She was going insane, imagining the worst, and too afraid to find out if it was true. All morning she must have been torturing herself. How had she managed to call Madge, and presumably Heather's mother too? She sounded anxious, poor thing, Madge had said.

Heather took her phone from her bag. 'I'll ring. I'll go out to the hall and ring, OK? OK, Christine?' She got a wordless nod in return. She set Pip back in his playpen and left the room and walked to the end of the corridor. She dialled the number and heard the last thing she wanted to hear.

'He hadn't been sleeping well,' Phoebe said. 'We knew that, he'd told us that. And then, when John went to work on Saturday, he discovered that Chris hadn't shown up. He phoned me and asked me to check his room, and he wasn't there.'

'So …'

'He was found later, down by the quays. Someone called

an ambulance, but he was already gone. He must have taken something, we don't know yet. Maybe he went looking for something to make him sleep, and maybe he got something bad. There's going to be an autopsy ... I would have rung Christine, only I didn't have her number.'

'She was too afraid to ring you when she got the postcard.'

'Ah, the poor girl, she'd have known it couldn't be good. He was doing so well, that's what's killing us. John was delighted with him at the bakery. He got on with everyone. He told us all about Christine, showed us her postcards. He was counting the days until he could visit her, and we were hoping, we were both hoping ... We don't know what happened, why he suddenly decided ... It just came out of nowhere. His mother's in bits.'

His mother. Another life destroyed. Heather thanked her and offered condolences.

'He had a Christmas present for her,' Phoebe said. 'Should I send it? I don't know what to do.'

'Maybe hang on to it for now,' Heather said. 'Maybe January would be better. I'll talk to her, find out what she wants.' A present from him arriving in the post could send Christine over the edge, if she wasn't there already. 'I'll call you,' she promised, 'after Christmas.' What else was there to say?

After that she made a hurried call to Madge. 'I didn't know there was a boyfriend,' Madge said. 'She never mentioned him. The poor thing.'

'I must get back to her,' Heather said. 'Shane will collect Jo.

Talk soon.' She hung up and paced the hall, not wanting to deliver the news – but Christine already knew, didn't she? She knew the worst had happened, didn't need to be told.

At the sight of Heather's face she gave a long, low, despairing moan, causing Pip to erupt in fresh frightened wails. Heather lifted him from the playpen and sat by Christine with Pip on her lap, trying to soothe both of them, wanting to weep herself at the waste, the tragedy of a young life lost, leaving at least two hearts broken.

Time passed. Pip's cries turned to tired hiccups, and eventually he slept. Heather brought him to the bedroom and tucked him into his cot with Blue Rabbit. She left the door open and returned to the kitchen, where Christine hugged herself and went on rocking, face chalky now, eyes empty. Heather pulled her chair closer and drew small circles on her back, and didn't talk. Talking would come later.

Her phone rang more than once. She ignored it. Mom, she guessed, wanting to complain about having to make her own lunch.

Shane would still have been in bed when Heather had phoned him earlier, but he never slept through his mobile. Part of his paramedic training: always alert, always ready for an emergency. Want me to come? he'd asked Heather when they'd spoken earlier. Always there for her.

He was dependable. He was what the Irish called sound. He was the kind of person you turned to in a crisis, the kind of person you knew wouldn't let you down.

He wouldn't run away when times got tough. He wouldn't be careless enough to get a girlfriend pregnant in the first place.

She thought about seeing Manfred again, and found she had no desire for it. She thought it was probably a good thing he'd deserted her all those years ago. She couldn't imagine what she'd seen in him.

Eventually Christine whispered something that Heather didn't catch. 'What's that, sweetie?'

'My sponsor.' Her voice sounded rusty with crying. 'Would you ring her?'

A good sign, looking for her sponsor. 'Sure I will. Give me your phone and remind me of her name.'

Ethel, her name was. Heather rang her in the hall and briefly filled her in. 'God love her,' Ethel said. 'I sensed there was something between the two of them. I was so sure Chris would make it – he was full of plans, and so positive, and clean for a long while too. Will you pass me over to Christine?'

Heather surrendered the phone and went out to see if the rain had stopped. It had. She stood at the front door, glad of the fresh air. The plants in the raised bed were dripping and bedraggled after the downpour.

She must look a fright; her hair frizzed if she didn't dry it with a brush. Her dress was still damp and unpleasantly clingy: she longed to pull it off and breathe again, but none of Christine's clothes would go anywhere near fitting her.

She was about to close the front door when a man came along the path and stopped at the small gate. She watched him swinging the gate open. Forties, she thought. Denim from head to foot, new-looking sneakers. Hair buzzed close to his scalp. She gave a quick downward tug to the dress as he strutted his way up the path.

'Looking for Christine,' he said. 'Does she live here?'

Stocky, shorter than her. Tough cookie. Heather folded her arms and braced everything. She put on the face she used when Lottie gave her lip, and moved to centre herself more in the doorway. 'Who wants to know?'

'She phoned. She put in an order.' He looked past her into the hall. 'Is she here?'

An order. Lord above, he was a dealer. Christine had put in an order, unable to cope with not knowing what had happened to her man. 'Who wants to know?' Heather repeated, more sharply. She'd taken some karate classes at school, a million years ago. The dress might rip if she attempted a roundhouse kick, but she figured its days were over anyway.

The man scowled at her. 'Is – she – here?' Leaving gaps between the words, as if she needed help to understand them.

She held her ground. 'You should go. Christine is clean, and she's staying that way.'

His eyes narrowed. 'Listen, bitch,' he said angrily, 'she ordered goods from me. I'm going nowhere until I talk to her.'

It occurred to Heather that he might have a knife. If he got mad enough, he might whip it out. Where was Shane when you needed him? 'She changed her mind,' she said steadily, aware that her legs had begun to shake. 'She doesn't want anything. It happens. No harm done.'

He cursed and took a step towards her. Heather widened her stance, trying to remember the long-ago moves. Knee up, elbows tight into the waist, fists raised and ready, standing leg swivel, bend and kick out with the other. If he wasn't armed, she'd send him into next week.

'I don't want anything, Frog.'

Heather whipped around. Christine stood there, pale as a ghost. 'Sorry, Frog. I made a mistake.' Her voice low and hollow. 'I'm trying to stay clean.'

He reached into a top pocket of the denim jacket and drew out something he concealed in his downturned hand. 'On the house,' he said, holding it out. 'Take away the pain. Go on, Christine.'

Heather moved to stand between them. 'Are you deaf? She says she doesn't want it.'

'Shut up, you fat bitch.' Shifting sideways to see Christine again. 'Here you go, Christine. Come on.'

Fat bitch? Heather felt a surge of hot rage. Again she changed position to block him. 'If you know what's good for you,' she said, tightly and slowly, 'you'll leave and take your shit with you. I'm in the NRA, and I'm packing right now, and I know how to use it.'

She sounded like a bad cop show. She wasn't sure her legs were going to keep holding her up, so violently they shook. Blood pounded in her temples. Her face felt like it was going to catch fire. 'Go on,' she said. 'Beat it. Don't make me shoot you.'

He bared his teeth then, like an angry dog. 'Screw you, Christine,' he snarled. 'Don't come looking again.' With one last glare at Heather, he turned on his tail and stalked back down the path, swagger gone.

She couldn't believe he'd swallowed that fairy tale. Any fool could see she couldn't fit a toothpick into this dress, let alone a lethal weapon. 'Come on,' she said, putting an arm around Christine's shoulders, guiding her inside. Back in the kitchen she made a pot of strong tea and poured it into two mugs, and spooned plenty of sugar into both. She'd have killed for a large slug of brandy, but that would have to wait.

'I'll stay tonight,' she told Christine. 'I'll get Shane to bring Jo around, and we'll sleep in the spare room.' She wasn't taking any chances, in case hard man Frog returned. What the hell name was Frog?

He could slash her tires after dark. Might help him claw back some of his bravado. The thought didn't bother her. Tires could be replaced – hell, the car could be replaced if he chucked a can of gas over it and set it alight.

'I'm sorry,' Christine said, elbows on the table, head in hands. Her voice low and defeated. 'I shouldn't have phoned him.'

'You shouldn't have had his number,' Heather replied. 'Let's dump it now' – and she watched while Christine deleted *Frog* from her contacts. It guaranteed nothing. She knew that. If Christine wanted drugs she'd find them easily enough, and the hunger for oblivion might well resurface whenever life threw her a curve ball. But damn it, she didn't need a dealer's number in her goddamn phone.

'You got any more of those hiding in there?'

Christine shook her head.

'You sure? Should I check?'

Christine handed over the phone and Heather scrolled through the pitifully few contacts. Any one of them, apart from *Dad* and *Ethel*, could be a dealer. She'd just have to trust that Christine was telling the truth.

'You want me to call your dad?'

Another shake of her head. 'He's got enough going on,' she said in the same dead voice.

Emily, she meant. The absence of Emily. Bill would come running, Heather knew. He'd go to the ends of the earth to save Christine, but for now they'd leave him in blissful ignorance.

'I don't think – I can't work for a bit,' Christine said then. 'Can you say it to your mother?'

Although Heather thought it would be better for her to keep busy, she said OK. Let her have a day or two to let the initial shock settle, to focus on Pip and try to come to terms with her loss.

After the tea they ate beans on toast, Heather practically force-feeding Christine until she managed a few mouthfuls, and after that she was persuaded to have a bath, and while she was in it Heather phoned Shane again, ignoring the *eight missed calls* message. Whoever it was would have to wait a while more.

'Your mother's looking for you,' he told her.

'Thanks. I'll call her in a bit. Sorry to land you in it. Sorry to wake you up earlier. You got the kids?'

'I did. So what's going on?'

She gave a condensed version of events, leaving out Manfred. 'I'd feel better staying here tonight,' she said. 'Eoin will manage the other two. Will you pack an overnight for me and Jo, and bring her over when she's fed?'

'OK.' There was a small pause. 'Madge said you were meeting a friend for lunch. You didn't mention it.' Not accusing her, just putting it out there. Maybe he'd found her clothes in the dining room, the jeans and sweater she'd taken off, thinking to be back in them by the time he was up.

'I'll tell you everything when you get here,' she said. He'd see the dress on her. She'd come clean about Manfred, like she should have done from the start.

She disconnected and filled a hot-water bottle for Christine. After she'd tucked her in, with the bedroom door ajar and the light off so Pip wouldn't wake, she sat on the edge of the bed and reached for Christine's hand in the gloom, and cradled it in hers.

'I'm so sorry this happened to you,' she said softly. 'It's so unfair, and you didn't deserve it. It's going to be really tough, but remember that you have people who are rooting for you, and who want to help you. You have Ethel, and your dad, and me. And you have Pip, who needs you. He's just found his mom – he can't lose her again. Don't let that happen, Christine. Don't do that to him.'

She couldn't see Christine's face, turned away from the sliver of light that was coming in from the hall, but she knew from the patchy breathing that the tears were back. She squeezed the hand she held.

'You're a far better mom than mine was. Pip's a lucky little boy. The two of you have so much good stuff ahead of you, once he gets old enough that he doesn't make you want to tear your hair out at least once a day. Wait till he starts to talk. Wait till he can call you Mom.'

'Mum.' So quietly Heather barely heard it. 'He calls me Mum.'

Good: she was listening. She was here, not locked away in a place Heather couldn't reach.

'Hey, that's great. Clever little man. Wait till he can wipe his own behind, and tie his shoelaces. Wait for the first time he cleans his teeth all by himself. Wait till he's able to tidy his room – not that he will, unless you bribe or threaten him. There'll be stepping-stones like that all along the way – and they might make you sad, because they'll mean he's moving away from you some, but honestly, it's such a journey, living with a growing-up kid. Such a wonderful, exciting journey. And I have a feeling he and Jo will be best buddies, like Lottie and Jack.'

And some day, if you can stay clean, if you eat healthy and look after yourself, someone else will come along, and you'll be what they need, and they'll be what you need.

That part she left unsaid.

'I was proud of you today,' she went on. 'The way you told that punk to get lost. I don't mind telling you I felt a lot more scared than I acted. I thought he might have a knife, and I didn't fancy bleeding out on your doorstep. You never know with those guys.

They're not good for your health. I was trying to remember my
school karate. Probably a good job I didn't need to use it – in this
dress I might have dislocated something.'

She went on talking softly, a lullaby of talk. She told Christine
about Manfred, because it didn't matter now. When it seemed
Christine had drifted to sleep she pulled the bedroom door
closed and returned to the kitchen. She took out her phone and
saw that the eight missed calls had become thirteen, and only half
of them were from her mother.

She'd completely forgotten Dad, arriving today from the States.
She decided to start with Mom.

'Heather, what on earth is going on? Your father and I have
been calling and calling. We were thinking of going to the
police.'

'Wait. What? You've been in contact with Dad?'

Her mother sighed. 'He's here.'

'He— Where? Where's here?'

'Your old house, of course – where do you think?'

'But I booked him a room in Fleming's. I told him that.'

'Yes, he checked in there and had a nap, and then he wanted to
touch base with you, but he couldn't because you weren't picking
up, so he called a taxi and came here. You had told him I was
staying here.'

'Yes … and he remembered where it was?'

'He didn't need to remember – he had the address. You gave us
this address, Heather, before our last trip to Ireland.'

'Right … and you let him in?'

'Of course I did. I'm not uncivilised, Heather. He was hungry, so we ordered Chinese.'

Her parents had had Chinese food delivered. They'd eaten a meal together. She'd had more than enough drama for one day. 'Is he still there? Can I talk to him?'

'I'll put him on in a minute. And another thing: Christine didn't show for work today. I had to make my own lunch. She didn't even have the manners to call and let me know.'

'I'm at her house now. She got some really bad news. Someone close to her died, and she's very upset. She's sorry about today, but she needs to take a few more days off.'

Another deep sigh. 'Well, I'm sorry to hear she got bad news, but actually I've decided I'm going to move into the hotel after all, Heather. This house is a little basic, if you don't mind my saying. And with your father there, I'll have some company. Will you tell Christine I won't be needing her any more?'

'Mom, your timing's not great, just when she's had the worst news. Will you at least compensate her for letting her go? Say a week's wages in place of notice?'

'Yes, yes – although the fact that she didn't show today—'

'Oh Mom, have a heart. So you're moving to Fleming's?'

'Your father thinks it's a good idea. We have lots to talk about.'

'Right.' Her head was spinning. She felt the beginnings of a headache. A car door slammed outside just then. It was either Frog back with his lighter and a can of gas, or Shane. 'I've got to go, Mom. Tell Dad I'm sorry I missed his calls and I'll talk to him tomorrow.'

It was Shane, with an overnight bag and no Jo. 'I dropped her back to Madge. I thought you might have your hands full here.'

'OK.' She saw him noticing the dress. He didn't comment. 'Come in,' she said.

She told him about Manfred's letter, and her response, and the exchanges that followed. She told it straight, no evasions. 'I was stupid. I let myself think ... maybe there was something better for me. You and I felt a bit stale – or I thought we did, and when he got in touch, I began to wonder if it was Fate.'

He nodded. 'I knew you'd gone off me.'

He hadn't brought it up though. He didn't do confrontations, not after being married to his ex. 'Not gone off you,' she said, 'or not permanently. Just, I don't know, I had a dip or something. A temporary dip.' She stopped, took a breath. 'I'm really sorry,' she said. 'I've been impossible lately.'

He gave a little grin. 'You're still miles ahead of Yvonne.'

That bar was low. Yvonne had physically abused him, kicked and scratched and punched him. Being miles ahead of that wasn't much of a compliment, but Heather took it. 'I got a bit bored. I forgot how lucky I am. I'll make it up to you.'

'Shush,' he said. 'I know I can be a bit of a crowd-pleaser. Force of habit, I suppose – it was just easier that way with Yvonne – but I can try to be more manly.' He made a fist and flexed his arm in a show of muscle that wasn't there, and she had to laugh.

'You don't need to change,' she told him. 'You're good as you are. I need a reality pill, and we need to reconnect. Maybe we could take an overnight somewhere in January, just the two of us.'

'Maybe,' he said, giving a funny little smile. 'What about Lottie though?'

'What about her?'

'I think she needs to know about her dad making contact.'

'She does. I'll tell her.' She dreaded it – would Lottie insist on getting in touch with him? Would she drag him back into the picture? If it happened, Heather would have to respect it.

'I forgot to tell you about the drug dealer,' she said, suddenly remembering. She described the scene with Frog. She made it sound funnier than it had been, because she didn't want to worry him, but still he was horrified.

'He could have killed you both. We've picked up our share of ODs. Those dealers are evil.'

'Right – but I'm a big girl. Literally, I was about twice his size. And I know karate.'

'You do not.'

'Well, I used to, at school. I figured it was like riding a bike.'

He gave her a look. 'In that dress?'

It made them both smile, and she knew they'd be OK.

After he'd left she stretched wearily. It wasn't late, not yet eight o'clock, but after such a full day she was ready for sleep.

She'd get Madge a little gift in the morning to say thank you. She'd admired the Tom Ford scent lately: Heather would get her the eau de parfum, because Madge was a treasure and worth every cent.

The bathroom mirror was a shock. Her hair stood out in bushy tufts after drying without help. The mascara she'd put on for

Manfred had run in the rain. She looked ghoulish and terrifying: no wonder Frog had made himself scarce.

And Shane, ever tactful, hadn't said a word about it.

She was getting undressed in the tiny second bedroom, finally pulling off the dress with relief, when she remembered Manfred's envelope. She took it out of her bag and found a sheaf of pages inside, folded and stapled together, with a handwritten note paper-clipped to the front.

Dear Heather,

I hope you will be interested in putting some money in this great opportunity. It is a new plan I am joining, and I must now find two more persons to come with me. You told me when we were together that you were waiting for a lot of money from your parents, so I think you will be interested – and perhaps they will too? Please read and then we can talk.

Yours truly,

Manfred

What? *What?*

She dropped the note onto the bed and turned to the pages. *Great opportunity!* she read. *High return guaranteed!* With growing incredulity she skimmed through graphs and instructions and testimonials. She saw words like *recruiting* and *foolproof* and *co-operation*. She read *building on shared investments* and *thousands of happy clients.*

She reread his note. She remembered him making some

comment about her parents' big house in one of his emails. She must have told him about the trust fund, all those years ago. She must have boasted about her parents' wealth, like a kid would do when they were trying to impress someone. I'm going to be very rich, she might have said, or words to that effect. Trusting him absolutely, wanting to share it with him.

And he'd remembered it. He'd filed it away in his head, and it had sat there quietly for over ten years. And then, when he'd decided to jump into what sounded like a dodgy pyramid scheme – wasn't that how they worked, people recruiting other people? Weren't they illegal now? – he'd thought of Heather and her trust fund, and he'd made contact.

But he'd done it so badly. He'd been too impatient, too greedy. He'd played his cards much too soon, right after meeting her. He hadn't even tried to rekindle what they'd had, hadn't given her a chance to fall for him again. He'd hopped on a plane from London, figuring it was worth the trip if he could get her on board with all her money.

He'd hardly mentioned Lottie today. He hadn't once asked about a photo. He couldn't care less that he was a dad, and still she would have to tell Lottie about him.

Would she?

She stuffed the pages and the note back into their envelope, and returned it to her bag. She took out the pyjamas that Shane had packed for her and put them on.

She climbed into bed and closed her eyes, daring sleep to evade her.

Christine

SHE LAY IN BED. IT WAS THE MIDDLE OF THE NIGHT, and Pip was asleep in his cot, and Heather was probably asleep in the other room, but Christine was awake, and felt like she was bleeding on the inside. She lay in bed and recited the mantra in her head.

I am clean. I am strong. I am confident.

I am clean. I am strong. I am confident.

I am clean. I am strong. I am confident.

The words she'd begun her days with in rehab. The words they'd chanted in group, the words that had helped her through the recovery programme. She'd taken them with her when she'd left; she'd started and finished every day with them since moving in here.

They didn't work any more. They'd lost their power. Now they mocked her. She was not strong, and she was not confident, and she was clean by the skin of her teeth.

All she'd wanted when she'd rung Frog was to escape from the panic. She couldn't bear the clawing fear, the anxiety that had begun to screech at her like nails on a blackboard as soon as she'd read the message on the postcard that should have come from Chris, but hadn't. I need something, she'd said, and he'd told her he'd be over later.

And while she was waiting for him Heather had arrived, and she'd phoned the number that Christine couldn't, and the panic and fear was swept away by a tidal wave of pain that was far worse, and all she had wanted was to lie down and let it fill every space in her and drown her. And Heather had tried to help, had tried to make it better, but nobody could help, nothing could help except the oblivion she craved.

And then she'd asked Heather to phone Ethel, not because she'd thought there was anything Ethel or anyone else could say to take away the pain, but still she'd wanted, needed, to hear that calm, warm voice. Just to steady her, she'd thought, until Frog arrived.

And Ethel, strong lovely Ethel, had cried with her, and called Chris a beautiful person. Don't give in, she'd begged, when Christine said she had to take something. Don't let them win, Christine. She'd reminded Christine of the pledges she'd made in rehab, all the hard work she'd done there. Don't throw everything away for a fix, Christine. Please don't undo it all.

And then she'd asked where Pip was, and when Christine told her, she'd said, Go and look at him, Christine. Go and look at your child – and Christine had walked down the hall and into her bedroom, and she'd looked at his sweet innocent sleeping face, and at the orange wellingtons Heather had left sitting on the floor by his cot, and something had shifted inside her.

And because of Ethel, and because of Heather, and because of Pip, and her dad – and maybe because of the orange wellies, she'd been able to tell Frog she'd changed her mind. And he'd looked mad enough to hit her but he'd gone, and she'd watched him walking away and wondered how he could possibly have fathered a child as beautiful as Pip.

But it was so hard to keep going, to keep trying to be strong. It was hard and it was cruel, and she didn't know if she could keep fighting.

She'd bought Chris a Christmas present, back at the start of December. She'd taken Pip into town after leaving Heather's house one day and she'd picked out a watch. It wasn't very expensive but she'd liked the look of it, black face with gold hands and numbers on a black strap. She'd thought it looked classy.

And he would never see it. She would never admire it on his wrist because he was gone. After all his promises, all his talk of missing her, and how he couldn't wait for January, and how he was dying to meet Pip, he was dead and she would never see him again.

She turned onto her side and closed her eyes, and tears found their way out and soaked her pillow all over again, and eventually she fell asleep.

'I must go,' Heather said in the morning, after she'd washed and fed Pip, after she'd boiled an egg for Christine that Christine hadn't eaten, after she'd said more of the stuff she'd said last evening that was meant to help, but didn't. 'I need to pick up Jo from Madge and get some groceries, and check in with my folks. I'll come back this evening. I'll stay the night again if you want me to.'

'OK.'

'Will you call your dad? He's off today so he can come and be with you. Will you please, Christine?'

Heather didn't trust her to be on her own; it was obvious. She was afraid Christine would leave Pip and go to find a fix. 'I won't,' Christine told her. 'I won't look for stuff.' Because she was clean, she was strong, she was confident – except she wasn't. She didn't know what she was any more, or maybe she did.

I am broken. I am destroyed. I am angry.

But because Heather pleaded again with her to call her father, and because Heather had squared up to Frog for her yesterday, she did phone him.

'Can you come around?' she asked, and he said yes, without asking why. 'I'll be there in ten minutes,' he said.

'He's coming,' she told Heather, and Heather hugged her and said for the millionth time that she was proud of her.

'Stay strong,' she said. Everyone telling her to stay strong, when she wasn't strong to begin with. After she left, Christine pulled the small bundle of postcards out from under the cutlery tray and ripped them up without reading them again. She put the pieces into a cereal bowl and set them alight in the sink, and watched them burn with new tears spilling silently down her face, and after that she scrubbed the bowl clean and drank the coffee Heather had poured for her, which had gone cold.

'What is it?' Dad said, when she opened the door. 'Is it Pip?'

She shook her head. 'It's me.' Over fresh coffee she told him in little halting pieces about Chris, and he held her and called her his darling girl, and she leant against him and kept on wanting to die.

Later, much later, when she was too exhausted to cry any more they sat side by side on the small sitting-room couch, in front of the fire that Dad had lit. Pip sat in the playpen that they'd brought in from the kitchen, wearing his wellingtons and talking to Blue Rabbit.

'Tell me about Mum,' Christine said.

'What about her?'

'Everything.'

So he told her how they'd met when he was fourteen and she was sixteen, a friend of his sister Grace's. He spoke of how he'd loved her silently for four years before he'd finally plucked up the courage to ask her out. 'We went to the cinema,' he said. '*The Field* was the film we saw. I couldn't concentrate on it, I was so nervous. That was my first ever date, with anyone. I was so shy you wouldn't believe.'

He spoke of their wedding, five years later on a day of rain.

Thirty-two guests, mostly family. He named the song Grace had sung during the ceremony in the church. He described the reception in the same hotel Mum's parents had used for their wedding. He'd forgotten nothing.

None of this was new to Christine – she'd heard it all from Mum in bits and pieces over the years, but the familiarity of it, the ordinariness of it, the predictability of it, was as soothing as a lullaby. She leant back against the couch and closed her eyes and listened.

'When you were born,' he said, 'I was completely terrified. I hadn't a clue how to be a dad. I was afraid I'd drop you, and you'd break. Mum laughed at me when I told her, called me a scaredy-cat. She'd never been a mum before, but she seemed to know exactly what to do.'

But he'd been the best dad. He'd done everything right and hadn't dropped her once – and then the woman he loved had died, and the daughter he loved had gone off the rails. How had he coped? How could Christine have done that to him, when he'd been as heartbroken as she was, or maybe more, after Mum's death? She'd been the worst daughter. The thought brought more tears – how could there be so many tears in her? She dropped her head onto his chest and let them soak into his shirt.

After another age had passed, she said, 'I want to ask you something.'

'What?'

'Why did you and Emily split up? Really, why? Please tell me.'

She listened to the soft thump of his heart beneath the shirt. She felt the rise and fall of his breathing. 'Dad?'

Another silence, and then: 'I'm afraid,' he said. 'I'm still a scaredy-cat, Christine. I don't think I could go through it again, or risk going through it again, with another child, and Emily ... wants children.'

She sat up slowly. The cheek that had been resting against his chest was hot. The skin around her eyes felt tight. The taste of tears was still in her throat. 'Are you serious, Dad? You're afraid if you have another child it will become an addict like me? That's the reason why you and Emily broke up?'

He didn't answer. He didn't have to.

She shook her head. 'But that's not going to happen,' she said. 'I won't let it. If you have another baby I'll tell it the truth about drugs – I'll put it off them for life. I promise you it won't take drugs. It'll be the last child in the world to take drugs, believe me.'

He looked at her. She could see he wanted to believe her, but couldn't trust that she meant what she said. And how could she blame him, after she'd shown herself to be so untrustworthy?

'I want to tell you something,' she said. 'When I got the postcard from ... When the postcard arrived yesterday, and I knew it couldn't be good news, I was too scared to ring and find out. I phoned a dealer I used to use, I still had his number, and I asked him to bring me something. I wasn't thinking straight, I was panicking, I didn't know what else to do, and he said he'd bring something around to me.'

Her father's face changed. He looked as if she'd just told him Pip had died. 'You phoned a dealer yesterday?'

'Dad, I'm telling you because I don't want any more secrets.'

'You would have gone back on drugs if Heather hadn't been here.' He looked like he might get sick, might throw up there and then on the sitting-room floor. 'And Pip was with you. This is exactly what I'm talking about, Christine. This is what I can't go through again.'

'No,' she insisted. 'Listen. I didn't take anything – don't you see? I really wanted to, and I asked for something, but when the dealer showed up I heard him at the door with Heather – I was on the phone with my sponsor. I went out, and I told him I didn't want it. I said I'd ... changed my mind. And that was the first time I said no, Dad. The first time since I started on drugs. He was offering them to me, he was holding them out to me, telling me they were on the house, and I said no. I didn't know I *could* say no to them, not when they were literally being handed to me, but now I do.'

'And he left, just like that?'

'Well, Heather told him she was in the NRA. She said she had a gun, and he must have believed her.'

Bill blinked.

'Dad, listen to me,' she repeated, even more forcefully, because she could see he still wasn't convinced. 'I'm *not* going back there. I'm not. I'm going to fight it with everything I have. They're not going to get me again. I'm clean, and I'm staying clean – and now I know I can.'

'I hope so. You don't know how much I hope you can do it.'

'I *do* know. I know how much it means to you. I made your life miserable, twice, and I'm never going to do it again. It's not going to happen, Dad – I swear it. Ethel has names of counsellors. I'm going to follow that up and get help. And I'm not going to let you ruin things with Emily. Please don't make me responsible for that. You have to fix things with her. You *have* to.'

And after that she wept a little more, because it was all so horribly hard, and she was filled with grief and loneliness, and weary from crying, and Dad held her and rocked her and didn't say much, other than calling her his dearest child, his precious daughter.

And then they ordered a pizza, and ate it by the fire – and since she'd skipped breakfast, Christine was glad of it. And later Heather arrived with an apple crumble and a tub of whipped cream, and they ate that too.

'Mom was very sorry when I told her what happened,' she said to Christine. 'She sends her best, and she's going to move into the hotel for the rest of her time in Ireland, because she wouldn't be able to manage without you.'

'She doesn't mind?'

'Not at all, she understands completely.'

She'd been OK to work for. Not friendly like Heather, but Christine hadn't minded that. She'd miss the money, but that didn't seem like something that mattered now.

'She's going to pay you an extra week's wages because she feels bad about letting you go. My dad's staying in the hotel too. They have separate rooms, but I think they mightn't get a divorce after all. I've given up trying to understand them. But I want you to come back and clean my house when you feel able – I still need you badly, and you'll have no trouble getting more work once I spread the word.'

'I will,' Christine said. 'I will come back.' She'd need all the friends she could find, and all the work too, to keep her busy.

And while Bill was washing up, and Christine and Heather were putting Pip to bed, Ethel phoned to see how she was doing, and Christine told her she was really sad, and really angry, and really tired. 'But I'm still clean,' she said, 'and I'm going to get counselling. You can send me the information you have.'

'That's my girl,' Ethel said. 'Don't let them win, darling. You can do it.'

And in this way, slowly and with love, she got through the day, her first sad, lonely day without him.

And in bed that night, listening to her son's rapid little breaths and reminding herself how much she had to live for, she came up with a new mantra.

I am clean. I am grateful. I am determined.

CHRISTMAS DAY,
FIVE DAYS LATER

AS SOON AS IT HAD STOPPED RINGING, EMILY'S phone started again. Don't, she begged silently. Leave me alone. I don't want you to wish me a Happy Christmas. I'm not able to be your friend, not yet.

The ringing stopped for the second time – and immediately resumed. Was he going to keep calling until she answered? It looked like it.

She picked it up. She let it ring three more times, and then she pressed the green button. 'Bill, I can't do this.'

'Emily, I'm outside. I need to talk to you.'

She looked at the closed door, as if she might see him through it. She glanced at the window, but the angle was wrong. All she saw was the back of the wooden seat she'd painted tangerine, with nobody sitting on it. 'What do you want?'

'Let me in. Please, Emily.'

'I won't change my mind.'

'I know that. I'm not going to ask you to.'

She disconnected, and for a few seconds remained standing quite still. Then she summoned her courage and went to the door, and slid the bolt across.

He needed a haircut. He couldn't go more than five weeks without looking dishevelled, his hair almost as impossible to manage as her own. He'd nicked himself shaving, a short red line between mouth and chin.

She stepped back wordlessly to let him in. They stood facing each other. She could feel her pulse beating in her temple.

'Emily,' he said, digging hands into pockets, 'I was wrong. I want another child. With you. I want more than one. I want lots.'

She was afraid to believe him. 'What's changed your mind?'

'Christine,' he said simply. 'She asked me why we broke up, and I had to tell her. And she said I shouldn't be afraid of another child of mine turning to drugs, because she'd make sure it didn't happen. She'd tell it, when it was old enough, about the bad stuff. She'd put it off drugs for life, she said. And when I thought about it, I realised that ...' he stopped, began again '... even if she goes back to them, that would send its own message, wouldn't it? Either way, I need to let go of that fear. I can't let it be the end of us, the end of you and me.'

She wanted so much for it to be true. From the kitchen, she heard the oven timer going off. 'I have to baste the turkey.'

He walked after her. He told her, as she spooned melted butter and juices over the meat, about the chef in the transition house that Christine had met and lost. The news astonished her. She'd never imagined Christine having feelings for another person. She'd thought her completely self-absorbed, chasing her habit with no thought for anyone else, not even her own child – but this was a new side to her.

And Pip was content with her. She was managing to be his mother, and that was as it should be, and Emily must accept that, and be glad of it. Christine was taking responsibility for her son, and that could only be good for Pip.

'Is she OK?'

'She's devastated, but she's also determined to stay clean. She's going to start counselling – and she ordered me to fix things with you. She said she couldn't be responsible for us splitting up – and she's right, I can't have her carrying that burden. She's my daughter and I'll always love her and fight for her, but you—'

He broke off, and she saw the emotion, the love and the pain in his eyes.

'Emily, you're everything to me. Without you, they may as well put me in the ground. I can't promise I won't worry, if I'm lucky enough to get you back, and if we do have a child. I'll worry like hell, but you'll just have to put up with that, and hopefully Christine will stick around to keep it on the straight and narrow, like she said.'

Emily closed the oven door. She set down the baster and wiped her hands on her apron. She reset the timer and put the pudding on to steam, and all the time she was conscious of him watching her, hands in pockets. He'd die without his pockets.

Finally, she turned to face him. 'You won't change your mind about this? You're certain?'

'I won't change my mind. I can't function without you. I bought a shirt,' he said, 'a couple of weeks ago. It's horrible.'

She laughed. For the first time in weeks, the laughter bubbled out of her. 'What colour is it?' She wouldn't let on she already knew.

'Brown.'

Her eyes filled with happy tears. 'That colour isn't good on you.'

He smiled. 'See? I need you, so I don't make other bad fashion choices.'

She hugged him. He hugged her back, and followed the hug with a kiss. 'So you'll come home?'

Home. 'I will, tomorrow. I need to get this day sorted out.'

Her parents would not welcome the news of this reunion. There wasn't much she could do about that. They'd be pleased to get a grandchild, when the time came. More happiness accompanied that thought.

She'd missed happiness.

'Is Christine up to coming to dinner today?'

Bill shook his head. 'It's too soon. I'm going to spend the day with her and Pip. I'm sorry to miss it, but—'

'Can I ring her? Can I talk to her?'

'If you want,' he said doubtfully, so she took his phone and sent him into the dining room with some balloons to blow up, and she called Christine.

'Dad.'

A dull note to the voice that Emily recognised. The sound of grief, loneliness, emptiness. 'Christine, it's me, Emily. I just – wanted to say I'm so sorry. Bill told me what happened.'

Silence. Emily hurried on: 'And I want to say sorry too for how I've behaved towards you since you came back. I wasn't welcoming – I was afraid you'd disappear again, and I was trying to protect Bill, Pip too.' Stop making excuses. 'I should have been more generous. I should have been more helpful, and I wasn't. I'm really sorry, Christine.'

She paused again. Still no response.

'And when you took Pip, I resented it. I'm sure you could see that. I was terrified we were putting him in danger, giving him back to you. I didn't trust you like Bill did – I was afraid to trust you. But Bill tells me you're doing very well with him, and I'm glad.'

More silence. Was she still there?

She was. She spoke.

'I was scared too, when I took him back.' Quiet, little more than a whisper, but not so quiet that Emily missed hearing the tears that clogged her words. 'I wanted to try to be a proper mum for him.' Pause, to let out a sob. 'I felt bad about you. I knew you didn't want me to take him, but I'm his mum, so ...'

Yes. However much Emily loved him, he would always belong to Christine.

'And I'm still learning, I still don't have much of a clue ... not like you and Dad. I don't always do things the right way, not the way they're supposed to be done, but he's doing OK, and I think he's happy with me.'

Emily closed her eyes. It was good, she knew it was good that he was happy, but still the words pierced.

'He looks for you,' Christine said then. 'He asks where you are. I know you don't want to come here, but—'

'I do,' Emily said quickly. 'I mean, I'd like to, but I was afraid, in case …' In case I wasn't wanted. In case it was too hard for me to see him with another mother. His real mother. In case I couldn't be nice to her.

'You can come any time. He'd love to see you.'

Emily took a breath in, let it out. 'Thank you.'

'I wanted to ask you before, but I didn't know – well, and then when you and Dad split up—'

'He's here,' Emily said, unable to stop the news jumping out. 'We're going to try again.'

'Good,' Christine said simply, and nothing else.

'He told me what you said about … any children that might come. About making sure they stayed away from drugs, I mean.'

'I had to, when he told me why you'd broken up. I couldn't cause him any more hurt, and he was hurting without you. You make him happy. I'm glad he had you when I was – when I went away. And … I never said thank you for looking after Pip. I never said it properly, but I am really grateful.'

'I loved it,' Emily said. 'I love him.'

'I know.'

A beat passed. 'You could bring him here today,' Emily said. 'I know you mightn't feel like meeting anyone, but you could just have dinner and leave straight after. Heather would love to see you' – was she even sure Heather was coming? – 'and Lil will be here, from the library. Bill told me you go to her storytimes.'

Another silence.

'Just if you want to, if you feel able. Dinner will be at half three. You can think about it. Bill will be with you in a little while – he'll be leaving here in a minute.'

Another pause. Emily pictured her on the other end of the conversation. Twenty-seven, with enough suffering behind her to last a lifetime, and now coping with another blow while she was still learning how to be a mother.

'I hope I'll see you later, Christine. I'll have a place ready for you, and a high chair for Pip, but I'll understand if it's too much, and I'll ring you in a few days if you don't come today.'

'OK.'

'Take care, Christine.'

'She didn't say no to dinner,' she told Bill. 'She didn't rule it out. See what you can do.'

When he'd left, before she could think about it and change her mind, she called Heather. 'Happy Christmas,' she said. 'Are we OK?'

'Happy Christmas to you. Of course we're OK – why wouldn't we be?'

'Well, we've drifted … and I texted you last night and you didn't answer.'

'Yes, I did – hang on.' She listened to tapping, and Heather came back. 'Sorry – never sent. I think my phone needs putting out to pasture. And as for drifting, yeah, there's been a bit of that – but we're able for a drift, right? We can survive the occasional drift.'

Emily laughed. 'Of course we can. It just seemed lately that I was losing everyone.'

'Honey, you're stuck with me. Get over it.'

'I'm glad to hear it. Bill and I are back together, so it looks like I'm stuck with him too.' She couldn't keep the smile off her face. 'He's had a change of heart about babies.'

'Hey, that's great news! I'm so happy for you – and if I'm not asked to be godmother I'll write you out of the will.'

'Oh, come on – who else would I ask? By the way, he told me about Christine.'

'Yeah, that was a big blow. She had high hopes of that.'

'I'm ashamed of how I treated her.'

'Now don't beat yourself up. She's trying hard, but she's still a work in progress. You couldn't be blamed for being scared.'

'I talked to her earlier. I asked her to come to dinner today if she feels up to it. Bill is on his way over to her now.' She thought of something else. 'Did your father arrive as planned?'

'He did – and get this: the divorce is off.'

'What? I don't believe it!'

'Long story – I'll tell you when I have time, which won't be today. He and Mom are staying at Fleming's – and Mom is planning to wear Oscar de la Renta this afternoon, just to put us all in the shade.'

'Golly, better remember to take off my apron.' She paused. 'And what about you?'

Heather laughed. 'I know what you're asking, and that's another long story for another time. We'll be busy catching up – but for now, all you need to know is that the German turned out to be a big disappointment, and Shane and I are back on track.'

'I'm delighted to hear it. Did you say anything to Lottie?'

'I did. I figured she had a right to know. I told her I'd heard from her dad and she could get in touch with him if she wanted – and you know what she said?'

'What?'

'She said she already had a dad – why would she want another one, especially one who ran away? I told Shane, and he's still preening.'

'Wow. Clever girl. So I'll see you all soon?'

'You will – brace yourself.'

A text arrived five minutes later from Daniel.

Happy Christmas. We'll see you for dinner. D xx

So Nora was going to come. Still hollow, still grieving, but willing to put in an appearance. *Wonderful*, Emily typed, *and just to let you know you're losing a lodger. Bill and I are trying again, so Barney and I will be moving out tomorrow* – and within a minute, *Happy days, great news* came back.

Time passed. She turned on the radio and basted the turkey again, to the accompaniment of 'Santa Baby'. All it had taken to bring her and Bill back together was Christine telling Bill what he needed to hear. Emily must find a way to say a special thank-you for that.

She parboiled the vegetables and topped the trifle with cream and sang along to 'White Christmas'. She took the ham she'd boiled the night before from the fridge and sliced it. She laid the overlapping slices on two oven trays and covered them with foil, ready to be reheated when the turkey came out. She danced around the empty kitchen with a broom as her partner when 'The Christmas Waltz' came on.

It was that time of year, when the world fell in love.

She knew all about love. She was an expert on love.

Heather and her family were first to arrive, at a few minutes after three. One look at Emily told Heather all she needed to know: happiness restored.

'I love your dress,' Emily said to Heather's mother. 'Very classy. You put us all in the shade,' which was exactly what Mom loved to hear.

'Great to see you again,' she said to Heather's father. 'I hope you brought your appetite.'

She was so good with people, Heather thought. Christine she'd had trouble with, but it sounded like that was going to come right.

'I met Manfred,' she murmured to Emily, as the others were settling themselves at the table. 'I can tell you here because you can't get mad in front of everyone. Suffice to say he was a huge mistake, and it's over.'

'I'm not mad, I'm relieved – but I still want all the details.'

'Oh, you'll get them.'

She'd tell her late some night, after a few glasses of something nice. They'd have a laugh about the pyramid scheme. Her moment of madness was over – and thank goodness, Lottie had turned out to have far more sense than her mother. After hearing that she was quite happy with the father who was there for her, Heather had sent a curt email:

I told my daughter about you. She's not interested in meeting a man who ran out on me when she was on the way. Neither of us wants anything to do with you in the future. If you contact me again I will report you for harassment.

And so far, so good.

'Guess what Shane got me for Christmas.'

'A new house. I don't know.'

'A weekend in the Cotswolds in England. We're staying above a pub in a little village – I've forgotten its name, but he's shown me snaps and it's very pretty indeed. And get this – there have been no new houses built there since the 1600s, so this American is very excited to see it.'

'That sounds great. Just the two of you?'

'Just the two of us – he's sorted all the kids. Middle of January. Weather won't be great but that's OK. We can hunker down and become reacquainted.'

They'd begun the process a couple of days ago. Shane had come in from work and got something to eat and looked after Jo while Heather had dropped Lottie and Jack to school. When she'd come home, he'd gone up to bed. All par for the course –

but after she'd put Jo down for her nap Heather had taken off her clothes and joined him in the bed, and woken him up quietly.

It had been a while, but they both remembered what to do. They might make another baby sometime, just to keep Emily's company.

❖

Lil hadn't been sure what gift to bring, so she'd played it safe with champagne and chocolates. Emily looked radiant in a blue dress, hair pulled into a loose knot and secured with clips that twinkled when she moved. 'Thank you so much,' she said, pulling out chairs for Lil and Tom. 'I'll put you here, next to Heather and her parents.'

Heather's parents seemed curiously companionable for a couple in the middle of a divorce. Sitting side by side, his arm resting along the back of her chair. Putting a very good face on things: Heather must have warned them well. Her mother's dress was stylish, if a little over the top. 'Oscar de la Renta,' she told Lil, when Lil admired it. 'I pull it out every now and again, just to give it an airing. You're wearing a pretty dress yourself.'

'Thank you.'

'Lil and Tom got married a couple of weeks ago,' Heather told her parents, and they congratulated the happy couple, and Emily poured champagne for a toast. As conversations resumed, Heather told Lil that Christine needed work as a cleaner. 'She's going through a rough time right now, so I'm trying to help. Maybe she could put a notice in the library.'

'She certainly could – and Tom and I could use her once a week in the apartment,' Lil said. 'It wouldn't be for long, though – Emily needs it when our lease runs out at the end of February. We're trying to find somewhere else, but there's not a lot around.'

'Actually, I think there may be good news on that front.' Heather told Lil of the reunion, and Lil looked again at Emily as she poured lemonade into a beaker for Jo, lifting her head to laugh at some comment from Shane.

Pure happiness in that laugh. She should have known. Lovely that they'd made up in time for Christmas.

She rose from her chair, unable to wait. She hovered until Emily noticed her. 'Lil – everything OK?'

'Heather told me,' she said, 'about you getting back with your partner.'

Emily smiled. 'Word travels fast.'

'I'm delighted for you,' Lil said, 'and cheeky enough to ask if it means Tom and I can stay put in the apartment after February.'

'Oh – yes, of course. I totally forgot about that, I'm so sorry. Yes, please stay.'

Lil smiled and thanked her, and assured her that they'd be happy to stay. Tom glanced up as she returned to her seat.

'OK?'

'More than OK.'

She told him. She watched his face light up with relief. She'd tell him later, or maybe tomorrow, about the email that had come from Sarah while they were getting ready for this dinner.

Vivienne has gone back to the US. Dad heard from her mother yesterday. I thought you might want to know. I passed on your letter.

It didn't tell them much. They still didn't know which version of events was true. Maybe, like Gran had said, the truth was somewhere in between.

It didn't matter. She lifted her champagne glass and sipped, and it was cold and tingling and delicious.

❖

'Come with me,' her father said. 'The change of scene will be good – and I'll bring you home the minute you want to go.' And because she'd run out of places to clean in the cottage, and because she didn't think she'd feel any worse in the restaurant, and because she liked Emily's cooking, and because Emily would love to see Pip, and because she knew Dad wanted to be where Emily was, for all those reasons she said yes.

He wiped Pip's face and got him into clean clothes while she put on her one and only dress and packed a bag with nappies and wipes and soother and spare trousers. She added the orange wellies, just in case.

It was coming easier to her, being his mother. It felt like she was slowly growing into clothes she'd never been sure would fit.

They stood outside the restaurant door, Pip in Bill's arms. 'OK?' he asked, and she nodded, and he rapped on the door.

'Christine,' Emily said. 'I'm so glad you came.'

'Thanks for inviting me,' Christine said. 'Pip, look who's here' – and he put out his arms and Emily took him from Bill and hugged him with her eyes closed. 'Pip,' she murmured, 'my little Pippety,' and Christine was happy he had someone who loved him so much.

Inside, Emily introduced Christine to Heather's father and Lil's husband, the only two people she hadn't met. Heather's father was dark-haired and tanned, with the same smile as Heather, and Lil's husband looked a bit like Jake Gyllenhaal.

Heather's mother, who was wearing some kind of fancy ball gown, patted Christine's hand and told her she looked lovely, when anyone could see that Christine looked anything but, and called her 'dear' for the first time. Christine wanted to thank her for the money that Heather had delivered yesterday, a week's wages for no work, but was shy in front of everyone.

'Here,' Heather said, 'you take this place, Bill, and talk to Tom and Lil. I need a chat with Christine. We can swap around later,' so they did as they were told, and Christine was glad to be sitting next to Heather.

A high chair was produced for Pip. 'Put it next to Jo,' Heather instructed. 'Christine needs a bit of time out from mothering. Shane, will you keep an eye on them?'

'Do I have a choice?' he asked, but he didn't sound like he

minded, and Christine hoped Heather didn't boss him around all the time, because she suspected he'd be easy to boss around. She thought she'd like him if they got a chance to become acquainted. She'd met a few paramedics during her time on the streets, and they'd always been kind to her.

'Well,' Heather said. 'Hanging in there.'

'Hanging in there,' Christine agreed.

'I'm glad you're here. I'm glad you came.'

'Me too.'

And she was. She was glad she'd made the effort to be here in this gathering. Her father had told Christine about Emily's restaurant while she was pregnant with Pip. It's where people can come together to eat, he'd said, people who mightn't have anyone else to eat with – and at the time Christine had thought it sounded lame, and she'd turned him down anytime he'd asked her to go there with him, but now she thought she understood it. Here, around this big table, she wasn't alone. It didn't matter that she hardly knew some of the others, it just mattered that they were there.

She'd phoned a counsellor who sounded nice, a bit like Ethel. Her voice was calm and gentle. They were going to meet in three days for a chat.

I am clean. I am grateful. I am determined.

There was another rap at the door, and Emily opened it to admit a couple Christine didn't recognise. He turned out to be Emily's brother, and she was Nora. Yes, Shane's daughter: there was a resemblance. She'd lost a baby recently, Heather had said, and Christine recognised the darkness in her eyes. Kindred sadness.

The couple took chairs across from each other, Nora slipping into the one beside Christine.

'I like your top,' Christine said. 'It matches your eyes.'

'*Your* eyes are amazing,' Nora replied.

They exchanged tremulous smiles as Emily topped up glasses and proposed a new toast. 'To love and hope this Christmas,' she said, and they echoed it all around the table, and Christine saw her father meet Emily's eyes as glasses were raised.

And directly afterwards, he turned to look at his daughter, and gave her a smile that was full of tenderness.

Yes, she was loved. He had never given up on her. And Pip, she thought, was beginning to love her. They were beginning to love one another.

And seated around a table with people whose lives had halted momentarily to connect with hers, she felt the time might come when there would be hope again.

Acknowledgements

Thanks to my invaluable editor Ciara Doorley, and the entire hardworking and friendly crew at Hachette Books Ireland. Long may you prosper.

Thanks to my agent Sallyanne Sweeney, vigilant, attentive, and always professional.

Thanks to my copy editor Hazel Orme for her wonderfully thorough work, and to my proofreader Aonghus Meaney for the final checks.

Thanks to all who helped when I came to them with a query during the writing of this book: Gabrielle Monaghan, Julie McLoughlin, Judi Curtin, Brian O'Gorman, David Casey and Barb Kates, and blushing apologies to those I've forgotten to mention (always, always).

Thanks to my family for their unwavering faith in my abilities, with a special mention for Mam, still my most faithful reader at the age of 95.

Thanks to you for doing me the honour of choosing this book: I sincerely hope you enjoy it.

Roisin x

www.roisinmeaney.com

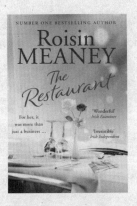

When Emily's heart was broken by the love of her life, she never imagined that she would find herself, just two years later, running a small restaurant in what used to be her grandmother's tiny hat shop. The Food of Love offers diners the possibility of friendship (and maybe more) as well as a delicious meal. And even though Emily has sworn off romance forever, it doesn't stop her hoping for happiness for her regulars, like widower Bill who hides a troubling secret, single mum Heather who ran away from home as a teenager, and gentle Astrid whose past is darker than any of her friends know.

Then, out of the blue, Emily receives a letter from her ex. He's returning home to Ireland and wants to see her. Is Emily brave enough to give love a second chance – or wise enough to figure out where it's truly to be found?

Also available on ebook and audio

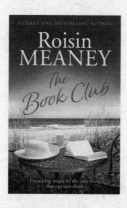

In the small seaside town of Fairweather, the local book club – a tight-knit group – is still reeling in the aftermath of a tragic accident.

Lil Noonan hasn't spoken a word since, and her grandmother Beth is worried that she plans to spend the rest of her life hidden away with only books for company. Beth, meanwhile, is trying to keep busy with the running of the local library and decides to make a fresh start by renting out her daughter's now-empty house to a newcomer in town.

Tom McLysaght tells the book club that he's eager to escape his high-flying life in London. Closer to the truth is that he's hiding a much bigger secret, one he can't escape from, no matter how hard he tries.

As the months pass and the book club continues to meet, Beth starts to open up to the idea that the future might still have some happiness to offer to her grand-daughter – and to her as well. But will they have the courage to reach for it? And will Tom trust them enough to reveal his secret?

Also available on ebook and audio

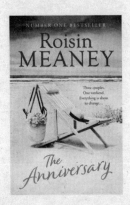

It's the bank holiday weekend and the Cunningham family are escaping to their holiday home by the sea, as they've done every summer for many years.

Except that now, parents Lily and Charlie are waiting for their divorce papers to come through – and have their new partners in tow.

Their daughter Poll is there with her boyfriend and is determined to make known her feelings for Chloe, her father's new love. While her brother Thomas also has feelings for Chloe – of a very different nature …

And amid all the drama, everyone has forgotten that this weekend also happens to be Lily and Charlie's wedding anniversary.

Will any of the couples survive the weekend intact?

Also available on ebook and audio

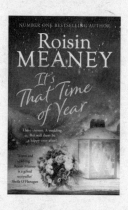

It's the day before the wedding ...

Three strangers arrive home to Ireland to the house that gave each of them refuge when they needed it most. They are there to celebrate the winter wedding of their beloved Annie, the woman who fostered them in their childhoods.

Now Julia is a world-famous singer living in luxury in Paris and Eddie is a chef in London, while Steph spends her days on a remote Greek island, running a writers' retreat with her older lover.

All three have moved on from the past, but as the wedding celebrations get underway, certain truths come to light. It turns out that some hurts last longer than others ...

As Annie says 'I do', with an unexpected twist for her wedding party, will Julia, Eddie and Steph discover their own happy-ever-afters in time for the big day?

Also available on ebook